THESE LONG TEETH
OF THE NIGHT

THESE LONG TEETH
OF THE NIGHT
THE BEST SHORT STORIES 1999-2019

ALEXANDER ZELENYJ

Fourth Horseman Press

These Long Teeth of the Night
by Alexander Zelenyj
Published by Fourth Horseman Press

First Edition, November 2022

Cover Artwork Based on "Muscinae" (1904) by Ernst Haeckel
Cover Designed by Elizabeth J. M. Walker & Brian A. Dixon

ISBN: 978-0-9883922-2-9

Fourth Horseman Press
http://www.fourthhorsemanpress.com/

For David Rix, founder of the Dark Valley,
with much respect and gratitude.

ACKNOWLEDGMENTS

Thank you to the many editors whose belief in these stories gave them their various homes in magazines, anthologies, and books in years past, though the following editors are deserving of a very special thank you:

Brian A. Dixon and Adam Chamberlain of Fourth Horseman Press.

David Rix, Douglas Thompson, and Alice Howard of Eibonvale Press.

Alessandro Manzetti and Jodi Renee Lester of Independent Legions Publishing.

Trevor Denyer of Midnight Street Press.

Though your ongoing support, enthusiasm, and friendship can never be adequately repaid, I hope that this collection goes a ways toward showing how grateful I am.

Thank you also to Nick Cato and Sami Airola.

A big thank you to my friends, most especially Lindsay McNiff; Rachel Eagen; Andrew Murphy and Lucifer's Voyage; Roger Wurdemann and Louise Davis; Claudio and Catherine-Mary Sossi; Nick Angelini; Greg Maxwell; Liam O'Donnell; Peter and Brittni Brinn; and the Deathray Bradburys.

And, of course, thank you to my family: Dan, Cindy, and Max Zelenyj; Tom and Lorrie Zelenyj; my mom and dad; David and Elaine Walker, and the rest of the Walker Family; my wife, Elizabeth: thank you for everything; and the critters: Daisy, Callie, and Dune.

TABLE OF CONTENTS

"The night is a tunnel...
a hole into tomorrow."

—Frank Herbert
Dune

INTRODUCTION
BRIAN A. DIXON

For twenty years, Alexander Zelenyj has been writing rare and remarkable fiction. From out of the crooked crevasses of his visionary mind have clambered all manner of characters: damaged warriors and depraved brutes, startling beasts and prophetic apparitions, pests and pixies and maladies-made-flesh. Through him, they've told us their stories. The narratives are unique and achingly familiar. From the first line, we are lured into a shared hallucination with his promise of the fantastic, but we soon find that the teeming jungles and twisted labyrinths he guides us through are haunted by our own secret hopes and fears. Establishing new mythologies at the same time that they reveal the truth of our world, the stories he has crafted are extraordinary. Such stories deserve to be celebrated.

These Long Teeth of the Night has been curated for just this purpose. With this book, Fourth Horseman Press honors two decades of unforgettable fiction from Alexander Zelenyj. Each of the stories and novellas in this anniversary collection have been selected by the author, many of them revised and expanded for the occasion. Together, they represent the range and impact of a remarkable career.

As a publisher, I've worked closely with Alex ever since I first came across one of his stories—"The Demon Takeover of Windsor, Ontario"—atop the slush pile of submissions for *Revelation* in 2004. So suited was his fiction to the magazine of apocalyptic art and literature that he became our most prolific author, publishing seven stories over a span of ten years. The bio he submitted along with that first story told that he "watches the skies fearfully." He soon had me watching, too.

As an educator, I have seized the opportunity to bring Alex's stories into the university classroom, offering the likes of "The Prison Hulk" up to classes of literature students. The results were often remarkable. Students are discerning and demanding, and their attention and interest are not easily won. The strangeness and the mystery and the revelation of these narratives, however, have proven irresistible. The classroom discussions inspired by them were spirited and full of ideas, conversations in which students confronted all of the challenging questions they pose regarding art and the life that it imitates. To study the writings of Alexander Zelenyj is to test the perceived limits of narrative. As the author explains in the introductory note that he has written for this volume, there are no reassuring genre conventions here.

These Long Teeth of the Night offers unique insight into the creative process behind these weird and wonderful tales. Each of the twenty-eight stories in this celebratory collection is prefaced with an introduction from the author himself. Some of these notes serve to reveal the inspiration for the story. Some of them depict the peculiarities and challenges inherent to the writing process. Others have been crafted as bizzarro narratives in and of themselves, serving to deliberately obscure that imagined line between narrative and reality, between the startling nightmares and wondrous dreamscapes captured here and the truth and anguish of our everyday lives. In the end, there are no comforting distinctions between that which is imagined and that which we know to be true.

The title and cover artwork conceived for this volume are, by design, enticing but also disconcerting. They convey a sense of the encroaching darkness in the primeval jungle. It is the darkness that permeates so many of the collection's stories. There are monsters to be confronted in these incredible tales, and the most disturbing of them all are those hideous archetypes of human evil that are so disturbingly familiar. Some of the stories are whimsical. Others are sobering. Still others depict evils so base and so pure that they will shake your convictions and stir deep-seated fears. The horrors in these stories may disturb but, with Alexander Zelenyj as your guide, you will learn of the incredible power that comes from peering into the darkness and finding the strength to confront the most uncomfortable of truths, to recognize such evil for what it really is. This is the power of all great literature.

The man himself has given us the best possible description of this collection, a warning of sorts, and a promise: these are "stories that coddle, stories that bite." Brace yourself as you prepare to delve into the narrative depths of these great tales. The stories of Alexander Zelenyj are stories of the night. And it has teeth.

AUTHOR'S NOTE
MY WEIRD BROOD

Welcome to this twenty-year retrospective of my published short fiction, spanning 1999–2019. These are speculative fiction stories, usually cross-genre. I won't get into genre specifics too much here and, with a couple of exceptions, I don't do that in the brief introductions I've written for each of the stories either. I rarely consider which genre I'm writing in while I'm writing, so it would have felt unnatural to dissect them in this way. I will say that my love of reading across all genres no doubt lies at the heart of the natural inclination I've always felt to draw from all over in my own writing, and to cross-pollinate among those sources, sometimes in search of something beyond genre boundaries, something that might not be easy to define. Some call this mixing of genres *slipstream* writing. For me, it's essentially a case of using the various tools and inspirations at my disposal to tell stories about people, no matter how bizarre or alien the backdrop.

Mostly, though, these stories are just my weird fiction babies.

It feels more appropriate to talk a little about what these stories are about, in an overarching sense. The great James Tiptree Jr./Alice B. Sheldon said: "For how many of us, me in my way, you in yours, are not our pens the weapons with which we can do something—a tiny something—about wrongs? Even if only to name them?"

This resonates with me because I decided long ago to never shy away from dealing with very dark, difficult, and explicit subject matter in my writing. (Provided the work in question calls for it, of course. Sometimes I'm inclined to write about much lighter subjects). It's out there in the world, happening right now, to someone, somewhere: any number of terrible things that encompass the damaging of lives. Apocalyptic subject matter shouldn't be glossed over, made easier to bear by filtering through a PG lens. Our hurting of one another is a theme that recurs in these stories because, though I may not have the power to stop these things from continuing, this focus at least shines a light on them for anyone who might be reading. Because we *should* see. Because acknowledging those wrongs makes the goodness that exists in the world that much clearer, too, and something to strive toward.

When the extremes of harsh reality and the fantastical are juxtaposed, a clear picture emerges that reveals the true horrors of the former and the wonder and strength of the latter. And I take great solace in the unlimited potential offered by speculative fiction when living in a world seemingly staggering closer to apocalypse every day. It might even have helped me maintain my sanity in this modern existence of ours, and when reflecting on some difficult personal experiences that affected me profoundly.

Where *did* all these stories come from? I suppose the obvious answer is that they came from me, and my collective experiences and inspirations, but exactly *how* they came to be born I could never begin to try to explain. Over the years, the ritual has been a pretty simple one even if its results have been, to me, somewhat inexplicable: I sit down at my desk—sometimes with an idea percolating in my mind, sometimes not—and let my fingers type. Sometimes it's an easy walk down a smoothly paved road; sometimes it's a trek across an unkempt, weed-choked field; other times it's a long, circuitous navigation and climb over a monolithic mountain—and then a new story exists that didn't exist before.

I hope you enjoy this selection of my strange fiction babies from the greater brood of my writing. Be forewarned: as I suggested earlier, some of them are rotten little bastards, merciless and feral and long-toothed, who won't hesitate going for your jugular. But others are gentler companions and provide good safehouses along a dangerous route. Still others are in-between these extremes, and are just plain oddball kids, a little deformed, a little peculiar (occasionally with uncanny abilities), but sometimes with a whole lot of heart.

Welcome to the fam. You're invited to spend the long night here with us...

MARIA, HERE COME THE DEATH ANGELS!

Oh, Maria, if only this story didn't have to be.

But it's a good way to begin this compendium of my published short fiction of the past two decades. It sums up my suspicions about why the world might be the way that it is. So, here it is.

I've written dozens of stories that revolve around the Vietnam War, including a chapbook mini-collection entitled Forgotten Hymns of the Death Angels *(Eibonvale Press, 2014; reissued 2018). Why I always find myself returning to this particular historical setting in my fiction I really don't know. I just feel compelled to go there again and again and again. Is this chaotic time and place done with me yet? No, I don't think that it is. Originally appearing in my second full-length collection,* Songs for the Lost, *published by Eibonvale Press in 2014, "Maria, Here Come the Death Angels!" was later reprinted under the title "Maria" in editor Trevor Denyer's Midnight Street Press anthology* Hellfire Crossroads Volume 5. *This led to an ongoing relationship with MSP that continues to this day.*

The most important thing to me here—and I know this with complete certainty—is that the darkness depicted at the story's centre is still out there, right now, deep in the depths of the wilderness, just waiting for the chance. Likewise, it's also currently hunting through the city—mine, and yours, too. It always has been, and always will be. And, truth be told, it's lurking inside the vast majority of stories in this book. Maybe all of them. Maybe every story I've ever written and will ever write. And it's important to me that I never forget these things.

Dig your foxholes deep, pals. The sky's dirty with incoming, and the night's going to last forever.

The jungle reeked. Its pungent stench, a miasmic brew of competing flora species and rotting vegetation, reached the outskirts of the village.

The weary men were gathered in a loose circle there. This, their makeshift camp of two days wait, baked in the torturous air. The weeks behind them—of slinking like animals through the wilderness, and fighting there, too, and fighting there and fighting there—weighed on them. They were the ragtag remnants of Rogue Angel Company. Tired, weak from hunger and malarial fever, most of them wounded. They each of them owned lost eyes.

In the distance, the village children stood huddled, watching the men curiously, whispering among themselves.

A man, turning onto his side where he lay in the grass, groaned. The bandage encasing his thigh was stained red with blood and brown with dirt. Then drowsy quiet returned while each of the men drifted between the place they were and those places they yearned to be.

Into the dead silence, Private McCall's voice carried like an unexpected beacon of light. "You know, I've seen angels here. I mean it. You boys looking at me like I'm nuts, but it's true. The real McCoy, with my own eyes."

The men were indeed looking up from where they finished their meagre rations or habitually cleaned their weapons or lay with eyes squinted against the angry molten glare of the air. Their murky eyes cleared as they examined their companion but still they eyed him with suspicion. Still, their weary expressions haunted them.

McCall finished, a song in his voice. "And here they come to save me again."

The men followed the Private's gaze, staring over their heads. There, in the bloody dusking west, hung a murder of great mechanical birds.

Choppers! Rescue! Salvation!

Everyone erupted into joyous cries, ecstatic at the sight of their deliverance so close at hand, the deathly pall of their dark mood lifted at last. The village children, following the direction of the men's gesticulations, pointed and cried out excitedly, too.

"Angels! Yeah, McCall, you got it, brother!"

"We're saved, boys!"

"Fuck yeah, we are!"

"Dustoff!"

"From up high, here they come!"

They leapt from their rocks and logs and finished their duties with renewed energy, as if their bones and muscles and hearts knew no ache. Some threw their dirty helmets skywards in celebration.

"You boys want to join me in Heaven?" McCall went on in a mighty voice rising over their clamour, fuelling everyone's relief and elation at the sight of the machines and the transient escape they represented. The captain eyed him approvingly and clapped a hand on his back.

Private Dobbs, though—off to the side of the group and thumbing once again through the handful of photographs he kept stashed inside his shirt pocket—caught something in his companion's eyes which seemed to betray a deeper knowledge or meaning that the rest of the platoon hadn't noticed.

"Thank you, Lord," McCall muttered under his breath, to himself and no one else but for Dobbs, who heard, and would wonder about it for the rest of the day. "Thank you for my time on this ripe Earth." And then he'd slung his Ithaca 37 across his shoulder and was on his feet, eyes in the sky.

Soon, the host arrived, and with it a great wind that whipped about the men like a storm.

Night-time Pattaya was awake and in the throes of living. The bar was tiny and congested with smoke and the stench of the humanity filling it to its corners. Soldiers crammed the room, rejoicing in their shore leave with prostitutes riding their knees while waitresses wove among the throngs carrying glasses-laden trays to and from tables.

Dobbs watched his pals, Lambton and Calling and Cartier, stagger off with a boom-boom girl apiece. He smiled, genuinely happy for them. Placing a hand over his pocket, he sipped his tepid beer.

He felt his eyes on him. Looking from his drink, he found McCall leaning backwards on his stool, his empty glass on the table before him, filled with cigarette ashes. Dobbs smiled at him and winced when he saw McCall's eyes lower to where his hand hovered lovingly over his breast pocket.

"What you always hiding in there, pal?" His raspy voice came through the music and conversation like a knife. "Huh, pal? I bet she's a pretty thing, whoever she is. Am I right? I'm right, ain't I?" He was smiling, and Dobbs laughed sheepishly.

"You got me figured, McCall. Yeah, you do. She's a beauty if I ever seen one. Makes me the lucky man I am."

McCall nodded approvingly. Turning his attention to the smoky air, he reached a hand out, closed his fingers. Dobbs watched, impressed, as McCall opened his fingers and the giant black fly flew from his hand.

"You're a magician, brother," Dobbs laughed, swallowing his beer and waving at a passing waitress to bring them both another.

McCall only shook his head. His voice cut through the din again: "She got a name? You got a picture you can show me?"

Dobbs put his glass down and retrieved the pictures. Pride filled him. He loved showing her picture and did so whenever he could. She made him better in the eyes of others, he'd always thought. She made him a man when he usually only felt like a boy playing soldier alongside men. Passing the pictures across the table he said, "Her name's Maria." Watching McCall scan the photographs, seeing his appreciative appraisal of each in turn, cajoled him into revealing his greatest desires to his fellow platoon member, though they didn't know each other very well at all. "I'll be done here in six months, God willing. Shit, I can't wait to see her. It feels like forever. I just can't wait, brother."

McCall whistled, holding a picture towards the overhead light for clearer inspection. "I *bet* you can't wait. Boy, I ever had a girl like that, I'd be counting the days 'til I got to fuck her brains out the minute I was back, too."

They laughed together. The waitress brought them their drinks and they knocked their glasses together in a toast to Dobbs's Maria and to beautiful girls everywhere. They watched soldiers dancing with whores to "My Boyfriend's Back" spinning on the jukebox and crackling the old tinny speakers. They chugged their beers and ordered again. The night was long and easy. Dobbs thought that he could live with nights like this if he

28

had to, where he didn't have to worry over shadows in the grass that might snipe him homebound in a bag. Nights like this would do until he was home again with his friends and his girl and the food he liked to eat and the things he liked to do.

His reveries urged him to call across the table, "Hey, McCall. You like baseball? You a baseball man? Who's your team? Who's your best player?"

McCall eyed him strangely. He laughed, shaking his head. "Nah, brother, I don't know baseball worth a dime. I never could play. Never wanted to, neither."

Dobbs nodded. Drunk and less inhibited than he would have been otherwise, he ventured, "You know, I don't even know your hometown, brother. You look like a county fella somehow. Don't ask me why. Just a feeling I got."

McCall, wearing the same pensive expression, said, "Come on, brother. I need some air. This place stinks to high fuckin' Heaven of sweat and smoke. Sneak your beer, though. No one's looking."

They slipped from their stools and out the tavern's back door, surreptitiously toting their glasses. The voices they left behind sounded ecstatic.

The late evening air was cooler but humid still. Mosquitoes annoyed their eyes but they were drunk and didn't care. They were used to hungrier mosquitoes besides, out in the bush, and bullets hungrier than any creature.

They wandered a meandering line out back of the tavern and beyond its small gravel lot into the thick elephant grass. Beyond the trees they could glimpse the morose lights of the ghetto district. Following the gurgle of the water, they found the river a minute later, dark and spotted with reflected stars. They stood there, looking into its depths, drinking their drinks.

"What did you say was her name?"

"Hmm?" Dobbs shook his head, chuckling, wondering at the languorous mood come over him, as though the water enchanted him, or else he'd only just caught up with the fact that he'd drank one too many.

"Your girl?"

"Maria."

29

Maria. Even her name he cherished. The way it conjured to mind everything about her. Her voice her smell her ways, how she looked as pretty with short hair as with long. *Maria.*

"Maria," McCall said in a protracted way, sounding as though he was savouring her name just as Dobbs was savouring it. "It's a nice name she's got, for sure."

They lit cigarettes and smoked in silence, enjoying the moonlight. The hum of the nearby bush was there with them, too, like some great electrical thing.

Into the nocturnal calm: "She ain't never gonna see you again, Private."

It took a moment for the words to seep through Dobbs's muddled thoughts. When they did, it was in conjunction with the burst of sensation that tore through his stupor. His eyes cleared and he stared with mute horror at the dagger hilt protruding from his stomach. He examined it until he understood the fact of it piercing him. He felt its blade ruining him inside. A growing pain emanated from the spot. The sight of his blood pouring from the wound and running the length of his pants stunned him. It seemed queerly as though he was divorced from this happening, as if he were watching a film of this violent act committed not upon himself but upon another person, but for the pain. He'd never smell her smell again. This great loss was his.

McCall's breath was rank as sewage as he leaned close to his ashen face. "Maybe they are angels, Private. And maybe I'm the strongest of them all. Maybe I'm the great deceiver now, and I can't wait to get back into the jungle to do what I do best in the world. I love the jungle, Private. It's where I met the Master, okay? I fuckin' *love* the jungle. With all my wrathchild's heart."

McCall curled his fingers over the worn dagger hilt. He wrenched it from side to side. Dobbs fell to his knees from the pain. He felt the blade slicing through his insides, the obscene collision of this razor-sharp intruder with his delicate, unguarded veins, muscles, organs, his crumbling architecture. His agonized cry was swallowed behind McCall's hand as it clamped over his mouth. He extricated the blade slowly and then plunged it into the Private again and again and again. The blows opened Dobbs's neck wide, and his belly, too, to reveal his tangle of intestines coiling in the mud near the river's edge like a grotesque orgy of serpents.

The moon moved across the sky. The forest grew loud, violent in its animal clamour, and then, after a time, became somnolent-sounding. McCall stabbed and stabbed.

A while later, McCall sheathed the dagger in the scabbard he wore beneath his shirt without wiping it clean. He examined the body gleaming in the lunar light. Minutes passed and he proceeded to drag it into the shallows of the river and roll it out into the water like one would a log. Dobbs's devastated corpse bobbed briefly before submerging beneath its black surface.

McCall looked into the waves. The stars shook frantically there. He was still watching when the water grew calm and the stars had fallen into stillness, to haunt the river with their frosty, otherworldly light.

A subtle tremor on the air gave the spy away. McCall spun and found the Thai boy huddled behind a skeletal berry bush nearby. Realizing he'd been discovered, the child stepped out from behind his meagre cover and hovered anxiously in his place, looking as if he were steeling himself to flee but was unable due to his fear. The wooden fishing pole he held quivered on the air in his small, trembling fist as though in the throes of a frenzied, invisible fish.

McCall sized him up with hard eyes. He undid his pants and pissed into the mud, watching the boy unwaveringly. "You know who I am, don't you, boy?"

The boy nodded, his eyes moons of terror in the darkness.

McCall nodded in return, as though satisfied with the honesty of the child's response. He finished his piss. He gobbed into the mud. He murmured, "Off with you now. Maybe we'll meet again one night, in the forest, in the city. Beware of me, boy."

The boy scampered mouse-like into the shadows.

The soldier turned and strode into the night.

The boy, having nearly reached the relative safety of the scraggly tree-line abutting the lot—and his village not far beyond—dared to slow and look the way he'd come. With fearful eyes, he searched for the soldier but nowhere did he see him, despite the wide open space of the lot with the river flowing on one side and the squat, ramshackle tavern a ways in the distance. A chill crawled the length of the child's spine. He understood then that he would have to be strong in the world. In his peripheral vision he discerned a shadow pass across the stars and blight their glow but when he looked there was nothing, only the night sky, dark and immense.

THE POTATO THIEF BENEATH INDIFFERENT STARS

This story originally appeared in the anthology Unparalleled Journeys II, *published by Journey Books in 2007. Ironically, it almost never saw the light of day because, if memory serves, I wrote the story in a blur one very late night and then immediately shelved it, completely forgetting about it in the days following. It was only months and months later that a friend chanced to notice the story file saved on my computer amid a slew of other files and, intrigued by the title, asked to read it. She enjoyed it and urged me to submit the story somewhere. I decided to send it to Journey Books editors Edward Knight and David M. Fitzpatrick, from whom it received a favourable response (and acceptance for the above-mentioned anthology). Two years later, I used it as the opening story of my first collection,* Experiments at 3 Billion A.M., *published by Eibonvale Press. And here it is again.*

It also offers a glimpse of what, for my money, one might call Paradise. Which is why, wherever the potato thief of the title comes from, that is the place I want to go, too.

He found her nibbling at potatoes in his field at dusk.

The purpling sky colouring her gently. The thin, agile fingers daintily holding the dusty vegetable. Her slim frame amid the dirt clods and grass spikes, fragile and child-like. The small circular eyes like obsidian marbles above the little mouth. Her skin the colour of green apples out of season, wan and ethereal in the settling gloom.

She was beautiful, he realized, even as his hand with the spade instinctually leapt out and swatted her down into the dirt. One swipe with the rusty tip and over she fell, dropping her potato-treasure in the soil beside her. Her delicate body was limp and unmoving, like a strange fossil dug up in his vegetable garden bordering the field, harkening backwards to a past unimagined.

He stared down at the thing, stirring a moment later at the soft knocking sound on the air: the metal tip of his spade where his trembling hand caused it time and again to brush the ground beside his boot. He dropped the tool and knelt close to her, anxiety overwhelming his movements and making them seem prolonged and too slow.

A smell of vegetation drifted to him, potent on the still, humid air.

He gathered her up a moment later and hobbled towards his backyard patio door. He glanced quickly in all directions as he went, to make certain no distant neighbour stood with hands shielding their eyes from the day's final sun-glare, wondering at his strange cargo. Certain that he was alone, as he was always, he slipped through the patio door, bringing the perfume of vegetation with him into his sleepy house.

He'd seen as he'd laid her gently on the basement sofa: the slight protuberance above her bare buttocks, the subtle suggestion of a tail.

The blanket he'd covered her with rose and fell evenly and he exhaled deeply with relief. He hadn't struck her too hard, only stunned the live fossil he'd discovered rooting about in his dirt patch potato garden. The soil-dust still coated her fingers, he saw, as he leaned close to where her hand lay across the blanket. He marvelled at their length and the nimbleness they suggested. He stared, awed at her colour, which was like summer almost in bloom: the last night of Spring manifest and curled silently on his threadbare couch.

He knew instinctually and without doubt that it was a female, although he'd seen no physical indication of gender while examining her earlier. Female and young, only a child. This he'd glimpsed in the silent startle of her eyes when he'd discovered her. Their bright astonishment as the foolish old man had swung his primitive stick toward her in his own shameful terror of her strange beauty.

He watched her sleeping and was struck anew. Truly, she was a beautiful creature. And in that instant, he named her, for her skin, and he wished her a silent wish: sleep well, Spring Apple. Whatever you are.

And he climbed the rickety narrow staircase, each slat of wood shrieking like a pained animal. Framed in the doorway, he clicked the light off and left the green girl in darkness. Closing the door silently so as not to disturb her slumber, carefully pulling the heavy meat freezer across the kitchen linoleum and leaning its great weight snugly against the door. He felt shameful in the act, as though he needn't behave in so wary a way—as though he needn't have anything to fear from something as delicate and fragile-looking as the sleeping creature. And yet he made certain to stack both a microwave and toaster oven on top of the freezer, and he retired to wakefulness on his living room chair with his rifle pulled down from the wall and resting across his lap.

And when he secured his meagre few minutes of sleep, it was only when sunlight returned, savage and like fire, seeping through the tightly-drawn curtains and reddening his face where he rested, poorly vigilant, in his chair. He'd managed to dream during the brief spell, only a fragment, but when he woke from it he woke with a start and with the image still stirring in his tired, unfocused eyes.

The deep verdant stretches of a jungle. Trackless in its depths, and himself lost in the endless green.

He sat a moment longer in his chair, sucking in air perfumed with the scent of just this dream place. Vegetation air. Emerald air. And he rose with a creaking in his knees and, awed and hungry for the taste he was breathing in, whispered toward the blockaded door which led into the basement.

His ear against the wood of the door told him and eventually he believed. From within, from below in the basement:

Birds.

Their music stirred him deeply. He'd always adored songbirds, since he was a very young boy. The surrounding county had reawakened his old love when he'd retired here several years before and listened once more to the A.M. symphonies held daily in the trees; and from the rooftop of the old derelict barn he kept to store his truck and all the many relics from his past which could find no place in his house; and from the roofs and rain troughs and scattered telephone wires of the small Leamington downtown strip which he visited weekly.

He clenched his eyes tightly, tried restoring logic to his reeling mind. There could be no such music below his home, in the basement, in the earth where cool air remained even during the most stifling of summer days. But his ear remained pressed to the door wood and he eventually could deny it no longer. From below, the symphony continued unabated.

The strangest birdsong he'd ever admired.

Like something electric. Like pure energy sizzling through a thousand robins or blue jays and merging with the music each species had stored in special genetic code inside of them. Altered by the unknown energy source, made more beautiful by it. Made more foreign through its presence surging there within each note. An alien soundtrack from below, and yet he recognized it clearly, like a song from his youth remembered bitter-sweetly. And he was wiping at his eyes where salty trails wound their way down and across his dusty cheeks.

Breath pent up, heart a hammering cacophony in his chest, he turned the dulled bronze doorknob. Slowly, he pulled, and pulled more, moving the freezer one inch and two and then two more, until the dark crack between door and doorframe grew large enough for him to step through, and deep enough for him to fear. He stood there, looking downward into the inkiness, and he was assailed by the sound, now grown louder, more real and indisputable.

His knees buckled again. His heart played a louder thrashing.

Something flitted past his face, startling him and urging a small cry from him. The flitting thing circled about him, a crimson sizzle whirring through the air at a velocity too fleet for his bulging eyes to follow. Then another whizzing thing zipping past his ear, and he cried out again. He searched for it but could barely follow its quick, erratic flight through the kitchen air, its nervous path hugging closely to the adjacent living room ceiling. Only a flash of colour like its sister sizzle, only this one a bright spot of purple too fast for the eye to contain.

From below, there was more singing, familiar but unknown, an old song through alien singers. He paused a moment, gathering himself, and he descended the squealing, uncertain steps.

She'd grown a coat sometime during the night.

He stared at her, awed all over again. Her beauty was overwhelming this morning. He marvelled at her new colour, thinking distantly that perhaps he'd misnamed her, too quick in his romancing of the strangest discovery he'd ever stumbled on. Deeper, her colour, the lush emerald hue of living things. And he peered with incredulity at her amazing new verdant coat of fur. The tiny hairs covered her everywhere, fuzzy and soft-looking, a true summer fruit dozing in the A.M. birdsong.

Around the small couch upon which she reclined he saw with disbelieving eyes the tangled foliage creeping upwards along the wall. The spreading of these leafy tendrils several inches along the ceiling, too, and massing on the bare concrete floor in bunches and tangles. He jerked his hand to his head as the colour-spot flashed close to his cheek: another red thing sizzling through the air. He looked about the cavernous room and saw.

There was a dozen or more of the strangest birds he'd ever seen, flashing like beacons from their perches in the creeping vines, among the tangles draping over the couch arms and cushions. Several more were making colourful arcs through the air. He peered closer at one he discovered resting from flight near to him, stepping gingerly from foot to foot along its little sward of green vine.

It was blue and bright, with unfolding wings like a butterfly's, fragile-looking and silky. He wondered how those tender wings could carry the creature through the air, its rotund body almost like a perfect globe. But before his eyes, with an electric singing which signalled its intention, the creature became a motion blur of blue and zipped through the air, lost in the basement reaches. It was soon replaced by another, this ball of bird lemon yellow and just as anxious in its foot-to-foot dancings.

When he looked to her again, he found her awake on his couch with her fingers in her mouth. She was licking potato dust from her hands, with a frightened glare in her dark eyes. He thought it beautiful, how she still savoured this garden residue. Like a child suckling its thumb for comfort. Like a hungry child asking silently for food.

He motioned with his hands upraised in an ineffectual gesture of peace. She still eyed him silently and without moving from her tense position on the sofa. He hurried uneasily upstairs and fetched a pail which he took several minutes to fill with potatoes from the garden. When he returned only several minutes later, she was cowering on the couch still, although now with a newly-risen canopy of greenery offering her cozy shelter. He presented the pail to her tentatively, the same slow way in which she eventually accepted his offering. Reaching forward hesitantly, tempted by the uneven landscape of vegetables, eventually snatching one with fingers as dexterous as he'd imagined them to be. She ate with aplomb, munching heartily on one potato after another. Her mouth and fingertips grew dusted with field dirt like an earthy powder or make-up. Her eyes watched him watching her through the entire repast.

He stood and stared from his vantage several feet from her until she'd finished off the entire pail and was sucking her fingertips again. He dared to smile at her black eyes, and to try for words in that surreal moment.

"Hello."

His voice sounded strange in his throat, and its odd presence in the room made him realize that he hadn't spoken at all since discovering the creature in his garden. He winced as she recoiled a little at the noise, eyes suddenly larger, rounder in her emerald features. Again, he raised his hands on the air uselessly, trying to convey his peaceful intentions even while she shrank deeper into the old folds of the sofa and her own leafy embrace.

He ventured, in a much smaller voice, "I won't hurt you. I never hurt anything. See?" He looked to his hands and offered a weak smile, feeling foolish and amazed, sleepy and dreamy. Again, he dared to offer her his voice. "I can see that I named you too quickly. You're more Summer than Spring. I see that now." He chuckled. She cocked her head towards the sound, her round eyes relaxing into a curious expression.

He became conscious of the dull ache in his knees then, and gingerly made his way to the ratty love seat beside the couch. He made sure to watch his own shuffling steps so that the green girl would understand his motion to be harmless. He groaned himself into the old cushions, feeling springs prod him through the worn material. Sighing, he looked to her and was amazed all over again.

Had she become greener during his several-second trip across the room? Was her complexion that much more like the deep lushness of jungle foliage? He smiled at the transformation, if that was indeed what it was, and was pleased to see her cock her head towards him once more. Mouth open to say some soothing thing or another, he paused as a flame landed on his knee. He started a little, focused his eyes on the round bird-like flyer stretching its butterfly wings towards the ceiling. It chirped its electric chirp and it made him smile. He looked to the girl, feeling the boy hidden inside of his ancient skeleton settle into his skin and take over the smile he smiled. A wide smile, and open.

"It seems you've brought friends with you, haven't you?" The flame bird darted its small head up at his words, hopping gingerly from one foot to another as it examined him. It lingered, making its little noises like energy-chirpings and watching him with curiosity. He turned to the girl and, pointing slowly to the pail on the floor, said, "I'm glad somebody likes my potatoes besides me. It feels good, you know? To share my garden with someone again. It's always better than eating alone."

He recalled his wife, dead now for several years, and their children off in the cities to the east and to the south, who worked their city-jobs and had no time for home-grown vegetable feasts. He remembered the look of his darling kneeling in garden dirt, with daffodils stirring in the air around her. He recalled Montgomery, his faithful dog of unknown lineage, which he'd buried himself in the garden after discovering its inert body lying sideways among the daffodils, heart failure among his flowers. His own heart had almost burst among them that day, too, slamming the shovel tip into the soft earth and feeling somehow cruel in so doing, deepening the hole to fit one wonderful animal among the crumbly, moist dirt and earthworms burrowing their tunnels.

A soft sound stirred him from his reverie. A tiny rumble, a gurgle, and he looked to the green girl's belly and smiled at her. She looked to her stomach, too, placing a hand over its small, rounded curvature. "That's one too many potatoes, I'd guess."

And he chuckled. He actually was able to laugh a little in her presence, an act he realized in that instant he hadn't enjoyed since Maria died years ago. Laughter, and the sight of the strange creature with her large, stunned eyes examining her noisy stomach made him shake with it. It was delicious, and he thanked her with the tears in his eyes and with words, too. "Thank you, thank you so much, Spring. Spring Into Summer. I didn't even know how much I needed that medicine."

The green girl continued to watch him closely, though he thought he saw her posture relax. Eventually, she pulled the pail from the floor and cradled it in her lap, savouring the lingering aroma of earth and potatoes. He felt ashamed when he noticed the slight swell on her otherwise smooth head, where he'd knocked her a good bump and sent her to sleep. He winced too when he remembered the rifle he'd pulled from the wall and left leaning at the base of the staircase, in case the beautiful thing he'd found hid something un-guessable and dangerous. He watched her hugging her pail and saw her docile nature. He saw it in her mysterious yet kind eyes while she watched him back, just as openly, just as wondrously.

His dreams had been serene and when he woke he discovered himself in a jungle.

Fronds were thick and waved into his eyes. The whirring of invisible insects surrounded him. Something grazed his arm and he looked and saw a flying silver stick hover close to him and then drift off into the greenery, its transparent gossamer wings nearly indiscernible on the air.

He stood from his chair, now covered in creeping vines and small flowering buds, wiping the vines from around his wrists and where they'd bunched about his thighs. Something stirred in the bushes at his feet and he glimpsed a large, six-legged shrimp scampering along the floor, which was no longer bare concrete but peeked through the greenery as a rich-looking layer of earth. He stumbled speechless through the foliage, bumping his knee softly on the sofa, now cocooned in leaves and chutes and an abundance of small, silky-petaled flowers, the species unfamiliar to him. He wondered at the thick clump of these flowers on the spot directly before the buried sofa, their pointed scarlet and green striped petals reminding him of Christmas. Then he realized, the potato pail, and his absent green girl.

40

He looked about for her but saw only much smaller movements: the gentle bobbing of some strange emerald insect as long as his hand among the fronds; a squadron of silver sticks drifting past in the distance, alongside a towering hedge of bushes and vines that it took him a moment to realize was his cocooned furnace; another of the shrimp runners padding along between his feet; a bizarre, rodent-like creature with silver-specked furry body and fleet feet that carried it silently beneath the green layers of the sofa. And a thousand invisible shufflings and tickings and whisperings in the jungle around him.

He turned and was startled to knock his crown against a newly risen tree, thin and black-barked. He stared in wonder at its tangles of branches and their cargo of miniature, oval-shaped buds, like purple and red-spotted alien fruit. It took him several minutes, but he eventually found the staircase and ascended it, slowly, because its new floor of grass was slippery with dew.

The upstairs was similarly jungle-conquered, too. Butterfly-birds circled in his kitchen and nested in his cupboards. From the living room came the cacophony of monkeys or some things which recalled to his ears the frenzied cries of simians. He nearly became tangled in the long, green, caterpillar-like thing like a bright feather boa which barred his path to the back door.

He found her, of course, among his potatoes, munching quietly, a mellow sheen over her eyes. The small earthquaking inside her belly sounded in the cricket stillness, too, comforting him somehow in his awe.

He squatted down beside her, cracking his knee joints and aching his lower back. His whisper was laboured. "You're an amazing little girl, aren't you? I feel as though you've brought me through the old rabbit hole."

Her throat gurgled in response, and her delicate fingers plucked another potato from the earth. He watched her nibble it and saw her tiny teeth sparkle in the early evening moonlight. He turned his eyes to the heavens and watched the stars slowly emerge, one by one, then hundred by hundred. Soon, the star field was everywhere, and he realized that he didn't keep his vigil alone. He turned to her, saw that she was scanning the sky, round eyes roving slowly from east to west.

Those small, black eyes reflected constellations whose names he'd forgotten but whose youthful romance lingered in his heart still.

"Which way?" he whispered to her, and though she made no response, he was happy to note that she no longer shrank from his too-loud old man's voice, the hoarseness of his attempted whispers. "Do they call to you? Which one is yours, or do you call the underground here your home? You certainly do seem to enjoy playing in the dirt."

The green girl gobbled her potato and breathed in the dust it left floating on the air.

The old man returned his eyes to the sky. He once knew the names of many constellations, had recited them like poetry for his darling Maria in the days of their courtship. He remembered telling her once, not long after they'd been married, that he saw a secret design among the stars which reminded him of her. He'd pointed and made his declaration to the night sky: *Maria. There you are. Between the archer and the bear. Being brave and strong and beautiful for the world to see, if they only happen to look up.*

He recalled the feel of feathers on his cheek after he'd recited these words: her lips, warm and soft, making his meagre poetry worthwhile. He hadn't thought of it in quite some time, because he could no longer enjoy evening skies like he once used to. He felt the old ache throb inside his chest, and he winced at its familiar pain. But he murmured the words then, upwards to the stars. "I miss you, my darling."

When he turned to look at the green girl, he found her eyes watching the shimmering black overhead along with him, a potato forgotten between her fingers. Her black eyes reflected that shimmering sadly, and he believed he understood at least some part of the mystery they held.

He found her star-watching on most nights.

Clambering through the dense green maze of his jungle-home, he passed the strange creatures occupying his grassy steps and soil-covered linoleum. He passed the sing-song trickling of water from somewhere in his basement, a secret water source he'd searched for on several occasions but had yet to stumble upon. Always climbing through his vine-draped patio doorway, fearful of the presence of some horrified distant neighbour waiting astonished for him in his overgrown yard.

But the old man rarely had visitors on his humble plot of land, and his children, all grown and busy inside of their own lives, called only infrequently. Only the green girl, with her black eyes fixed all over the sky. Her posture disappointed with slumped back and sagging shoulders. With earth-dust around her mouth and a rumble in her belly, her coat of emerald bright and lush in the darkness, she was a healthy and thriving beacon drawing his admiration each time he gazed on her, but no acknowledgement or signal from the sky.

He'd taken to sitting with her outdoors every night, even during the chilly final weeks of August. He'd laughed and shown her that she needn't fear the arrival of fireflies in the county, catching one in his hand and cupping it there gently for her to peek through his fingers and admire. Eventually, she plucked them gently from the air, too, and held their pulsing bodies close to her eyes, cocking her head side to side as if bewitched by their light.

One night, while watching her examining a night crawler poking itself from a hole in the lawn, he'd murmured, mostly only to himself, "What kind of powers do you own, that you can grow so much in my little home on a diet of potatoes and dirt alone?"

In answer, the green girl had rocked backward and forward in a funny little dancing motion where she sat near to him in his lawn chair. Her eyes were closed tightly—as if in mirth or joy, he wasn't certain. But a beautiful moment it was, and one that he thanked her for heartily. "Thank you, child. I haven't known magic like this in too many years." And then he added, almost as an afterthought, "We must grow you some more vegetables, and soon. Or you'll lose your bright colour."

And he cried softly, while she watched his tears with inscrutable eyes.

He found her watching the grass one quiet morning before the crickets had awoken for their playing, staring fixedly at the spot upon which her small green feet were planted.

He was surprised to realize that it was the site where he'd buried Montgomery three years before. "Yes," he murmured softly. "It's a special spot, isn't it, my dear?"

The green girl only continued to watch the grass and feel its warmth with her curling, furry toes.

The next morning, he discovered a bouquet of flowers growing on the spot. Yellow, like daffodils and sunlight, only brighter and much more beautiful for his eyes to look upon.

●　　●　　●

Leaning on his walking stick, the old man ventured about his property in search of some sign of the green girl's arrival, finding nothing.

No craft like a star-plucked steel leaf nestled among corn rows, immobile and depleted of some un-guessable fuel. No wreckage or debris looking alien among the wheat, and no other wondrous summer apples wandering the fields and bushes with wide, black eyes desperately searching the county horizon.

There were only tractors making deep ruts in the earth, and ordinary gatherings of crows on wooden fences. There was the hum of invisible insect life in the grass and trees, and the crackling sound of summer afternoon heat baking the corn and wheat rows.

And he returned to his little plot of land, remade in its new splendour, and it was like returning to another time and place entirely. His knees brushed exotic and vivid petals and fronds, and a million unnameable smells filled his senses. He drank them in gladly, and his thirst was satiated, and no coat of dust bothered his tongue and the back reaches of his throat any longer.

He found her in the dirt, examining beetles black as her eyes, allowing plump bumblebees to land on her soft-furred fingers, and cocking her head at a pair of orange cats watching her surreptitiously from among the wild grass.

He saw that her tail had grown. No longer nub-like, it now made a little curlicue where it lay modestly curving her buttocks, and the delightful sight of it made him adore her all the more. He descended his weight into his lawn chair, creaking its rickety frame or maybe his own, and watched her bury her feet in the soil in delight. He was tired from his walk and felt the tremor still stirring inside of his ancient knees.

He squinted into the bloody late-afternoon sun, a frown worrying his wizened features, and he murmured, "What shall we do with you, my dear? Whatever shall we do?"

They lingered in the yard, and when the first stars emerged against the deep purple backdrop of dusk, he saw her stare forlornly into the sky.

He watched her in her melancholy vigil, and ached for her, understanding all too well. He said, with a sad glimmer in his eyes, "I know, my dear. It's a terrible ache, isn't it? To be so alone, and no one visits you? It makes even the stars less beautiful."

His jungle house in the sleeping county grew, and no farmer or other retiree could guess the beauty he grew there. Or the nature of the first wondrous seed, the small frail child with the bottomless eyes and the coat of green, like a celebration of summer's best qualities.

He wondered if others wondered, distant farmers shielding their eyes from the trickery of sunlight making oasis mirages in the heat-shimmering distance: is that a new tree in the old man's yard over there in the hazy distance? I don't recall that row of bushes bordering his house on the east side. Where did it come from? And that strange new sapling, only a trick of the light surely, but its leaves look so dark and strangely-shaped from this distance. Did it spring up overnight?

He continued to wonder himself, and his worry for the girl grew every day. Who could tell what might happen if the wrong person noticed the miracle in the county? Visitors would travel from far and wide to witness the spectacle of this unknown geography, and for a glimpse of its amazing maker.

He braved the unknown one night himself, while his throat was parched but his legs too tired to walk him indoors to refill his empty glass from the flowers-obscured kitchen tap. Reaching over his head, he plucked the round, black fruit from the overhanging branch of the new tree. He brought its furry skin to his lips and slipped his dentures deep into its surprisingly soft body. Its delicious moisture refreshed him, its taste vaguely reminiscent of pumpkin only much sweeter, yet with the refreshing tang of orange and some indefinable other ingredient which brought to mind visions of palm fronds and other greenery. And he didn't crave water for the entire rest of the evening.

He'd caught her watching him silently, though, from among the tall spikiness of a strange new cluster of purple flowers with petals like cartoon lips. Tilting her head one side to another. Looking tranquil in her roost. Looking somehow pleased.

● ● ●

He found her as dawn burned the jagged field horizon line.

Her small body was torn and rent, curled up among the daffodils and weeds. Her colour vanished, green to pale off-yellow, nearly white. The awful transformation had transpired sometime during the earliest A.M. hours, while he'd slept soundly in the indoors jungle. Her small eyes clenched tightly in her final moments, frozen in her departing terror.

He judged the teeth and claw marks to be those of a dog. A roaming animal from one of the outlying farms, perhaps, happening on the strangest creature it had ever encountered in any of its nocturnal travels. Startled, perhaps, in its discovery, striking instinctively at this unknown thing resting where only field mice and raccoons and grasshoppers were known to roam.

He remembered the haunting feel of the shovel connecting with her small, green skull on the evening when he'd first discovered her rooting about in his garden. The deeply regretful feeling of examining her child's body with shaking fingers, stomach churning at the sight of the darkening welt atop her head.

A numbness settled into him, touching his bones and thoughts as he stood staring. Only his heart burned, with an ache he recalled from years ago, when his wife had gone to sleep and never awoken again, ruining the peaceful picture of evening skies for him forever; making grass-watching and potato-gardening easier tasks than admiring shimmering constellations of his own invention.

The salty taste of tears, where they rivered down into the corners of his mouth, stirred him.

He gathered her wordlessly in his arms, as he'd done once before, and carried her to the garden. She was cold against his skin, shivering him in the still cool morning air. Her lifeless touch made him recall the morning several days ago when he'd awoken in the lawn chair to find her asleep across his lap, the warmth of her sleepy form making him tranquil and drowsy while the sun rose and illuminated the awakening day around them. Spring, Summer, Life. This was his green girl. She'd never known winter because wherever she'd come from there existed no such season of icy death. This he knew, like he knew a few things about evening skies.

He dug her a hole, beside the grave of Montgomery, and placed her there with tears ruining his vision. He wept for a long time afterwards, his tears keeping his cheeks clean of the dirt that powdered his hands and nose. When his legs grew too weak from his digging work, he knelt down before the grave with a popping of springs in his knees, and wept there for a long while, too.

He looked to the new day's sky of sun and distant, wispy clouds, and felt the lingering chill of the night goose pimple his skin. It was the end of August, and he knew now that summer was truly ended.

The old man began calling his children on the telephone, not so much as to become annoying, he hoped, only so much so that they remembered that he was alive and well. His weekend rings became tradition and he made certain to speak with cheer even if he was feeling a little bit glum.

He spent time in his backyard, watching the ordinary birds in his old tree, and listening to the violining of crickets as dusk settled over the fields each evening. And he star-watched with great dedication, too, spending time with each shimmering speck he could find before his old eyes became too tired and he was nodding off into sleep.

The jungle had crept out of his home as stealthily and mysteriously as it had arrived. The morning he'd discovered her among the daffodils even, he'd noticed the limp look of the strange cluster of silvery flowers beside his patio door; the drooping vines looking forlorn and lifeless everywhere; the withered fronds and pale grass, and the silence among the bushes where hidden things had stirred and rustled only days before.

Where the grass had gone to, he did not know. Where the rich soil layering his linoleum and carpets had seeped, he couldn't begin to guess without convincing himself that senility had arrived with his many years to claim him once and for all.

But he frequently visited the spot in his neatly-manicured lawn, beside the grave of his old trusted dog, where he'd once dug another, similar hole, and filled it with a dying beauty. He stood before this spot on the remaining afternoons of lingering summery haze, and even on occasion during chill September evenings when the breeze shook him, making him nervous and rattling the dentures against his gums. And he admired with wondrous eyes, not unlike the wide-open gaze of a child, the strange and amazing tree growing from that very place in the lawn. Very foreign its supple green trunk like a large plant-stem, furred like a tennis ball only much softer to the touch. Unmistakably alien the way its thin, curvaceous branches grew ripe cargoes of round, similarly-furred and delicious fruit among their rich emerald and obsidian leaves. Flowers bloomed there, too, along the trunk and branches, and particularly at the tree's base, where they flourished, clustering wildly and in vibrant profusion. Their crimson and violet hues were radiant, their delicate, silvery markings shone in sunlight and moon glow alike.

He took his time standing upon this spot, savouring the sight of the strange flowers stirring in the breeze, and the fruits bobbing in their places, like lush, living ornaments celebrating a season past. And a bittersweet ache pained his heart during such moments and made it very difficult not to cry.

But in the evenings, he found himself less unhappy than he once was. Maybe this was because he could name several more constellations each night that passed, as if the simple act of watching their twinkling light held enough power to part the collected time of years and make recollection easier to bear.

And when his children asked, on occasion, why his happy tone, or what the secret of county living might be that he sounded so hopeful during their telephone talks, he startled them first with laughter, robust and hearty—and then also with his words, spoken with zestful wistfulness, if such a thing could possibly exist in the universe.

"There are bushes and there are trees everywhere," he told them. "Everywhere. And they never wilt and die, not really. Winter arrives and ravages the land, surely, but Spring always returns. And those bushes and trees, well, their cargoes sing. They sing songs of beauty that are hard to imagine for city people like you and you and you. And there are flowers that grow out here, and they move to those songs, too. And if we're lucky enough, and we listen very closely, we hear their secret rhythms and we dance with them, too. And I have one very, very special tree, my darlings. It grows in my yard near to my potato garden, and it is a strange and beautiful tree. It's quite an alien and amazing specimen, and the fruit it bears—oh, the fruit it bears! There's no other tree quite like it in this world, and of that I'm very certain!"

His children invariably chuckled good-naturedly at his words and made promises to visit him in his amazing county country.

And he always made certain to add one other wonder of the land to his prodigious list. "The stars, my darlings," he told his children. "The stars here are better than anywhere else. Here, they shine and twinkle and tremble, and you can see every constellation that ever formed. One is even able, on occasion, to discover new ones, and old ones emerged again after many long years hidden." Then he added, "Although, it must be said, that it's always a prettier sight to watch them with someone else beside you. Someone who sees the big sad romance in a picture like that."

And they heard the wistfulness in his dreamy words, and they promised once more to come and visit, and sometimes they found time in their busy city lives to do just that. And when they did, their father gathered them on the grass beneath evening skies, and together they marvelled at the good perfume of the flowers and trees and county air.

"You're right, Dad," they invariably agreed. "It's so peaceful out here. And quiet. And beautiful."

The old man nodded at their words, and said, "Oh, there's beauty, my darlings. Beauty and mystery deeper than anything."

And they smiled at his dreamy, romantic words.

And he pointed into the night sky, there and there and there, and he showed them.

THE PRIESTS

The main character here—and he's a strange one—was born in another manuscript. He's a minor character in a novel I took many years to complete, and whose peculiar tale, I thought, deserved its own time in the spotlight. His is a story about beauty and magic in a brutal world where goodness has been mostly extinguished. It's a world you may recognize as our own, though his story takes place quite some time in the past.

There's a scene in which the character is reading a book. That same book has always been a great comfort to me, too.

Oh, to close your eyes, and when you reopen them to have awoken in a different place...

"For the Son of Man came to
seek and to save the lost."

—Luke 19:10

I: THE HOUSE

Pastor Geoffrey Garfield was rinsing the pewter donation bowl behind the rectory when he saw the figure shambling in from the field. It used the narrow, balding footpath that wound through the wild grass and the woods beyond, and which led to exactly where Garfield stood, brows knitted together as he squinted in the milky-aired dawn. Initially, he'd thought it was a small group of men with arms wrapped about one another, perhaps friends, perhaps drunken revellers, though the town, with its main street of taverns and brothels, lay in the opposite direction from which they came.

Soon, though, he understood that it was no group of men.

It moved in a peculiar manner, partly shuffling, partly swaying, and seemingly turning about full circle, time and again, as it came forward. At first Pastor Garfield thought it an ungainly method of locomotion, but the longer he watched, bewitched, he understood the fluidity and alien grace of its movement.

As the figure drew closer, the pastor's jaw dropped and the pewter bowl fell from his fingers to land with a flat wallop in the mud at his feet while he clutched the silver crucifix hanging about his neck through his vestments.

"I have heard of you," Pastor Garfield said. "The name they call you has travelled this land far and wide, though most— myself included—might not have believed the stories."

They were standing facing one another within the rectory. It was swathed in a patchwork of ill-fitting, dirty rags, their stench hanging in the warm air. It clutched a grimy satchel protectively in one of its hands. The pastor stood with his back to the entrance to the church proper, where tapers cast an inviting glow in the expansive room.

"Yes, I seem to have become the stuff of urban legend or nightmare," said one of the voices of the figure before the pastor.

And another of its voices said, "Though I believe the main of the tales you hear are not very accurate."

And the third of its voices said, "Which name do you refer to, Father? *Horror? Monster? Sideshow attraction?*"

Pastor Garfield said, "Men call you... the Priests."

"Ah yes," said all of its voices in unison, a strangely sibilant sound. "They call me that as well."

Indeed, its name had travelled by word of mouth over the years, and grown to become something like a dark tale by which mothers and fathers would coerce their wayward children to go to sleep—sleep, children, or the Priests will come for you in the wee hours, and take you far south of Heaven. The Priests was, though, no figment of the imagination but rather, as Garfield now

52

saw, a real-life abnormality, a freak of nature, a strange being comprised of three bodies linked as one like a bizarre Siamese triplet. Each of its bodies was joined at the shoulders and faced inwards, with its heads bowed eternally together, giving the name by which it was most known, for its resemblance to a trio of men leaned together in earnest prayer, though many frowned upon such a sacrilegious moniker.

Pastor Garfield, still awed by the reality of the creature, sought to introduce as normal an atmosphere between them as he was able. Gesturing to the couch he said, "Please, sit." And then, "Can you... That is to say, are you able... to sit?" He felt foolish asking, felt that it was surely an imbecilic question, but then he had never met with such a scenario before.

"Yes," said one of the Priests's voices, though the pastor couldn't tell which body had spoken. Its other voices echoed, "Thank you, Father." "Thank you."

He watched amazed as the creature drew itself upon the couch in a complex yet graceful movement of its peculiar body, folding its limbs queerly so that two of its bodies rested along the edge of the couch cushions, their combined weight holding aloft the third body, whose legs lay crossed on the cushion while its torso remained suspended in the open air beyond.

"Are you... comfortable?"

"Yes."

"Very much so."

"Thank you, Father."

Pastor Garfield seated himself across from the Priests, in the sister wood and plush armchair. Folding his hands across his lap, he looked at the creature levelly and said, "Where did you come from, my children? And what... what exactly are you, if I may be so bold?"

"I do not know," said the three voices of the Priests as one. "I only know *that* I am." One of its voices added, almost as an afterthought and with a hint of mild amusement, "You may refer to me in the singular, Pastor. For I am one person."

Another of its voices said, "One."

A third said, "Three-in-one."

"Oh, yes, I see," said Pastor Garfield. "I apologize. Please forgive me, my child. I've never met with someone quite like you before."

"No," said a voice of the Priests.

53

"You have not," said another.

"Three-in-one," said a third.

"Why... Why have you come here?" said Pastor Garfield.

The Priests paused and after some deliberation, during which the pastor had the distinct feeling that the being wasn't so much considering its words but conferring among each of its individual bodies or minds, one of its voices said, "Why do I go anywhere?" and another voice answered, "I seek salvation," and another voice said, "If salvation is to be found in this world." And then together, in a manner that unsettled the Pastor, the three voices in unison said, "Perhaps fate brought me here. Perhaps one such as I, whom the world has given the name of the Priests, was destined from the beginning to conclude its journey in a place like this, an oasis in the heart of this world where oases are very few and far between."

A pained expression came over Pastor Garfield's face. "This world... You must know of its savagery," he said. "The world is a hard place for most men."

The Priests nodded its heads, and Garfield guessed the expressions it wore were creased with bitter remembrances. He'd initially wished to be able to see its individual faces, to look it in the eyes, but in that moment found himself relieved that he could not.

"A place of hardness," said one of its voices.

And another said, "And sadness."

And a third said, "And wickedness everywhere."

The Priests, weary from its long journey, sagged on the couch as if sleep were pulling it down, and yet the need to unburden itself of its long tale kept it awake. And so it talked and talked, and the things it spoke of seemed very foreign and unreal to the Pastor, yet rooted in a reality all-too believable given what he knew of humankind, so that it felt as though the Priests spoke from some strange midway point, some place between dream and reality. And oh, what a place it was. What a sad, aching country it was.

II: WHAT THE WORLD SAID

"One body belongs to an idiot—it cannot think! It drools and it gibbers and it jabbers!"

Individual voices rose above the crowd's general murmurings. "Let's see it!"

"Show us the monster, barker!"

"Freak! Freak!"

The carny, smiling triumphantly, stepped aside in perfect synchrony with his assistant, a gaunt, pimple-faced twelve-year-old boy he'd trained well in his simpleton's tasks, who pulled heavily on a rope as stout as a grown man's forearm. The tattered brown curtain behind them lifted upwards from the wooden stage floor. Voices rose from the greater murmur of the crowd, throwing themselves toward the small wooden stage erected along one side of the stained tent. Smoke hung in a dense cloud over the heads of the people, billowing upwards into the domed curvature of the small tent's ceiling.

"Behold!" the carny shouted.

Gasps and shouts and whispers of disbelief and horror from the people, as the Priests lay revealed, standing naked underneath the plain light of the gas lamps mounted on either side of the tiny stage.

The carny struggled over the crowd-voice: "One of the beings has a great intellect and that, ladies and gentlemen, is a true tragedy, for it is trapped between the idiot and... the *other*!"

The carny's wooden stick smacked one of the Priests's heads viciously. The crowd gasped, held spellbound by the dark origin of the being that spilled from the carny. He spat, "And this final body, oh! this final body is the *truly* horrifying one, for it hungers for human flesh and for the soft flesh of babies most especially! It feels only hunger and fury and lashes out in violence whenever opportunity arises! Beware, ladies and gentlemen!"

The shouts of the rowdy crowd grew more unruly still. They were eager to see proof of the spectacle of the horror, to decide whether it was grotesque enough for their satisfaction and worth the price of admission into the gloomy tent. The carny, his spiel timed to perfection after the many long months of touring the carnival circuit, roared, "Turn it around! Show the people the horrors!" And he and his young assistant slipped wooden sticks among the intertwined bodies of the Priests and pushed it and pushed it, turning the helpless being around in a circle for those gathered to see. It spun and it spun, its three pairs of bare, callused feet pattering along the wooden stage floor, its penises releasing the streams of urine that its bladders could no longer contain for the fear filling its pounding hearts.

Cries of horror and disgust rose on the smoky air. Fruit and stones and crumpled papers pelted the Priests as it cowered its three bodies closer together in a futile bid for preservation. Its voices whispered beseechingly all throughout the assault:

"It's not true—I am no monster."

"I am a man."

"I have good in my hearts."

But no one heard through the emphatic din.

III: WHAT THE WOMEN SAID

In the warm cave darkness, a voice said, "I have the need."

"Yes, the need is strong," said a second voice.

The third said, "I'll have a tug."

"Three tugs. Three-in-one," said the second, getting to work by swivelling its left arm down and grasping the flaccid penis of the first, and vice versa, until each penis of the Priests was held by a hot hand. Three bodies; one gestalt, a single home of connected limbs. Like any other person, it satisfied itself when it needed to.

The Priests's breathing grew louder in the cave. After a moment, the voices spoke together. "This is no good. I need more."

"Do I dare?" one of its voices ruminated.

"Yes," another said. "Yes."

Without further discussion, the Priests slipped from its alcove set into the hillside along the edge of the woods, where it had found shelter after fleeing the carnival, and made its way towards the lights of the town glowing like embers at the base of the hill in the hot summer night.

The toothless prostitute slipped between the Priests's web of arms and legs. Standing there in the midst of the three bodies, she looked claustrophobic. Fear and revulsion vied for control of her features, but her need for money won out and she smiled grimly.

"What's your boys's pleasure?" she said.

"I am but one," said the voice in her ear.

"Three-in-one," said the mouth beside her.

"One," said the head which she faced inside the meat-web. "Well, if you want it, you gotta pay for all three of you. That's about fair, I'd say."

After a moment of deliberation, the Priests said, "As you wish." In a life of abject poverty, the meagre hoard of coins it had stolen over the years was a treasure, and difficult to part with. But some needs had to be met no matter the cost.

"But know that I am, in fact, one."

"Three-in-one. Three-in-one."

The prostitute, with raised eyebrow, began unlacing herself and said, "Okay then. How would you like it, sir?"

The Priests passed her around between its three bodies. While one filled her from behind another would fondle her large swaying breasts, holding her in place, while the third stroked her thighs or ran fingers through her curls. The laboured breathing from its faces was loud and hot in the confined space.

When it was finished, the prostitute disengaged herself from the weird embrace of the Priests and stood beside it in the alley, counting her money with hands that trembled, making the task difficult.

The voices of the Priests said:

"Thank you. You are a beautiful woman."

"Beautiful."

"Thank you for being with me, one with three-in-one."

She watched the being as it moved deeper into the alley darkness in its strange shuffling-spinning manner, like a wheel made of interlocked men. The Priests watched the prostitute too, for as it moved it spun about, giving each of its pairs of eyes the opportunity to see the woman standing in the fringe of streetlight glow that invaded the narrow alley. The Priests could tell by the expression on her face that the memory of the thick and otherworldly embrace she'd experienced would haunt her, though something else in her eyes betrayed some deeper, more troubling thought. Perhaps no one in all her years of such clandestine meetings had ever called her beautiful.

IV: WHAT SCIENCE SAID

"Okay, let's have a listen."

The Priests briefly came into the care—though the Priests would have called it *possession*—of a physician. Dr. Walter Stokes had discovered the Priests as part of a traveling sideshow and purchased its freedom from the show's proprietor. Immediately upon securing the Priests, he'd brought it to his office under cover of nightfall for an examination.

Reaching a trembling hand inside the space made by the Priests's connected bodies, he moved his stethoscope with great —if unsteady—deliberation from one of its chests to the next to the next. As his hand moved the little silver device, his mouth moved as if of its own volition, murmuring words like, "Incredible," "Amazing," "Miraculous," and culminating with, "Sweet Lord, can this be, can this really be?"

After a moment, Stokes straightened and, staring with wide eyes, said, "Have you but one personality or three?"

"I have three, each of which is distinct from the others, though we each want the same things. We do not squabble, we do not argue, for we agree on all things."

"But you experience those things... individually?"

"In a manner of speaking, yes," said the three voices of the Priests as one, "Though, as you can see from the way in which I answer your questions—as one—I am of one mind. My personalities give comfort to one another, and strength, but they all inform and speak of one mind. Somehow, I am, and have always been... three together as one."

"As with any other person in the world, many different moods and characteristics make up who I am," added another voice of the Priests.

The physician stared at the Priests raptly. "Amazing," he said again. "I'm finding it difficult to understand, but I am fascinated beyond words." Then, fiddling with the stethoscope, moving it along one of the Priests's backs, he said, "Have you heard of Joseph Merrick? The so-called Elephant Man?"

"Yes," said one of the voices of the Priests, while the other voices murmured agreement too. Then a second voice from within the circle of the being said, "I feel sorrow for Mr. Merrick. Great sorrow."

"Yes, great sorrow."

"My hearts go out to him."

A curious and rather indignant expression seeped its way into Dr. Stokes's features. He said, "And why do you feel sorrow for Mr. Merrick, who has shown such courage in the face of his condition, and such an unguessed and admirable predilection for the arts?"

"Because he is alone," said a voice from inside the circle of the Priests, silencing the doctor.

"Yes, alone."

"One. Only one."

The night outside the physician's office window had grown quiet. The moon seemed frozen in its sky of pitch, never to crawl into the west again.

"Will you let me study you?" said Dr. Stokes.

"Yes," answered the Priests as one, disliking the lie it so easily gave the doctor, knowing, of course, that it could do nothing else if it were to survive, for it had seen the look in the man's eyes: a cold and calculating avarice the likes of which it had seen plenty of in its years among men. By morning, it had slipped away undetected from the cheap motel room the doctor had rented for it, no doubt leaving its short-lived personal physician wondering whether the madness of his previous evening's appointment had actually transpired at all, whether something like it had any place in the bright day-lighted world he knew, where nightmares didn't really exist among his usual patients with their everyday sicknesses and complaints.

It was hours after making its escape under cover of a sudden and violent rainstorm, while the Priests was taking a rest from its trek through the sodden, thundering night, that it crossed paths with a drunk man stumbling toward his bed somewhere. The man stopped short, squinting through the rain and shadows at the strange form hunkered down alongside the wall of the squat building in the alley, cocking an ear at the sound of its voices.

"Who's that?" he called, and then, more belligerently, "What the hell are you whispering over there?"

"A prayer, friend," said one of its voices.

The man staggered closer. In the brief illumination thrown from a flash of lightning he saw the Priests in all its strangeness. A gasp escaped him, and he hissed, "What demon prays during a storm like this?" The man's eyes were wide with horror. His hand went instinctively to his hip, where a knife was undoubtedly hidden beneath his shirt.

"Perhaps we pray for all of us."

"You and I, and everyone."

"All."

The man's expression of fear turned to one of disgust, and though he opened his mouth to speak, no words came, for he knew not what to say. Confusion came over him, which angered him, and so he only spat at the Priests and said, "Go to Hell, you fuckin' ugly demon! God save us from you!"

And the man stumbled on his way, careening from the rough brick walls of the buildings he passed, casting fearful glances behind him as he went.

The Priests remained where it was, making no effort to find shelter from the storm. It stood very still in the deluge, in the centre of the widening pool of muddy water in the centre of the alley, as if waiting for a word or sign from the tumultuous sky, or perhaps waiting to feel cleansed.

V: WHAT THE CHILDREN SAID

"Has anyone ever loved you?" said the little blonde-haired girl, eyes wide and probing.

The Priests looked down on the child from its place inside the observation tank on the small wooden stage. Through the scratched face of the thin protective glass, the girl was queerly elongated, making her face mean and severe, unless of course this was the beginnings in her face of the future woman peering through.

The Priests's answer fell quickly and sure in the stuffy air of the display case, rising into the heights of the barn beyond, in which the observation tank had been erected in this small town whose name it would never learn but whose people seemed so much like those of all the other nameless small towns through which the carnival show passed.

"I have myself."

"Three-in-one."

"One."

The little girl considered this for a moment. Then she said, "You're so ugly, I think no one ever loved you or ever will."

And she turned quickly on her heel and marched the length of the barn and out its open doors, to where her parents waited for her. Their laughter reached the Priests inside its tank, sounding muted and nervous but no less vindictive.

In a single hushed voice, the Priests called after the girl, "I'm sorry for you, child. But it is you, beneath your pretty cherub's face, that is truly and deeply ugly."

VI: WHAT THE FAMILY SAID

But there was goodness in the world, too, the Priests learned. Rare people, like Reginald Bonnycott Bendum, ringmaster of a traveling circus and father to its menagerie of strange men and women and children and beasts. The Priests had approached Bendum when the freak show it was a part of crossed paths with his own, much larger traveling spectacle. The Priests, expecting much the same reaction from him as it received from most people, was surprised at the man's warmth and the friendship he offered without any hint of avarice or dishonesty.

"When you join my traveling show," he'd proclaimed with a great smile on his lips and the twinkle in his eye for which he was known far and wide, "You become a part of my family."

The days that followed were good ones. The Priests made friends, shared sympathetic stories with troupe members, felt acceptance for the first time in its life. But over the months, something grew inside the hearts of the Priests, which it took quite some time for it to recognize as a great unrest, and a great need for knowledge that its newfound life—as wondrous and good as it was—could not satisfy.

One evening, the ringmaster welcomed the Priests into the study of his lavish trailer following its appearance in the freak tent several hours earlier. He left the room and returned a moment later with refreshments for himself and his guest, and stopped short in the doorway. Peering between the Priests's connected network of limbs he saw that it had retrieved a book from one of the shelves which lined the room. It was holding the volume between its heads and, cocking an ear, the ringmaster discerned its voices taking turns speaking softly, one after another after another.

"'I opened my eyes upon a strange and weird landscape.'"

"'I knew that I was on Mars.'"

"'Not once did I question either my sanity or my wakefulness.'"

Into the silence following the Priests's voices, Reginald Bonnycott Bendum said, "My Lord, you're able to read!"

The Priests quickly lowered the book in its hands. "Forgive me, sir. I hope I have not been rude and too liberal in reading from one of your books."

Another of its voices, equally flustered, said, "Your shelves hold so many volumes, it was hard to resist investigating them further."

"So many books," said its third voice. "So many voices." Indeed, the ringmaster was an avid reader, and loved strange and wondrous tales best of all. He'd been a collector of books for many years, and his travels to different cities afforded him the luxury of visiting many different bookshops.

"Of course you haven't been rude at all, my friend," Bendum said. "Please feel free. I just... I'm only a little surprised that you're able to read, though I suppose I shouldn't be—your eloquence should have told me."

"Books have been a solace and escape for me often throughout the years," the Priests said, "Though I have not been able to read nearly as much as I would have liked, for books are difficult to come by."

Another of its voices said, "I no longer recall how or when I learned to read."

And a third voice finished, "But I've been grateful for the gift as long as I can remember."

"You'll find no better escape than that which you hold in your hands now," the ringmaster said. "Mr. Burroughs is a master of taking his reader away, whether into time-lost jungles or places beyond the stars."

"Yes, I can see that," said the Priests.

"I feel the refuge in these pages," said the Priests.

"Refuge," said the Priests. "Haven."

"The book is yours," said the ringmaster.

The Priests sucked in its breaths as one. "But sir! I cannot accept such a generous gift..."

"You can, and you will," said Bendum with conviction, a glimmer in his eyes. "Please, my friend. Consider it... a farewell gift, from one friend to another."

"Then you know that I seek answers that your nomad caravan cannot give me," said a voice of the Priests wondrously, sadly.

"I thought as much, my friend," conceded Bendum. "I had a feeling that's what you wanted to speak to me about this evening." Then, "Who raised you, when you were a child? Have you no ties to this person or persons today?"

"I do not know," said a voice of the Priests.

"I no longer recall—it was so long ago," said another.

A third voice said, "I remember a woman—a very old woman—but the memory of her is seen as if through a fog. I do not know who she was, but have always known in my hearts that she was not my true mother."

"I have always believed," said another voice, "That bringing me into the world was her final act, for she surely must have died during what was certainly a very difficult childbirth."

A grim chuckling came from the Priests at this, conjuring horrifying visions in the old man's eyes, though he couldn't help but chuckle himself at the being's dark humour. Bendum nodded. "If I may ask, then, what do you remember from your early life? As a child? Of the people whom tended you?"

"My earliest memories," said the Priests, "are pain-filled."

"Cages and strangers all the time."

"Men staring, disgusted, women horrified."

"Some images are only half-formed, it seems."

"For I may have buried them."

"Deeply. In deep, deep places."

"For bad memories are best to be interred as deeply as possible."

The old ringmaster thought of his travelling circus, and the countless visitors to their show who came to gawk at the spectacle of them all in their collective strangeness. They survived as any family should, through the simple solidarity of standing up for one another, always. Strength in numbers and familiarity and love, so that at times it even seemed to be the case that the outside world, and not the strange, closed-off internal world of the traveling show, housed the true freaks and horrors.

"I wish you would stay. You have a family here anytime you want it," said Bendum. He was thinking of his beloved menagerie of misfits: the dog boy; the mermaid; the monkey-boy; the octopus baby; the bearded woman; the clowns and geeks and acrobats and sword-swallowers and masked ballyhoo players. And this unique being before him now, a person like no other, but for its hearts, which were good hearts, like those of his other troupe members.

"I have a family here," said the three voices of the Priests as one.

"Three-in-one," said one of its voices.

"Three-in-one," echoed another.

And together, "I seek greater answers, from a greater source, about this world in which I live, and about other worlds elsewhere."

The ringmaster stared with wonder at the Priests. A great respect for the being filled him. "My friend. My dear, *dear* friend," he said. "You are a beautiful creature. And a miracle among us all. I'm so grateful for—I'm so *honoured* by—the time you've spent with us." And he wept.

The ringmaster and the Priests cried together in the murky trailer, while the world outside marched on.

VII: THE KINGDOM

Into the warm air of the rectory, one of the Priests's voices said, "There is so much more I have not even begun to tell, Pastor Garfield. So much more, in the years following my self-exile from my circus family...

"Once, years ago, a gang of drunk men found me seeking solace in a little-frequented alley in a town whose name I can no longer remember." Two of its voices fell silent, and a third voice continued its tale, "These men were horrified at the thing they discovered seeking shelter amid the refuse and rat nests, but hid their horror behind their anger and false bravado." And another of its voices finished the dark tale: "These men took turns raping each of my bodies, three men at a time. Their dark game went on and on."

Another of its voices said, "One of the men broke a bottle across the back of this head." The Pastor watched in mute horror as one of the Priests's heads waggled slowly from side to side.

Indeed, a long and thick, time-faded lump scarred the head from crown to nearly the base of the neck.

A different voice said, "And once, long ago, came a time I sought salvation in a place of monastic peace."

"Yes," it said with another of its mouths, and it was all it said, as if the subject was too difficult to continue, until its third voice said, "But even the good monks of the monastery barred my way at their gates, believing me to be an aberration of another world that would seek to harm them in their stronghold of peace."

"Perhaps they were merely frightened," it said, "for maybe they saw me as a strange and gruesome broken reflection of themselves?"

"Yes, perhaps," mused its third voice with what sounded like embittered amusement.

A cynical laugh escaped one of the Priests's mouths, though the Pastor knew not which. Garfield felt a great weight in his chest. As a rule, he sought to understand and be compassionate to his fellow man; but when man proved time and again the unending reserves of his barbarism, it was a Herculean task, and one that the Pastor found more and more difficult to achieve.

"I'm... I'm so very sorry for the things you have suffered," he said, knowing of course how paltry the words were.

One of the Priests's voices said, "Many times have children screamed in horror." Another voice, "And ran away screaming still." Another voice: "Or pelted me with stones, and spit on me and cursed me." But the first voice amended, "But they are children, and children, being pure beings, only become sullied by what they learn from those around them. They are to blame, the teachers of children, never the children themselves."

After a moment's pause, one of its voices said, "But there are some who are good. The ringmaster, Reginald Bonnycot Bendum, for one."

"Yes," said Pastor Garfield. "He sounds like a good and honourable soul."

"Yes," the Priests said together. "A rare soul indeed."

Garfield fretted, knotting his fingers behind his back. "I wish I could do something. But I wonder, if a good soul like your ringmaster friend was not able to give you what you seek, in a place of care and understanding, then... what can *I* do for you, my children? My child? What am I able to do for you? Why have you sought *me* out?" He felt fear envelop him, as though the task was a challenge set before him by the Lord, but what if he hadn't the strength to complete it?

A voice of the Priests said, "I need to know whether my belief all these long years has been a foolish one. Whether what my hearts have always told me is wrong."

Another of the Priests's voices said, "Is there a place?"

"A place?" said Garfield.

The voices said:

"A place of salvation."

"A place of sanctuary and refuge."

"Is there Paradise? Does the fortress of Heaven truly exist beyond this world that is burning away in the great fire of its own making?"

Pastor Garfield considered the weight of the things he'd been told by the creature; and he considered what he knew of the world's dark history; and of the few good-hearted people to whom he preached each day and whom he considered true friends. And he answered honestly.

"Yes. There is such a place. There has to be, or else why would any of us be here at all?"

The Priests said, in a single sibilant and imploring voice:

"Show me."

Pastor Garfield nodded. Something flared into life inside him. His mission lay revealed. He'd received the Call long ago, when he'd still been a young man, but this, this was a renewal of his true purpose. He opened his mouth to speak but the Priests stopped him.

"But first, Father, I must confess, for I have sinned."

Pastor Garfield listened to the Priests's tale, of a dark winter's night in a small, nameless town; a tale of another hard-hearted man—a tavern-keeper, angered by the vagrant he'd found sheltering from the cold within the alcove of his establishment's rear doorway; horrified by what he found when he'd kicked this sleeping bum awake, sending the strange creature stumbling out into the alley where the moonlight revealed it in all its gruesomeness. This man had followed the Priests as it fled down the alley as if intoxicated with the vision of it, unable to leave it be, hounding it with the terrible things he called it, growing angrier and bolder in his bullying until, finally, he committed the crime no other had ever done to the Priests—he squeezed himself through the tangled, interconnected web of the Priests's fused limbs and taken up vile residence in their midst so that he could look into each of its faces, and he spit scornfully into each of these faces of shame. Helpless, unable to escape with the invading man tangled inside of its limbs, the Priests did what it had to. For it was this final violation of its private self, the only space it had ever had to itself as a shield from the prying eyes of the world, that proved too much for the Priests to bear, and it acted on its humanity—proving that it indeed had the hearts of men—and it held the man tightly in its three-bodied, unyielding embrace, and used the teeth of its three mouths to tear the man's throat out. Three-in-one, strong in the throes of the pain filling its hearts, against one weak and heartless man.

In the wake of its story, the Priests stood silently, shuddering with the weight of the words it had finally spoken aloud to another man after years of silence.

And Pastor Garfield, his jaw trembling and his eyes hard and inscrutable, said, "No, my son. You've committed no sin at all. For some men are Lucifer Himself, risen up from the molten pit to which he was banished, to spread the fire of His burning heart in this beautiful but harsh world."

The weeping that then poured from the Priests undid Pastor Garfield, for it was a joyful weeping the likes of which he'd never before heard in his long years of preaching the good Word; and he wept, too.

Later that night, something awakened Pastor Garfield from the dark dream he dreamed—a dream of fire and darkness engulfing him—and he sat up in bed, sweating a cold sweat and listening to the wind whispering in the eaves. Then, beyond its insistent voice, he discerned another sound. Listening hard, he slipped from the bed and, donning his robe, drifted across the room and into the hall outside. He followed the sound, coming to the rectory doorway and facing the church beyond. There, lit in a halo of warm orange light thrown from the sputtering candles in the candelabra, he found the Priests kneeling on the wooden floor, heads bowed together as ever. Its synchronized whispered voices came to him: their recitation of the Lord's prayer comforted him, warmed him in the chill air.

Garfield listened to the Priests's prayer, its physical deformity and its place before the altar imbuing it with the appearance of a secret cabal conducting some clandestine rite. And he reprimanded himself for his wrongful judgment and fear when he'd first met this creature, and smiled in acceptance of what it truly was he saw convened within this house of the Lord he humbly tended: beauty, in all of its awesome and unexpected splendour.

And he went in silence to a place beside the Priests, and he knelt there too and added his voice to the prayer filling the room.

They turned at the knock on the heavy oak door, and the echoes it sent reverberating into the church's lofty reaches.

"Father," called a woman's voice from the other side of the door.

A note of hysteria edged the voice.

"My child," Pastor Garfield whispered to the Priests, eyes full with agitation.

"I understand," said the Priests as one. "I don't want to alarm this visitor with my unexpected presence and... strangeness." And it rose smoothly from the floor, making quickly for the shadows of the rectory to one side of the altar.

Pastor Garfield raised a hand, said, "Thank you, my child. If you could please wait within the rectory, only until I see what the trouble is." He hurried through the aisle formed by the pews to the door, pushed it wide to find Beatrice Salisbury shuddering in the wind, a blanket-wrapped bundle in her arms.

"Beatrice," he greeted her, smiling and stepping aside for her to enter the church.

"Hello, Father," she said. "I'm sorry to have disturbed you at such an hour."

"Not at all, my child, not at all," he said. "How may I help you?" Her distraught expression chilled him. She held aloft the bundle and with one hand drew back a veil of blanket to reveal the child within. The soft skin of his face and neck was splotched with angry red spots. His eyes were puffy and mired shut with the same deep crimson marking.

"I'm scared for James, Father," she said. "He's been like this for days. Dr. Samuels examined him, and what he first took to be measles... well, it's proven to be something else. He doesn't know what to make of it. He said he's never seen nothing like it in all his years of medicine. And earlier this evening, James's cough worsened and... I found blood on his blanket."

She broke off, weeping, shoulders shuddering.

The Pastor placed a hand across the child's forehead, took it away quickly. "He's burning up!" he breathed.

"His fever broke a day or so ago, but came back last night worse than ever." Her eyes pleaded. "Father, I don't know what to do. Thomas thinks it's a curse, and the doctor couldn't help him, so I thought maybe you could offer... a good word, or prayer?"

"Of course, my dear." Pastor Garfield took the child from its mother. With great care, he parted its blankets to reveal his features more clearly. The child's face, he saw, was swollen and inflamed, and a dark black bruising had begun along the periphery of the red markings, calling to his mind cases of bubonic plague he'd seen photographs of in books. He knew not what the child's affliction was but knew in his heart that it was deadly.

Beatrice turned at the soft sound behind them, and saw the Priests standing within the shadows of the vestibule leading into the rectory. She stared with wide eyes a moment before a scream tore from her, its echoes rebounding throughout the vaulted chamber. She drew back a step, faltered, and fainted, crashing to the floor before Pastor Garfield who, with the infant cradled in his arms, was unable to catch her.

"I'm sorry, Father!" said the Priests as one. "But I heard what the woman said and wanted to console her."

"I wasn't thinking, Father," cried one of its voices.

"I'm so sorry," it said again. "I should have known what seeing me would do to her."

"Hush, my friend," Pastor Garfield said. "And wait here a moment." The baby wheezed thickly as he placed it gently onto the floor, lost inside the voluminous folds of its blankets. He then turned to administer to Beatrice, pulling her to a sitting posture leaning against the nearby pew. He went to retrieve some water and a towel from the interconnecting washroom, and as he returned into the main chamber, saw.

The Priests shuffled and spun with its peculiar grace to a place before the infant, and then carefully and with great deliberation stepped a pair of its legs over the baby so that the child lay directly in the midst of its three bodies. In this way the

Priests was able to see the child clearly with each of its three pairs of eyes looking down upon it in its centre.

Garfield stood with towel and water in hand and listened to its hushed voices carry across the echoing chamber.

"A beautiful child!"

"Oh, sweet baby boy, look at your golden curls!"

"A miracle! Just look at him!"

"Hush, little one, and save your strength."

"Yes, be quiet, child, and rest yourself."

"Hush, and soon your fever will go away."

"Hush, child, and sleep to awaken another morning—the world will be yours, some day."

"Yes, you have so much ahead of you."

"A long path."

"A long and good path."

"Sleep, and dream good dreams."

"You are not alone—you will have love in your life."

"Great and infinite love."

"The angels, they sing of you, and for you."

"Sleep, child."

"Sleep and be well."

"Sleep."

As the Priests fell into silence, so too did the child, his soft burbles eventually turning into the steady rhythmic breathing of deep sleep. The Priests continued to stand over the baby, its voices whispering a soothing melody, and though the pastor couldn't make out what it said, the sound itself was a gentle, a nurturing, a peaceful sound, the rhythm and sound of impassioned prayer. And within the protective house of the Priests's tangle of limbs, the child slept on, undisturbed.

Baby James's fever broke by the following morning. By the evening of that day, the red spots on his face and neck and arms were subsiding, and no fever burned his brow. He slept fitfully at first, but then long and well, to awaken in the early evening with a mighty appetite and a healthy voice crying for his mother's breast. The child also spoke his first word that night, looking up into his mother's face and smiling: "Good," he'd said, and it had made both his mother and the Pastor cry. And then James slept again, burbling drowsily as he dreamed and dreamed his way towards the next day and a long and healthy life.

To the child's mother, Pastor Garfield explained that what she'd seen the night before was no abomination as she'd believed. He assured her that it was but a poor soul, with a good heart. And he explained what he'd witnessed himself, and given that baby James had recuperated so quickly in the aftermath of it, well... He left that up to Beatrice to decide for herself. Watching her weep with thanks told him her answer, and for this one step for all mankind in a better direction he was pleased. He implored her to make no mention of what she'd seen to anyone, to allow him the task of introducing his newfound companion to the townspeople at large; and though Beatrice had nodded in agreement, he doubted she would be able to resist telling her husband, Thomas, of what she'd seen, who would no doubt see witchcraft and curses at work, and in turn would spread this untruth among those who would listen.

But Garfield could only thank her for her understanding, hoping in his heart that she truly did believe and understand what he'd tried to explain to her, and watch her leave the church and head home with her recuperating child bundled in blankets against the chill November air.

It was later on in the morning when the pastor opened the door to the small storage room he'd made up for the Priests the evening before. He found the creature sleeping, positioned in the same queer posture he'd seen it sitting in once before, one of its bodies forming the base upon which its second body leaned partway, with the third body sitting upright, leaned back as far as it was able and in this way pulling against the weight of its companion bodies and serving to prop itself up. The Pastor stared in renewed wonder at the tangle of limbs, trying but failing to comprehend how this creature could have survived in the world for as long as it had, shuddering at the things it must have suffered through.

He noticed the book then, resting on the mattress among the protective shelter of the Priests's limbs. The light from the ajar door helped him see its tattered cover, and the faded picture adorning it, of a man and woman standing together on a barren and alien landscape, with a star-stippled sky reeling over them. By the light he read its title and author's name—*A Princess of Mars* by Edgar Rice Burroughs—and a smile creased his face.

This, then, was the Priests's Bible, its long-standing book of refuge and salvation. In that moment, Pastor Garfield understood truly the power of words and the gift of escape they could give those in need.

He remained there a while, tears on his cheeks, the sound of the Priests's three breathings soothing him where he stood watching from the doorway.

"I hope your dreams are good dreams," he said.

At this, one of its heads, belonging to the body sitting semi-upright, stirred. Straining to see behind itself caused the other heads to stir too.

"I'm sorry," said Pastor Garfield, wiping at his eyes. "I know you must be tired. I just came to check on you, is all."

One of the Priest's voices, muddy with sleep, said, "No. Thank you for waking me, Pastor."

Another of its voices said, "I haven't slept this well in a long time. It must be nearly dawn. I feel refreshed."

The third of its voices said, "Thank you for allowing me lodgings here."

"It's nothing," Pastor Garfield said, waving his hands on the air. "I was washing up in the washroom down the hall but am finished now. Feel free to use it if you wish to clean up before breakfast. You can find me in the rectory whenever you're ready."

"Thank you, Father," said the Priests as one.

They were seated at the small, round oak dining table in the rectory's kitchen. The silence of the church proper beyond the door was a deep and heavy one. They'd spent the day reading, immersed in scripture, and felt rejuvenated, though their eyes were red and sore from strain.

"I've slept little and have thought long and hard, and I have two things to say to you, my child," said Pastor Garfield.

The Priests waited, silent and still.

"Firstly, whether or not what I saw and what transpired here last night was miraculous, as I do believe it was, it did tell me one thing: that you are a child of Heaven, and that He has seen fit that you walk upon His earth. You are loved. You have good in your hearts, and you are loved."

He paused a moment, emotion seizing him and making words difficult. Then he went on.

"And secondly: you may stay here if you wish. You have a place here with me, in this House, to work and study and to continue to do good while we wait together for the better place after the world we've known here, with its slow thinking and sadness and savagery."

"But Father," said a voice of the Priests, saying what was in the Pastor's heart: "What if others see me, and do not understand?"

"Yes," said another of its voices, "What if men come here, as they surely will now that my presence is known, and see and see only horror?"

"What if they come back with noose and torch and rifle?" said its third voice. "To vanquish the evil thing that they see, and the good man who fell under its spell and saw good in its hearts? Once the woman tells them of me, this thing may very well come to pass, as it came to pass so many times before, causing me to flee and seek refuge elsewhere only to learn, time and again, there was no refuge to be found, anywhere, but for perhaps the haven of a touring freak show traveling the dark lands."

"If only I too could fall asleep and wake up on Mars," said its voices together, and the pastor saw that the Priests was cradling its treasured Burroughs book to itself.

Pastor Garfield nodded solemnly. When he spoke, his voice was hard as iron. "Let the people come. This House is a new and better House today than it was before. Let them come." And it was all he said.

He saw the shuddering of the Priests's shoulders and knew that it was crying. He waited a moment, cleared his throat, and said, "One other thing. I've been thinking. You have been called many things in your life, and yet you've never owned a true name. I think it only appropriate that you have a name, for no good man should go without. You are a special and unique person, and after witnessing last night's miracle, it seems to me that perhaps you represent a step forward, in a new and better direction for us all. And so, I propose we call you... Adam."

He could foresee how his superiors in the church would react to such a choice; but then he knew how right it felt in his heart, and this was a voice with which he could not argue.

And although Pastor Garfield couldn't see the faces of the Priests as it sat huddled before him with its heads bowed towards each other, he was certain there was a great joy—like a miracle, like the light of true Paradise itself breaking through barriers of cloud to touch down on Earth—pouring forth from its three pairs of weeping eyes.

Father Garfield said grace and they ate their simple but good dinner in a silence punctuated only by the caterwauling of the wind through the high eaves of the church outside the rectory.

It wasn't long before the murmur of voices and movement carried through the night, the crunching of many feet through the autumn leaves littering the road leading to the church's steps. Pastor Garfield and the Priests looked up from the book they were reading together and made their way to stand at the threshold of the rectory's doorway and looked out across the pews of the church. The flicker of torches and the shadows of those who wielded them played a violent dance on the stained-glass windows, casting gruesome demonic shadows crawling and leaping like blasphemy inside the immense room, across its walls and altar. The great murmuring voice of the crowd sounded much like the voices of the many crowds that had come to witness the Priests in the past, though perhaps louder now, and somehow angrier.

The Priests said, "Thank you, Father, for your kindness."

And, "Thank you for listening to my story."

And, "Thank you for sharing your House with me."

"Thank *you*," said Pastor Garfield, "For sharing your story with me. Now be strong, and trust in the strength and goodness of this House."

Adam, in a single voice, said, "Then let us pray together now, and wait for His answer."

The two men, side by side, recited the strongest words of salvation they knew in the darkening church, their four voices striving to be heard over the growing din of the people gathering outside the walls.

A GIFT FROM THE WORLD

This story appears here for the first time. It was the first story I wrote in 2019. It's about what the world is capable of giving to people. I wish it weren't so, but it's true. Even the best of us—even the very strongest of us—are no match for it.

Bizarre-as-shit things happen. Of course they do: we live in a strange world.

This thought swam through Carter's mind as he stared down at the catch the day had given up to him. He had found the small fish as he was passing through the grass alley that ran between houses in his east-side neighbourhood, not too far from his new house. It was a quiet, early afternoon: birds sang from the canopy of spruce branches overhead, the scant sunlight escaping their tangled leafy fingers to stipple the path with a malnourished light. The engineered perfume of fakeflowers from the many gardens in the different backyards dizzied him with their potency. Bumblebees droned past, pausing at these deceiving imitations of the flora that had once flourished in the area, before moving on in their lethargic, disappointing quests. Flies buzzed in his ears like electricity in shorted circuits.

And then the fish.

The first strange fact about the creature—he wasn't sure what kind it was, as he knew very little at all about fish—was finding it where he did: lying in the centre of the grassy lane, on a small beach blanket, as if it had been placed there with great purpose, almost reverentially. Its scales glimmered blue-green in the bright light. Its dead stare looked at nothing. Clusters of stunted tendrils hung flaccidly from its belly and sides, grotesque mutations from living in the chemical-ruined river.

He looked up and down the grass alley. Nothing stirred at either end but for the distant gauze of heat-haze. There was no sign of children at play, or adults tending to their diseased lawns and wilting gardens. Only the fabricated lilacs and roses struggling through fence slats and chain-links, and the pair of sunflowers that towered over the backyard fence beside him, peering over its edge as if spying on him like a pair of weird, alien sentries. Somewhere, a hissing of a sprinkler carried through the thick air.

The second strange fact relating to his discovery was that, though the river was only a ten-minute walk from there, there was no sign of fishing gear nearby, no bait or tackle, no children eager to preserve their weird catch in a bucket filled with water. His mind turned to tales he'd heard—tall tales, presumably, though again, it was a strange world and who could tell for sure about such things—of inexplicable incidents of creatures falling from the sky: rains of frogs and toads and snakes. Much more common—though certainly no less extraordinary—were the countless meteors striking the Earth after voyages of millennia in the eternity of outer space. Why not a single mutant fish dropped from the heavens on a sweltering August afternoon?

But then he considered the bright, multi-coloured beach towel on which it lay, a sure sign of human agency, with the fish arranged neatly dead-centre, as if on display.

Again, he peered along the quiet lane.

No one moved in the backyards. The muted sunlight lay heavy and oppressive on everything. The humidity seemed to have increased perceptibly in the last few minutes. He felt his t-shirt clinging to his back. He wiped sweat from his brow with the back of his hand. He'd set out on his morning walk over an hour ago when the temperature had still been comfortable. Had he known the humidity index (he kicked himself for not having checked the weather channel before leaving) he might have stayed inside the cool comfort of his house.

He'd actually been enjoying his weekend off work, relished putzing around the new house doing this or that laidback activity (catching up on his reading of the paper, say, or surfing the sports channels) or ambling out in the neighbourhood with nothing in particular to do. He'd been relying on his weekends more and more to help him stay grounded, sane; he needed to just Goddamn relax, to decompress after the stressful week behind him. All in all, he was pleased with his decision to buy the house in this relatively quiet east-side suburb, away from the downtown core, and so different from it that on days like this the city centre seemed almost unreal, a fragment of a dark dream he'd finally woken from after suffering through a long and troubled sleep. Sometimes, on days like this, he almost felt like living here might cure him of the voices that haunted him, the whispers and barked commands in his ear while he was on duty, fighting hard to focus on the case at hand while playing it cool so that Delaney wouldn't notice, and worry about him.

He shook his head, wondering at his reverie. He blamed the heat like a hot blanket draped over him, smothering him into incoherent thinking. He was taking a step forward to continue on his way—to home, and air-conditioned luxury, and possibly an afternoon nap before Delaney came over for their pizza and card-playing night—when something compelled him to reach down and grab the fish from the beach blanket. Its scales were slippery, and he nearly let it slide through his fingers and flop onto the grass. He found himself cradling it to his chest as he walked and thought how funny he might look to someone happening to be watching from a backyard window: a burly, sweaty, flustered man hurrying down the grass alley burgling a fish in his arms. He wondered what Delaney would think—as far as partners went, she was as laidback as they came, but then, technically speaking, wasn't this act theft, a certified crime, however small an offense in the greater scheme of things?

He couldn't say exactly why he'd done it. Only that he'd *had* to do it. As if something had told him that the fish had, in some way, been left there specifically for him to find. A gift, from the day. A sky-gift from the strange world, and who was he to deny a miracle like this?

He'd nearly reached the mouth of the grass alley when he felt the fish move.

It was still alive!

He stared at it in awe, indeed saw its little tentacles curling on the air, its gills fluttering as it struggled to survive in the blistering afternoon heat. Its eyes remained as emotionless as before, of course, staring blackly up at him as he continued on his way, though he imagined the hint of an imploring expression in its gaze, as if it were begging him for help or an end to its misery.

He hurried on his way, keeping a watch out for roving sky-eyes and nearly stumbling over the rough patch of weed-choked grass outside the gate to his own backyard. (Try as he might, some mutated strain of Creeping Charlie had continued to creep across both front and backyard lawns, and now even beneath the fence to infest his portion of the quiet green lane.) He slipped through, using his foot to gently close the gate to behind himself, and walked briskly across his lawn to the small white shed in one corner. Its door was ajar, and he nudged it open with his leg. He squinted into the mossy-smelling gloom, found the pale outline of the plastic bucket sitting among a clutter of yard maintenance tools to one side of the door.

He grabbed the bucket, careful to not let the fish slip from his fingers, and hurried to fill the container from the hose at the side of the house.

He laid the fish gently into the bucket. He watched, entranced and thrilled, as it came to immediate and renewed life. It swam enthusiastically back and forth in the few inches of water and, though its space was confined, he was pleased that the water had rejuvenated it after the heat had seemingly leeched all life from it.

He was filled with a happiness in that moment that he hadn't felt in some time. It was nearly child-like, insofar as he could remember feeling similarly excited when he'd been a boy discovering crayfish in the dry summer creek bed, or catching fireflies inside the prison of his cupped palms and watching their manic lightshow glowing through his arched fingers. With work a constant hardship, and things in the city—Hell, things in the whole world—getting worse all the time, well, out and out happiness was a real rare commodity these days. And so, he found himself inwardly rejoicing at this unexpected joy that had overcome him and decided in that moment to surprise Delaney with a home-cooked dinner rather than the pizza delivery that had been the plan.

It was a sign, he reasoned, a good sign, that it was the right time to share with her the thing that had become a growing concern for him and that he'd been putting off confessing to her: the things he'd been seeing throughout the city more and more

78

these past few months; the visions, or hallucinations, or maybe they were real, which was maybe the most frightening possibility of all. And the voices, Goddamn them: the voices, too. But telling Delaney would be a big help. Getting the weight of it all off his chest would be good, and together he and his partner would solve the dark riddle of it the same way they'd solved so many cases he'd lost count.

He stirred from his thoughts, turned to the fish. He gave it an apologetic look. "Sorry, buddy, but something caught you and made a gift out of you. You'll make a fine supper."

The decision was like a revelation. It made the small guilt he felt at taking the animal's life easy enough to bear. This wasn't a selfish gesture. This was meant to be. The waters of Heaven don't give up their gifts without good reason, after all. Right? Right. Indeed, he no longer questioned the fish's origin. Despite the evidence of its river-mutation, in his mind the thing had come from somewhere else, somewhere special that cancelled any fear he might have had about actually eating a potentially radiation-saturated creature.

He went out onto the backyard patio and fired up the grill. Then he hurried inside to fetch some plates and utensils and condiments. He had thirty minutes or so until Delaney was due to show up, and she was never late for anything. He wouldn't be able to finish the meal, but he could have it well underway when she arrived.

Delaney passed through the side gate to hear the unexpected sound of Carter out on the backyard deck. She could just make out his elongated shadow stretched across the grass, could hear the creaking of the wooden floorboards beneath him as he moved about. She followed the cement path leading to the backyard. Peering around the corner of the house, she was surprised to find him fiddling at the controls of the barbecue. Sensing her, he turned around.

"Hey," he said, a grin materializing on his face. "I thought I'd surprise you. Sorry it ain't finished yet—I'm only getting started. It's slow cooking on this old relic." His running-shoed foot knocked a gentle percussion on the dented frame of the barbecue.

Delaney smiled. Just when she started thinking that the two of them had gotten stuck deep and good in the tedious routine of their grim job, he surprised her with something like this: a small gesture, but so well-timed that it became a much greater gesture at the same time. It had been a long week of work for them both. Hell, it had been a long year so far, and it was only half done. Sometimes it looked like there might not even be a next year coming at all.

"Hey, that's awfully nice of you, Chef Carter. What's on the menu?"

"Fish!" He was beaming as he said it, more uncharacteristic behaviour for her usually taciturn partner.

Her eyes widened. She was impressed. "You went all the way to the market for dinner? Thanks, Carter, but really, you shouldn't have gone to the trouble." She chuckled at his enthused expression. He reminded her of a big kid. Standing there then, he might have been a cub scout prepping his first catch to share with the troop, though there probably never had been a cub scout flaunting two gleaming mech-arms.

"No," he confessed. "I didn't do all that. But still, it's going to be fish for supper tonight."

She frowned. There wasn't a deli counter at the small grocery store down the street, and obviously he wasn't going to be cooking boxed fish out on the barbecue. "But where did you get it? You didn't go fishing, did you?" Her eyes widened theatrically. Her stomach was already tightening at the thought of the chemically-tainted waters of the nearby Detroit River, the "EXTREME HAZARD: SWIM-AT-YOUR-OWN-RISK" signs peppering the nearest beach, and the growing number of radiation-mutated fish in the years since the Cloud. *Eat a fish from those waters*, she'd said to him once when a case had taken them out this way, marvelling at the locals they'd seen fishing from off the pier, *and you might grow a fin or two yourself.*

"Nah," Carter said, though his smile had disappeared. "I'm no angler. You know that." Then, seeing her consternation, he added with a mysterious narrowing of the eyes, "*Our fish fell from the sky.*" And he felt the truth in it.

Her frown deepened, but then she relented. To Hell with it. It had been a long week, after all. Let him have his victorious—and mysterious—dinner fish. She'd enjoy it too.

She chuckled. "Okay, Carter. Sounds good to me."

"Great. Dinner should be ready in about fifteen. But we can have a beer before we eat."

"Yeah," she said. "*Yes.* A beer—or two—would be perfect." She sat down on the edge of the deck, stared out across the backyard, not commenting on the weed-besieged lawn. Instead, she sighed and said, "It's only a ten-minute walk from my place to here, and in that time I saw two sky-cams sweeping the neighbourhood. I don't like." Where sky-cams flew usually meant that crime wasn't too far off, and the thought of any criminal element infiltrating this relatively safe neighbourhood was a truly disheartening one.

Carter, focused on fiddling with the knobs on the barbecue, said, "I don't like it either, Del. Luckily, no eyes saw me and the fish."

She glanced over, wondering again at her partner's unusual enthusiasm for preparing supper. Then she scolded herself silently. Why the Hell was she bringing up bullshit like sky-cams when they should be just relaxing on a day away from the squad-house (even though they both knew they could never be fully free from their work)? They both needed a breather from talking about things that conjured up thoughts of the job, where the sky was infected with sky-cams and the awful things they witnessed. Carter had been at his new house for only a few months—it was still a relatively new comfort for him, so his uncharacteristic cheer made sense, and she was going to try her hardest to let it infect her as well.

She looked back to the cement walkway leading to the side door of the house. "Where's Baxter? Inside?"

"Yeah, he was being a whiner out here earlier, begging for food like it was nobody's business," Carter said, grabbing a spatula from where it had been resting on the grill's small side-shelf. "So, I had to put him inside. Let him out if you want to say hi. But watch out—as soon as he smells the cooking, he's going to be drooling all over."

Delaney laughed and, getting up off the deck to go get the dog, bumped her foot into the white plastic bucket sitting at the corner of the house, between the deck and path. She hadn't noticed it coming up the walk. A sloshing sound came from inside it. The perforations on its lid were dark, betraying nothing of the interior.

Carter saw, and explained. "Sorry, Del. That's our dinner-to-be. I stuck the lid on top a second ago. It seemed the direct light, muted and gross as it is, was making the water too hot. Wanna see him?"

She gave him a look. "No. I won't want to eat him after I see how cute he is."

Carter laughed. "Suit yourself."

They were both turning away when the bucket rattled. Rattled *hard*.

Delaney jumped.

Carter turned to look at the bucket.

She said, "Wow. He sounds... big. What, did a *shark* fall from the sky today?"

"Stranger things have happened," Carter said, a great distance in his voice.

Delaney looked to him, watched him closely.

He suddenly wanted to peek in at the fish. Maybe it was too congested inside the bucket with the lid on. Maybe the direct daylight would have been better. What did he know about the caretaking of fish? He was a cop, not a fisherman. Sure, he knew how to beat a perp with the nightstick in his fist until the guy shit blood in his pants, but the caretaking of a little fish? No clue. Digging up clues leading to the arrest of the evil men operating a youth prostitution ring from the confines of derelict warehouses on the city's outskirts: sure, he could help sniff those out right alongside the best detectives in the precinct. But pick up a clue or two on how to keep a fish in good health right up until the moment he severed the head from its body with a butcher's knife and threw the scaly critter on the grill? Nope. Clueless, with a capital "C". He was as helpless in the kitchen as he was helpless in losing ground to mutated Creeping Charlie taking over his lawn more each day passing. He was as helpless in the kitchen as the homeless woman had been helpless in the alley the other night after his shift was done, when he had put her out of her misery with a pair of sustained taser blasts that left her convulsing in her nest of cardboard boxes and filth until he witnessed her spirit leave the broken shell of her and lift toward the rectangle of sky framed between the buildings. *That's* how helpless he was when it came to all things culinary.

Or maybe he was just helpless.

This thought, as always, sent an icy finger crawling along his spine, a cold breath gusting over his heart.

The bucket shook again, tearing him from his reverie. A loud thumping accompanied the shaking, and a more violent sloshing of the water within.

Delaney stared at the container, then looked to Carter.

Without thinking, acting on some adrenaline-fueled, peculiar impulse, Delaney reached down and pried the lid from the bucket.

Her eyes went wide. Her breath sucked in with a hiss. She stared.

Time paused then, as if the whole world was held still and unmoving, except for the three of them; the world dreaming its late afternoon siesta-dream before waking for the summer evening bacchanal to come.

And though she'd reflexively flung the plastic lid up in front of herself like a shield, what she saw as she peered guardedly from behind its curved rim remained, no matter how long she looked and questioned its reality and what it might mean, about her partner, and about the world in which they lived:

A blue-skinned human baby struggling feebly in the shallow, dirty water of the bucket.

A ROMAN PLAGUE

This is one of the stories that I had the most fun writing. The tale of a troupe of Roman Legionnaires who meet a deadly stranger one dark night along the ramparts of the fort they guard against invaders. It's a story about temptation, and the nasty things embedded deep in the hearts of the best of us. It's about the apocalypse inside every person, and that we breathe out into the world all the time.

I wrote this immediately after completing an essay I contributed to an amazing anthology devoted to Chris Carter's Millennium *television series (one of the great TV programs) entitled* Back to Frank Black: A Return to Chris Carter's Millennium, *published by Fourth Horseman Press. My essay focused on the character Lucy Butler, portrayed by the talented Sarah Jane Redmond. My piece posited the theory that Lucy Butler is the Devil Himself. So, I had the Dark Lord on my mind a lot around that time, enough so that He found his way into this story, and into the seductive form found therein.*

March! Onwards! Have at them! And beware...

A plague ate its hungry fill
of Dura's mighty Roman ranks,
drowned too Italcus, whose red river banks
saw no more Romans left to kill

The tempest she had a name
Some named her Cacus, the fire-spitter
others the serpent and witch
But these titles? Too meagre to give her
For a woman so named
Could ne'er own eyes so wise
so righteous
so beautiful

—*Song of Joy*
Persia, circa 256-57 AD

"Dura-Europos has fallen, brothers. The Persians own the city."

The Legionnaires of the colonia, Italcus, listened raptly and with grave features to their fellow soldiers standing before them, weary and wounded from the bloodshed they'd left behind. These three men were survivors of the sacking, defeat defining their sunken postures, shame in their eyes.

"The Sassanids are desert devils," said the man beside the first, shaking his head in astonishment. "Mining 'neath the city, filling the tunnels with poison gas, choking our brothers. The Euphrates, she runs red..." He drifted off, a stunned look in his eyes.

"We've come to spread word of the defeat," said the third man, a desperate look seeped into his sallow features, as if yearning to prove the wisdom in their retreat, the courage in their hearts. "Those who survived have been taken to Ctesiphon. Slavery awaits them."

"*Barbaricum* filth," spat Aquilinus, captain of the colonia, grimacing with disdain, eyes smouldering. The raised, smooth-skinned scar running a crooked line from left cheek to chin shone white amid his livid, burning features. "News of this will see the Gauls calling along the border, and the Huns and Visigoths, and others, all while Rome answers this affront. Hadrian's Wall, I fear, is not so strong to repel them all."

"My lord, we must make haste and bring word of this massacre—Rome must know!" Marianus was ashen-faced beside his old friend, clutching the sword hilt in the scabbard at his waist. He was a veteran of countless campaigns, many won and some lost, and the gravity of this defeat shook even him.

86

Aquilinus's eyes were hard as he surveyed his men. "We remain here this night and ride at dawn."

In the west, thunder sounded, like a bugle calling for battle.

Moonlight paled the grey stone walls of the garrison, the wild grassland beyond.

The Legionnaire Valentinus stiffened at his station along the wall, an inexplicable chill of dread snaking along his spine and making his nape hairs rise. Something was amiss; something in the night that had been as it should be was now wrong. He gripped his javelin tightly, looking to east and west from his post, but he found no sign of enemy, no shadow of Sassanid or Gaul slinking low to the ground in the berm between ditch and wall, moonlight glinting from drawn blades, only the shadow-drenched land of grass and granite stretching away in all directions, the forest hulking in the east like a great and impregnable wall.

When next he looked up, he found her silhouetted against the red gibbous moon, standing within the nearby parapet. Utterly naked, her skin white as snow, her long hair wild, windblown and blood-red. Valentinus stifled a cry and staggered back a step, aghast, when the phantom figure stepped from its perch on the edifice and descended like a moth upon the air toward him.

She drifted down and down until her small feet alighted upon the stone floor without sound. He saw then her eyes: feral and hungry. Her tongue lolled from between her succulent lips, a corpulent, grotesque muscle the deep blood-colour of raw meat. Her erect nipples were sharp black darts stabbing through the queerly charged air at the Legionnaire even as she opened her arms to him.

"Halt!" he commanded her, tearing himself from the bewitching paralysis that had overcome him and raising his pilum toward the woman's chest. But the glimmering in her eyes mesmerized the soldier, taking fast hold of him once more as she approached soundlessly to stand before him, the barbed iron tip of the pilum pricking her between her breasts, letting loose a thin line of blood, jet-black and viscous as oil.

She opened her mouth wide and the voice of a hundred wolves bayed at the soldier, freezing the blood in his veins, loosing his bowels. Among the feral cacophony came another, human voice, masculine and deep, coarse and guttural:

"A storm is come, to mock and make mud of the towers of men, so that you may better see the greater paths before you."

Thick clouds rolled across the moon, deepening the night's dark.

A red rain awoke the troubled Legionnaires of Italcus.

It beat with great violence upon the roof of the barracks and pounded the dirt of the open courtyard, making of it an immense pool of crimson-slicked mud. The deluge lasted but moments but the force of it awakened the fort, its uncanny nature sending rattled sentries scrambling to sound an alarum of bugles.

The soldiers emerged wary from their barracks, pulling on tunics and scale armour and fastening sword-belts around their waists; while the sentries, holding torches high, stared stunned from their posts along the stone walls surrounding the outpost, all seeking to fathom the ghastly nature of the precipitation; until slowly, through a fog of incredulity, understanding came over them all: for among the great crimson pool owning the courtyard they discerned one of their own, recognizable only by the shreds of his tunic, his crushed bronze cuirass and shield scattered among the ragged remnants of the man's body torn asunder into a million pieces, limbs and organs and naked bones and a sickening brew of unrecognizable, pulped remains. His pulverized helmet lay in the blood-puddle's centre, its once-imperial crimson plume sullied with his gore.

Men cried out, unsheathing shortswords and seeking to look in every direction at once—among the dense shadows beyond reach of the torches's glow, into the crooked towers and ramparts, even to the sky itself—but could not find the unimaginable enemy in their midst.

And then she was in the centre of the blood-filled courtyard, among them all. Her red lips smiled. Her wild eyes blazed, appraising the soldiers hemming her in. Her hands were dripping crimson. Blood clung to her arms to her elbows, too, and splashed her breasts, and made a thick circle around her leering mouth. A long, shredded strip of flesh lay tangled in her red locks. The glistening necklace she wore was the Legionnaire's intestines.

The captain, Aquilinus, glowered at her. "I woke from a dream of you, witch, and saw you crawl forth from a black hole gaping in the earth!" he swore, tearing his shortsword from its scabbard at his hip.

Beside him, Marianus cried, "Nay, my lord, I swear to you I saw the witch with mine own eyes, when a black star fell from the sky only minutes ago! And then the screams of our brother, not long after, and the dark rain!"

A soldier stabbed his sword towards the intruder, exclaiming, "Look! It is Cacus, the fire-spitter!"

At mention of the demon's name, the men shuddered; they shuddered as they saw the woman's hands raised upon the air, palms towards them, a plume of fire smouldering in each; they shook with dread when she opened her mouth to show them the fire glowing within.

She mocked them with vile laughter—the voice of a cackling hyena pack, a brood of screeching gypsies casting dark magics in night woods—silencing them all. Into the great bestial clamour, the woman's hoarse voice sliced like an assassin's dagger. "Your paltry empire, your frail walls, your weak skeleton army of brittle bones and trembling hearts and small hungers: a greater fire shall sweep you all away, for there is always and always a mightier flame. Far mightier even than that wielded by little brothers Cacus and Vulcan."

The Legionnaires raised their weapons threateningly.

She tittered at the gesture and crooned grotesquely, "Soldiers, I only want us all to be together, for together we *could be* the army of fire to burn away weak veils of peace the lands over. We could rule the Earth, forever, and forever, forever, and forever."

Aquilinus stepped forward. He beat a fist upon his iron cuirass and aimed his shortsword at the woman. "Rome rules the world, witch, and you would do well to know it. We know not whence you came, but swear that you shall pay for this vile blasphemy of magick."

At this she spat blood and embers into the dirt. A serpent slithered forth from the black tangle of hair at her groin. The fires in her hands flared higher, excited. She took a step forward, menacingly, and they saw her left foot, cloven now, and black-furred.

Aquilinus gave the command: "Cut this whore to pieces."

89

The Legionnaires rushed the pale woman, bristling steel.

Their swords whirled about her but she moved faster still, an impossibly fleet blur that bewitched the eyes of the hardened soldiers, slowing their muscles and blunting their weapons's kiss. Among the clash of their arms the woman's weird, imploring litany echoed in their ears and hearts, over and over and over:

"I only want us all to be together. We could rule the Earth."

After a time many of the Legionnaires's swords had found a comrade's flesh, slashing a throat wide in a torrent of blood, lopping off an arm at the elbow in a geyser of crimson; for weird visions materialized in the heart of the chaotic fray, causing confusion and panic and fear the likes of which were unknown among those disciplined men of war: one soldier, Albus, screamed shrilly as the gigantic black scorpion scuttled upon him to spear him clean through his torso with its tail like a colossal scythe slicing crops; his comrade beside him, Longinus, stood helpless and transfixed by the poison-eyed stare of the basilisk that descended from out of the star-studded sky to snap his legs in half with its gargantuan serpent's fangs; the young, brash soldier, Thracius, flailed in the dust, screaming shrilly as two long rusty nails impaled his eyes, though none witnessed where they had flown from; a spearman's head was decimated by the jaws of the great black bear that strode bold as a king into their midst upon its hind legs, fifteen feet high its countenance of fury roaring into the darkness; this beast dispatched another Legionnaire as well, crushing him like kindling beneath its long-clawed foot, scattering his throwing-darts in the red mud; and even brave Aquilinus, in the end, was held spellbound, shortsword hanging low toward the earth, by the spectacle of the hulking, horned blasphemy blanketing him beneath its shadow, its awful demonic visage glaring down upon him with immense molten eyes, its smouldering volcanic maw opened to devour him with all the rabid hunger of the world.

Among the carnage, she danced a lithe dance, pirouetting easily on the air, slipping and feinting and turning fluidly, unkissed by sword or dagger or javelin. Her engorged crimson lips smiled all the while, rapturous as she rejoiced in the screams rising moonwards.

Blood flowed like a river undammed; fire rose high enough to lick and scald the stars trembling in the early morning sky.

• • •

A day of great celebration arrived in the Sassanid village, Al-Salihiyah, near Dura-Europos, only several miles from the final Roman colonia, Italcus, along the frontier between Rome and Persia; minstrels plucked their harps and sang with jubilation while the people danced and cheered, for news carried swiftly among that long-harried people of a plague that had befallen the Legionnaires who guarded this neighbouring symbol of draconian Roman rule, Italcus, as too their fellow soldiers at once-proud Dura-Europos had been destroyed. The irony did not escape the Persians, who had long referred to their would-be oppressors as the pestilence that had decimated their numbers over the centuries, seeking always to squash their culture, their dignity, their history, their own right to rule the world. Over time, this great vanquisher was likewise named Justice; and Retribution; while some named her more simply, Fire, and she would grow to become that whispered ghost, those dusty lines joining history and myth.

Some villagers of Al-Salihiyah, who had been awakened by the sounds of fighting, claimed strange visions that long night of mysterious slaughter: a child watching from its bedroom window saw a pack of hyenas loping through the village streets long after midnight, each with a human infant gripped between its slavering jaws; a woman filling an ewer from a well swore to have watched an immense bat, pig-sized, flitting helter-skelter low over the rooftops, chattering madly and spitting fat blood droplets onto the houses like the wickedest of curses; an elderly farmer wept with hands clasped together and a prayer of thanks upon his lips as the woman glided through the thoroughfare, her naked breasts gleaming in the moonlight, her fingers aflame, her serpentine torso undulating in the dust, leaving a wet trail in the wake of which followed a phantasmagorical mirage:

The troupe of Legionnaires, marching wearily, heads bowed earthwards—bloody; charred; chained.

BLACKER AGAINST THE DEEP DARK

I was walking home from somewhere when the idea for this story came to me. I remember stopping to jot down the framework for the story on a receipt I'd found in my coat pocket, which I worked from later that night to write the story. It was one of those tales that seemed to write itself, which is always such a joy: before I knew it, the story was finished.

"Blacker Against the Deep Dark" was originally published in an anthology called The Beauty of Death, *from Independent Legions Publishing, the Italian publisher that published the digital eBook edition of my second collection,* Songs for the Lost, *in 2016. That same year, I read the story as part of a summer arts festival called the Stone & Sky Music & Arts Series that took place on Pelee Island, Ontario. After my reading, as I was gathering my things, an audience member approached me. An older gentleman, he clasped my hand in both of his and told me that the story had made him cry. He went on to explain that the story struck a chord with him, commenting on its portrayal of the awful things we, as human beings, are capable of doing to one another. He thought it was important that people be reminded of the darkness that exists in the world, so that we might be inspired to be better human beings ourselves. It was one of those incredible moments when I was fortunate enough to experience firsthand the positive effect that something I'd written had had on another person.*

Two years later, when I was sequencing the stories of my third collection, this story felt like the perfect choice to begin the book, and to serve as one of its bookending pieces, framing the eclectic and melancholy weirdness between. In fact, the story represents the overall collection so concisely that it lent its title to the book as well.

"The temple bell stops but I still hear
the sound coming out of the flowers."

—Matsuo Bashō

Mr. Yashimoto was tired. It had been another seemingly endless day at the office. The investment firm for which he worked specialized in asset management, and his newfound role as assistant manager and team supervisor kept him much busier than he liked. Long workday hours were generally followed by his having to bring aspects of his work home with him, ruining his weeknights and spoiling the former luxury of weekends he'd enjoyed before his promotion. He was grateful for his job and the life it afforded him and his family, and yet he couldn't help but feel gloomy on days like this, early in the week and trudging home with another long slew of days exactly like it before him.

"It's not very *disciplined* of me," he muttered, thinking of his parents, long since passed away, in whose efficient house with its strict regime he'd so often felt ill-fitting, misplaced, his head circling in fantasies of things he might be doing rather than the schoolwork that he was neglecting. And he added, feeling young and emboldened and angry all at the same time, "But I don't care." He set off again, shoulders slumped petulantly, fists clenched and swinging at his sides, his steps moving faster along the sidewalk.

Suddenly, a voice said:

Be free, son, for you are free.

He spun round, looking in all directions for the speaker, but look where he might he could find no one. The street in both directions lay empty of vehicle and pedestrian traffic. The porches of the houses across the street were un-peopled, shuttered against the sunset. The sheer brick face of the building along which he stood—a long-derelict schoolhouse—reared upwards, dark and windowless and mute. At its base, a handful of virgin white lilies stirred in the breeze, looking misplaced in the desolation of sun-bleached scraggly weeds and ancient brick.

At last, as if resigned to do so, as if he'd known all along that he must do this thing, he turned his eyes upon the shadow blasted into the stone wall before him. The shadow's human shape could not be denied, no matter how strongly he sometimes wished he could successfully deny it. Its round-shouldered, bowed posture, head inclined toward the ground as if it were being buffeted by a very strong wind, a frail arm raised before its head in futile defence. He passed the same place each day, twice, both on his way to and from his job, and always his eyes were drawn to it, though he often only looked quickly before turning away and refocusing his thoughts on the importance of the work day ahead or the importance of finishing his work at home, after he had supper with his wife and ten-year-old son.

His grandfather had introduced him to the shadow-people of Hiroshima when he was a very young boy, but he'd never forgotten that distant day of encounters. Wandering the streets by foot with his slow-moving grandfather, the old man's twisted bamboo cane tapping a sharp emphatic percussion everywhere they went, as if he were emphasizing each of their steps through a city the young boy had only then learned was inhabited by just as many ghosts as men.

The old man would offer occasional narration to the scenes they witnessed, pausing to point a quivering line with the bamboo cane toward a blank building façade or schoolhouse wall or a set of concrete steps rising to the door of a Buddhist temple overlooking the sidewalk, and saying things like:

"Thousands died, here and everywhere. The air grew dark and smelled like a charnel house. The sun was put out."

and

"Children died on that day too. Babies burned. The Bomb—that great Fire—did not discriminate."

and

"People suffered so. Their skin burned. Their eyes melted and came running from their sockets like spoiled milk. They vomited for days. And then they died. It was Hell fallen from the sky on a morning like any other, but like no other."

and

"Look, there and there and there, and see their spirits condemned forever to the face of a stricken city, on a stricken day in history. See them, and hear what they tell us."

These words chilled the boy, and because he never forgot them, they grew to chill him more and more as he grew to manhood, for he also grew to understand them more and more. His grandfather had passed on, and so had his parents, but always the old man's words stayed close with him, haunting and awful and yet not entirely unwelcome, much like the city's shadow-people themselves.

Finally, Mr. Yashimoto turned back to the brick wall. "I am ashamed," he said to the shadow-form in the wall. "I forgot my good fortune. Thank you for reminding me of the world."

All was still and quiet. No more voices spoke on the air. Mr. Yashimoto remained standing on the sidewalk beside the wall as dusk stole over the city, no longer feeling the same urgency to hurry home as he had. He waited and waited and waited. He heard the distant gonging of bells from the Shinto temple several blocks to the east. He smelled the miracle of the white flowers's perfume on the still air. He thought of his son, who would soon be old enough to be taken on a tour of the city and shown its long history and saga of shadows in every building, every temple, every home new and old, every tree standing tall in the face of the wind.

He'd hoped the descending darkness would blanket the wall before him, concealing its shadow-body, but even in the night the form stood out starkly, blacker against the deep dark. There was a lesson in this, too, thought Haruki Yashimoto, and with it clutched to his heart he bowed respectfully to the wall before turning and walking unhurriedly down the sidewalk in the direction of his home and family waiting.

HIGHWAY OF LOST WOMEN

This story had a very long gestation period. I'd had the idea for it years before beginning work on it and then picked away at it on and off for maybe a couple of years before sitting down to finish it. I was ecstatic when Midnight Street Press editor Trevor Denyer accepted it for publication in his fantastic anthology, Ghost Highways.

It's a bit of a different story for me, which is partly why I'm fond of it. It's about four women, life-long friends, and the ways in which each of their lives has met with insurmountable obstacles as a result of their gender. They embark on a road trip together, both as a means of reclaiming their friendship, which has fragmented over the years, as well as finding a deeper meaning to their individual lives. What they find is both utterly unimaginable and... well, you'll see.

I: EXODUS

"Oh. My. Fucking. God."

Sam had slammed her foot on the pedal and ground the car to a squealing halt. In the sudden, stunned silence of the killed engine, with dust settling down in a tinkling pall over the vehicle, her friends followed her rapt stare through the dirty car window.

A line of naked women stood in the heat-shimmering highway, barring the old Topaz from its southbound path. Where they'd come from the friends couldn't say—it seemed as if one moment the highway had stretched empty and desolate before them, and the next they were there. The women—there were fifteen of them, the friends would eventually come to realize—were holding hands, linked and stretching across the entirety of the road and past its shoulder into the fields to east and west. Their hair was uniformly dishevelled, their eyes vacant, lost. They were all extremely pale, as if they hadn't seen the outdoors for a very long time, as if they'd been plucked from some unguessable place of perpetual gloom and rematerialized into the heart of the brilliant, burning day. Their bedraggled hair and the triangles of their pubic hair were stark against their moth-like complexions, drawing the friends's attention and accentuating the figures's shocking nakedness.

The women stood, motionless and silent, facing the occupants of the stopped vehicle, while around them the lonely highway and miles and miles of bleak wild scrub country sweltered in the midday sun. In the nebulous distance, the blue haze-shrouded hills shimmered like anxious apparitions. Time seemed stretched, stilled.

Sam, her hand already on the gear selector, turned with the other occupants of the Topaz to instinctively look behind them, in the direction from which they'd come and toward the promise of escape.

"Oh, God," cried Alex and Darcy together.

"Fuck," Billie said, gripping the headrest of her passenger-side seat in a vice-like hold.

The road behind them held another line of women: identically lost-eyed; startlingly naked; porcelain-white and motionless and summoning the deepest, most profound dread in the friends's hearts.

II: DARCY, MAP-LESS

"Gotchoo!"

The girls turned to Darcy where she sat in the back seat, clutching something in the cage of her fingers. She parted her fingers a little to show them: it was a tiny, cream-coloured butterfly, fluttering its wings madly in a futile effort to escape back into the sultry air from which it had been plucked. Darcy had had her arm dangling out the window since they'd set out that morning, trying intermittently to snatch insects from the air as they sped down the highway.

"How can you even see anything shooting past the car?" Sam exclaimed, eyeing her friend's reflection in the rear-view mirror. "We're going, like, a buck-twenty out here!"

But Darcy only laughed and continued squinting into the bright air as they tore down the highway, the wind whipping her pale blonde hair everywhere.

"Holy shit," said Billie, turned around in the passenger-side seat and looking with awe at the butterfly in Darcy's fingers. "You actually got one."

"I got lots," Darcy said, smiling. "This makes maybe a dozen. But I let them all go as soon as I catch them and say hello."

She laughed and let the butterfly go. The others laughed too, amazed at their friend's luck or skill or strangeness.

Darcy was the "quirky one," which was alright with everyone because she was really and truly quirky and not just pretending out of a juvenile need to be unique from those around her; a genuine weirdo of the highest order; the girl who collected rocks and acorns like boys collected hockey cards, and made bizarre arrangements of the items on her bookshelves; who more often than not chose to stay home Friday nights to read books and cuddle with her cats, foregoing the noise and sloppiness of weekend bar-hopping for quiet bookworm evenings with old friends Bradbury and red wine; who caught highway butterflies in seemingly impossible ways and then acted like it was the most ordinary thing in the world, as if she didn't know magic of some kind.

She squinted, eyeing the path ahead, and a moment later closed her fingers, feeling a soft something in her hand. When she pulled her arm back inside the vehicle, she found herself clutching a single white flower petal and wondered where it could possibly have come from. She didn't mention it to her friends, and after a moment of staring at it quizzically she dropped it from the window.

Then she retrieved the book from the handbag between her feet and opened it to its bookmarked place. She tried reading but was distracted: she kept seeing him; a pretty boy, a grocery store clerk who she'd met a few days before and seen twice since their first meeting in the vegetable aisle. He was shy and funny and had nice eyes. But then he had told her about his ambition, of finishing the business program at the university so that he wouldn't have to stock shelves for the rest of his life. She hadn't retorted that she herself worked at a small, independently owned convenience store doing exactly the same, and that she liked it, and that she felt no superiority over anyone else working jobs like theirs just because she had a useless university degree (English Language and Literature, BA Honours). She hadn't even told him about her degree until their second date two days later, just before they'd kissed goodnight outside of her three-storey apartment building overlooking the Ganatchio Trail that wound through the quiet evening streets. But his mind had been on that upcoming kiss—she was sure he'd felt it coming just like she had; the imminence of it was huge, cataclysmic even, the electric expectant build-up before a summer lightning storm—and after the kiss and the subsequent telephone conversation before she'd left on the road trip, they'd talked of other things, and the whole subject of her English degree and her job and her view of things like education and work and the kinds of jobs afforded those with certain degrees versus those with certain other degrees continued to be glossed over.

That was okay though. They would talk again soon, once she was back from the road trip with her friends. She and the boy would talk, and have another date, and she would find herself fallen in love with him the way she'd only thus far in her thirty years of life on Earth ever been in love with full moons on July nights, and moth cocoons lying suspended from an oak branch and catching the final sunlight of a dusking day like a solar flare curling up from the edge of a life-sustaining sun. Or she wouldn't love him at all, and he wouldn't love her either, but that would be okay, too, because there were other miracles rampant in the world everywhere she looked, even if she was the only person who ever seemed to see them. Even if she felt it more and more those days: a loneliness the likes of which she'd never before known, one that went somehow beyond—somehow deeper— than cuddles with cats and hours spent escaped inside of books could ever take away.

The four friends had settled back into their mellow untalking rhythm, nodding along to the Mazzy Star song crackling from the car's old stereo speakers and watching the 401 and the desolate heat-scorched country continue everywhere the eye could see. In the lazy moment, Darcy closed her book and closed her eyes to the world in favour of the dream-world behind her eyes, the place where things were always perfect, where boys were good and pure and the rest of the dream-population was no different from her, and where she felt at home, always and always at home.

INTERLUDE

It had been a road trip of necessity: girls-only, exclusive members of the original gang going back to grade school days, pointing the car down the highway and gunning it northwards, leaving the ghosts of shitty summer jobs and shitty summer boyfriends and more pressing problems than those long behind them. It was dead centre in the middle of a scorching July hotter than any of them could remember, and they unanimously agreed that it was the best decision they'd made in a very long time. This decision and this certainty they'd each clung to in the days leading up to the trip, a beacon signalling a break from it all and the ambiguous hope of something better waiting for them at journey's end.

Their ultimate destination they'd left vague, like most things in their lives. Up north had been the consensus, but exactly where they'd left open. Port Elgin, possibly; or further north toward the Muskokas if they felt inclined to drive a few more hours; and if they felt especially bold and craved their escape to last longer than initially planned, maybe even Tobermory at the tip of the Bruce Peninsula overlooking Lake Huron. Somewhere green and on the water had been Sam's only stipulation, on which all four friends agreed.

That morning, as they'd pulled onto the 401, Alex, Billie, Sam, and Darcy looked together down the highway leading into the shimmering miles ahead and felt it, that combination of excitement and relief and fear: Who knew what lay ahead? Who knew where they might go?

Billie craned her head to glance at Alex where she sat behind her. "I'll bet if we tried Darcy-magic that we'd just end up catching hornets or wasps in our hands, huh?" She laughed, but her friend only murmured something inaudible by way of agreement and continued staring into the wasteland of barren fields and scrub brush stretching around them as far as the eye could see. Billie scowled, a little irritated that Alex should bring along personal baggage, whatever trivial thing it might be, on a trip meant to free them from their worries; but she saw also the small, somehow frightened look of her friend huddled down in her seat, and understood that look only too well, so she let it go and turned back to the sun-glazed road ahead.

As she watched the fields of sun-devastated corn crops racing past them, she wondered what her friend was thinking about. She worried about her when she got like this. Alex was quiet generally but quieter than usual these days. Some people interpreted her quiet way as aloofness, or snobbery, or shyness; all of these were wrong. She just preferred listening to others first and foremost and added her two cents when she felt it appropriate. In life she cut corners not out of laziness but from the desire to streamline a too-busy and overwhelming world into manageable chapters. She compartmentalized her life to preserve her sanity. She was economical and open. And quiet about it. This her small circle of close friends knew and loved about her. And if they knew just how much she sacrificed for something like taking a road trip with her friends in the middle of her stressor-filled life they'd have been even more grateful for her willingness to try and get back some of the magic they'd made between them long ago in their younger days together.

Sam said, loudly over the music, "Okay, ladies, I say we find the adventure today we set out to find. I mean it. Like, if we feel like pulling over and getting lunch at some off-road, mom-and-pop diner, let's do it. If we feel like robbing the friggin' place, let's do that too! If one of you feels the need to tell me to turn off the road and plow straight through the field and head for the forest on the horizon, you tell me and I'll do it, I swear I will. We set out to get away, right? So that's what we're going to do!"

Sam was the most driven of their gang, but driven only in mundane pursuits for which she felt no true passion. Rather, it was the simple doing of the thing that gave her reason to get up in the morning, and to feel good about herself. She was the opposite of Darcy, with her arcane pursuits—everything she did gave her some new knowledge to add to her ever-expanding repository of esoteric experiences—whereas Sam's interests were dictated more by the frantic need to be doing something, anything, it didn't really matter what; because a state of non-movement constituted boredom and the admission that she had no real interests at all. And so, of course, she was just as adrift as the rest of them, maybe even more so for her awareness and acceptance of how people saw her and the inability to find anything meaningful to dedicate herself to.

Darcy took her up on her offer. "Okay, Sam, you said it: I feel like a snack, so let's pull over."

They saw the fast-approaching wooden roadside farmer's stand and its selection of fruits and vegetables. Sam slowed down and eased the car onto the shoulder. They got out and saw a frail old man rising like a scarecrow from a wicker chair on the adjacent house's shady porch. They perused the fruits as the man hobbled down the gravel driveway toward them. By the time he reached them, they'd each selected a peach—even Billie, who replaced the blueberries she'd chosen with a peach at the last minute.

"Hullo, angels," said the farmer in a croaking, bullfrog's voice.

"How much for four?" said Billie, holding her peach for him to see.

The old farmer deliberated, then smiled a toothless smile. "They're yours. A gift. Safe travels, and good luck."

"Oh, we can't take them for free," Darcy said, smiling.

But the man raised a liver-spotted hand on the air in farewell and was already limping back to the shade of his porch.

"Thank you, sir," called Sam, echoed by the others.

Feeling humbled and lucky, the friends walked back to the car. Only Billie held back, eyeing the departing farmer with troubled eyes. It felt somehow un-right to her, taking something without paying for it; as if, like she knew from past experiences, such a gift meant they were now obligated to reciprocate in some unspecified way, at some point. She didn't like owing anybody anything. She pocketed the peach inside her hoodie, brooding.

"What a perfect day," proclaimed Darcy when they stood outside the car, her arms upraised in luxurious acceptance of the sunlight pouring from the cloudless sky. "We couldn't have picked better weather."

"The sun is my enemy today," Billie said, squinting in the bright air and raising a hand over her eyes as if to ward off the sunlight. "And this heat is brutal." She plucked the sunglasses from where they were clipped to her shirt collar and slipped them over her eyes.

"The sun's never your enemy," said Darcy, her good-natured admonishment failing to cheer her friend.

"Sure, Mother-Earth Darcy," Billie muttered. "Peace, love, and sunshine for all."

The words stung. Darcy stammered, "I'm sorry, Billie. I didn't mean it like... I didn't mean anything bad when I..."

"Don't mind her," chimed in Sam, shrugging off her flannel shirt and tying it around her waist. "Billie's just being bad-ass Billie."

Billie cocked an eye at Sam. "What's that supposed to mean?"

The suddenly charged mood hung uncomfortably over them.

Sam raised her hands on the air. "Peace, Billie. Peace. I was just saying."

"Just saying what exactly?" Billie said. "And what's with all the hippy-peace bullshit today?" She looked around at them all, found Alex watching her feet, arms crossed tightly across her chest as if to stave off a chill wind, biting her lip nervously. "How about you, Al? Are you a member of the new hippy power movement too? What's next on the fucking itinerary, Alex Starchild?"

Alex scuffed a toe in the gravel, holding her peach in limp fingers, as if she'd forgotten about it entirely. "Um... Let's just start driving again."

"Sounds good to me," Billie said, rolling her eyes towards Darcy and Sam and climbing into the baking car. She pulled the peach from her pocket and took a vicious bite from its juicy body that cracked the silence.

Darcy watched her helplessly, said, "I just meant that the sun's out today and it's nice." It had no effect on Billie, sitting stoic and silent in the car. Darcy added, sounding petulant and weakly combative, "The sun isn't anyone's *enemy.*"

Sam smiled inwardly—she adored Darcy, who just then reminded her of her parents's Chihuahua, anxious and frightened of the world but bold enough with the backyard fence separating it from the neighbour's German Shepherd to bark indignantly at its larger counterpart. But Sam only made a cutting motion across her throat meant to convey to Darcy to not bother; to leave Billie alone because once she was in one of her moods it was no use trying to reason with her; to let Billie hate the sunshine as much as she needed to.

III: BILLIE, THE BLACK HOLE

"Billie, you're nuts."

Sam immediately regretted the words—it was always risky to take even a light-hearted jab at someone as volatile as their friend. She glanced quickly from the road to Billie beside her, caught the frown crease her features even as she slipped back inside the vehicle from where she'd been leaning precariously through her window, with only her legs inside, her sneakered feet tucked beneath the questionable safety of her seat—Darcy had spotted a white butterfly clinging to the hood of the car and pleaded with Sam to pull over so they could dislodge the creature, and Billie had wordlessly slipped halfway out of the speeding vehicle to pluck it off with a ginger hand while her friends argued about it. No amount of protesting from the others could have persuaded Darcy that it wasn't necessary to rescue the insect, that being capable of flight ensured that the insect would be fine. (The butterfly, Darcy argued frantically, would be relocated to a place too far away from its local habitat if they left it where it was.) So, Billie had done what she had to in order to silence everyone's arguing.

Billie held her gently cupped hands over her headrest. "There you go, Darce. You do the honours." Her voice was patient or tired, Sam couldn't decide which.

105

Darcy, beaming, accepted the gift of the white butterfly from her friend's fingers. "Thanks, Billie! You saved her!" And she cast the insect from her open window like a spell, watching it get sucked off into the air currents.

Though Billie's eyes were hidden behind her sunglasses, Sam knew the look in them as surely as she knew how badly they'd all needed to get away for a while. Anyone who knew her at all knew that the determination—the hardness—never left her eyes, as if it were safeguarding something else hidden beneath, some weakness Billie would never let out for the world to see and exploit.

They'd known to pick up Billie last that morning because she was always the last to be ready so they figured she'd need the extra fifteen minutes it would take them to hit her place *en route* to the highway. Her lack of punctuality was appropriate, because she of them all had grown up the least, if you were going by outward appearances alone: she still wore her mascara and eyeliner high school Goth girl thick, wore the same choker she'd worn in those days, and the same heavy metal band t-shirts, even dyed her hair punky colours from time to time, as if daring her bosses to fire her because fuck that telemarketing gig anyways, and that part-time fast food cashier gig too—rebel rebel, hear her yell. Someone—an ex from years back, one of the many, and there were many—had jokingly called her Billie-Wolf, for her love of an old werewolf movie and the midnight hour, and the nickname stuck, not for the same reasons her ex had called her this but because everyone had agreed that it suited her in some difficult to articulate way.

Sam glanced at Billie. The look on her friend's face told her not to bother trying to talk to her, she was in a deep and brooding place from which she didn't want to come out. So, she turned back to the road reaching into better places and, eager to combat the anxiety that had suddenly come awake inside her, she pressed her foot down a little harder on the gas.

They all made poor decisions. This they agreed on and this was the common thread that had linked them all throughout the years, no matter how distant from one another they'd grown geographically or emotionally. They were the same in their old way of investing too much trust in other people, and so they'd

106

changed in the same way too over the years, so that they'd grown to watch everyone and everything encroaching on them with a wisely wary eye; though, just as unwisely, as if helpless to do otherwise, they continued making the same mistakes they'd always made.

Billie turned in her seat and seeing her friend immersed in the book cracked open in her lap, said, "Darce. What are you reading?"

Billie squinted at the cover of the book Darcy held aloft: *Away From Night and Into Light: The Ascension of the Sirius Group.* "It's about a UFO cult," Darcy explained. "Do you remember the Magahatti Massacre?"

Billie did. The cult had been led by an eccentric and rich lunatic named Michael Boreal, who'd led hundreds of disciples in a mass suicide that promised revelation and ascension to a cosmic paradise of some kind. She'd been twelve years old and had obsessed over the event for months after it happened, which her mom had found alarming and her friends thought was Billie being Billie. Billie herself had never decided on why she'd been so drawn to it.

She said, "Yeah. I remember it." She scrutinized the cover, an old black and white photograph of the cult leader, Michael Boreal, standing at a lectern draped with a cloth that had his group's symbol sewn into its fabric. He looked as if he were addressing a group of his followers—eyes manic, hands raised emphatically in the air, opened mouth inches away from a slim microphone—though the photo showed only him. She wondered if he'd been a lonely person or whether he'd truly found happiness in his followers and his mission. She said, "Why are you reading it?"

Darcy scowled a little and clutched the book to her chest protectively, as if her friend's question had threatened it in some way. "Why not? Is Darcy not allowed to read anything besides New Age hippy self-help books?"

Billie looked at her friend a moment, decided she liked her response to the question—as close to an admonishment as she was likely to ever receive from perennially sweet-as-sugar Darcy—and smiled before turning back in her seat and watching the highway rushing at them at over 100 kilometres an hour.

● ● ●

Billie sometimes felt like the female version of the cowboys she'd seen in the old Western movies she used to watch with her kid brother, tough and resilient with a pistol on her hip, free with the open horizon calling her name like nothing else had ever called her before. But that was mostly surface stuff, the façade she knew everyone else saw and that she'd cultivated over the years to keep other, less resilient things about herself hidden down deep. No one else had ever gotten it right, except for once, back in high school, and of course it was Darcy who had nailed Billie spot-on with a defining name, though Billie had ignored it like a pro so maybe over the years even Darcy had begun to question whether she'd been as insightful as all that.

They'd been in tenth grade, enjoying the limited freedom of an afternoon of free expression in art class. (That meant Mr. Simon, their teacher, hadn't wanted to teach that day and was in and out of the room throughout the class, hitting up the staff room and cafeteria.) The teacher's instructions had been simple: let whatever's inside you out onto the paper. They were allowed to use whichever medium suited their fancy, within reason: coloured pencils, markers, brushes and watercolour paints, construction paper and glue, glitter, whatever.

Billie could still remember Darcy's artwork clearly: at first glance a pencil-drawn bouquet of lilies that she coloured in violet with a hand so gentle they were for all intents and purposes white. It was only when you held the paper far enough away from your face that you realized there was more to it than that. Among the leafy tendrils of the flowers's stems, a face materialized that had given Billie a start. It was a beautiful face, neither masculine nor feminine but equal parts both genders, whose distinguishing feature was a long, grotesque, and deadly-looking pair of horns which rose from its high regal forehead to curl and become intertwined among the flowers's stems. Its eyes, too, petal-shaped and peering from among the foliage, held a vicious glimmer that seemed impossible to have sprung from any high school student's pencil.

Darcy, seeing Billie's jaw drop and eyes widen at the discovery, had subtly squeezed her friend's elbow and placed a finger across her lips. Billie had turned back to the image,

108

impressed in a way she'd never been impressed by her friend before, although "awed" might have been a better word to describe how she felt.

She was awed once again by her friend several minutes later when Darcy, peering over Billie's shoulder at her finished artwork, succinctly defined both the image and its origin in the artist when she said, "It's beautiful, Billie. It's a black hole. It sucks stars into itself and swallows them. Like we learned about in Mr. Landsdale's astronomy class, except scarier. I think we all have one inside of us, except some people's are bigger than others."

Billie had succeeded in laughing and rolling her eyes at her friend, then hiding her face behind her long, newly-dyed black hair while pretending to embellish the giant black circle covering her sketchbook paper with the coloured pencil in her fist. But she'd stared into the depths of that black hole on her page, and in that moment knew she'd successfully completed her assignment because she felt that yawning black hole—had always felt it—inside herself. If Mr. Simon only knew, he'd give her perfect marks like she'd never received before.

It was only after the bell had rung and while they were packing up their things that Billie, coming out of her shaken state a little, had thought to ask her friend about her own artwork. "Hey, Darce, how come you put that face hidden in your flowers?"

They were slipping into the rear of the line forming at the classroom door when Darcy, smiling the perfectly sad and open smile that would mislead many boys into believing they'd found their girl, said, "Because there's always bad hidden in with the good."

That was all she said but to Billie it had sounded like the highest and most profound of wisdoms. Even then, as a teenager who occasionally thought she knew everything, Billie understood how inadequate she was at expressing those things she knew in her heart to be true. She was glad to have a friend like Darcy, who could do that for them both. She was glad to have someone like her on her side, someone who knew Billie's secret—that she'd been consumed long ago by just such a dark cosmic power, that infinitely huge black hole eating her inside every day passing and which she'd miraculously been able to commit to paper—and that her friend could still see some good in her despite that.

Billie had been so grateful for her friend that she scored some pot from a guy a couple of grades older and brought it over to Darcy's later that night. They'd snuck out her bedroom window, climbed the chain-link backyard fence, and crept through the field down to the nearby river where they smoked for the first time. They talked about many things that long night—school, boys, parents, music, books, religion and science, cosmic powers beyond reckoning, good and evil and night and day and the immense differences between these opposing forces—and they were comforted. They were comforted by the river's trickling voice; by the electric voice of the crickets in the field; by the familiarity of each other's voices, the solace in them no matter how dark and difficult the subjects that they conquered.

She'd been ten years old when she met the Devil and learned that He lived inside every ray of sunlight making the world a golden and warm and deceiving place.

It was the summer that Billie had been introduced to the lake, that same strange, black-sunned summer of her final days being a little girl. She'd fallen in love with the lake then: Lake Huron, with its deep, green waters holding her and her father rocking gently in their little motorboat each afternoon; the distant green shoreline's destinations of mystery, containing secret paths through unmapped woods. She would pretend the forests contained pixy tribes whom only she could see, and who only revealed themselves to people who'd never stopped believing in magic. At night, peering through the flap of the tent she shared with her brother, she saw them too, drifting their elegant air-dances among the lesser fireflies bobbing erratically amid the black silhouettes of the trees. She'd snuck out of her tent and followed the dancing lights until she stood among the cattails along the shoreline, her breath taken away by the sight of the heavens above reflected in the placid lake beneath. As above, so below, and the universe inside the lake had held her under its spell until the sun peered its head over the horizon, bloodying the water and burning away the majesty of the cosmos.

Sometime over the years, Billie had started thinking of her parents only in relation to their days vacationing on the lake, a regular summer-time occurrence, as if they were somehow native to that place and no other; her mother dappled in sunlight, wending her way barefoot beneath the canopy of branches like an Amazonian queen, leading her and her father along the narrow path as if she knew the way to wherever they were going; smiling down at her, face flushed with the heat, eyes gleaming with what Billie knew instinctively was love; her father owning the prow of the motorboat, hurling fishing lines out onto the water, the king of the lake and guardian of her and her brother's and her mother's safety, until. Until.

In the early days of that first vacation, it felt as if they'd never truly lived in the world outside of the safe green embrace of those deep woods and comforting waters. Years later, it would seem as if they lived there still, that this place was where Billie's parents's spirits retired after they'd exited their destroyed bodies crushed like pulp among the wreckage of the station wagon and the pickup truck that had weaved across the grass median and smashed them headlong into darkness on the day Billie was preparing to leave home for the first time and try the college path; because this path, doubtful at best, seemed the only escape from a home that had stopped feeling like home nearly ten years before.

It was a cruel life to have exposed ten-year-old Billie to the fairy-tale splendour of a place like this, only to snuff it out in a single afternoon's evil on her family's final day vacationing in its green heart. But then this was how the world was—unexpected and savage and cruel—a lesson she would come to learn again and again in her days. And so that endless afternoon on the final day of the family vacation was a brutal stay in eternity for little Billie, as her father raped her on the boat bobbing in the middle of the sun-speckled placid lake, her sun-bathing mother and the beach and the colony of the forest pixies as far away as Heaven was from Hell.

INTERLUDE

The relentless droning of the car's engine; the monotony of the road spread forever before them; the bright air suffusing the car; the heat seeping into their skin, thoughts—it all combined to make them feel sleepy, too tired to speak or move or otherwise fight their lethargy. They simply drove on, their tires eating the kilometres, making the car seem like the only moving thing in the midst of that timeless, static, burning afternoon.

"Remember that time we spent the entire day 'fishing' on Little River?" Sam said, apropos of nothing. She was making air quotes with her hands, where her palms rested on the burning steering wheel.

Her friends stirred from their somnolent reveries. They all laughed quietly in remembrance.

"We were the best sports fishermen in all Windsor," said Darcy, laughingly. "We caught some crayfish, if I remember."

"*You* caught the crayfish," corrected Alex. "Of course, Miss butterfly-catcher." She squeezed Darcy's knee beside her, mostly to show she's wasn't teasing her, received a return squeeze from her friend to show that Darcy understood. Not everyone was as touchy as Billie.

Sam found Darcy in the rear-view mirror, smiling bashfully and looking at her small hands resting in her lap, and said, "That's right, Darcy—see, you can't deny your magical abilities with us. We have history."

Darcy only said, "I remember we found a family of them—a crayfish family—in the grass along the shore. And we were amazed that they'd been there with us all along, without us knowing about them, or suspecting they were even there. And then we let them all go."

It was a good memory, one safe with innocence and secure in its secrecy among them. A Vault Memory, that only members of the girl tribe needed to know and recollect.

They'd secretly borrowed Billie's father's fishing line and, using jelly worms as bait—even then, as fourth graders, they understood the ridiculousness of this, and did it more to amuse themselves than anything else—and spent a morning and good part of an afternoon idling along the break wall on the river. Skipping stones across its still, chemically green, scummy surface; talking about school, their classmates whom they hated and crushed on, the coming school year, distantly exciting but, up close, more frightening than anything else.

Truthfully, they'd hung out on the river a lot growing up. It was the refuge of the tomboys, and the girls who didn't mind playing with the tomboys, or at least appreciated the privacy afforded by being tucked away in the wilds behind the townhouse neighbourhood where no one else from school could see them hanging out with undesirables like these.

"Yeah, those were the days," Billie said, immediately feeling the bittersweet nostalgia of the reminiscence overcome her. Everyone else felt it too, and the conversation flagged after this.

They drove onward. The sun crawled across the sky. Heat rose from the road ahead in shimmering, smoky waves as if it were burning up. They passed a bouquet of flowers tied with twine to a sapling bending toward the road, the only sign of a human hand they'd seen in some time. Ironically, it was likely a memorial marking the site of a fatal accident.

Nobody said anything as they left the flowers behind them. Darcy reached a hand and placed it on Billie's burning shoulder, squeezing her briefly. Billie didn't return the gesture, or even look back at Darcy, but, keeping her eyes on the road dead ahead, nodded slowly in tacit acknowledgment that something good had been passed between them.

IV: SAM, NO ONE

It had been Sam's idea from the outset: she'd needed an escape plan, had used the trip as the excuse for it, and arranged all the details, co-ordinating their respective schedules months in advance to ensure that it would work for everyone.

She still wasn't certain what it was that she was escaping from, though it didn't feel as though it mattered much anymore. Her job as a bank teller was tedious but steady, with the potential for some slight upward mobility, although there was no sign of that for her—she'd been working there in the same position for five years and the only thing that ever changed were the faces of the customers she saw every day. She'd briefly considered going back to school but then dismissed the idea just as quickly. What would she take anyways? Her four-year degree in psychology had yielded her nothing but the bank job, which some co-workers of hers had landed without having to sacrifice four years of their lives to academia, not to mention paying exorbitant tuition costs. Choosing psych as her major had seemed wise, maybe because it sounded like an important field of study. Exactly how inexact of a science it was—and how useless a bachelor's degree in it would prove to be—she'd learned only in the long years afterward.

Maybe the gathering of the old gang again was what mattered, more than anything else. It certainly wasn't their destination, as they had none. This had been part of the allure to each of them: the not knowing, the discovering along the way of any treasure they might find. Maybe they were all still children at heart, tomboys in adult bodies pining for the days of adventure they'd left too far behind, lost and tangled in the weeds and webs of the many years.

"I need a coffee," she muttered, scanning the distance for signs of a roadside diner or convenience store but seeing only naked fields and the forest that had been following their progress for the past hour edging closer than ever to the road. Up ahead, she saw the tree branches touching over the road, creating a green tunnel through which they were imminently to pass.

Billie said, "We've got our bags in the trunk. I've got my thermos in there." She tapped her fingers along the plastic lid of Sam's now empty thermos squeezed into the space between their seats.

"Thank God for you, Billie," said Sam, immediately slowing down and turning the car onto the soft shoulder. It struck her as a very dramatic thing to have said, and she felt a little embarrassed, wondering where it had come from. When she saw Billie's expression beside her, stoic and hard, it made some sort of sense to her and she said nothing more.

They all got out, stretching and getting the kinks out of their backs, necks.

Sam popped the trunk, grabbed Billie's thermos from where it stuck out of her gym bag's exterior pouch, uncapped it and took a long swig. "I needed this," she said after a minute, and tilted the thermos to her lips again. Billie stood beside her, leaning against the car and staring at Darcy—she was standing a few metres to the rear of the car, her sandaled feet off the shoulder and in the knee-high grass. Dandelion seedlings clung to her dusty jeans, drifted languidly about her legs. She was staring off into the trees before them with rapt eyes.

The friends exchanged looks both amused and uneasy. Mostly to break the unsettling atmosphere, Billie called to Darcy, "Hey, butterfly girl—you're okay over there?"

Darcy's mouth moved but whatever she'd said was spoken too softly for the friends to hear. They exchanged the same mildly spooked looks and sidled over to her.

Sam said, tentatively, "Darce? You okay?"

Darcy didn't answer. They followed her looking into the woods, faced the deep green wall of the wilderness looming over them. The trees stretched as far back as they could see, becoming a green wash of vegetation in the distant depths of the forest. It struck them instantly, the great quiet emanating from the woods: empty of birdsong or the chatter of squirrels or the buzz of insects; and the road behind them, of course, desolate and lonely.

Darcy said, chilling them all, "This is wrong. Mother Earth isn't in there."

Billie turned to appraise her, had her lips parted to make some sarcastic remark—this kind of happy-hippie-horseshit stuff was ideal material—then remained silent, thoroughly unsettled by the look of her friend, small, frail in the face of the immense trees hulking over her. Instead, she said, "Come on, guys. We better get going."

Darcy said, "Where did she go? She's supposed to be living in there, right? Where is she?" She turned pleading eyes to Billie beside her who, discomfited more than ever, shrugged her shoulders and looked away. As she was turning her head, she saw it. Her friends sensed something amiss and followed where Billie looked.

A ways into the woods, a bouquet of lilies, identical to the one they'd seen on the highway, was wound around the base of the tree trunk with a piece of fraying rope. The virgin petals were like snow in the lush summer green of the weirdly hushed woods.

Billie felt her friends watching her—indeed, they'd all instinctively turned to her, the queen tomboy of the old gang— and she felt annoyed at the implication of that needy look. Too uneasy to remark on it, she said simply, "Come on," and led them back toward the car, thinking as they crunched through the gravel how strange it was that in a deep part of her, she'd been half-expecting to find their car no longer there, but whisked away to some dark place, stranding them there to walk the endless road together.

•　　　•　　　•

They drove on. The sun hung in the molten sky, baking the earth and the road and time itself, stretching the minutes into hours and the hours into days and the days into forever and forever into the road trip itself like an odyssey the four friends had embarked upon, for better or worse, a lifetime ago.

V: ALEX, LOST IN THE WORLD

Alex had promised herself that she'd leave work behind but, in her heart, had known this would be an impossibility. Work was too ingrained in her life, in the matrix of who she was and who she'd been raised to become, for her to shrug it off in favour of a frivolous trip up north with friends. *I'm so fucking Japanese*, she thought grimly as she scanned the field racing past her window without seeing it, resenting her parents and the strict and disciplined household regime she'd hoped to escape when she went to college, but of course hadn't, couldn't.

Part of her, as ever, felt pulled back to the only thing she seemed to know, which was the dedication to her job. She was part of a battery research team working within the great conglomerate of the Chrysler Corporation. She was lucky to have gotten the job but hated the commute from Windsor to Detroit every day, the long waits each early morning at the tunnel, the routine rigmarole with the border police. (Usually they let her go without too many questions, but occasionally they held her for more questions than seemed necessary, a fact she always assumed had to do with her ethnic background, though why they had anything against the Japanese in this day and age of Middle Eastern bias and paranoia she couldn't begin to fathom.)

The job itself was lacking in ways too. She had little passion for the work, and the projects she was allowed to work on were commandeered by those above her, all of whom were male and seemed always to treat her contributions as less significant than their own, when they deigned to allow her input at all. She'd heard much of the glass ceiling encountered by women working in the science fields while she'd still been in school but had figured she'd be lucky and avoid it, or that her diligence and hard work would help her circumvent obstacles like these. She'd been wrong.

"What the fuck?" Billie's voice had risen over the white-noise crackle of the radio, jarring Alex from her reveries. "I honestly have no fucking clue where the Hell we could possibly be on here." She was holding the map against the dashboard, tracing a line across it with a finger before scanning the road for signage that wasn't to be found.

Sam tapped a finger across the GPS resting in the centre of the dashboard. "Still dead," she said, frowning. They'd noticed it an hour before, its screen inexplicably gone dark.

"Here, let me see. I can read maps," Alex said, sounding cross and bossy.

Billie turned slowly around in her seat and cocked an exaggerated eyebrow at her. "Oh *thank you*, Miss Smarty-Pants. But hang on a second, Dum-Dum Billie can try her hand at reading lines on a piece of fucking paper too, can't she?"

"I didn't—" Alex began, then shook her head and left it.

"I didn't know you Japanese kids were good in other subjects besides math, but if geography's your thing then, by all means, have a go," Billie went on.

"What the Hell, Billie, that's racist," Alex said. "Very nice."

Billie laughed sardonically and turned back to the map in her hands.

Maybe it made her a bitch, but Alex didn't care that she wasn't that sorry about her behaviour toward Billie. Her thoughts were on more pressing things, like the journal article she should have been working on at that very moment instead of embarking on a frivolous trip with her old friends, friends who didn't even know her anymore, or didn't care enough to try to learn who she was and what she was fighting so hard to do with her life and career. One of her position's many requirements included meeting a quota of publications each year, an area in which she'd fallen sorely behind due to her busy schedule that precluded any post-work devotion to research. And beyond work, there was the increasing desperation she felt—and the pressure from her parents—to find someone, an appropriate partner; a successful man; a Japanese husband to complete her in her parents's eyes, though of course she secretly yearned for this fictitious man to

117

truly complete and complement her so that she wouldn't suffer the same fate as her mother, subordinate to a man she'd never truly loved or even knew. Or maybe these ambitions were only pipedreams unworthy of a responsible adult and she should focus her energies on the daily tasks at hand, which she let slip away from her more and more all the time, the present moment being the best example.

She only came out of her reveries when it became clear the car was slowing down and her friends were straining forward in their seats to get a clearer view of something. She looked over Sam's shoulder, a hand raised to shield her eyes from the glare of the sun.

They were coming up to a crossroads of sorts, marked by a seemingly purposeless wooden pole—it carried no signage nor light—to which someone had affixed a bouquet of flowers with a narrow loop of fraying rope. Once again, as in the forest and on the road earlier, they were white lilies. The intersecting road was paved and led as far as they could see. In the distance, it shimmered in the heat, the same gossamer veils lifting into the air that they'd been seeing all day.

"Well," said Sam thoughtfully, "It *is* heading straight up north. Short-cut, maybe?"

"Is this on the map?" asked Darcy hesitantly, leaning forward to look at the map in Billie's hands, then turning to study each of her friends' faces in turn.

"No, I don't see it..." Billie said, then called over her shoulder, "You want a crack at looking for this, Miss Maps?"

But Alex didn't notice the mocking words, feeling only an anxiety while they sat idling at the mouth of the road. "Should we?" she said. "I mean, the 401 would get us there eventually anyways." She heard the subtle, pleading tone in her own voice, hoping someone would naysay the idea, because she hadn't the courage to do so herself.

"Do we dare?" Darcy said, a mischievous glimmer in her eyes.

After a second of rumination Sam declared, "Of course we dare! Today we dare the world!"

Billie cocked an approving eye on her. "Right on, Sam." She punched Sam's knee gently, squinting through her sunglasses down the empty road yawning into the hazy distance before them.

Sam smiled. She felt good, bolstered by her boldness and Billie's validation, not noticing Alex scowling in the backseat, eyes staring broodingly out the window into the hushed woods.

She turned onto the unmarked road and pressed her sandaled foot hard on the gas.

INTERLUDE

They'd been driving hard for over two hours.

Their initial exuberant conversation had given way to listlessness, sleepiness, and soon enough a subtle fear that swept through the friends and left them each feeling utterly alone in the world, more so than they'd felt in the days leading up to their expedition. And though no one said a word about it, the thought haunted them all: they hadn't passed a single town, gas station, or vehicle at all during the entire two hours after they'd turned onto the unmarked highway. Not even signage of any sort met them on their way, no speed limit postings, directional signs, nothing. Only the empty road unfurling in front of them, and the blank wild country of fields and hulking forests and occasionally sloping hills rising on either side of the road.

Darcy tried hanging an arm out her window but there were no butterflies to catch anymore.

Alex said, "Hey Sam. Did you want one of us to take over driving for a while? You must be tired."

"No, I'm okay," Sam said. "Thanks though."

Alex had been studying her friend's face in the rear-view mirror and saw how she hadn't looked into the mirror at all in acknowledgement.

Sam's eyes remained looking defiantly straight ahead down the highway, as if she were willing the road to end and their location and destination to finally become clear.

They drove on through the heat and stillness, eating the kilometres.

At some point Billie wiped the back of her hand across her sweating brow and murmured, "Fuck already. We're up north—

isn't it always cooler up here in the summer? It's like we're driving through Goddamned Hell. Fuck."

Nobody said anything. They just stewed in the claustrophobia-inducing air of the car, hanging arms outside their windows in a futile effort to cool themselves in the furnace wind whipping them as they sped onward down the highway. Darcy had stopped trying to catch butterflies as they drove— something told her that not only would there be none there, but that anything she might catch would do her harm.

Since there hadn't been any signage indicating an impending rest stop, they pulled over and took turns squatting and relieving themselves in the bushes alongside the road.

Alex had just finished wiping herself with the last of her handy-wipes and muttered under her breath. "What a fucking fiasco."

Billie, standing along the shoulder nearby and staring off into the woods, caught it and laughed a harsh laugh. "Well, listen to Miss Maps—such language! Would Mr. and Mrs. Tanaka approve of their prim and proper daughter cussing like a lower class white girl cusses? Then again, would they approve of her pissing in the flowers and wiping her vag with leaves?"

It was a combination of everything that in that moment added up to driving Alex to do what she did. Hot, sweaty, uncomfortable at having to piss in the grass like a dog, disgusted with herself for embarking on a trip with someone like Billie, a supposed friend who couldn't bother trying to understand her plight or needs or concerns, she marched along the shoulder, a defiant glare in her eyes. She stopped in front of Billie and said, "Why don't you shut the fuck up, you fucking cunt? One more word and I'm going to slap that smile off your trash face."

But, of course, it was Billie who dished out the violence, as she seemed predestined to always do; Billie who reacted as a person with such a predisposition to violence would in the same situation of challenge and threat, who without thought lashed out and delivered a closed-fisted blow across her friend's cheek. Alex crumpled to the gravel. Their friends cried out and ran toward them.

"Jesus, Billie!" said Sam. "Fucking relax!"

"Oh my God, you guys!" said Darcy, hands clutching her chest as if she'd received the blow herself. "What are you doing?"

From the dirt at Billie's feet Alex looked up at her assailant. A cruel, bloody smile creased her face as she said, "That's perfect, Billie. You piece of white trash."

Billie hauled back and kicked her friend, hard. Her foot caught Alex in the breast, eliciting a sharp cry from her. Sam leapt between them and Darcy fell to crouching beside Alex, coddling her. They both cried shrilly. Sam barred Billie's way, hands raised defiantly against her chest. "Don't, Billie. Unless you want to beat up me and Darcy too." Sam felt fear prickle in her at the possibility of suffering Billie's fury; she'd admitted as much to her with what she'd said, and saw something in Billie's eyes register at the admission. Maybe it was the question: even though she'd be able to beat the shit out of her friends, was that something she really wanted? Something else awakened in Sam in that queer, paused moment: she suddenly knew that she no longer wanted to be the glue binding them all together, as she had been since childhood. Maybe it would be best to let them drift apart the way people always seemed to, childhood friends and families fractured by the countless things in the world that existed to thwart once-reliable bonds.

Billie stared into her eyes for several seconds, lips quivering in fury, fists clenched at her sides. Then she turned without a word, walked out into the centre of the road, and screamed a throat-wrenchingly hoarse cry that sent shivers down the friends's spines. It was an animal cry, something so primal-sounding that they were shocked to learn it could come from inside their friend, even one as tomboy-tough as Billie. This was Billie-Wolf unleashed, the naked animal come out of its burrow deep in the earth, from deep inside itself. They watched Billie-Wolf in its aftermath, shoulders tensed and bunched, fists still clenched, shaking all over like a creature in the throes of some sort of hideous and agonizing transformation; a minute passed, and then she straightened her posture, walked casually back to the car, got in, and eased the door closed.

Overhead, the sun seemed suspended in the same position it had been in for the past several hours, relentlessly burning the landscape and summoning phantoms of heat-mirage to swim languidly in the uncertain distance. The leaves of the trees alongside the road were made brilliant by it, the emerald gulfs beyond glittering with golden lanes of light.

In a small, stunned voice, as if to herself, Darcy said, "There aren't any birds. The trees are quiet. And no more butterflies. There's nothing out here."

"It's the heat, Darce," said Sam half-heartedly, failing in her effort to comfort either of them.

They stood in the huge, lifeless silence, the sun beating down on them ferociously.

The three friends drifted back to the car after a few minutes. They got in, and Sam started the engine. She eased them back up to a steady 100 kilometres an hour, eyeing the gas gage: they were closing in on an empty tank with no gas station in sight, or even within hope.

After several minutes, Alex surprised everyone when she said into the stunned silence of the car:

"Billie."

"What's up, Alex?" Billie said from her passenger-side seat, eyes watching the road.

"I don't think you're a racist, and I don't believe you're white trash."

"I know you don't. Because you're smart enough to know I'm not. I'm an asshole, though. That's what you believe."

"Are you?" Alex said, a little challengingly.

"Oh, yes," Billie said. "That I certainly am." And then Billie surprised them all. "I'm sorry, Alex. I'm sorry for hitting you, and saying the things I said, and for a lot of things."

They digested this, and eventually Alex filled the pregnant silence and said, "I know."

Conversation between the friends stopped then. Sam absently fiddled with the radio but couldn't catch a station no matter how long she surfed the radio band. Trying to play the CD they'd had on earlier didn't work either, resulting in a savage static noise that she shut off quickly. The GPS remained dead. It was as if some atmospheric disturbance was interfering with the car's electrical equipment. Even their cell phones remained unable to register signals. Billie, the only one of them wearing a watch, tapped its plastic face with a finger, unsettled that its hands had stopped moving sometime within the past couple of hours, though she said nothing about it. The only sound was the engine, and the tires over the road, and the whipping wind

122

through the open windows, sounds of illusory movement in a moment that seemed stretched, prolonged, eternal.

A sliver of time passed then during which all four of the friends happened to have their eyes closed simultaneously, though they'd never know it—Billie nodding off with the map spread across her lap and an angry grimace on her face; Alex anxious and upright in her seat but too weary to fight her lethargy; Darcy, mellow in the sunlight, her sleepless night of fictional lovemaking with the fictitiously perfect grocery store boy catching up with her where she lay with her head bumping along on the underside of the window-frame, her book about suicide cults forgotten and tucked beneath her leg; even Sam, hands gripping the hot wheel, closed her eyes for a second, or maybe two or three seconds or a million years, and felt the luxurious relief of a break from the monotony of focusing on driving, the warm embrace of the car enveloping her all over and making her feel deceivingly cozy, coddled, loved—

And then Sam opened her eyes, and the world, and everything in it, was changed.

VI: GOING HOME

The highway beyond the line of naked women was empty as far as they could see, heat-shimmering and lonely. The sun was finally descending in the west, reddening the distant rolling hills of what should have been the Bruce Peninsula, though it felt strange and unfamiliar to the friends. Somehow, a long time had passed between the friends's car being stopped by the appearance of the women and now. They weren't sure how this could be but were certain it was true.

The friends's voices in the great engine-less quiet were immense with fear.

"Oh. My. Fucking. God."

"What the fuck is this, Sam?"

"I don't know, but it's fucking insane."

"Where the Hell did they even come from?"

"Oh God, please let's turn around."

"Maybe, should we... should I talk to them—?"

"Are you fucking crazy, Darcy? Turn us the fuck around, Sam, and—"

"The engine died—"

"Shit, my phone still isn't working—there's no signal—"

"Oh, fuck, guys. Holy fuck!"

They turned and followed Darcy looking the way they'd come: another line of naked women stood there, motionless and silent, hair tangled, with the same dead eyes watching them caught in their dark highway dream.

They each saw the other visions that appeared but said nothing, denying their reality in that moment when their great fear might only have been conjuring mirages that were not and could not stir there: the fires that had burst into life in different places in the fields on either side of the highway, spitting and flickering furiously; a coyote holding a plump brown hare in its jaws in the wild grass beyond the gravel shoulder, the animal struggling briefly and then growing limp, a stream of yellow-red blood and shit pouring from its anus; the sun sending out visible rhythmic pulses as steady as a heartbeat that warped and fractured the light, making it somehow whiter, hotter, muddier, tangled and jumbled and more difficult to see through. The fields on either side of the highway were covered with white lilies, creating an illusion of cold, as if a snowy landscape miraculously stood untouched by the relentless heat. The coyote remained there in the wild grass and snowy flowers, eyeing the spectacle burning in the road as if bewitched; looking unreal wavering in the heat, as if its image were being transmitted from some far distant place.

Alex said, "Maybe we can talk to them, and ask them if they need our help," hearing the weakness of her frail voice and the foolish and cowardly idea it sought to convey even as her friends heard it too. Because who was she to offer help to anyone when she couldn't even help herself? Who was she to offer help to these women beyond helping, who were like some dark reflection of themselves?

Darcy said, "I don't know what to do," and in that moment felt free, for it was the first time she'd ever admitted it to herself: she was adrift in the world and had always been. Nothing could change that: no trip to a forested paradise, for no such paradise existed; no other person advising her with her best or worst interests at heart; no program at a school somewhere far away and no book with harsh lessons about the world because those lessons always taught her the same thing, that for some the world was an uninhabitable place and that she was one of those lost people destined to never fit in.

Billie-Wolf instinctively reached inside her backpack that sat on the floor-space between her feet and pulled out the small revolver. The sun glinting from its steel nose caught Darcy's eye. "Oh my God, Billie, what the Hell is that?"

This is a weapon, dad—do you wanna fuck me now? Do you wanna put it in your dirty little mouth for me?

"It's okay, Darcy," Billie said distantly, seeing her friend's frightened face emerge from among the old phantoms gathered before her eyes as she hefted the barrel level with her chin. Sunlight continued to flash from its steel, mesmerizing Darcy and somehow prolonging the dream-like moment. It had been a gift from her mother, remarkably enough, given to her on her sixteenth birthday, as if she'd been acknowledging without words the necessity of her daughter keeping vigil against the unnameable evil in their shared world. Billie had both been grateful and hated her for it, and for her mother's sickening mixture of courage and the cowardice that diluted it. She hadn't gone anywhere without the gun tucked inside her bag since that bittersweet sixteenth.

"Don't worry," Billie said to her ashen-faced friend. And then she reached into the backseat and squeezed Darcy's hand warmly and said, "Darcy, you're the most amazing artist I've ever known. I've been meaning to tell you that for a long time."

Billie's three friends were all watching her with terrified and hopeful eyes. She knew they wanted her to lead them, to be the one with the plan. But she had no plan. She'd never had a plan in her entire life and had never led anyone. She saw them then the way she often remembered them: her secretly damned family enfolded in the deep green embrace of the forest of her childhood, accepted among the benevolent pixy tribe who ruled that secret kingdom, though her parents deserved none of that splendour. Somehow, their evil had deceived even the enchanted fairy peoples of her memory; and then, of course, they'd gone and died on her, so that they could never try to atone for any of the evil they'd put into her life.

"Oh fuck, holy shit guys!"

They followed Sam's wide-eyed stare.

The line of pale women in the road ahead was advancing. They looked behind them and the women there were likewise walking forward—soon they would merge and hold the car between them. The sense of being surrounded filled the friends with a quickly mounting panic. Sam turned the ignition frantically but the engine remained dead.

Desperately, the friends looked to each other.

Sam's voice was high and wavering with hysteria: "Oh god, oh fuck, they're coming closer, look, look, look, do you see, do you see?"

They saw, and couldn't look away from the vision: the women drifting inexorably closer, the heat waves shimmering from the highway tarmac making their feet appear as if they were several inches above the road. They saw their vacant eyes like deep holes, lost-looking and desperately in need of something they could never have.

Sam felt something begin its change in her. Ebbing away was her fear, replaced each second passing with emotions she didn't initially trust to be there at all: eagerness; ecstasy; a sheer and unbridled relief.

Darcy remembered her date, in two days's time, with the supermarket boy. But her heart suddenly acknowledged what she'd known to be the pointlessness of that and other misguided meetings. Why? Why bother? Who cared? She felt tired. Weary of people and their complicated ways. She needed to sleep. She needed to sleep and wake up in a better place, or at least a different place than the places she'd known.

Billie dropped the revolver into the floor space at her feet. She was no warrior, only the daughter of warriors, savage and grim and cold as winter. That was the real joke on her: she wasn't like that at all. She wanted to be held, in a green place by good people. She wanted to shed the disguise of sturdy tomboy and be a little girl again, but even as she wished this wish she knew it could never be.

Seeing this, her friends felt a collective relief come over them: Billie had made a decision of some kind, and an important one. They were closer to something now, the next step in this dazzling, impossible moment; the next chapter in their story.

Alex, numb all through her body and feeling adrift on a cushion of sweltering air, thought: *We're home.* The old gang was

126

together again, older and more mature, women grown from the flowers of the ungainly girls they'd been, but really the same now as always. The world was still the same vicious and savage animal as it had always been, as it would always remain. Nothing was changed—they were the same people after all, the same tribe today as they'd been since as far back as they could remember— though they themselves were ready to move on from all that they'd known. And all the anxiety she'd felt suffocating her from the moment they'd set out on their trip together—the chokehold of her responsibilities to work and to build a family and to win her parents's approval—it all evaporated like a mirage of ghosts drifting upwards from the sun-blasted road and into the burning aether.

Turning to her friends, Sam was relieved to see it all around her, reflected in their faces, their ecstatic eyes like unexpected windows to a far different place than those places they'd come from. These were the friends she knew, had known her whole life, had grown up with and lived through joy and heartbreak with. This was the old gang. This was the close circle. And now, finally, after all the long years of their friendship, she felt ready and able to relinquish her role as their namesake leader; she no longer needed to be the glue binding them all together, because their fate had been decreed and they would be joined forever, like the best of families remained, the strongest of tribes. They were home. They had each other, and they were home. And she'd led them here—if nothing else, she'd proven herself a good leader, and after countless wrong choices and mistakes had led them here to this moment on this day.

She heard her own voice like a revelation floating up from the depths of a dark dream she was finally waking from, and finally leaving behind her:

"What else were we going to find out here?"

The procession of phantasmagorical women, now merged into a tight circle surrounding them, continued to edge closer to the car at its centre. The women's lost eyes beckoned them. Without further word, the four friends opened their doors and went to meet them.

ON TOUR WITH THE DEATHRAY BRADBURYS

The following message was written on the back of a Deathray Bradburys ticket stub I found on the grassy hill that overlooks Little River Pavilion in Windsor, Ontario, the day following the band's performance on the night of August 25, 1999:

Tammy,

I believe too. Here's to us,
leaving the Evil behind.

Love, Dana

The two girls—17-year-old Tammy Chalmers and 16-year-old Dana Holloway—were among the eighteen people who went missing in the wake of the concert they had all attended. Romantic local folklore claims that on certain clear nights we might be able to find them all, dancing in the constellations. I can believe it. Because sometimes salvation—even the most miraculous—is for real. (Was it chance that the concert of a so-called UFO suicide cult took place in the shadow of the hill that locals have been calling "Suicide Hill" for reasons lost to time?)

To the above inscription adorning this gift from one friend or lover to another, all this author can add is a heartfelt...

Long may they live, the mighty Deathray Bradburys!

———————————————————————

"Good evening!"

The silver-masked singer stood before the microphone, his gloved hands raised ceilingward in a grand gesture of salutation. "And welcome thee to this night when the skies and Heaven above shall open wide and bleed down and down and down their light and love unto this soil, and into the red, red, red, red world below! And in this middle-country, oh, in this right-here right-now lieth you and us! And you are beautiful, and we are the Deathray Bradburys, and this world—oh, this sad, lonely, wicked, vengeful world—oh, she is no match for us! For tonight we are gathered here to offer you celestial salvation from your woes! The Twins are burning and the Twins are calling! Paradise awaits! Join us, brothers and sisters—*this is our night!*"

The sparse crowd milling in front of the band in the gloomy, cigarette and pot smoke-congested basement bar roared their approval. Most wept openly, while the handful of regular patrons merely chugged their beers, treating the spectacle as they would any other band playing the tiny, decrepit venue.

Feedback erupted from the battered amplifiers. The similarly silver-skinned bass player, his wings spread like an immense metallic curtain behind him, shouted a count-in into his own microphone: "One-two-three-four!"

And the Deathray Bradburys brought their rock and roll salvation to their disciples one final time.

THE DEATHRAY BRADBURYS: A BRIEF HISTORY, AN ETERNAL MYSTERY

555:

The binary star Sirius, also known as the "dog star" or "Big Dog" because of its place in the constellation Canis Major, is the brightest star in the sky and has therefore long been revered by peoples throughout the world. Its very name comes from the Greek word *seirius*, meaning "scorching" or "searing," its brilliance and prominence in the sky earning it a long-standing place in occult symbolism and the mythologies of some of the world's most pre-eminent empires. The ancient Egyptians's entire mythology and religious system, for example, revolved around Sirius, owing largely to the fact that their ancient astronomers observed that the Nile flooded whenever the sun was aligned with the star, providing fertility to the land. Known as the Nile Star, Sirius was said to be the birthplace of their most prominent deities, including Osiris, Isis, Seth, and Horus, and its rising formed the basis of the Egyptian calendar.

The mystery of humankind's connection to Sirius deepened in the twentieth century. In 1931, French explorers and anthropologists Marcel Griaule and Germaine Dieterlen first made contact with the Dogon, a small, reclusive tribe living in Mali, West Africa. The anthropologists discovered that the Dogon's folklore included a rich and elaborate mythology revolving around the star Sirius. This mythology was based on information said to have been passed down through generations as far back as 3200 B.C. and included an extensive and inexplicable knowledge of the science underlying the star. With advances in European and Western astronomy came proof that much of the Dogon people's knowledge relating to Sirius was accurate, a seemingly miraculous fact considering their Stone Age society's complete lack of scientific discipline.

How, without scientific equipment of any kind, could the Dogon have known that a smaller star, now recognized as Sirius B and invisible to the naked eye, orbits Sirius, that its orbital cycle is exactly 50 years long, and that it rotates on its own axis? It was only in the 1950s, after all, that a telescope was developed that was powerful enough to see Sirius B, and it wasn't until 1970 that it was first photographed. Further, the Dogon showed knowledge of Sirius B's immense density and classification as a white dwarf star—this primitive people named the star Po Tolo ("Tolo" in the Dogon language means "star" while "Po" is the smallest seed known to their society) and referred to it as the "heaviest star," describing it as being white in colour.

The Dogon also claimed knowledge of a third star orbiting behind Sirius B—they called it Emme Ya, and its existence was conclusively proven as recently as 1995, when French scientists Daniel Benest and J. L. Duvent detected motions in the Sirius system that they attributed to a possible third star. It is now commonly referred to as Sirius C and remains a point of intense interest for astronomers.

The Dogon said their knowledge of astronomy was long ago passed to them by the Nommos, an extraterrestrial race of intelligent amphibious beings sent as emissaries from Sirius. Descriptions of the Nommos can be equated to mermen and mermaids of ancient legend, and can also be found in Sumerian, Babylonian, and Accadian myths. Most accounts of the tale describe these beings as having arrived in an ark-like craft amid great thunder and fire. Their purpose, according to the Dogon, was to act as spiritual saviours for the human race, bestowing their metaphysical and astronomical knowledge to those who would listen. For this reason, the Nommos were also called the "Teachers" and the "Monitors." The Dogon claimed that the Nommos would someday return to Earth, taking control of its waters and ruling the world, in this way making the world "clean again." It was also said that the Nommos make periodic visits to the Earth, and reward followers for their devotion by bringing them back to Sirius, which the Dogon believe to be a heavenly realm or paradise.

Over the years, it has become accepted that the Dogon could not have acquired their vast scientific knowledge of Sirius without contact with a technologically advanced civilization— whether this scientific knowledge was terrestrial or extraterrestrial in origin has never been conclusively determined, although there is a great deal of evidence in support of the latter. The tribe's inexplicable and astonishingly advanced scientific knowledge is given incontrovertible proof in the form of a 400-year-old Dogon artefact which bears a clear depiction of the Sirius configuration, as well as the Dogon's ceremonial celebration of Sirius A and B's cycle, a ritual dating back to the 13th century.

Sirius continues to enthral people the modern world over, as it has since before times of written record. This long and rich history has infused the unprecedented events revolving around the Deathray Bradburys and their alleged spiritual connection to the binary star with an added scope and an ever-deepening mystery.

132

666:

The enigma of the Deathray Bradburys has endured over a decade and could be compared to sifting through the ruins of a once thriving civilization that inexplicably vanished without a trace, leaving a proverbial ghost town for bewildered fans and researchers to examine and re-examine and speculate over in its wake.

Very little is known about the Deathray Bradburys. The seminal band's career was short-lived: the five-piece formed sometime between 1995 and 1997 and concluded their recording and touring existence in late summer 2000. Although their place of origin isn't known for certain, it's speculated to be somewhere in the greater Windsor-Essex County area of South Western Ontario, due to the fact of their playing an exorbitantly large number of performances within this geographic region (though the band did tour throughout other parts of the country in their later days, as well as into the United States). The most prominent cities frequented by the band included Windsor, Chatham, London, Hamilton, Kingston, and Toronto, and smaller towns in the vicinity of Windsor, such as Belle River, Comber, Woodslee, Harrow, Leamington, and Kingsville, among others.

Stylistically, they played a raw and minimalist form of garage rock, with a heavy nod to the frenetically-paced, three-chord punk rock of the late 1970s and a melodic sensibility reminiscent of 1950s bubblegum pop and doowop. They precociously merged this with an overtly psychedelic guitar and keyboard influence— along with typically reverb-drenched vocals—which embellished the band with a distinctly spacey quality in keeping with their overall cosmic aesthetic.

They were famed for their unabashed embracing of B-movie inspired imagery. Each band member wore retro/pseudo-futuristic silver costumes and masks (complete with antennae, goggles and, occasionally, wings!) so that no one ever learned their identities. Interestingly enough, the band members never disclosed their names, either real or stage names, preferring the mystery that came with total anonymity. They likewise refused to do interviews, although admittedly any noteworthy print publications that would have been interested in giving the then little-known band coverage were few and far between; the only forums known to have written about the band were fanzine-type publications with very limited circulation, most likely passing from person to person at live performances, through small independent record shops, or via other underground channels.

Yet the Deathray Bradburys would become most famous in underground circles—and ultimately to the rest of the world—for their lyrical fixation, an obsessive focus revolving around themes of escape from a decadent, increasingly violent and racist world to a paradisiacal place of salvation. This haven, at first glance a seemingly fictitious creation, was repeatedly reinforced as an authentic place by the group's proselytizing on-stage banter and the recurring mini-essays and poetry-like texts found as liner notes in their recordings, describing the tenets of this belief, as well as a timeline establishing a set date for a planned exodus from Earth to this paradise.

Going to a Deathray Bradburys concert was much like attending an evangelical sermon, complete with a self-proclaimed prophet—in this case the band's lead singer/frontman, delivering impassioned between-song orations imploring the band's followers to embrace the higher power of which they sang—and throngs of spellbound followers in rapture of the spectacle unfolding before them.

The basic story proposed by the Deathray Bradburys in their cryptic lyrics described a future mass exodus that they themselves were destined to lead. (Exactly how the band came about this knowledge was hinted at but never fully disclosed.) Those chosen to accompany them were individuals with a deep emotional and spiritual need to escape their own personal woes, and more generally the misery inherent in life on Earth. As the tale went, those who followed the band and believed in their promise of salvation would likewise be saved alongside their musical heroes, ultimately to be transported—some believed spiritually while others believed physically—into this heavenly paradise among the stars: the "light" of the Sirius binary star system. The group's lyrics speak of Sirius in fanatically reverential terms and show a foundation based in the historical and mythological roots relating to the star.

The exodus was scheduled to take place, for reasons once again apparently known only to the band itself, on the final night of August in the year 2000. Debate continues concerning the means by which this "ascension" was intended to occur—many analyses of the group's lyrics and literature speculate that mass suicide represented the medium through which the salvation promised by the group was going to take place, as evidenced by recurring references to the drinking of "potions" of ambiguous "energy." Suicide is indeed a recurring theme throughout the band's body of work, specifically repeated allusions to the "freedom" it provided from unrelenting misery and sadness.

The song "Robert the Mighty," for example, seems to be an ode to pulp writer Robert E. Howard, elevating his life and subsequent suicide to divine proportions in accordance with the Deathray Bradburys's belief in the transcendence afforded those who take themselves from the mortal world.

In "County Road 26 to Infinity," tribute is paid to "the angels Boreal and Wood," a worshipful reference to both cult leader Michael Boreal, the founder of the Sirius Group who led his disciples in a mass suicide on the island of Magahatti, as well as James William Wood, infamous for his abduction of the fifteen women who would come to be known as the Essex Fifteen, each a victim of forced or assisted suicide (debate still rages as to which) and promised ascension to a heavenly realm: Sirius.

Members of the so-called Essex Fifteen are likewise mentioned throughout the DB canon, such as in the songs "Peace-Star for the Lost Sixteen" and "Maria 16"—a reference to the youngest victim of the Essex Fifteen, Maria Reed, the numeral appended to the name in the latter echoing the title of the former and signifying the band's sympathetic belief that Wood himself should be included in the group of suicide victims, bringing their number to sixteen victims rather than solely the fifteen women.

Topically, the band wove an eclectic number of subjects within the greater tapestry of the recurring and unifying themes of suicide and escape from a violent world. References to lilies recur throughout the band's lyrics, providing a link to the inexplicable phenomenon of this flower species growing in abundance at the site of the Essex Fifteen group suicide in Essex County, Ontario. The flower became symbolic of the band, and fans attending their concerts would reputedly wear them in their hair or throw them onto the stage during performances.

Constant comparisons are made in the band's lyrics between the decadence of modern living and the purity of times long past, the beauty and splendour of bucolic environments versus the perils of the modern city, and our modern-day insistence on

135

(often dangerous) technological advances. A similar theme is explored as well: the contrast between the innocence and wonder of childhood and its inevitable loss in adulthood. These ideas draw a neat line to the band's namesake, famed author Ray Bradbury, whose work delves into these very themes.

Interestingly, given the Deathray Bradburys's quasi-cult/religious stance, their lyrics make no effort to deny the existence of God or Satan but rather suggest that their own prophetic visions offer their disciples an alternative to both. Biblical references throughout their literature to the Devil, angels, and giant figures reminiscent of the Nephilim (the Biblical giants said to be a product of the union between the sons of God and the daughters of men) suggest an acceptance of the tenets posited by a variety of organized religions, while simultaneously giving equal credence to subjects rooted firmly in scientific foundations. These include the scientific experiments and aspirations of trailblazing inventor and physicist Nikola Tesla; the age of the dinosaurs, an epoch spoken of in romantic terms for its absence of humankind, often described as a violent and ruining force; interstellar phenomena such as stars, wormholes, and space travel; and more arcane sciences, such as ancient numerology, alchemy, and occult mysticism.

Mythological subject matter recurs in the group's lyrics as well, ranging from allusions to the Greek myth of Icarus to ancient African lore, with the story of Tombanik, an active volcano long said in the folklore of the region to be inhabited by a god fallen from the sky. Interestingly, these myths involve themes of flight and celestial phenomena, both seen elsewhere in the band's writing. References to the sea and ocean abound in their lyrics, also—the Greek sea-god Proteus appears in several songs, as well as direct references to the amphibious, sea-dwelling Nommos and their promise to reclaim and purify the Earth's oceans.

Aesthetically speaking, the Deathray Bradburys evoked a unique combination of imagery in their lyrics, ranging from the cosmic to the pastoral representing the positive side of the spectrum, and the modern world/society—specifically the city—as its antithesis. This, and the need (and means) to escape from a world rife with emotional suffering and anguish, marked the foundation of the band's message.

Fantastic as the premise of the group's promised ascension sounds, its appeal to a subset of the underground music community was profound: fans of the Deathray Bradburys treated the band as some religious devotees treat their faith, with absolute conviction and fanaticism. This lyrical subject matter— as well as the prayerful, angry, and outraged manner with which it was often expressed—found particular appeal among disaffected youth, as it offered a sympathetic voice while speaking very clearly to an end of suffering and a promise of rescue from an oppressed existence. For this reason, the band began drawing increasingly loyal crowds to their concerts at small bars and all-ages community centres even before the release of their debut album, sowing the seeds of their future legacy. Rather judiciously, the band omitted certain details of their invented story, lending it a deliciously cryptic and enticing air that allowed for fans to fill in gaps as they liked.

Knowledge of the Deathray Bradburys's seeming sincerity about the proclamations they made grew through word-of-mouth, defining the band's agenda and setting them apart from their peers, as well as any rock and roll groups that came before them or have come since. The group's entire catalogue—comprised of a single full-length album entitled *There is a Place* (self-released on Saucer Records in July 1998, reissued as a tenth anniversary special edition in 2008 by Ryko Records), as well as several obscure 7" singles releases and countless bootleg recordings—presents this agenda very clearly. Sometimes the lyrics come at the listener with a gleeful simplicity and vulgarity appropriate to the band's punk roots, but more often with a breathtaking poeticism worthy of their literary inspirations and the grand and grave subject matter of which they sang so obsessively. The Deathray Bradburys's eclectic style ran the gamut from anthemic rally calls giving directives to their followers and praising their collective spiritual beliefs, to impassioned tributes to their literary and scientific influences, to poignant philosophical dissertations on the nature of living in and seeking haven from a difficult and uncompromising world.

Some have argued that their obsessive focus and seductive rhetoric made the band as much a cult based on charismatic manipulation of its adherents as they were a group of musicians. Whatever their agenda, the band's musical prowess can't be discounted. With a variety of tightly crafted, deceptively simple

137

anthems drawing influences from a variety of genres, they represented an anomaly in the music world: a garage band of immense talent and originality whose chief objective was not only light years removed from the lofty goals of fame and fortune that so many other bands aspire to attain but the purported fulfilment of spiritual ideals they pursued to the utter neglect of a burgeoning career.

In the process, they provided a source of spiritual hope for their small but madly devoted fan base.

777:

It remains unknown what became of the members of the underground band the Deathray Bradburys following their final performance at the Coach and Horses in Windsor, Ontario on Thursday, August 31st, 2000.

For all intents and purposes, the band—along with a reported thirty local missing persons linked to the event, and one hundred ninety-five people from throughout other areas of the province— quite literally fell off the face of the Earth, coinciding with the date set for their preordained, fictitious(?) exodus. An extensive, province-wide search was undertaken throughout the months following, yielding no clues whatsoever as to the whereabouts of those missing. The case, a decade on, remains unresolved while debate continues as to whether this represents one of the most elaborately staged mass-scale hoaxes in history... or something else entirely. As a result of these unexplained circumstances, the band's ever-growing cult status remains assured, as well as the legacy of mystery and romance—and grandly evocative music— they've left behind. It goes without saying that the group's body of lyrics continues to be scrutinized.

In positing theories as to the whereabouts of the Deathray Bradburys and their missing followers, perhaps it's best—if exceedingly romantic—to conclude with the enigmatic yet seemingly prophetic words of the band itself:

There is a place
Far beyond all of this despair
We promise you, friends:
There is a place for us all.

—from the song "First Colony"

First published in Underground Tracks
Volume 1, Issue 252, November 2010.
Author: A.B. Sossi

"*I* know," said the man to himself, closing the music magazine across his knee where he sat on the wooden bench overlooking the Detroit River.

He did know. The truth, more startling than any fabrication he could concoct.

He'd had a girlfriend in those days, when he'd been young and reckless and living a life he wished he could have back. She'd followed the band with a religious zealot's devotion and had gotten him into their music, too. He loved punk rock, loved B-movies, loved the fusion of the two to create the most purely fun music he'd ever heard. But she'd believed in the Deathray Bradburys in a way he'd thought went too far beyond their cool, B-movie aesthetic. She'd believed all their goofy, tongue-in-cheek rhetoric purporting to offer salvation to their followers and escape from their troubled lives if that was what they needed. She'd even gone so far as to have their symbol tattooed into her left breast: the oddly ancient-but-futuristic silver hexagon filled with a pair of darker rings. She'd never been one to fawn over her artistic heroes, either, so seeing her uncompromising devotion to the band was more than a little unsettling at times.

He recalled their argument that distant night, post-show, she begging him to accompany her onto the small tour bus, a converted school bus, along with a dozen other fans and the band members themselves. They'd argued outside of the venue for nearly thirty minutes while the band loaded their gear into the bus and the handful of their fans boarded along with them.

"Please, Matt. *Please?* Will you just come? Just trust me, okay? This is for real! All of this is seriously *for real!*"

139

Of course, jealous as he was of the band who'd succeeded in turning his girlfriend into an automaton groupie slave, he'd dismissed her, telling her indignantly to do whatever she wanted, but that she'd be doing it without him. He'd glanced back once as he went on his way, seeing the bus lurching from the alley behind the bar and onto the street, heading east. This was the last he'd seen of it, and his girlfriend, heading into the drowsy A.M. and a lunatic's promise of much, much more. Even then, though, before the great disappearance became realized—during the final days that the Deathray Bradburys were still considered by many merely a fun good-times band with a healthy dose of theatricality mixed into their repertoire—even then he'd felt a pang of guilt, remembering the secret darkness that his girlfriend hid from the world at large, the secrets of her home life which he alone was privileged to have been told. Even then, in the throes of his disbelief, he understood her own need to believe.

"The joke was on me," he muttered, staring at the stars reflected waveringly in the scummy river. "Fuck." There was no escaping their light, so he cast his eyes resignedly skyward, dismayed at the completely cloudless view in all directions: stars everywhere, a billion remote points of light everywhere his eyes roved. It was a view he sought to spare himself as often as he was able. He murmured, "I miss you, Katie. I miss you, baby. I'm sorry I didn't hear good enough."

He was crying then, for himself, the unfulfilling, lonely day behind him, and for his great blunder over ten years before. But eventually a smile worked its way through his regret and melancholy, as it always did when he reminisced about those long-lost times: a smile for Katie, who was at peace, somewhere.

JOURNEY TO THE END OF A BURNING GIRL

The tale of a pair of detectives trying to solve the mystery of a deadly, otherworldly drug that legend says holds the power to open the gates to Paradise (the downside being that it also seemingly kills its users in extremely horrific fashion). It's also the tale of one man and the ghost of a girl that won't leave him alone. But the real heart of the story is a vision of a world of the not-too-distant future that is so irrevocably without hope that it's left its people with one final dream for salvation: suicide.

This story wouldn't leave me alone, either—the seed of it appeared in my mind years before I began working on it. I let it grow, and it flowered into this strange novelette, part dark science fiction, part near-future noir, part surreal apocalyptic story, part psychedelic fairy tale, part bizarre horror.

It's also grown into a full-length novel, which I completed work on not long before sitting down to write these introductory words to the stories of this volume. You plant a seed, and you never know what might blossom...

And yeah, I saw the news today, too. And yeah, I know things may be looking dire and hopeless, but please, let's all hold on just a little while longer:

Clark and Kessel are on the case, and they're the best in the Goddamn business.

"I am fire... I am death."

—Smaug the Dragon
from *The Hobbit* by J.R.R. Tolkien

I: THE WEEPING CITY

A fire the size of a mountain consumed the screaming population of the dream, as it swallowed them in every dream he dreamed.

They perished in an unholy agony, and the ashes left behind were the great cloud hanging over his waking life, too.

"I'm looking for someone," Philip said through his muffling rain-suit, striving to be heard over the din of the storm.

"Who you lookin' for?"

The eyes watching him through the narrow slit in the metal door were uncompromising, unsympathetic, as if they were much accustomed to refusing the pleas of others.

"I'm looking for Vern."

There was a pause. The eyes remained unperturbed, perhaps only growing harder. Rain sleeted down, slapping hard on the alley's floor. Thunder cracked across the dome of the iron sky. "I can't help you."

The slit in the metal door slid shut with an angry hiss.

He stood there in the buffeting rain, frantic, uncertain of what to do. He knocked on the door. His fists fell with a disheartening flatness. He pounded harder on the metal. "Hello? Hello! Please, I need to talk to someone. *Please.*"

He waited and waited, but no answer came from behind the dark door. He stood before it a while longer, shaking in the cold, feeling his despair mounting. He was tired. He was so very tired but knew he wouldn't sleep that night, if ever again.

142

Helpless to do anything more, he turned and slipped through the alley toward the labyrinth of the city streets beyond.

The 6th Precinct buzzed with an unusual amount of Monday chatter. Anxiety hung in the air like an electrical charge, fuelling a persistent preoccupation with the televised and online news, at whose centre lay their police force and its recent struggles. The ongoing investigation into the most inexplicable and difficult case in recent memory plagued the detectives and police officers, with seemingly no end in sight, so that the usual routine of processing collared prostitutes, small-time dealers and other, more dangerous offenders carried on while the gossip bug ran like contagion through the precinct.

Detective Kessel rubbed at her bloodshot eyes and turned away from the photographs of victims spread across her desk. She'd been examining them obsessively for hours, as though staring at them might wring some clue or truth from the case that had been mystifying her and her partner for the past five years. She clicked off her com-screen, which had been displaying a gallery of those self-same photos like some horrific reflection of the physical evidence at hand. She preferred hard copies, whose tangibility—whose realness—she felt closer to.

She guzzled the remaining black coffee in her mug and stretched. She would pour herself another cup—her fourth that morning—and attack the evidence with clearer eyes. She stood and refilled her mug from the bare-bones coffee and donut station at the rear of the squad room. On her way back to her desk, she took a moment to feed the House's scat-sucker, something she only ever did out of sympathy because nobody else bothered.

She loathed the sight of the things. Every House had one on hand for interrogations deemed red level-significant, their necessity meaning they were kept readily accessible at all times so that they became fixtures of squad room décor, like fish in an aquarium, but hideous suspended in their cylindrical glass containers like immense amniotic fluid-filled test tubes.

"Here's your disgusting breakfast, Gabrielle," Kessel said, reaching a hand to the small circular opening on the top of the container and feeding a couple handfuls of powdered nutri-meal through the grill. The flakes stunk like shit and, nose wrinkled,

143

she watched them pepper the surface of the water. The scat-sucker immediately swivelled its eyeless, corpulent pink- and grey-speckled body and sent a half dozen of its pudgy tendrils to slither among the food debris. Seeing the thing spasming in pleasure, and especially hearing the grotesque sucking sounds it made, caused Kessel to grimace and quickly return to her desk. She muttered, "I deserve a raise for being the only one around here brave enough to feed the damn thing."

Her partner, Clark, watched her from across his cluttered desk adjacent to her own. He said nothing, just sat chewing pensively on a pen. The pouches under his eyes told of his own battle with insomnia since they'd been assigned the case. He closed his eyes, leaning forward with his elbows on the desk and his chin in his hands, but Kessel knew he wouldn't be dozing.

The tinny voice of the radio, plagued with white noise from the bad weather and the weird electrical language of the Cloud, had ended its song block and had begun playing its thousandth re-airing of the daily news. Kessel tuned in.

"—but the drug has been on the Canadian underground market for a little over five years, and already its reputation has grown to mythical proportions among the general public. Its reported properties are unheard of in other psychotropic drugs, sounding like the pseudo-scientific lore of pulp fiction stories. But the startling evidence in each of the known cases can't be denied, and it's been puzzling researchers since its first appearance.

"Its name is VERNTELLUS, stylized in most fringe literature and newspaper sources in all upper-case characters. The origin of its name is also unknown, although it's believed that it may be a hybrid of the Norwegian word, *vern*, or 'protection,' and the Latin word, *tellus*, or 'earth.' The recent—"

Clark let out a long, slow breath, drawing Kessel's attention. She broke in over the report. "Clark. You want me to shut it off?" She'd grabbed the remote from her desk and was aiming it toward the radio across the room.

Clark, eyes still closed, unmoving from his position, said, "Maybe we need to hear it again."

Kessel didn't know how serious he was. She frowned, worrying about her partner. He was taking the case personally, and letting it follow him off-duty. But then they all were. Andersen and Bester, and the Loot, too—and seeing one's

144

lieutenant overwhelmed by a case meant things had gotten real bad. And this on top of the usual insanity of living under the Cloud. She replaced the remote on her desk, wishing she knew what to say to make things better. Wishing she could finally get some insight into the mystery.

"—drug's inherent danger lies in the promise it offers that no other drug available on the underground market can: escape in the truest sense of the word, mental and emotional and, some claim, *physical*. It's said to be ingested in pill or capsule form, but its ingredients and origin remain unknown. Evidence—"

Kessel looked from the radio speaker to Clark, but he hadn't budged. She knew he felt it like she did: helplessness. Because, quite literally, all leads pursued by the detectives over the months had led nowhere, and everyone knew it.

Clark's relic Old World desk phone rang. Eyes still closed, he took it from its cradle, listened intently to the receiver pressed to his cauliflowered ear. He hung up. The radio's voice was immense in the squad room.

"—even more distressing is the remarkable fact that the drug seems to be completely untraceable, because it's never been physically confiscated. The party or parties responsible for the distribution of the drug remain unknown, a shadowy bogey-man continually eluding the best efforts of the police to—"

Clark opened his eyes and leaned back in his desk chair, his huge body making the chair's frame squeal. He removed his sear gun from the holster on his hip and aimed it at the radio speaker. Kessel raised an eyebrow. She snagged the remote from her desk and quickly clicked the radio off in mid-sentence.

"Just in the nick of time," she said. "One less casualty in this whole mess." And that was just local news, she thought, thankful they'd missed the world news broadcast that preceded the local program, with all of its inevitable coverage of the escalating conflicts in the New Vietnam War and in the Middle East crisis, and of course the ongoing terrorist strikes plaguing the other side of the border.

Clark turned to her, lowering his gun. His expression was equal parts grave and sardonic. "Kessel. We got another one." He shook his head and holstered his weapon. She felt the same despair in her heart that she saw in the gesture.

"Let's go," she said as stoically as she was able, grabbing her coat and rain-suit from the back of her chair and crossing the

145

room toward the door. Clark followed, swinging from his chair with an ease that always impressed her, given his immense size. They donned the protective suits, waiting for the scoop-tube to arrive.

A moment later they were standing inside the rubber-walled tube, being zipped down to the street. Kessel said, "This makes an even two dozen reported Vern victims in the city." And, of course, there would be countless numbers who would remain unreported and forever unknown. And this was on top of nearly the same number of victims across the river in Detroit, which was suffering its own epidemic. It was disturbing in the truest sense of the word.

"It's fucked," said Clark as the scoop-tube came to a stop and its door slid open for them. "But then what isn't in this town these days?"

What no one knew—least of all Clark—was the degree to which it disturbed her. She hadn't slept well in months and when she did her dreams were hounded by burning shadows moving inside the matrix of the dream-streets down which she drifted.

Together, they stepped into the rainy street.

The rain turned the reflections of streetlamps and police vehicle headlamps into grotesque, shape-shifting smears on the glistening cement. Overhead, the great Cloud stretched everywhere, its belly pulsing with weird green effulgence. The fact that the heavy precipitation fell from the Cloud made it potentially deadly, necessitating the use of the form-fitting bubble-umbrella rain-suits that had become standard issue for citizens.

Clark and Kessel crossed the small lot and climbed the rain-slick steps of the steel fire escape that led to the roof of the downtown transit terminal. They wove among the network of rusted gantries and lattices, their flashlights reflecting from the steel and brick and casting a wavering aura that penetrated into the hungry, starless darkness beyond the building.

"I hate these Goddamned things," Clark said as his rain-suit scraped the rough brick of the wall hard enough to worry him. He paused to examine its durable plastic fabric and, relieved to see that it hadn't been punctured, continued warily on his way, muttering under his breath.

146

Kessel didn't comment, knowing it would only anger her partner further if she pointed out that his physical size was a major contributing factor to his problem navigating the narrow fire escape—Clark even had to have the House's Science Division guys tailor-make his B-U to fit his huge, muscular frame.

They climbed onto the puddle-plagued rooftop, ducking beneath the crime scene tape cordoning off the area and passing through the milling police officers sweeping the southern side of the building. There they found the tell-tale signs of the drug-death: the scorched shadow of a person impressed into the wet shingles. The imprint curled upwards along the edge of the figure, and a stagnant burnt smell clung on the thick air, despite the wind. A forensics man was meticulously scraping along the periphery of the shadow with his tool in one hand and a plastic baggie in the other.

Clark stood staring at the shape outlined in the shingles, hands on his hips. "This is... insanity. What can do this?"

They stood together, staring at the unfathomable shadow scorched into the rooftop. It was the shape and outline of an adult human body, likely male judging from the build, spread-eagled near the roof's edge.

"It's like Hiroshima. It blasts them—burns them—right into the ground. Jesus fucking Christ. No matter how many times I see it, I just can't believe it."

Kessel said, "It's almost symbolic. Taking the drug here, on top of the transit building."

Clark scoffed, spat into the rain. "Yeah, this poor asshole sure got *transported* to a better place. Goddamn fucking druggies. So desperate they believe every pile of bullshit their dealers feed them."

Kessel said nothing, only stared at the ashen signature burned into the warped, shingled roof.

Beside them, as if in response to some dark-humoured and perfectly orchestrated cue, an immense city shuttle lifted upwards along the south side of the building from the airway below. Its roar of engines and tail-fire gusted a wind across the rooftop, sending bits of litter fluttering in all directions. Its smell of fire and fuel thickened the air.

The detectives watched it rise over the buildings and sit on its cushion of fire a moment before orienting itself northwards and drifting across the thundering sky. The faces of passengers in the

147

lit-up windows gawked impassively downwards at the rooftop commotion. The citizens were accustomed to scenes like this. It was one of the many inter-city shuttles taking passengers and freight across the river and into a variety of American townships beyond. The drug had found its way there, too. Their American counterparts in Detroit had found no concrete evidence of the drug either, though they were reticent in sharing any progress they'd made in their own investigations. It was a rapidly growing embarrassment to the police forces of both cities, and had served to initiate an unspoken-of but growing rivalry—who would crack the case and discover the true properties of the drug.

It saddened Kessel the more she thought about it. She'd grown up with her grandfather's exciting and virtuous tales of man's conquest of the moon. Her own parents, although never avid followers of such news, had lived through the interstellar breakthroughs of establishing the first U.S. colony there and manned expeditions reaching Mars. Any competition between nations then had been, at least so far as she could discern, for the greater fulfillment of mankind's potential exploration and expansion among the stars. Now she was part of nothing more significant than a banal competition to solve a criminal case in what everyone around her believed revolved around a drug inadvertently leading to violent suicide.

And yet its purported properties spoke to the child in her, who'd grown up with these other, more altruistic missions of humanity. So her hope remained—if any of the drug's supposed properties were real, wouldn't that make its discovery and usage the same altruistic goal? Possibly even more important, something the science of today might use to leap forward for the betterment of all?

The wind picked up. Rain continued to lash the city, unleashing the chemical stink seeped into its concrete buildings and garbage-filled alleys, stirring it from the depths of the deadly, polluted river.

Kessel squinted into the sombre sky. "The radio said this rainfall's a record. There hasn't been a storm like this in this area, ever. It's been over a week straight of this. They're saying it's likely a result of the Cloud."

The radio had described the hundreds of rats seen floating in the parks along the riverfront, drowned out of the sewers, as well as a homeless man who'd sought refuge from the cold and rain

148

among the underground network of sewers and drainpipes. The man hadn't owned a B-U, so his long-term exposure to the elements would likely have caused him irreparable harm.

"I saw a drowned dog a couple days ago," she added, recalling its bloated look, as if it were close to bursting open and disgorging its bellyful of sewage water.

"The city needs a good rain. Maybe it'll clean up some of the filth out there, even if the rain's as dangerous as they say." Clark's voice was tired. The dark grey pouches under his eyes had become more pronounced, corroborating the evidence of his sagging posture.

"It would take a million-year rain for that to happen, Clark. But I appreciate the sentiment."

"Maybe someone's trying to cleanse us," he said, his voice deadpan with irony.

"Yes, maybe they are," Kessel said, watching the rain.

"Good luck with that job," Clark said.

A fresh-faced police officer walked up beside them, his eyes eager behind the mask of his B-U suit. "Vern's back again, huh?" he said, his eyes held by the signature burned into the roof.

Clark muttered, "Vern's here to stay, unless we crack this insanity. It's a fuckin' drugocalypse out here." He looked at Kessel, added, "Some smart-ass reporter should use that, make himself famous for being so clever."

He shoved off through the other loitering officers, shaking his head. Kessel looked after him, saw his burly outline a moment against the sheeting rainfall before he descended out of sight along the fire escape.

When she turned back to the shadow-form in the rooftop she wasn't only uncertain of what she saw there, but also of how it made her feel.

The dive bar was dimly lit and sparsely populated. Customers —mostly a handful of loners tucked into shadowy booths or seated at the bar with their heads turned down in studied examination of their drinks in front of them—didn't look his way. Philip sipped his beer at the bar, waiting for the bartender to catch his eye. When the man sidled a little closer to where he sat on his stool to scratch at a small notepad with a pen, Philip cleared his throat.

149

"Excuse me. Uh... Is... Is Vern here?"

The bartender turned away to wipe the countertop with a rag he grabbed from somewhere beneath the bar. His hand, Philip saw, was mechanized, an ancient model, a relic with its tell-tale unnaturally spasmodic movements. Most people would have upgraded years ago—those who didn't in this day and age either couldn't afford the newer models or else weren't allowed to make the upgrade. Maybe the man had served time and was thus prohibited from anything other than the most Old World tech-integration. He wondered vaguely whether the limb was a result of some accident, or the more likely possibility of cancer, the city's most tenacious illness. Maybe it was even a product of the new breed of illness, the super-diseases that had made their appearance not long after the calamity across the river had sent forth the Cloud to engulf both their city and its city of origin, Detroit.

Philip had actually seen one of them, once, and that brief glimpse had changed him: to know that he lived in a world where such nightmares had been made flesh—possibly been *created*, by men like himself—and this thought had validated the need that already consumed him, to exit the city and the greater, darker world of which it was a tiny insignificant mote. He remembered it now, and shuddered: looking out across the parking lot from his sixth-floor balcony one humid summer night, staring beyond its boundary at the monotony of cars and shuttles traveling into and from the Core, when a movement closer to him drew his attention. Looking down and seeing it, directly below his aerie, moving furtively and with great deliberation close to the face of the brick building: a lurching grey shape the size of a large dog, scuttling on its cluster of legs, a small, mushroom-like appendage that may have been its head nearly lost amid the horrid bouquet of limbs like gnarled branches sprouting from its top side.

And then it was gone, disappeared from his sight somewhere below, though its predatory posture and movement had haunted him all that night and many after. He'd retreated indoors, closing and locking the balcony screen door and the heavier glass door, though he doubted either could stop the thing he'd glimpsed hunting in the nocturnal city. He'd gotten as far as picking up the telephone with a mind to reporting the sighting to the police, wondering how he'd explain what he'd seen and how that would sound. This was at a time when such things were only beginning

150

to be reported and existed more in the realms of pseudo-science and conspiracy theory than reality. So, he chose to hang up the phone and suffer the first of several sleepless nights while imagining many-legged things crawling across his ceiling directly over him trembling in his bed.

He shook his head, annoyed at his wandering thoughts. He took a sip of his beer, and then a bigger gulp, before replacing the glass on the bar top. He eyed the bartender again, gathering his resolve.

"Sir? Excuse me?"

The bartender continued wiping, engrossed in his work with his hand's subtly herky-jerky rhythm. His heavily pockmarked face betrayed no emotion. His silver hair, tied back in a long, greasy ponytail, glistened in the dim orange overhead lights. The man closest to Philip at the bar, and within earshot, slipped from his stool and drifted toward the bathroom to the rear of the room.

Philip stole himself, thinking of his great need, and the immeasurable pain he lived with every day and that followed him into dreams. He said, "I need to see Vern. Please."

The bartender looked up. His eyes lingered a second on Philip's haggard face, seeming to absorb the sight of his bloodshot eyes, the dark pouches beneath them. "Nobody by that name hangs around here. Sorry."

"I was told I could find him here," Philip said quickly, excited to have initiated conversation with the reticent man, "and that I might be able to learn where to find the Saint."

The bartender eyed him coldly. "You were informed wrong."

"Please, sir, I—"

"This is a rough area. I got a direct line to the cops here." He pointed to the old-fashioned rotary phone hanging on the wall behind the bar, another relic from a bygone era. "I don't know anyone by that name but you keep askin' and I start dialin'. I'm a retired blue-shirt myself. The only reason I ain't called you in just for askin' for Vernsy is because I don't believe in no justice out there no more, so I don't give that much of a shit either way. But don't push me. Drink your beer, then get out. Or just get out."

Philip turned away, stunned, and looked back into his glass. He lifted it to his lips and guzzled the remainder of his beer, tasting nothing, then eased from his stool and hurried through the murky tavern to its side door that let out into the narrow alley.

In the adjacent street he watched a streetdroid drift past, doing its best to suck up the wet, mulchy detritus lining the gutters. Its dull, graffiti-spattered hull made him depressed. He thought of its programmed, forlorn circuit of the downtown Core, the people it passed, the garbage it ate in the wee hours when pedestrian traffic was lowest, but for the lost city denizens like himself. It drifted out of view behind a building, the laboured wheezing of its engine lingering on the wet air.

Feeling utterly defeated, Philip turned from the street and, pulling up his collar and fastening the seals of his old B-U suit, slipped down the alley, merging once again with the wall of rain lashing down from the pulsing, iron sky.

"Hey, man."

He looked up from the newspaper. A teenage girl, no more than sixteen years old, was smiling nervously down at him from where she stood beside his table. Her dyed platinum hair framed a narrow face. She wore a small skirt, navy stockings, army boots, and a worn leather jacket opened to reveal a Deathray Bradburys t-shirt and a very small pair of breasts. The B-U suit she clutched crumpled in her hands was dripping—evidently she'd been out in the rain for some time. A stale smell, of wet soiled clothes, drifted from her, though her clothes were dry.

"Yes?" Philip said.

"I was wondering—and feel free to tell me to get lost—if I could sit with you, and maybe have your leftover fries?"

She was looking now at his plate, which he'd pushed to the edge of the table for the waitress to pick up. There was a handful of French fries soggy with ketchup and a small corner of halibut he'd been too full of beer to finish.

"Sure," he said. "Of course. Help yourself."

The girl popped herself into the booth across from him. "Thanks." She began plucking fries from the plate, eating them quickly. He felt awkward, not sure whether to continue reading the newspaper in front of him or talk to the girl. She made the choice for him.

"So, what's your deal?" she said. "I've seen you around a few times. Here at the diner, and walking around downtown. You seem like a loner." She watched him with a candid expression,

152

then added quickly, "That's cool, though. I'm one too. A loner. As you might be able to tell."

Philip nodded. "Yes, I am, actually. Always have been. I, uh, guess I prefer it that way. How about yourself?"

"Yeah, same here," the girl said. She'd finished the fries and was eyeing his half-full glass of cola. He pushed it across the table toward her and she thanked him with a pretty smile.

Watching her down the remaining pop, he said, "What's your story?"

"You first," she said, returning the glass to the table. "You didn't actually tell me."

Philip said, "There's not... There's not much to say. Not much you'd want to hear, at least. Trust me on that."

Maybe it was what he'd said or the way he'd said it, but the girl only nodded, accepting this as fact and persisting no more. "Well, me, I'm what they call a teenage runaway. Yup. It's true. You're looking at the real deal. A genuine couch-surfing runaway and high school dropout trying to stay away from her fucked-up home—well, ex-home, I guess—and survive until something... better comes along? Something like that? That's the abbreviated story."

"What... do you do for money?" He steeled himself, hoping he wasn't about to meet his first-ever child prostitute. The city was filled with them, human and half-mech both. One could see them every night strutting the downtown's west-side corners and side streets. The squalid residential areas tucked into the downtown Core's bosom like cancerous pods were the worst for it. He tensed, feeling the awakening murmur inside of him, the voice of that great furious cleanser of the sullied whom he was trying so desperately to put to sleep forever. *Vernsy, where are you?*

"I steal when I have to. Pick pockets, pick purses. I broke into some car and shuttle meters before. Usually I freeboot."

Philip's relief showed as he unclenched his fingers from where they rested on the tabletop. He saw that she noticed and was watching his hands with a raised eyebrow.

He said, as nonchalantly as he could manage, "I'm not familiar with the term. Freeboot?" It put him in mind of the pulp stories that he'd read as a boy, featuring the mercenaries of ancient days or of fictionalized future times, making hazardous livings thieving and fighting in the service of rebel armies.

153

Picturing the skinny girl in this role was amusing but somehow not altogether incomprehensible.

She said, "I jack into computers, steal files, run codes for people who aren't supposed to have that kind of access. Stuff like that."

"Where did you learn that skill?"

The girl shrugged dismissively. "My parents are tech designers. Software, hardware. I grew up around that stuff."

Philip said, "So your parents have done really well for themselves." He was taken aback—his notion of runaways had always led him to believe they more often than not came from an economically destitute background.

She caught his meaning. "Money's not everything, as they say." She scratched a congealed ball of ketchup from the tabletop with a dirty fingernail.

Philip, watching her closely, said, "You're a smart girl."

The girl said, "Yeah, I am. My name's Donna, by the way."

"Philip."

"Cool. Well, thanks for the fries, man. I'll let you get back to your paper if you want."

"No," he said. "I'm done with it. I was just about to leave anyways."

"I'll walk with you?" she said.

Philip shrugged, nodded. As he was slipping his coat on the words came out. "What are you running from?"

Donna eyed him avidly a moment before firing back, "What are *you* running from?"

"Who said I'm running from anything?"

Donna said, "Your eyes say it." She gave a disarmingly sympathetic smile, added, "I can tell."

Philip said, "The same thing as you." And then the thought occurred to him, and since he had nothing at all to lose from inquiring, he said, "Do you know where I can find VERNTELLUS?"

Donna's reaction surprised him. "I'm not *that* good a freebooter. I've tried, lots of times, for a few different people. I've run codes, tracked dealers. But no luck."

"Did you—do you—want to meet Vern yourself? Is that why..."

She eyed him queerly. "I don't want to *die*, if that's what you mean. I... I used to want to, but then I ran away. And now it isn't

154

so bad. It's not good either, but it's better. So... I'm not sure I need to see Vern, if he's going to kill me."

"What if you knew he wasn't going to kill you? And that everything you'd ever heard about him was true?"

She watched him evenly, then shrugged and turned to step into the legs of her B-U suit.

He was stunned enough by this personal admission, surprised that a young girl he'd chanced to meet like this was so familiar with the drug at all. But he was completely unprepared for Donna suddenly and without warning bursting into tears. She cried quietly, head bowed before him as she struggled with the rain-repelling suit.

"It's... It's okay," he said, uncertain what else to say or do.

"No," she said. "It isn't."

"No," he said. "It's not."

They stood this way, Donna crying and Philip standing over her and trying to protect her from the eyes of the handful of late-night patrons in the diner. A couple seated at a nearby booth, though, noticed and were eying him suspiciously.

The woman called toward them, "Is everything okay there?"

"Yes, we're... we're fine," Philip said awkwardly. The woman's authoritative tone unnerved him. Her voice was husky and deep, vaguely masculine. Her eyes were hard, unafraid. Challenging.

The woman looked at Donna. In a softer voice, she said, "Are you okay, honey?"

Donna nodded.

"Are you sure? You can tell us."

Philip was sweating beneath the scrutiny of the man—his grizzled features and hard eyes frightened him nearly as much as the woman's accusatory tone. He was a big one too, broad in the shoulders and with hands like battering rams resting on the tabletop, both of which gleamed dull silver: mech-hands.

Donna nodded again, more emphatically this time.

"Okay, sugar," said the woman. "You take care now, okay?" Turning to Philip she said, with as severe a tone as before, "You take care now too, sir."

"Thank you," Philip managed, looking to Donna expectantly. She wiped her nose with the back of her coat sleeve and nodded once, as if signalling that she was prepared to leave.

He led the way to the exit, held the door for her as she pulled the hood of her suit over herself, the whole while feeling the burning gaze of the couple watching him. They slipped into the raining night.

The tires of the cars driving past made loud hissing sounds on the cement. They saw half a dozen drowned rats floating in the gutters, bobbing in the rushing, brown-watered current washing into the sewer grates and into the subterranean darkness beneath the streets. The night was continually pierced by thunder murmuring, its voice shuddering within the concrete under their feet and the buildings surrounding them. The sky pulsed its angry green, here, there.

As they walked, Philip felt only a brief twinge of warning, as he'd felt earlier while in the diner when he'd managed to quell its presence inside him. Maybe the catalyst had been all their talk of running away from bad things, or perhaps the inquisition-like questioning by the woman and her silent, brooding male partner. In any case, he failed now to stifle the thing from where it stirred in his heart. And Philip was displaced, and *it* was awake inside him again, owning the shell of him completely.

The fire.

The king fire-bringer was awoken and hungry for cleansing, and the spreading of the fire into every place of sullied innocence there was.

Ten seconds later he was straddling the smart and pretty and terrified teenage runaway, choking her life from her narrowing windpipe and taking her away from all of this. He'd yanked her violently into an alley they were passing and delivered her a vicious and unexpected close-fisted punch in the mouth. And now he was taking her away from all of this. He was giving her the gift of taking her away from all of this. He was telling her one chapter of his story as he took her away from all of this.

"She's not even mad, Donna," he said between gritted teeth. "She's not even angry and doesn't hate me for what I did. She's just... *with* me. Always. Every second of every day. I wake up in the morning and she's curled up beside me, like I was her dad. She looks at me. She *looks* at me. I think maybe she just wants what I want. I need the drug, Donna. I need it for *her*. Do you understand? It's the only thing I can give her. Until then, what

156

else is there to do but give you what you deserve, too, the only way I can give it to you? I can take you away from all of this, too."

He saw the ghost-girl staring up at him through the eyes of the dying girl in his hands. He squeezed tighter, feeling Donna's windpipe bend beneath his dragon-strength. Foamy drool was gathering at the corners of her mouth, her eyes were bulging and filled with terror or delight, he couldn't decide which and it didn't matter. Alive or dead, he would carry her off and cleanse her in fire the way an innocent girl like this deserved.

Philip chanced to catch sight of a flurry of movement in his peripheral vision; he turned and watched the fight breaking out among the youthful bar-goers on the midnight sidewalk directly at the alley's mouth thirty feet away; heard their drunken, violent words cursing each other as *faggots* and *mechfuckers* and *cocksuckers*; heard the meaty sound of their fists committing violence on each other's faces; saw the blood streaking their faces and clothes and the sidewalk on which they fell, rolled, struggled with one another; saw one of the men's arms, exposed through the torn sleeve of his rain-suit, glinting a brilliant silver: a state of the art mech-limb, affordable only to the elitist of the elite. These young men, rich from their family's fortunes and bored and aggressive and foolish enough to incite bloodshed for fun.

It might have been the blood that drew him out of his own blood-spell. He recoiled from the sight of it, recognising the malicious place it came from, and collapsed backwards from the prostrate girl. When he looked at her then he saw only her innocence and the terror in her eyes. Her dark, bruised throat behind the crumpled rain-suit appalled him, and the lingering memory of his physical contact with her on his burning hands made him feel sick. Nauseous, he turned away and tore open the mask of his rain-suit just in time: he vomited violently into the garbage and weeds bursting up through cracks in the concrete. His vision swam chaotically, his ears rang with the river of his blood pounding through his angry veins, and with the shouts of the young fighting men on the street, and with the laboured, wheezing breathing of Donna beside him.

He watched her and through his tears saw her sitting up, blood on her mouth, coughing phlegm inside of her suit, watching him with those moon-sized eyes of fear.

"I'm sorry, Donna," he said. "This isn't the way I'm supposed to help you. I'm so sorry. You don't know how sorry. But I'm

157

going to be better. I promise you that. And then I'll help us both. I'll find you, and I'll help us both."

Miraculously, Donna, staring at him with wide eyes, gulping air hungrily, crying, gave him a gift: she nodded, easing the shame in his heart and confirming that he'd been correct about her, that they were alike in a very profound way. They were members of the same tribe. He wept and stood on violently shaking legs to stagger down the alley, deeper into the darkness where—for now, until he redeemed himself—he belonged.

At least the girl was still alive after having met the dragon that slept inside his heart. This was the only thing Philip could feel good about, though it was a small consolation. The promise he'd given Donna gave him the strength to renew his search for the Saint, and ask of him what so many others asked, but only few ever received.

Occasionally, the city coughed up a sliver of good fortune.

It was pure luck that Donna, stumbling down the sidewalk without looking where she was going, collided with the woman outside of the pawn shop on the street's corner a few blocks down from the diner.

She couldn't see clearly through her tears and the rain-smeared shield of her B-U suit but recognized the voice of the woman from the diner. "Hey, slow down. You're okay." Her hands on Donna's shoulders were unyielding but somehow motherly. Donna relinquished herself to her emotions and, wrapping her arms around the woman, wept with abandon.

The smack of rain pelting down hard on the cement was loud in her ears.

"It's okay, sugar," said the woman, louder than the rain. "We'll go someplace warm and out of the storm, and you can tell me all about it, okay?"

Donna nodded, blinking her eyes hard, wishing she could properly wipe her tears away but unable because of her cumbersome B-U suit. Taking the woman's offered hand, they hurried off together through the downpour.

As they walked, the woman said, "What's your name, honey?"

"Donna."

"Nice to meet you again, Donna. I remember you from earlier tonight, at the diner. My name's Johanna."

158

●　　●　　●

Another sketchy trash bar, another fruitless conversation with a reticent bartender.

Philip crouched in his lonely booth, sucking on his bottle of piss-tasting beer and wondering what to do, when a woman slid into the booth beside him. The old leather cushions wheezed beneath her supple buttocks. The open neckline of her dress showed off her huge breasts. Her narrowed eyes were conspiratorial as she leaned into him.

She said, "I overheard you earlier. You want to see V? I know where he is. And I know where the Saint is."

Her smile was suspicious but Philip, of course, had nothing else in his bleak world to which he might cling. He smiled back, uncertain but hopeful.

"You do? Please, I'll do anything if you—"

"Information, of course, costs," she said, her desirable smile never once leaving her face.

"Of course," he said. "Of course."

She laughed. "You know, you're kind of sexy, in a weird sort of way. It'll cost you a little more, but we could go upstairs. Ronnie's got rooms for rent. Real cheap? I've been serviced and re-fitted..."

He'd heard of mech-upgraded prostitutes but never thought he'd meet one, let alone be propositioned by one. His initial curiosity about her mechanized sex grew quickly to a deep revulsion toward the world at large, and the ways of that world he was frighteningly familiar with.

You wouldn't want me like that—dragons eat stupid, worthless cunt-whores like you for lunch. We eat them then spit you out and burn you up with our fire and then devour your burning shitty fucking remains all over again. There's no other way to cleanse a whore.

He thought these thoughts but, holding on to the remaining shreds of decency in himself, politely refused her advances. "Thank you, but I really can't. I'm just... I'm all fucked up. That's why I need to... to see Vern. To meet with the Saint as soon as possible. You understand?"

"What's your name?" she said.

"Philip."

159

"Ain't I hot enough for you, Phil?" she said teasingly.

I could burn you to shitty, dirty, smoking, fucking bits: that would be the only way to clean up someone like you.

"You're very attractive, yes."

"Yes I am, Phil. It's gonna cost you double for saying no to Mary-Ann MacTavish. I'm pretty damn famous in this part of the Core. Double, *and* a Harry Chinger waiting for me when I get back from polishing my chrome." She laughed her practiced laugh and excused herself, taking her time crossing the smoky-aired room for the restroom.

When she returned to the table ten minutes later, she found an elastic-bound wad of bills resting on the cushion where she'd sat and the illegal vodka-lizard blood cocktail she'd requested waiting on the table.

"Is this enough?" Philip said, knowing that it was. It was a good chunk of his meagre savings, but she was a common whore, after all.

"Enough for me," she said mysteriously and, tucking the wad of bills into her small leather purse, raised her glass to her lips. She watched him steadily as she drained its contents in several efficient gulps. Replacing the glass on the table, she stood without a word and led him through the bar to the rear door. Once outside, she continued wordlessly across the small parking lot, and then down a dark street, past rows of sleeping brownstone tenements. She wasn't wearing a rain-suit, but then most prostitutes didn't bother with them—they ruined their sex-appeal, and the average whore didn't give too much thought to her health or future. Turning down an alley, she led him to the rear lot of a squat, unmarked building. She motioned to a brown metal door. "That door. In the early morning. Be here. Because it'll be a different door the next day. It's never the same door twice."

He nodded, staring at the door, eager and afraid.

She left him there with, "You'll never know what you missed," and a coy smile he found both repulsive and strangely inviting. He watched her saunter off down the alley, the clacking of her heels sending sharp echoes rebounding from the surrounding walls. He imagined he saw a halo of fire encircling the whore, but when he blinked it was gone, and only the whore remained.

He had nowhere to go—home no longer felt like home to him—so he curled up alongside the opposite building, among

160

the stiff weeds and wet newspaper pages stirring in the wind, preparing to wait out another endless night. Above him, he watched as a rat nimbly crossed the length of a sagging cable strung between the buildings, like a trapeze artist with no hopeful destination at all.

He was stumbling through the choking smoke. His eyes watered, his breath laboured as he sucked in the burning air, the ashes.

Then he was parting the curtain of the smoke and he saw her: a young child of no more than five years, crying where she knelt on the concrete floor in the centre of a ring of fire. Seeing him, she screamed.

His dream-self felt a helpless anger like heat boiling inside himself.

He looked again and saw the girl and she was on fire.

"Smaug!" she wailed, pointing at him. "Smaug!"

It came from him, he realized—the fire spouted from his mouth in a geyser that enveloped the shrieking child.

Within seconds she was obliterated.

Her screams remained behind, haunting the air, haunting his cranium where they would reverberate infinitely long after he woke from the dream.

He stirred and through frost-crusted eyelids saw that a line had formed. Six people waited alongside the adjacent building, huddled close for shelter beneath the narrow, rusted overhang: the first clearly a prostitute, with the tell-tale furtive eyes and cocky posture of her trade, as if she were spotlighted on a runway and ignoring the jeers of a bellicose audience, despite her ragged outfit of shapeless grey jogging pants and old runners; the next a business man-type, dapper in his trench coat and polished leather dress shoes; then a small Asian woman in a faded purple winter coat, blonde-dyed hair obscuring her features; another streetwalker, this one made up like the gaudily-dressed whores in 1980s movies about big-city street gangs, in faux leather mini-skirt, bright red high-heels and lipstick to match; a teenaged boy with baseball cap pulled low over his eyes, hands shoved in the pockets of his tattered jeans, shuffling his booted feet anxiously in the cold air, he the only one among them without the protection of an umbrella-bubble; and finally, a bent old woman, in her mid-60s or older, her toque and scarf and mittens doing little to help the cold, barren look in her eyes as she stared fervently at the brown metal door before which they were lined up, as if willing it to open.

When Philip creaked to a standing posture and accidentally disturbed the lid of a garbage can, it was this little woman who turned at the noise and called to him in a wavering voice. "Don't worry, sir. We know you were here first, camping out here overnight. You're first in line."

She received no argument from any of the others gathered there. Their sympathetic expressions baffled him. How had she— how had they all—known that he was here in this lonely A.M. alley to see the mythical Saint? That he wasn't simply a homeless person—there were so many in the downtown Core—or a drunk sleeping off a long night at the bar? Was it something in his face, the same thing he saw clearly in each of their faces? Or merely his presence among them at such an early hour and in such a remote nook of the city?

"Thank you," he said, straining his sleep-draggled, croaking voice to be heard over the wind.

He limped over to them, shaking from the cold that seemed to have seeped its way into the marrow of his bones. He took his place in line, stunned at this tangible proof that the Saint—and the myth of the escape he could provide—was *real*.

A warmth—a good and un-violent warmth—came over him and helped to stave off the cold that had corrupted his body through the long, raining night.

The wait in the relentless rainfall was a long one, numbing Philip so that he'd nearly fallen asleep standing propped against the brick wall. The sound of the metal door creaking open jolted him to alertness.

He stared at the immense man outlined in its dark mouth, wearing a dark red suit jacket encrusted with glittering rhinestones that looked like it had been borrowed from some long-distant glam era. Philip saw from his jerky movements that he was a fakeman, and an older model. His face, though partially

162

hidden in the gloomy interior of the building, betrayed the tell-tale un-human quality of a full-mech, somewhere between the unembellished features of a department store mannequin and a child's vision of what a mechanized man should look like.

The fakeman looked down the alley in both directions before silently beckoning to Philip with a large, ring-festooned hand.

Philip followed him into the warm darkness, and the others filed in behind him. Then the door to the outside world closed and they were locked inside the kingdom of the Saint.

II: SHADOW PROMISES

"There was a riot at Pile Prison across the river yesterday."

Kessel's words hung heavy on the air of the squad room. Clark looked from the report on his desk. It was late. The House was empty but for them and the scat-sucker gurgling moodily inside its tank.

"I heard. A dozen inmates died, and two guards. They got it cleared up fast though."

"Do you know what started it?"

He eyed her, an anxious look in his face.

"One of the inmates—a death row man—claimed another prisoner had VERNTELLUS, and was holding back from sharing it with him."

Outside, a departing pair of police cruisers filled the night with the cacophony of their sirens. It sounded somehow cataclysmic to the detectives staring wordlessly at each other across their desks.

"There was no one there. The building was empty."

Clark's voice was filled with awe. He and Kessel were sitting in the cruiser, examining the building alongside which they were parked.

Indeed, the entire warehouse had looked as though it had lain deserted for decades: the carpet of dust, thick and undisturbed; the abandoned crates and desks and chairs; the wooden floors collapsed from age in certain sections; its upper floors crumbling and home to nesting pigeons; the whole gutted

163

look of the place, another husk deadening the rapidly declining downtown Core.

They'd pulled back the hoods of their rain-suits, and the metallic clamour of precipitation on the vehicle roof fell louder without the muting fabric. Clark rolled down the window, lit a cigarette, and sucked on it hungrily, exhaling smoke into the night. "I don't know who this Saint guy is, or how he just disappears completely from hideouts we get complete and total confirmation on, from multiple sources, no less. It just... I can't figure it."

"I don't get it either, Clark. It makes no sense. It's like he's always just one step ahead of us. It's been like this from the beginning."

Kessel felt comforted knowing that the desperation so evident in her voice would be construed by her partner as stemming from her instinctually investigative nature. He would never guess her more personal desire—her *need*—to know the truth about the drug.

Clark understood something of the distress he heard in her voice though. "Johanna..." he said and then only looked at her helplessly.

Kessel laughed. "You've never called me that, Clark. Stop it. I know things are dire when you start calling me by my first name."

He chuckled too, retrieved his paper coffee cup from its holder under the dashboard radio, then tossed the nub of the cigarette into the street. "Sorry, Kessel. I just... It just feels so... This whole case..." He gestured through the rain-washed windshield, taking in the dark street before them. "I've never seen anything like this. And I've been on the job a long time. Too long. But this is different. This is... I'm not sure I'll ever figure it out. I'm not sure anyone can. The evidence is there in every burned outline of every druggie we find, but... what could *do* that? And all the claims about Vern actually taking users to... *another place*..."

He drifted off, shaking his head and looking helpless. "I just wish I could get my hands on the scumbag who first invented this shit, or who brought it over here from wherever it started." He clamped his palms together with a loud ringing sound that startled Kessel in the close space of the car. Clark had been a boxer during his younger, pre-mech-upgrade years, and a top contender in the city's welterweight division. More than a few

164

collars had gone down hard and fast from those big, scarred steel hands when resisting arrest on the streets. Something in the gesture of bravado now, though, saddened her. Maybe its futility in the face of whatever it truly was going on in the city. Maybe the helpless look of her partner huddled in the cruiser and unable to grapple this epic and elusive thing with those hands.

Kessel said nothing. She kept the fact to herself, that she felt some festering thing that she could only liken to familiarity—closeness—to this otherwise inexplicable, ongoing case.

Clark pulled her from her reverie.

"There."

She followed his line of vision. A figure was furtively vacating the building via the unmarked side exit and turning down the adjacent alley.

"Where the hell did he come from?" Kessel breathed. "We combed every inch of the place."

"I guess we need a finer-toothed comb."

They donned their rain-hoods and slipped into the rain, jogging down the alley after the man. They trailed him through the piss-smelling staircase of the parking garage, the echoes of his footsteps bouncing down the stairwell and helping to stifle their stealthy pursuit. A moment later and a metallic bang told them the suspect had exited through one of the heavy steel doors that gave access to a lot.

Peering through the glass window of the fourth-floor door, they saw the man approaching a car midway across the lot. He saw them though and, in panic, bolted for another stairwell on the opposite side of the floor. They raced in pursuit, and a moment later found the door leading onto the garage's roof, broken and askew on its rusty hinges, banging in the wind.

They saw the man at the opposite end, near the edge. He seemed to be scrutinizing something in his hands by the orange light thrown by the rooftop lampposts.

"I got this," Kessel said, padding ahead of Clark, her sear gun drawn on the man. "Don't move! Put down the drug, *now!*"

The man's eyes were frantic. He was crying. His hands shook violently.

"Sir," Kessel said in as measured a voice as she could. "We know what you're holding. Drop the drug and put your hands in the air. You don't want to do this."

The man stared at her, eyes astonished. "But I do. But I *have* to."

He had his rain-hood thrown back, and Kessel could see the collar of his shirt beneath, the tie knotted at his throat. Lawyer or accountant or techware man, she thought.

"Sir," she said. "Give me the drug."

The man stood shaking, crying.

Clark's hard whisper came in her ear. "Take out his leg if you have to. We need him alive to talk. And we'll finally have hard evidence."

The man raised his hand, trembling, as if with a great strain, toward his open mouth.

"Stop!" Kessel said, walking closer.

But she didn't shoot her gun and take out the man's leg and save his life. She'd been trying to fathom what the man needed so badly to escape from that he was willing to swallow a drug with such unknown and instantly deadly properties. She was thinking of what it felt like to be so lost—so powerless to quell the pain inside of you—that this seemingly magical and dangerous drug called to you so loudly.

The man clapped his hand to his open mouth and let himself fall backwards from the lip of the parking garage. The detectives watched his descent into the open air between the building on which they stood and the neighbouring warehouse, helpless.

Lightning flashed, radiation pulsed, thunder boomed.

The detectives scuttled and splashed across the rain-drowned rooftop to the edge of the garage.

"You didn't fire," Clark said.

"No," Kessel answered.

They were staring down into the chasm between buildings. The wind was circulating a large and dense cloud of ashes like dark confetti. The air around them was thick with it. Ashes floated everywhere, cindering particles that clung to their rain-slick B-U suits.

The wind soon dissipated the debris, but both detectives had seen it with their own eyes: among the chaos of ashes, the distinct burning outline of a man's body silhouetted in the roiling raining air, making a slow, languid descent to stain the dismal alley darkness below like an effigy.

166

•   •   •

The room was black as pitch but for the cone of orange light spotlighting the imposing figure seated on its simple foldable steel chair and the two fakemen guards standing silent sentinel on either side of him.

Philip, alone in the chamber while the other people waited in an adjacent anteroom for their own private audience, trembled.

"Are you the Saint?" he asked, knowing as he stared at the purple velvet-robed man reposing before him, that he of course was. The snow-white hair, combed back to reveal the high forehead, the glinting blue eyes like ice; the stoic, unperturbed expression beholding him as he prepared to tell his tale, make his request, grovel if he needed to—of course this was he.

"I have what you want," the Saint said by way of answer.

"I don't want it. I *need* it."

The Saint watched him evenly, unmoved by Philip's plaintive appeal. Certainly, he heard the same from many others, Philip reasoned. The Saint said, "I'm not sure you understand the nature of the thing you seek."

"I do."

"Tell me."

"It... VERNTELLUS... provides an escape. I... need that."

"What you fail to understand is this—VERNTELLUS, so far as anyone knows, physically removes you—erases you—from the here and now, and transports you, physically... elsewhere. This other place is completely unknown to us. No one knows for certain what happens to the user, namely where V takes a person, or what it does to them physically and mentally and psychically during the journey. Non-believers claim it's suicide, which of course can be a virtue unto itself. Whether it would be an agonizing demise, none can say."

"What do you believe?"

"I've never taken VERNTELLUS, have I? I've never taken it, though I value its permanent place on my person. But I've seen its effect. I've witnessed it many times. One moment the user is here, and the next, upon digesting it... they're gone. There is no sound, no sound of pain, no evidence of death. Only an inexplicable light, and their shadows—their *signatures*—left behind to mark the last place they stood in the world."

Hopeful, suddenly desperate to find some connection between himself and the Saint, Philip said, "Do you keep Vern on you, for yourself? Maybe if you did something like I did, so if the pain gets unbearable and you—"

"Don't ever presume you know me," the Saint said with quiet, measured fury. "Don't ever do that, and I'll give you the courtesy of not trying to figure you out either. The fact remains: the *drug*, as you erroneously call it, is in the truest, most unfathomable sense of the word, a gateway. To where we don't know. It's the hope in where it may lead that keeps me in business, and keeps men like you grovelling at my feet."

Philip felt sick again. His knees shook, and his stomach lurched. He was so close and yet he remained helpless. He bit his quivering lip, watching the concrete floor in silence.

He ventured, "Where... does it come from?"

The Saint said, "I don't know. No one knows where the gift of VERNTELLUS came from. One day no one knew of it, the next it was in the world, and labelled by the men who craved it and those who decried it as a *drug*, a term sorely inefficient in defining it. I'm but a causeway between here and where VERNTELLUS leads, wherever that may be."

Philip nodded. He swallowed, found it difficult, his mouth was so dry.

The Saint said, "More practically speaking, are you able to afford VERNTELLUS?" He was looking Philip up and down with a close scrutiny that said he was accustomed to appraising men in exactly this way.

With great effort Philip straightened his shoulders and spoke with conviction. "Yes. I will have the money—any amount of money—for when I meet with you again."

An amused twinkle shone in the man's narrowed eyes. "Will you? Really?"

"Tell me how much and I'll meet with you tomorrow."

The Saint told him how much.

The price was very, very high.

III: THE HUMANITY CURE

"—latest attack from what witnesses claim was one of the so-called super-diseases believed to have resulted from the Cloud and its atomic and experimental energy effects. The victim, 48-year-old Wallace Tremblay, has been taken to Downtown Metro Hospital, where he's receiving emergency mech-replacement surgery. Fortunately for Tremblay, the bites he received were restricted to a single area on his body—his right arm—making a mech-limb procedure a potentially much more successful one. Residents of the Core should take note: the assailant fled the scene when police arrived and has yet to be found. Officials have yet to confirm the identity of the attacker, but have said that he—or it, as many are arguing the case could be—should be considered extremely dangerous.

"In other news, seven more local disappearances and/or deaths associated with the use of VERNTELLUS have been reported in the past twenty-four hours.

"The remains of four of the victims were found in their homes, making identification somewhat easier. The remaining three individuals were discovered out of doors, including a homeless man, Ronald Durley, who was identified by witnesses who saw him taking VERNTELLUS in a vacant field abutting a supermarket. He was spoken of fondly by volunteers at the downtown mission and soup kitchen run out of the United Way church. The identities of the two remaining victims remain unknown, though based on examination of their signatures, police believe one was male and the other female.

"Brian Dixon, Professor of Psychology at Michigan State University, believes the prevalence of VERNTELLUS is a sign of a much greater condition in society. 'The rise in disappearances or deaths associated with the drug is reaching epidemic proportions. That says a lot about the mass psychology at work here, that so many people have turned to something that promises not only death via suicide, but a reputed tangible escape from the reality they know, an end—'"

Clark clicked off the television set with dread in his heart.

He was sitting, smoking a cigarette in his underwear, a glass of whiskey in his hand. The coffee table in front of him held the un-capped bottle of his morning anti-rad meds. He hadn't taken

169

this first of the day's doses yet, though he knew he should so he could get the pill's side-effects over and done with: the nausea and the vertigo and the shitting his guts out. This morning ritual that made him want to pulverize his alarm clock when it brayed at him at 5:00 billion A.M., and plunge back down into the solace of sleep, even though his sleep had been a troubled place for some time now.

He didn't want to go to work today. For the first time in his life, he believed he'd chosen the wrong profession. He should have worked harder at boxing, got a better trainer, someone who would have pushed him harder, challenged him to up his game and take on tougher fighters in the days leading up to his final, fateful match against the all-mech that had almost killed him in his bid to make it to the coveted Moon Fighters League. At least in the ring he'd had opponents he could fight with his hands.

But he would go to work. He would go to work and do what good he could, like his partner always did. Kessel likely didn't know how much he admired her dedication to the job, how often of late he'd looked to her persistence as inspiration to crawl out of his bed and enter the new day waiting outside his door, with all of its charred ghosts haunting the streets. The drug-dead, as well as the other ghosts he'd been seeing more and more, whatever they were—Hallucinations? Visions? Products of his long-term exposure living under the chemical shadow of the Cloud?—those fleeting spectres hovering in alleys and against the faces of buildings, shimmering and coalescing into people and creatures and objects that were there one moment, until he blinked them away in the next.

Or were they real? He lived in a city that was home to rain that burned like fire, and atomically mutated fauna, and walking, murdering super-diseases (things *couldn't* get any Goddamn worse and weirder than that, he figured), and a Cloud as big and unknowable as Judgment Day hanging over it all. Were his ghosts any less real than the other horrors he saw every day?

It was nothing new, of course, but the thought never failed to boggle his mind, that the population of the city had risen so dramatically in the years since the Cloud had initially driven so many away that it now surpassed its pre-Cloud numbers. Increasing numbers of immigrants were coming to the city all the time—illegally—seeking VERNELLUS, from places as removed from one another as Japan and the Middle East and Eastern

170

Europe. Knowledge of the drug had spread to all corners of the globe and, given its alleged properties, attributed to it a mythical status that extended to enshroud the city itself. The result was that many saw its place of origin as a new Mecca, and made the pilgrimage to procure the drug, something that said a great deal about the radically diminishing quality of life throughout the world.

He swallowed his remaining whiskey and refilled his glass by the light of the lightning-crossed, green-pulsing sky outside his apartment window. He had time for one more before facing the madness that had infected his city.

Philip stood in the rain-flooded alley, staring at the bag in his hands with the pistol nestled inside. The bank was directly around the corner of the alley to the west. He was going to stride in as bold as a man could be and get as much money as he possibly could, and then lose himself in the maze of alleys and side streets and rooftops of the Core. He'd emptied his savings but needed more. He had no other option left to him. If it didn't work out the way he planned, and bank security or the police or God Himself cornered him, well, he had the pistol in the bag to take himself out with. He feared death, but feared life more. He feared the dragon sleeping inside him and, so much more than this, he feared it waking again and razing another innocent from the wicked Earth.

He removed the pistol from the paper bag, afraid of its weight and the death it held inside its chambers. It was an Old World model he'd purchased illegally from a pawn shop owner several weeks before, their transaction taking place in a storeroom after hours. He knew nothing about guns and paid the man the sum he'd wanted, knowing that he very well might have been getting scammed. But desperation urged him, and he'd left the shop through its back door with the gun tucked inside of his jeans and a new determination in his heart: he was committed now. He'd gone this far, and was that much closer to securing his escape from the misery he lived with day in and day out. He sucked in a trembling breath, heedless of the rain drenching him where he'd left his rain-hood pulled back. He cleared his thoughts and was focused on the task at hand. Success in one form or another would be his, and that was that.

171

"Philip."

He stopped, heart smashing.

"Don't move. I'm armed. Put the bag down and your hands in the air where I can see them."

The voice carried loudly and clearly through the tumult of the rain smacking the pavement and the thunder murmuring in the clouds.

"I said: Put. Your. Hands. In. The. Air. *Now!*"

Helpless, thoughts reeling, thinking of a young girl turned to a blackened skeleton by the old dragon's infernal breath, he dropped the bag and gun and raised his hands slowly on the air. He would never be free of the fire smouldering in his heart. It would burn him up from the inside. He felt tears welling in his eyes.

"I've been following you tonight."

He'd heard the unseen voice before, though he couldn't place it. He stood motionless, teeth chattering in the icy air, the footsteps of his invisible assailant coming toward him. The tip of a gun pressed into the small of his back.

Her voice came loud in his ear. "I believe it, Philip. There is more than what you've known. There has to be. Here. Take it. Go away from here. But take her, too. If you really have good in your heart, then take her away from her memories, too, like you promised her."

The small, deadly pressure in his back was gone. He listened to the sound of footsteps receding quickly down the length of the alley. He turned, but there was no one there, only he and the rats and the rain. He saw the bundle sitting on the pavement. A dark, unmarked satchel. He lifted it in his quivering hands. It was heavy. He opened it and by the uncertain light of the single streetlight infiltrating the dark alley looked inside.

He stared and stared, no longer feeling the rain whipping down on him, unaware that for the first time in many years, he was smiling.

It was a different building—an abandoned automotive garage —but the same lost-eyed people milling at its back door. Philip had received the coded message that morning, with the location and meeting-time, and had rushed there to find several others already waiting.

A fakeman—different from any of the former fakemen he'd seen last time—appeared in the doorway, beckoning them inside with a silent gesture.

Twenty minutes later, Philip was ushered into an area of the garage where another makeshift meeting room had been set up. A series of battery-powered industrial flashlights had been slung along a cable stretched the length of the garage, illuminating the imperial figure of the purple-robed Saint seated on the rusty chassis of a derelict car, like a mechanical patient abandoned by its surgeons mid-operation. He was once again flanked by monstrous fakemen towering into the shadowy recesses, their telling eyes burning a cold blue in the gloom.

Philip had kept his appointment and stood shuddering before them.

The Saint looked with undisguised surprise at the bundles of cash strewn on the floor before him, spilling from the opened mouth of the satchel. Still watching the money, he spoke to Philip waiting politely before him.

"This looks like a fairly sizeable sum you've brought me," the Saint said, sounding as though he actually thought very little of it.

Philip said, "It was the most... I could get. I could get more..."

But, of course, he knew he couldn't get any more. He'd lost what courage he'd had when preparing to rob the bank, and he could expect no more miraculous help from mysterious strangers.

When the Saint said nothing, Philip said, "The news this morning said they found a hooker V'd away. And recently there was a homeless man, an elderly homeless man. These people—they couldn't have had any money at all, let alone enough to pay you the price you ask for Vern. Why did you help them?" He immediately regretted the accusatory tone in which he'd said it but could do nothing about it now.

The Saint turned his penetrating gaze on him. "I may be a business man, but I'm also a compassionate man. When I see a need that runs so deep that it's killing the very heart of the person begging me for my help, well... I may not be a saint, but I won't turn away someone withering away with a pain that I know all too well myself. This is why all of my agents that you've seen here are mech-men."

He gestured to the two stoic guards flanking him on either side. They loomed over Philip, eyeing him unwaveringly and without emotion, and he suddenly understood the truth in the Saint's words about these mech-engineered men. "All my friends wished for a better place, and so I gave it to them. They were my friends. My family. They *believed* in a better place than here. I would have done anything for them."

Philip stared at the Saint, taken aback, and awed. He said, "Then... Then you are a saint, truly."

"I'm a man," the Saint said. "I've tried to be a good one."

Philip and the Saint watched one another without words. Rainfall beat a savage clatter onto the roof of the garage. Thunder pealed a booming din that echoed in the huge open space.

"And that brings us to this moment, doesn't it?" said the Saint from his spartan throne. "There remains one final step for our transaction to take place. I need not reiterate to you that VERNTELLUS is an extremely valuable commodity, and so its scarcity is high, even to myself." He paused, letting his words sink in, his eyes focused on the money before him. "The last time we spoke you'd told me that you *needed* it. Prove to me now your *need* of VERNTELLUS—truly, that you're *worthy* of the salvation it brings—and it will be yours."

Philip had rehearsed the words countless times. There was only one way to tell the tale: truthfully, with every shred of beauty and ugliness the truth held.

Philip told him.

In exacting detail, he described where and how he'd saved each of the three people.

The first was a young woman he'd known from his administrative job at the border control office. They'd gone on a few friendly lunch dates together and once, via email, she'd divulged to him the secret of her father's abusive ways, her mother's blind eye to crimes committed in her household. Eighteen years lived in secrecy and shame until she'd been old enough to escape the house as an adult embarking on a career path, at which point she realized that though escape from the house had been possible, any true escape was impossible because the demons to which she'd been exposed couldn't be exorcised by physical distance and detachment.

Philip had gone to her straightaway, answering the awakened need in him to help her the only way he was able, and saved her by bludgeoning her into a better oblivion than the haunted life she'd known. He'd used a hammer he'd taken down from a peg in his garage and hidden in the sleeve of his winter coat, killing her mercifully with the first blow but hitting her repeatedly in the skull to make certain she was gone. He'd wept throughout it, and long afterwards too, once she'd been buried in the moist soil beneath the viaduct with its railway line thirty feet above.

He told of the second, only two months following the first: a shrunken little elderly man who'd given him the kindness of his smile when Philip sat dejected on a bus stop seat following a long and tedious day of dealing with cold and angry people at the tunnel border station. Beginning with mere small talk, the old man confessed to him during the bus ride that his wife had been murdered earlier that year in a home burglary gone much too far, and that the criminal had yet to be caught, and that he missed her very much and couldn't get used to her absence. Smiling his sad smile, he'd advised Philip that he should savour the time he had with the loved ones in his life, because one never knew when life would take them away forever. Something inside Philip ached at the pain he saw in the man's gentle gaze, which he recognized as his own, and he'd known before the bus spit them out at their stop that he had to save him. Philip held the elderly man's arm and helped him cross the street adjacent to the bus depot, and then dragged him behind the boarded-up convenience store to throttle the gentle life from his scrawny throat. Looking down on him, Philip had been glad to see the hint of a smile creasing the man's weathered, wrinkled features. And then he cried for the man, who'd been made to suffer so, and he cried for the guilt eating away inside himself like a cancer. What right had he to judge who fled from this wicked life?

He then told of the third, and this was the most difficult to tell of, because she was the one true ghost that lived inside of him: the young girl, whose name he'd never learned, but whom he'd been fated to find weeping in the rain inside the colourful tangles of a jungle gym only three weeks before. He'd been hurrying homeward following some errands. She'd been cradling a hardcover book to her chest—*The Hobbit*, by J.R.R. Tolkien. An ancient book, a classic beloved by many, which he remembered having read for school when he was a boy. The school on whose property the playground was located was a hulking mass of brown brick in the distance, to which the girl pointed, crying, as

175

she explained herself and the tears streaming from her eyes; she couldn't tell her mother and father because they would never believe her, or worse still, they might blame her, about her teacher, Mr. Morris, and the things he'd been doing with her after school since before Christmas; the ever-jovial second grade teacher loved by staff and students alike, who'd started touching her in a way that had always felt wrong to her and that she'd hoped and prayed would stop if she wished for it hard enough. The child's last words before she gave herself up to a renewed fit of sobbing would stay with Philip: *I want Smaug to come and burn Mr. Morris up.*

And Philip, imagining the life ahead for this poor damaged child, had acted without thought, but in acquiescence to the certainty of his heart's command. And he delivered the child one terrific blow to the head that had killed her instantly, followed by several more blows to make certain she was passed away from evil forever. He waited there with her until dark fell, and then carried her in his arms across the field to the alley along which his backyard opened. He dug her a deep hole there, and placed her gently into it, and it was then, while tidying her wrinkled clothes so that she would look pretty in her internment, that he saw the scars: all across her forearms were deep scratches, some old and faded with time, but many new and bright red and deeply scabbed. He pictured this poor child marking herself like this, as he knew some people did in order to deal with great trauma, and his heart ached anew. And he'd went inside his garage to retrieve the blowtorch, with which he razed the scars and made the girl pure and virginal again. Philip may not have been able to conjure the storybook dragon of the child's fantasy to destroy the acts of her torturer, but its fire could cleanse her body.

Each of these three people needed to be freed. The world was too dark a place to contain creatures so good, so fragile and ill-equipped to live in such savage times. And there were so many other good people suffering in the world who needed the salvation he could give them.

Philip's voice echoed in the black garage.

"It wasn't me that did those things. Physically, yes, it was me. My hands holding the hammer and blowtorch. My hands delivering the blows. But something got into me. It got deep inside, and took me over, and I want to be cured of it. It was *the world* that got inside me. I want to be cured of *the world*. I want to be cleansed of it. I need the drug. I'll give you anything for it. I need to be freed."

He finished his appeal: "The world infected me. It's inside me now. I almost took another just yesterday. I wanted to do it for the same reason I did it to the others—for *good*. To free her, from all of this. But I know that this isn't the way to do it. There has to be a better way, and a better place. I need to leave, and go away to that place, where I can be better than I was, and the best I can be. I want to take this one with me, to make amends for the things I've done wrong before. I want her to be happy, and free of the memories that haunt her. I don't need to be forgiven—I need to be freed, of the things I had to do, of the things I'll have to do again if I keep on living in this cruel world."

The dragon's apocalyptic fire needs to be drowned, or the haunted and good people will burn again, and again, and again.

The Saint watched him a moment with emotionless eyes. A subtle whirring emanated from somewhere within his body and sounded loud in the stillness, as if gears and cogs were working hard to process the information received through Philip's confession. He removed a small canister from somewhere inside his voluminous robes. Its silver skin shimmered in the sodium light. He twisted the canister with both hands, turning either end in opposing directions. A soft hissing sound issued from the cylinder as a small aperture opened in its hull. Philip saw where the Saint's robe had fallen down the length of his forearm, glimpsed the glint of metal skin—an unsheathed mechanized arm. And he knew then that the Saint was a mechanized man, a fakeman; and he knew that the man himself had went away, for his own reasons, and left the gift of this simulacra behind to help in this world.

"It's yours," said the spirit of the Saint. "May it quiet your memories."

Philip was unable to thank him through the ecstasy of his weeping sending emphatic echoes throughout the garage.

The late-night diner was reliably quiet.

Donna, ignored as always by the young cashier absorbed in her telephone conversation, sidled up beside the woman tapping

177

away at her handheld computer. She waited politely until the woman noticed her.

"Yes? Can I help you?"

"Hi, miss," she said. "Sorry to bother you. I was just wondering, if you don't mind—and feel free to tell me to get lost—if I could maybe have your leftover sandwich bits on your plate."

When the woman only eyed her in a combination of disbelief and disdain, Donna added, "I'm really hungry."

The woman simply shrugged and went back to her computer.

Mean bitch, Donna thought, grabbing the remnants of the wrap from her plate and shuffling towards the rear of the diner. Out of habit, she stopped beside the corkboard, eyeing the ads for part-time menial jobs and other, more sketchy communications. Something caught her eye. Her name, written in bright red marker on a small piece of paper torn from a larger page and half-obscured by a job posting for a dishwasher at a nearby Korean restaurant. She read the handwritten message beneath her name with surprise and fear and excitement and wonder. She read it again and again and again.

It made her feel special. No one had ever written her a letter before.

She touched the necklace of bruises encircling her throat and without hesitation left the diner and slipped into the storming night streets. She was so bewitched by the spell of the letter that she didn't notice the rain touching her bare face, her rain-hood flapping behind her as she hurried on her way.

This latest stakeout had turned out a wash.

They'd been watching the targeted building from their rooftop aerie for hours, but it had been quiet as the grave all night, its windows dark and sleeping. This fruitless vigil filled Clark with a steadily growing futility and despair. What was the point of this difficult job they did without respite or results? He grunted, settled into the siding-sheathed wall of the rooftop electrical shed against which he was leaning.

The rain had awoken a thick fog that rose around midnight and now hung like a great pall over the city everywhere they looked. Through its rolling tendrils the lights of the buildings and streetlamps were extinguished or were blighted to dim embers fighting a useless effort to push back the darkness. Only the sky's intermittent belches of green radiation filtered through vividly, amorphous, monstrous.

Clark shivered inside of his rain-suit. "It looks... spooky. Don't it?" He watched the fog apprehensively, thinking of the spectre he'd seen only the night before while staring out across the city from his bedroom window: a weird, luminous red smoke in the shape of a bird that blew slowly on the wind, bewitching his eye; drifting to a place directly across from his window, and then plummeting straight down, as though it had weight to it, to hit the concrete of the street six floors below with a concussive thunder that trembled the walls around him.

It had taken him a minute, but he'd convinced himself the noise was just the coincidence of a thunder-clap coinciding with a real bird happening to drop dead right in front of him. It was easier to swallow *that* pill than the idea of yet another vision fucking with him.

A moment passed, of rain beating down relentlessly, thunder cracking the endless spine of the invisible sky. An airdroid drifted past close by, the wheezing of its labouring motor audible through the roar of the storm as it went about its duty of inhaling the deadly carbons in the air. Most believed their efforts fruitless, yet the city continued sanctioning production of the machines, another pointless expenditure for tax payers.

Kessel's voice came to him sounding far away in the fog, even though she was directly around the corner of the shed looking out across the building's opposite side. "Oh, there are ghosts out there, Clark. The city's filled with them."

And the thought was suddenly there in her head: *I once killed a perp out of hatred, not duty.*

She let the memory overcome her and take her away to be relived, as she so often did. The man had been on the lam since his conviction, a pedophile she'd succeeded in tracking through the underworld network of crackhouse and juice-pit informants and hookers often tapped by the detectives. She'd cornered the son-of-a-bitch in the backyard of a west-side ghetto project two years before; with no one around but she and the man and the wicked, wicked spirit of that man whose evil she'd known herself as a young child. That ghost had never left her. And the trapped perp had raised his hands in the air, giving himself up with a look of surrender and shame in his face; and she'd raised her sear gun

179

and burned him five times in the chest; and she'd stood over the man and watched his life bleed from his destroyed body and still it hadn't been enough vengeance for the little girl she'd lost in her youth; so she burned him again and again and again; and still it hadn't been enough vengeance to quiet the haunting voice of her memory.

She planted a gun in the dead man's hand. It had gone down officially on record as a case of self-defence, but it had been the coldest of cold-blooded murder.

Kessel trembled, biting her lip. Around her, the fog swirled comfortingly dense.

Clark peered around the corner of the shed to see his partner staring out across the fog-shrouded streets. The lost look in her eyes where she sat huddled, her rain-suit's hood shrouding and casting her narrow cheeks in shadowy relief, only made him more uneasy. He wasn't sure what to say. He was better at hitting things—hitting people—with his steel fists than talking things through with them. He looked away from her, saying nothing.

They sat watching the storm- and fog-besieged city, the mist curling around them and between them and everywhere else they could see, with nothing more to say.

He'd been waiting in the alley since dusk. He was soaked through to the skin, having left his B-U suit at home. He no longer needed its protection from the chemical rain. He shook violently from the cold. He would have waited another hundred nights to atone for what he'd almost done. He huddled closer to the wall among his nest of sodden cardboard boxes and rusty garbage cans, watching the street at the opposite end of the alley.

The pill was small but its weight in his palm had startled him. He could barely hold it and was forced to clamp his other hand beneath it in order to hold it, and even then he struggled with it. Sweat broke out on his brow when he'd handled it, grimacing with the effort. He'd felt his muscles straining and a kink awaken and stab in his abdomen. He felt its weight now as a comfort nestled inside the pocket of his coat. He checked the alley but it was empty. He wrapped his arms around himself to help stave off the chill, but it was hopeless. He would wait for her.

"Philip."

180

He looked up and she was there. Donna, the teen urchin, haunting the alley as if she'd materialized there from another place. She hovered anxiously in place, moth-like and fragile between the immense dark brick faces of the walls towering above them. Her rain-hood was thrown back. By the streetlight's glow he made out the circle of blue and purple and black bruises around her throat. It hurt him to see.

Her voice came again, small and uncertain. "I found the note you left for me, on the corkboard at the diner. Telling me to come here tonight. Is it true? Did you find what you were looking for? Did you find... Vern?"

Philip smiled at her. "An... An angel helped me. She gave me the money for it."

Donna remembered the kind woman's husky but soothing voice, the motherly comfort of her arms around her in the cold rain. She thought about how she'd shared her story with this woman, feeling able to divulge everything about the dark story of her life like she'd never felt able to share it with anyone before. Maybe it had been the fact that she was a police officer—a real-life detective, who'd seen and who knew many dark and sad things—that had convinced Donna. Or maybe it had been the understanding in her eyes.

She said, "I know."

Philip retrieved the pills from his pocket. "I have one for you too," he called to her. "I didn't know where to find you, so I left the note at the diner. I knew you'd go there sooner or later because you told me you always went there, asking for food. I asked the Saint for two pills. I told him about you and that you were also running away, from the same things I'm running away from. And the Saint... he really is a saint. He gave me this, to give to you. If you want it. If you truly *need* it."

Donna came forward, splashing through the muddy puddles and scattering rats and railers with her steps. She paused, watching him warily. "You won't hurt me again?"

Philip said, "No one will ever hurt you again, Donna."

She held out her hand.

"Be careful. It's heavy. Unimaginably heavy."

She said, "I... I know. Somehow I knew it would be. I always imagined it that way. I'm ready."

He placed the capsule in her hand. She cupped both hands together and had difficulty keeping them aloft. She shook with

181

the effort, though she was smiling widely as she struggled. Philip marvelled at that smile, so free.

Around them, the city shook in the throes of the thunder and rain, the sound of giants delivering each other blows as they battled for a kingdom in the sky. He thought of the angel that had given him the gift of the money to purchase his escape from all of this, and from the memories of the world that had invaded his heart and made him into a different man than he'd once been. He thought of the ghost of the playground girl he'd saved, and thought, *I'll see you soon, darling. We're going to be free of all this now, and I know I'll see you again, in the better place. I know it.*

With great effort, two-handed, Philip lifted the impossibly heavy capsule toward his mouth. Sweat broke out on his brow when he handled it. He grimaced with the effort. He smiled at Donna. She was still smiling, too, as she struggled to raise the capsule to her mouth.

Philip placed the pill, slowly and with great reverence, on his quivering tongue. He heard a voice in his head, felt it like a candle sputtering into life and throwing back the darkness in a stifling, windowless room. That room was him. The voice was the ghost of the child, and her voice was full of joy.

Thank you, dragon.

Thank you, Smaug.

The early morning alley was ablaze with the frantic lightshow of police vehicles's headlamps. The rain hadn't abated. It came down in a deluge, whipping the buildings and streets and the police officers and detectives in their rain-suits. It brought up the fetid stink of the city, which hung in a miasma over the streets.

The two detectives stood staring at the scorched concrete.

There were three bodies outlined there: an adult's body (likely male, judging from its height and general build); a young adult or teenager's body, possibly that of a girl, based on her body size; and, in a much fainter outline, as though the signature had been burned into the concrete long before the others and been faded with time and the elements: a small child's.

A family, Kessel thought.

"This city," Clark seethed, scanning the bleak landscape of the alley with his flashlight, illuminating the overflowing garbage cans, the ugly brick facades of the enclosing buildings, these decades-old witnesses to countless clandestine and illicit meetings and crimes. A great rage had awoken in him at his feeling of helplessness. "There's a cult of lunatic fakemen out there who believe they're better than humans. Last summer we had a self-proclaimed avenging angel serial-killing his way down in the history books. We got baby killers and child murderers and child prostitution and rapists and criminally insane robbing banks with weapons as heavy-duty as the Goddamned army uses. If the rumours are true, we even got walking diseases on the streets, like something out of a loony's batshit nightmare. This city, this Cloud-cursed city..."

He trailed off, shaking his head, eyes lost as he stared at the raining, pulsing sky.

These were only a few of the department's cases of the past year, and the year was young.

"The city is the world," Kessel said, echoing the Loot's words, his oft-spoken refrain like a condemnation of everything they knew, in their city and beyond. Like a prophecy, of what waited tomorrow.

Clark exhaled loudly, breath steaming the mask of his rain-suit. "And now this." He scuffed the fire-tattooed pavement with his shoe. "What kind of a fucked-up drug does this to a person? Coke don't do it, meth and heroin and crocodile can't touch this. Goddamn juice can't even do it. And it even gets kids. *Kids.* It's wicked and unnatural and unknowable and... *evil. Evil* is what it Goddamn is."

"Maybe it's something else."

Kessel's words startled him. He turned to her, eyed her quizzically. "What the hell does that mean? What else *could* it be?"

"A cure."

She walked off, leaving him staring after her, and wondering.

The morning stayed dismal and grey. In the afternoon, for the first time in a very long time, the sun fought its way out of the clouds like a miracle, briefly throwing light into all the corners of the city.

But before long the darkness came back.

IV: LIGHT

The sun there held a new kind of fire, benign and welcome.

The waters there cooled his memories, made them easier to bear.

The woman detective had been right:

There was more than what he'd known.

Now he knew peace.

He smiled, basking in the light.

He looked forward to thanking her when next they met.

For now, though, he would celebrate the peace with his new daughters.

IN THE CITY WHERE DREAMS WANDER THE SIDEWALKS

A very dark story inspired by a personal experience that had a profound effect on me.

I'd been writing for a local arts and culture magazine and had been out on an assignment to take pictures. At some point, I found myself in the neighbourhood described in the story, on the periphery of the downtown core, just beyond the limits of the casino, where urban squalor immediately sets in like an infected wound at the edge of the opulent, expansive casino property. I was passing a decrepit car repair garage, many years unused, when something caught my eye. It was a piece of paper stuck up on the interior side of its grimy window. The paper stood out even at that distance across the street, being that it was bright and new-looking in the unlighted window and with the dark brickwork surrounding it. I crossed the street and read the message printed boldly on that piece of paper.

The essence of that message, more or less, is the same one that appears in this story. And it seemed to me—and still seems to me, and I've thought about it long and hard over the years since I saw it and wrote this story based around it—like the embodiment of some sort of darkness the likes of which it's truly terrifying to consider exists in the world, let alone much closer and in my home city. One of the greater, underlying messages of the story is that this thing—this evil—exists in your hometown too.

Let's take care of each other, and never ever feed our children to the darkness.

People who were once my friends mocked me and laughed, as if I were making it all up. *Your eyes tell you strange things.*

But I know something about the black centre of this everyday Southwestern Ontario city. About the man who takes the teenagers from their place in line outside of the Salvation Army Youth and Rehabilitation Centre. Who filches them from the sidewalks and alleys like candy from a store dispenser. And I know this: he's the closest approximation to the Devil we've got here in Windsor, Ontario. Because when they come wandering into the dead Sunday morning streets days later, the girls and boys have un-living eyes that look past you a million miles when they drift by on the sidewalk.

I've spoken with them, before and after their transformations, and I've seen their eyes and the humanity that always seems erased from them when they return from the man. And that man is a terrible legend among these homeless, old and young alike, while the children fear him most because what these street-people say about him is true: he prowls the streets, making circles of the blocks until he sees one he adores. It's always only a single one chosen each night; and then the passenger side door of his forbidding car is thrown wide and despite the rumours and fear riding the air in that sector of the city's downtown, they always slip inside as if enchanted, and close the door.

And they drive off together, the terrible man and his newest candy girl or boy.

And the new day's early morning streets are always checkered with slow-moving children with eyes looking nowhere, shuffling down sidewalks and filth-littered alleys with no destination anymore at all.

● ● ●

I saw my first abduction on a Friday evening in September.

I'd been staring from my third-floor bedroom window, blowing cigarette smoke through my window screen and into the chilly air. Absently, I saw them, two regular walkers of downtown sidewalks: the giant tattooed woman with limp and cane—two blue-ink tear drops ugly and sad running down her left cheek—and her daughter—or the girl I'd always taken to be her daughter, because why else would this biker lady with ancient wary eyes always shuffle along with the Downey girl ever at her side. I remember fixing my eyes on the girl, trying to discern from my high vantage those details which made her a different kind of human than the rest of us: the strange heavy-lidded eyes, the perpetually blank expression, and the webbing between her fingers. Of course, I could not see at that distance, but I knew they were there, these alien attributes. Because she, like her unsightly mother, was a fixture of the city's downtown country who I knew well enough.

When the long black car pulled alongside them, I figured it was one of the regular johns. One of the sicko demented fucks who paid cheap money to rape a retarded girl while the hideous mother supervised, waiting until it was over to collect their money. I'd been hearing the stories about the two for years—the Twisted Two, I'd always thought of them—hating the world a little more every time they crossed my mind.

The picture three floors below was familiar and awful and I was stamping my cigarette out and preparing to vacate my place at the window when the biker woman began wagging her cane in the air. It caught my attention, that flurry of activity from a usually slowly waddling mass of poor motherhood. I watched, saw that the Down's syndrome girl was already seated in the passenger seat and that both she and the driver, whose face I couldn't make out in the dim interior of the vehicle, were both gesticulating for the mother to get away from the car. Then, in puzzlement and mounting horror, I watched as the girl slammed the door closed with a quick, flat thud. I heard her mother's anguished scream clearly through my open window as the car rolled away down the street and beyond my view.

I sat watching the shrieking mother, waving her wooden stick in the air, and the picture of her sobbing regretfully made little sense to me, because hadn't she been offering her child up for cars to swallow for years?

I watched her for several minutes as she waddled back and forth along the sidewalk, an enormous panicked penguin, crying, confused, apparently unwilling to leave the site of her daughter's abduction. I felt horrible. My stomach became queasy and I considered waiting beside the toilet for my dinner to resurface. I stayed in the window, though, until the tattooed woman vanished in the darkness, and when my eyes became sore from staring into the night I went to bed and waited for sleep that didn't come.

Two days later, I was walking briskly to work and the world became half normal once again: there they were, the biker lady and her retarded girl, coming slowly towards me half a block away. I could pick them out at any distance, their familiar silhouette and odd, shuffling gait. But when I neared them, the woman's eyes were watching the sidewalk, not raking passing traffic for signs of prowling johns. And until that moment, I'd never realized the consciousness that lived in the faces of the mentally delayed because when I looked into her daughter's eyes, I saw that they were dead, and they hadn't been this way before at all. Behind the usual blankness there was something else, something more vacuous and un-alive than I'd ever seen there. There or anywhere else I'd ever looked. Pit-eyes, hollow and fathomless.

Those eyes have haunted me from that morning on. I see them in my thoughts when I'm rinsing dishes at work, and they watch me from the inside of my eyelids when I'm trying for sleep. I'm haunted, and the worst part is now that I've seen it once, I see it everywhere. Signs of this darkness slipping through among the lit world. All around me, right in front of us all, the same car drifting like a spirit down our streets, curbing the roads with passenger side door wide and beckoning to young men and women moving down the sidewalks.

I try not to see, but I always do. Maybe I'm running late for work or leaving the movie theatre with a girl, when a teenager with nothing at all behind his or her stare drags past us like a resurrected cadaver on the street. And I shiver—a profound tremor quaking through the deepest parts of me—and I know sleep won't come to me that night.

188

● ● ●

Two months after that first awful abduction, I sat chatting with a fairly well-known homeless man identified locally as the Fisherman, for the fishing hat he sports during all seasons, brimming with seagull feathers, like some strange, grubby peacock with no permanent residence but the sidewalks down which he travels. We were seated midway up the long concrete steps leading to the upper levels of the Ouellette University corner plaza which houses the theatre, a coffee shop and small deli, and a slew of vacant storefronts, part of the city's epidemic of bankrupt businesses. We were talking about the weather, because what better subject to discuss with a man of the outdoors while he doled out the small Ziploc bags of marijuana to his regular Friday night customers. My own stash, a half bag bought at sale price because he liked talking to me, was already snug in the breast pocket of my jacket.

Then, right in front of me, and I couldn't believe my perfectly terrible luck in happening to be freezing my ass where I was when I was: the waif was pretty, for all her thickly-caked eye make-up and tattered fishnet stockings and faded blue-dyed hair, all the requisite pop culture standards of punk rock vogue. Evidently cold with her arms wrapped around herself in ineffectual defence against the chill air, she appeared altogether doomed, leaning into the open maw of the long car hulking predatorily alongside her, its engine purring smoothly in the night.

I wanted to do something. Call out for her to stop. Urge the Fisherman to snare a hook in the girl's fishnet-stockinged legs and pull her to safety. But all that escaped me was a muttered "fuck" as I sat helplessly captivated by the spectacle. Beside me, the Fisherman thought he understood, and he laughed. He said, "I know, my friend. I'd like some of that young pussy myself tonight. Lucky bastard."

We watched as the girl clambered into the seat and closed the door after her with a small thud. The car drove through the green light, turning left and heading west; heading, I knew, to some incalculably dire night for her. I murmured, "I think that might have been the Devil in that car, friend."

189

To which the Fisherman replied in a subdued tone, following my stare and gazing off westwards, "You're right. I've seen him, too. I didn't want to say. In case it might ruin your night."

I stared at him, watched him carefully while he went through his stash of dirty dollar bills under the amber street light glow. I asked him, "What do you know?"

And I watched him as he didn't answer me, only continued counting his money, and then he got lost and had to restart at the beginning of his count, with a disengaged look in his eyes making his task difficult. He stood a moment later, his business done or maybe unfinished on the corner that night. And he nodded at me wordlessly and wandered off down the street, headed northward, toward the icy river somewhere in the night.

I thought: what plot *is* this, unravelling in the night every night under the city's unseeing eyes? And I wondered where it was, what dank sweaty place exactly was it that served as the place of transformation for all the children of the night; who returned to wander their old haunts like ghosts called back from graves. Darkness and chains and ropes and locked doors perpetually guarded this terrible site in my imaginings. I envisioned cluttered back rooms of small convenience stores or confectionaries where unspeakable pictures play out under the dim light of a single bulb. I imagined the second or third sub-basement level of a long-abandoned factory or warehouse where only mice and echoes live, in some feebly lit corner space, on a mattress stained ugly, marked with atrocity. It could be there, too. It could be anywhere at all in this small-ish city, so big, really, when you're seeking to pin-point the nesting place of something shitty and black to the core.

And *who* was it exactly, I wondered with growing awe, who was this abductor, and what did he do to his victims during the endless nights? Was he a crazy john strung out and riding jolting meth-highs? Or was he an archetypal family man, a community figure with pressed suits and perfectly radiant smiles for all those looking up to him? Or was he somewhere in-between these portraits on the endless spectrum of terrible chameleon humanity?

Or was it simply badness incarnate?

And this possibility somehow always made more sense to me than the others, although I was never certain why. I only knew that it felt awfully right, seeing it that way; like a thing risen from lightless subterranean places into the nocturnal playground of the city streets, and there it is, finally, seen. A dark secret revealed, for those few who see it. A long-festering malignity manifesting in the playgrounds and streets and alleys and wherever else we allow our children to become lost.

The Fisherman said it best, maybe, by not saying the words at all. By avoiding my eyes because probing into some things is best left undone. But it was a girl that summed it up for me, a girl I worked my tedious job alongside and who I began to know more and more over the months. It was wise Martha who said something revelatory apropos of nothing while we sat watching the river from her car one sun-splashed day, our fast food lunch remnants stuffed back into the paper bags in which we'd received them.

I remember how it looked that afternoon. One of the rare days when the world looked lit perfectly, almost so powerfully illuminated that it seemed as if you might be able to figure out anything. Decipher long indecipherable problems, slip puzzle pieces together so that larger structures lie revealed. Because it's always easier to find answers when you have a reliable light source peeling away the dark and brightening the remote corners of the world.

Just like that, in the easy space of silence following a quick meal, while the cholesterol attacked our bodies and we swished Coke around in our mouths to help dislodge the bits of french fry and hamburger meat from between our teeth. Just like that, as I sat there pondering the world distantly with sunlight making my eyes water, with the Detroit River sparkling the way it does only on afternoons like this. And she said:

"I've been having crazy dreams lately. About there being something... That there's an evil living in the world." And she looked at me then, which I was hoping she wouldn't do because of the fear I knew she'd see in my face, but she did and didn't notice, I guess, because then she added, "A pervasive evil. And it scares the Hell out of me, those dreams."

And she was done, and so was our lunch hour break from dish-washing drudgery, and I sat in numbed silence as her revelation confirmed for me my own nascent knowledge. Like a verification of my sanity in a world growing impossibly more

191

savage each day passing. I shuddered, watching the magically deceptive sight of the dirty Detroit River looking beautiful in noon hour sunlight. And Martha started the car engine and then we were driving back towards work and more dirty things to scrub clean.

My friends often laughed at things I told them.
Your eyes tell you strange things.
I stopped saying those kinds of things, ideas that would lead them to softly ridicule me, their steadfastly paranoid friend. But I knew about the black thing at the centre of the city even if they wouldn't allow themselves to acknowledge it. I'd caught glimpses of it, and saw it mirrored a thousand times over in the eyes of the broken young people I passed every day.

I discovered the clue years before but hadn't made any sense of it. I'd made no connection between this clue and the new brand of street life I'd been seeing, the avenues and alleys teeming with walking dead children. My epiphany arrived as I was passing through the rear exit of the restaurant and into the rat-plagued alley, having just completed my evening shift. I walked eastward without hesitation, knowing that it would still be there, in the same place I'd found it years ago, ruining the down-trodden neighbourhood behind the deceiving splendour of the casino even further.

I stopped briefly at the casino and used a payphone to call Martha, the girl who dreamed of evil in the world. When she picked up, I told her to come meet me. She asked whether I was okay. Maybe there'd been a tremor in my voice, or maybe it was just the words themselves. I said, "Do you want to see a clue? It's about the evil in the world that you dream about."

We hung up and I walked to the place we were to meet, in the semi-enclosed park wedged in between three surrounding walls of town homes. I sat on a peeling bench and waited, listening to the incessant vibrant chatter of ghetto children from the see-saw and sand box, sounding as if they didn't know yet about the sad truth of how the world is. There was an overturned Big Wheel on the small, narrow front lawn near me and it made me sad. It only added to the feeling of everything becoming worn down and useless, forgotten in the endless march of one hopeless day into the next.

192

• • •

Our walk to the site of the clue was short. We didn't say much as we walked. I think Martha sensed a little of my trepidation. I sensed dread coming from her in waves, as if she knew something she'd witnessed or suspected was about to be confirmed, suspicions validated.

Minutes later we were standing alongside the decrepit, hulking building. It sat low to the uncropped lawn, near to the traffic-teeming Riverside Drive, yet unnoticed too, for all its proximity to the machine hustle and bustle and stink of exhaust. It had once been a garage of sorts, an automobile repair shop gone bankrupt in some distant decade. Its windows were striped with rusted iron bars, and the scratch-pocked glass beyond them was filthy with grime.

I pointed to a spot in the window, partially obscured by a rust-flecked bar. It was still there, as I knew it would be. My friend leaned forward and with a crease in her brow read the message written in faded ink on the sheet of time-yellowed paper and stuck up to the inside of the glass. She read it aloud softly, an awed murmur in the settling purple dusk.

> Hey, kids. You're sick and tired of living at home and listening to everything your parents say to you and claim to do for you. You know more than they do. You know everything you need to know. You know that they don't love you. Get out. You don't need them anymore. You know everything you need to know to live and be free. You'll never need them again. Get away from them now. I'm waiting.
>
> —THE WORLD

She stopped reading, and I gave her the time she needed to re-read it again and then a third time, and then I let her mull it all over and consider what it could mean. Whether it was a twisted message directed to runaways in the area, attempting to lure them into service as prostitutes or dealers; or whether it might be her dreams made tangible and masking taped-up to a grimy window of a deserted building in the centre of a poverty-riddled neighbourhood, a corporeal message in front of her eyes

193

revealing her worst suspicions to be true. There was no contact number on the weathered-looking paper, no address even, and somehow this made it worse, the absence of any trace of human connection in the enigmatic message. A communication from the depths of some unfathomably and eternally dark place, to the innocent girls and boys destined to hear, those weary children lost enough in their own awful lives that they would find their way into its black heart regardless. Or who could do nothing but wait for it to come for them, a dark pre-destiny purring its spell-like motor-rumble through the streets of poverty and despair.

A moment passed and when she finally was able to speak, Martha said, "It's awful. My god, it's so *awful*."

We held each other's hands fiercely because what else could we do when beneath the pall of something so seemingly insuperable and embedded like a tumor in the fabric of the world. But even then, even during the comfort of holding on to each other, and though the vacant building was squat and not very much taller than us, it seemed to loom larger than that, dwarfing us in the certainty of our powerlessness.

We don't talk about it. We haven't since that night. We both know it's there, some kind of incontrovertible proof of what we've known for too long to live and breathe in the nooks and crevices of the place we live.

I see the car, black as night, with its shotgun-side door opened wide like a mouth for swallowing the children living on the sidewalks. We both see it, and the teenagers themselves, returned days later but never the same, the touch of humanity gone from their eyes, with their new, wan faces like chalk powder as they drag themselves through the streets like ghosts escaped from the shells of the people they'd once been. And we huddle ourselves inside of movie theatres and we eat dinners in restaurants facing away from windows overlooking the sidewalks, and when we talk on the phone, we keep it brief and remain inside topics of when's your next shift and what movie do you want to see next weekend.

And when I see the Fisherman with his scavenger birds's feathers pluming straight into the congested downtown air, I bid him a good evening, and we chat briefly about the weather changes and how the rain makes the air cool even if it's still muggy. And we make our regular exchange, dollar bills for clear plastic baggies of weed. And we say goodnight and wander away down the street in opposite directions, our eyes watching the cracks zig-zagging the pavement, as if all our steps weigh a ton and look at the damage we do whenever we walk in the world.

GLADIATORS IN THE SEPULCHRE OF ABOMINATIONS

Occasionally, I'm able to pinpoint a precise moment when inspiration struck for a story. This is one of them.

It had been the summer of 2007 and a friend and I had taken a daytrip out in nearby Essex County, leaving the smoggy city behind for rural farmland, cleaner air, and any wineries along the way.

We'd been driving through the flat landscape of seemingly endless crop fields for some time when I saw a lone brown cow standing in a farmer's pasture we were passing.

Something about the animal struck me as being absolutely beautiful—forlorn and lonely, yet big and dignified and strong-looking, and with the dying daylight shining in its sleek lustrous coat—and in that moment I decided that this was much more than a farm animal: she was a goddess.

I went home and wrote the story that night, pitting a deity against the worst of humankind.

The title is very Robert E. Howard-esque, muscular and bold and dark. I love Robert E. Howard, whose stories changed my life when I'd read them as a boy and made me understand that there was no form of art as compelling as a powerfully written story.

Long live King Robert and the gods and goddesses manifested in the world!

They are the fields where he learned to walk.

This scorched country of dying corn and sun-ravaged wheat, where he learned to walk and where, as an adolescent, he once dropped down from the power of the sun and had woken up with a broken ankle and a dust coat on his tongue. His father had carried him through the shimmering heat of the day and laid him in bed for his mother to pray and worry over and nurture back to health, so that he could toil alongside his father among the rows once more.

Billy squints into the savage sky, savouring the warm dirt browning his ankles with dust. He replaces the sunglasses over his eyes and feels the transient illusion of coolness cover him. His Ford Meteor is resting beneath a slowly descending dust cloud a hundred metres away, its mechanical insides still clinking from the long drive through the county. Bending to one knee, feeling the old tension needles in his wounded ankle, he scoops a palmful of dirt, breathing with great labour at this small exertion. Despite the shooting in his ankle bones, he remains there a while, close to the field. Dust sprinkles through his clenched fingers and a small cloud begins to rise about him. He closes his eyes and imagines it settling on him everywhere like a tangible manifestation of memories from the before-years, memories that have hounded him since he left this place long, long ago, and that pulled him back to these fields, this dust that he knows so well.

After a moment, he stands with a wrenching ache in his bones and staggers towards the wan promise of the derelict farmhouse and its adjacent barn looming dark in the distance. The horizon lines in all directions are uncertain, shimmering ghost-points heat-miraging in the silence with no sign of habitation visible anywhere. The nearest farm, he knows, is several miles to the east, and a sense of his great solitude settles over him like the inescapable dust of this place. Only the crackle of grasshoppers and crickets like electricity in the corn husks follows him.

The uneven earth slows his progress, but he doesn't mind. He walks with care, tentatively, gingerly side-stepping the larger dirt clods for softer, crumbly-looking spots in the field. Side-stepping also the occasional black beetles and earth-coloured grasshoppers stirring like dried leaves amid the parched soil. He stops often, squinting through his plastic lenses towards the brilliant blood-coloured late day sky. He takes his time during this perusal, as if waiting for something to appear there among the scant clouds, among the blinding red of the burning air. Maybe an image half-formed or partially suggested among the stray clouds like cottony shrouds.

A feeling of nostalgia creeps inside his awareness as he shambles on towards the decrepit buildings. And he no longer feels the heat of the August sun on his skin, as though his backwards-looking thoughts of long-past days have chilled the air and him passing through it.

The house is a skeleton picked clean by the elements.

What remains of its walls and roof have sunken inward from the elements and the years. The glass of its windows long ago shattered by rocks hurled by county children exploring this foreboding place, with its evil but tempting aura. Porch and interior floorboards parted at the insistence of weeds and wild grass and roots. Birds own its eaves, mice and rats its rooms. He creaks a loose section of floor in the living room and disturbs a brown garter snake from beneath the dust-blanketed, tattered chesterfield. He jerks his foot away, a cry strangled in his throat as the serpent slides past him. He follows its progress down the hallway, dimly illuminated by the stray sun-rays slashing in through the ruined ceiling. He catches the creature's volcanic stare as it lingers at the far end of the hallway, the quick and chilling flicker of movement that is its darting tongue. He senses somehow that it is a dark gesture, menacing and mocking, and then the snake disappears around the corner, in the direction of his old bedroom and his parents's room.

He shivers at the thought of it coiling in those places, beneath the beds and dressers, around the legs of his old desk where, as a boy, he'd worked diligently and with great patience to lay out his warring toy armies of doomed cowboys and Indian braves. Late nights, with such great rewards for his work each morning when

199

he awoke and he saw them lined up along the desk in their plentiful ranks, the hour late and his father's harsh rebukes ringing his ears and shaking the pictures on the walls.

His hand brushes a lampshade, crumbling it into its base with a dry groaning sound that startles him. Dust flies into his face, tickling his throat and nostrils. He sneezes, the loud jarring quality of the sound irritating him. He stands tense and alert for a moment, listening to the scratching of some unseen rodent inside the walls or beneath the floor. He turns and heads towards the kitchen, wincing at the groaning of the ancient floor beneath his boots.

He marches straight to the row of cupboards along one wall and, kneeling, opens the two central doors. There they are, exactly where he'd left them so many years ago, a stark obscenity filling the space completely. Massive and crudely sculpted, the pair of square cement blocks. Lying end to end they are maybe a metre long, their outer edges rough and notched. He stares at them, feeling a quiver along his spine at the sight of them. Revulsion in the form of acid rising inside his throat when he notes the dark stains showing through the film of dust. He reaches forward gingerly, steeling himself, and nudges the rigid brown leather straps protruding from the slabs. He runs a finger along the worn interior lining of leather drilled into its cement foundation, shivers. He envisions how it might feel to slip his hands inside those straps, past the wrist and midway up his forearms, and heft upward with all his strength, raising the blocks from their place for the first time in decades. To wear them ashamedly, and to wield them on the air, a pair of colossal cement fists. Gloves for hurting, the evilest of man-made tools he's ever laid eyes on.

The fists carry memories in their stained, notched hides. He sees his father lumbering in from behind him, ambushing his son in the barn where he'd happened on the strange objects lying among assorted tools on the worktable. His father's harsh words and quick hands, swatting him in the face and drawing blood from his lips. Offering no answer to his son's questions and protests, only further reprimands and blows from his hands.

Billy sees himself in another time, young and frail yet strong enough to have been able to carry the great cement weapons in his arms, hugged against his chest as if in some grotesque embrace. Staggering from the barn and up the porch and into the kitchen, stowing them inside the cupboard where they've rested for twenty years. From where no curious children exploring the derelict farmhouse throughout the years have dared to remove them despite their unique and bizarre appearance. Perhaps their weight and unwieldy size prevented such acts, or maybe only the black stains bled into their rocky skins.

He sees himself and shudders: young Billy, wheezing and trembling with the exertion it had taken, his youthful strength sapped, tears making paths through the dust on his cheeks. Shaking all over, while he recalled the screams of terror and pain he'd left behind him, in the barn, in the secret pit.

Without too much conscious deliberation, perhaps to avoid losing courage and changing his mind at the very last, Billy reaches quickly for the giant blocks. He hefts them from the cupboard with a groan caught between his teeth. They're very heavy. Only a very strong man could lift them without difficulty, hoist them onto the air like a child wearing a baseball glove.

He thinks of his father again, of his brawny arms and the damage they could do. He'd been a strong man. The strongest and most frightened man Billy had ever known.

Clenching his jaws with the effort, he grips the blocks by their ancient leather straps, one in each hand, and groans the floorboards tremendously on his way out of the skeletal farmhouse and into the fiery afternoon.

He stands in the burning patch of shade thrown by the barn towering over him. Its hulking form chills him despite the sweat beneath his arms, running trickling beneath his shirt. His proximity to the building unleashes all of his old fear. Its walls are ancient and worn, their once-red skin of paint long since flaked and fallen away. The mark of fire scorches the barn everywhere, a dull, deathly look. Dilapidated and dead, it is another husk amid this stretch of blistered corn country.

It catches his eye where it lies on its side a few feet from the barn door, amid a mess of splintered wood. He walks over and prods the battered, sloshing canister at his feet, kneels beside it and removes its cap: miraculously, the sharp stench of gasoline wafts to his nostrils; seemingly the sole lingering trace of moisture in this place of relentless heat and humidity. How long has it been here? Years? And why wasn't it salvaged? Certainly, teenagers have found the place throughout the years. Would they all say no to free fuel for their cars? Perhaps they would, at that. Billy understands how visitors would not want to take away any item as souvenir from the cursed place.

He listens and there is no wind. There are no scrabbling sounds of chickens in the wire pens, or squeal of piglets wading in mud or snuffling about in food troughs. No horses whinny nervously in the stifling air, swatting flies with their tails and snorting foam onto the dirt. Only the crackling of locusts scuttling through the fields and heat-ravaged crop-husks. Only the electric buzzing of cicadas in secret shelters among occasional trees and bush skeletons.

He is enveloped in the silence of the windless air and shudders. He remembers a great wind from the past, and its cacophony has not waned despite the chasm of years. The roar of fury and agony rides with it on the stifling air. With it in his thoughts, he crosses the yard and steps into the broken building before him.

The stable is a baking shelter, diminishing none of the afternoon's furious heat. Its roof, now partially collapsed, does little to hide him from the naked stare of the summer sun high above, just as it had done little to shelter him from the tenacious heat some twenty years before when it had been intact.

An afternoon of baking much like this one. He, a boy, deliciously naïve and eager for the adventuring which a summer day might yield while his father toiled in the fields and his mother hosed down over-heated cows in these stables. Abandoning his afternoon hour of schoolwork in answer to the adrenaline surge of excitement inside him. He and the crickets rustling through the corn. He and the invisible insect colonies and flying V squadrons of geese sailing in the August sky. A young boy amid his animal companions, discovering a secret that existed underneath his feet, where the volcanic sun's fierce light didn't reach. Beneath the soil, deep inside of the earth where he'd believed only ants marched and night crawler worms squirmed.

As if it had been there all the while. As if it had always been secreted there alongside him and the world he'd known his whole life, of his parents, the farm and its horses and cows and roosters. Among the fields and wood lots of his rural county home. There with him always. Maybe there in the earth from the beginning of time, or as long as evil deeds existed.

His father's role in the horror was the single act for which Billy had never forgiven him. He feels his presence there as he explores the old stables, the barn corners with their intricately-wrought webs and mammoth wolf spider architects. But then this is to be expected. This place of wood and dust has been a country of ghosts for many years now, and their presences all around him shiver Billy in his tentative steps.

His father's eyes had spoken that fateful afternoon even if his words provided no explanation to his young son at all. A litany of impassioned rationalization, but with eyes of awakening madness.

It is an abomination, son. The boys are only working off the strain of their hard lives. They are good men. Believers in God's will. Don't fret, son. Turn your eyes from it if you must, but do not hate the boys for this. It is an ungodly thing that they battle.

Billy fingers the crooked rusted teeth of the handsaw hanging from a nail on a blackened wooden beam. The minute motion stirs a large spider the colour of dust to cross nimbly around the corner of the pillar, disappearing on its opposite side. His eyes scan the upper reaches of the barn directly over his head, its high ceiling lost in deep shadows. Stray sunbeams slant in through slat cracks and pour through the gaping hole in the ceiling on the opposite side of the immense room, spotlighting newly stirred dust motes in their drifting, lazy movements. He sees that several bird nests dot the jagged rim of where the roof is gone entirely, victim to the fire which had climbed the long wooden timbres and collapsed them into the belly of the building itself. His booted toe nudges an old tin milk pail with its bottom full of webs and its tinny din echoes its rattling song into those invisible ceiling reaches. The noise freezes him in his place, eyes wide and staring into the shadows, ears straining in the newly descended silence, though he knows not what he's listening for. Nothing stirs, though, and he lets out the breath he wasn't aware he'd been holding in.

It is an abomination, son, his father whispers from the shadow-corners, shivering his son even twenty-plus years after the last moment they'd looked into each other's eyes before the moment of divine reckoning. Before the mist of choking black

203

smoke. Before the tumult and roar of fury and pain and a wind so savage he could only liken it to some Biblical force.

Billy steps gingerly around the overturned pail and tangle of thick, frayed ropes lying coiled and discarded on the floor beyond it. He makes certain to avoid brushing against the stout rusted chains lying limply across the gates of the stalls. Peering through the boards of each stall he passes, he finds large, blackened blocks that had once been hay bundles, massive objects congealed long ago from fire and smoke into these baleful, grotesque slabs. Like headstones, and the stalls, crypts of the dead. He spies destroyed food troughs there as well, splintered and ruined with time; occasional leather tethers and saddle gear; dark grey nuggets the size of stones which he knows are petrified manure piles; hills of pale bones amid the dirt and hay and crumbled walls; and the prevailing, lonely look of the compartments devoid of animal occupants.

Suddenly, an arrival of stagnant air into his nostrils, close and rank. Familiar and powerful. And he halts mid-step, unable to breathe.

He has made his way to the secret hole unintentionally. Having wished perhaps to prolong the inevitable in his explorations. Knowing, of course, that he would find it again, in its old secret place, because it was his true purpose for roaming this desolate farm country today. Its wooden double doors have long since crumbled with the ravages of time, leaving only scattered, splintered fragments in the dirt, and two long, scorched hinges jutting forlornly at odd angles. The long rectangle of black beckons Billy, chilling him simultaneously. It gapes towards him like the hideousness of an immense black mouth leading into the bowels of the earth. A wound in the ground and in the very fabric of this moment in which he sweats icy rivers beneath his shirt and trembles in his place, while ghosts speak compellingly to him from his haunted childhood.

Quaking at the threshold of the hole, his eyes follow the crude stone steps descending into darkness. He wavers there a moment, on the brink of it, the flashlight he retrieves from his back jeans pocket illuminating the narrow shaft and its distant bare floor of dirt and stones.

From the black mouth, his father's voice, like a spell luring him down.

Ungodly, the thing they battle.

204

Steeling himself, he descends into the maw, with the touch of ghost-flames licking at his heels with every faltering step.

The roar of the arena assailed him.

The riot of masculine shouts like declarations of war. Vindictive and violent. Vindicated by the power of the spectacle which they witnessed unfolding before them. Blood and thunder inside the bowels of the earth, hidden beneath ordinary crop fields and daylight.

Young Billy witnessed it, too, that strange day while the world baked outdoors and hid terrible wonders deep in its earth belly. A strange day of lesson-learning and astonishing discovery, when the young boy had first grasped a little of the huge mystery that was the world of which he was such an infinitesimal part. Like a mote of dust, he'd drifted by chance into a scene of impossibility, even for a boy with as vivid an imagination as his. It was also a day, as far as Billy was concerned, of learning about men and the black pits that they carried inside of themselves. The first day he'd truly seen his father.

Knees buckling with excitement and the fear of his father's fury if he discovered his meddlesome boy trespassing into the forbidden barn and its enticing secret hole in the floor, young Billy descended into the roar. Removing his dusty shoes for better stealth. Creeping barefoot and silently down the large stone steps, peering carefully beyond the perimeter of wavering light at their base. Whispering down and down in his seemingly endless journey to the basement floor. Padding unnoticed to one side of the staircase. Concealing himself there like another earth bug snug in the ground. Staring in amazement at the circle of men occupying the furthest corner of the cavernous room, their backs to him hidden behind the steps.

Torches trembled in wall sconces around the room, illuminating the men with their raised fists spiking into the air. Their shouts made him incredibly nervous, their violence was a thing that he'd never heard before, hadn't guessed that it could live inside the bodies of the farm hands who he thought he'd known. Quiet and melancholy, most of them, with eyes only for the hoes in their hands or the sky and promise of rain.

After a while of anxious spying, he glimpsed it.

Through the tangle of the men's arms and legs, and their heads jostling for clearer vantage. In the orange-lit corner space of the stuffy room, surrounded on three sides by the jeering, shouting on-lookers, backed against the basement wall. Harassed by one man in particular, it seemed, who darted within the ragged semi-circle, too, fists raised into the air and gripping or maybe sheathed within some large, misshapen objects. Brief snatches of some enormous living thing which held the throng's attention: an immensely long arm or leg, pale and taut, rippling with muscle; a rounded curve of shoulder and large tangle of hair tufts.

The loud, flat thud of some hard object striking flesh from within the crowd of men caused Billy to wince. The sound of blows landing, dull wallops without echo. Quick and meaty and awful. The constant clanking clatter of chain links being dragged across the dirt floor as some bound victim vied for purchase in the dust and rocks or swerved to avoid some vicious hand of punishment.

And then it reared up, induced in a moment of pain and fury to lash out madly, savagely. Fully three heads taller than any of the more than dozen men boxing it in, its enormous head scraping the rough ceiling and sending a rain of dirt cascading downwards. One massive shoulder grazing a wooden support beam, bending it askew and creating another storm of earth debris making clouds in the room. Its fur was a wan off-white colour, spotted with dark circles edged in a raw pink flesh hue. Its eyes were huge and moist-looking, obsidian ovals casting back the torchlight like visible reflections of its inner fury. Its bovine facial structure could not be denied no matter how Billy's senses reeled at the sight of it, resembling in most ways a massive cow-like animal. Hornless, a female, with flaring nostrils and giant jaws dripping blood beads like red rain in the glare of the torches. Standing somehow, inconceivably, on its hind legs, brandishing its hooves into curled fists like some alien pugilist or gladiator.

Billy watched awed as the beast delivered a quick blow with one of its legs, crushing the head of its antagonist and hurtling him through the air into the closely-gathered wall of his companions. A flurry of scrambling activity among the farmers and their arms, the dull clanking of chains across the bare floor where they pulled the creature's restraints tight. Billy saw the chains encircling the thing, the thick loops around its neck and

206

ankles and hooves, drawn rigid by its tormentors, holding it in place while a man stooped beside the fallen farmer at his feet. Standing a moment later with the enormous objects in his hands and lunging toward the animal: his father. The meaty crush of the objects into the thing's chest and skull as his father relentlessly delivered blows while his companions held the creature helplessly in place.

Billy saw her then, and his stomach lurched sickeningly at the sight: his mother, with different eyes, holding her treasured silver cross high into the oven air. The look of mania in her gaze as she shouted her voice hoarse like the men gathered there with her. Urging them onwards in their singular purpose. Basking in their meting out of punishment in the secret room.

The sound of meat being pummelled savagely, ceaselessly, filled the congested space. Young Billy crawling back into a corner, behind the staircase, among old wooden crates and discarded pieces of furniture, blanketed in shadows. Huddling into himself. Plugging his ears futilely with trembling fingers. The pained lowing of the thing's suffering filtering through and quivering him. And eventually Billy slipping away into an unconsciousness haunted by the terrible clamour he was unable to leave behind.

Awaking into silence and darkness, Billy thought for a moment that he was dead. He didn't know how many minutes passed of him scrambling frantically, blindly about the base of the stone staircase. Scraping his knees and palms where he scrabbled, stumbling and bruising his shins. Making his uncertain way up the steps, feeling the hammering frenzy of his heart when his hands pressed on the wooden door at their summit and met with unyielding resistance. Pushing with all his strength, but the wood holding firm while disturbed dust particles rained into his eyes. His breathing anguished and panicked in the inkiness, this sound of his terror frightening him all the more.

From the room below: a quick crackle of sound. A snort, a snuffling in the dark. Of some breathing thing.

He was alone with the thing. Alone in the world at that moment. His father and mother above, in the lit world of sunshine and farm animals and tractors and ploughs. They had left him behind unknowingly—foolish, curious, trespassing son. Tears flooded from his eyes, the taste of salt trickled in at the corners of his mouth.

From the black, a hoarse grunt. A deep and harsh throat-clearing sound. Young Billy's knees buckled at the noise, a high whimper escaping his lips, brief, terminated sharply in his fear at being heard by the thing. He listened intently, shuddered at the husky grunting which issued from below. He noted the threatening quality in the sound, felt it in his bladder like a hard and insistent pressure. The raspy growling came again amid a clanking of chains.

A moment of endless silence. Billy's breathing constricted painfully in his throat, his ears ringing in the huge quiet, his skull threatening to explode with pressure. Then, a mournful lowing from the blackness. The sound of pain and lament, like some awful funereal dirge. The sound of self-pity and agony in every timbre of the voice below. Billy became unravelled at the sound, unsettled in every way. He trembled within its cacophony reverberating in the large but confined space of the room. His eyes welled again, and he cupped a hand to his mouth as the miserable wailing rose and reached its terrible crescendo amid the tiny, whispery sound of dirt and small stones spraying from the ceiling and onto the floor and stairs.

The sudden, desperate urge to see coincided with the memory of the single renegade matchstick hidden in Billy's back jeans pocket; whispered surreptitiously from the kitchen table while father had left to answer the milkman's calling and his mother had her head in the cupboards over the sink, stacking newly cleaned dishes. Plucked from among its companions in the matchbook and slipped into his pocket, quickly and efficiently and with no little amount of fear throbbing Billy's temples, because father may have smoked like a chimney during winter but would hear nothing of his son fiddling with that sort of habit. The experts said it ruined the lungs, and young boys playing with fires only ever led to trouble besides.

Without thought, with only the pounding behind his chest and in his head, Billy padded down the staircase. Negotiating it easily with a hand ghosting the rock wall as he descended. His other hand holding the matchstick between tightly clenched fingers. Fear returning once he'd touched the dirt-floor bottom, and the snorting sounded from the dark once more.

208

Only this time closer.

The imaginary touch of spittle grazing his forearms where he stood trembling, stray droplets from the enormous snout of the chained thing. A swift rattle of chains, the dull sound of stout links dragging along the dirt, tapping against stones.

Steeling himself, Billy edged to the wall directly before the stairs, felt along its rough, uneven surface. Moments later, his fingers slipped onto the cool touch of the iron sconce. The small knocking noise of the wooden torch rattling its bracket as he clumsily mishandled it.

Silence boomed forth from the underground chamber. The silence of listening while his quivering fingers found the ashen end of the torch, still warm from being lighted before he'd lost consciousness. The gathering of his will, as Billy counted himself into the brave or foolhardy act of striking the matchstick against the wall and plunging it straight away into the blackened tip of the torch.

A moment later, torchlight flared the stone wall before him, dazzling his eyes. He shuddered, waiting anxiously for a great roaring to fill the room, or an imminent blow to crush him where he hovered, eyes clenched tightly, against the wall.

No sound or violence came. He turned apprehensively and looked into the secret room.

It was a pathetic ruin of a once awesome creature.

It cowered in the flickering orange glow. Huddled into itself, it was still massive. A mountain of sinewy flesh, it sat on the ground with its back against the rough wall. Its arms were long, corded with muscle despite their relaxed posture in the thing's lap. Its hands were hoof-like, but stouter than the hoofs of any animal he'd ever seen. He was awed at the agility and dexterity he glimpsed in those large digits, and at the power evident in its enormous, hunched shoulders and stout legs. A mane of thick white hair hung along the back of its neck, spilling across those shoulders. Its short coat of wan fur was filthy with dirt, the skin beneath a maze of old scars and fresh wounds, mottled everywhere with huge, dark bruises. Its gigantic skull was similarly battered, scabbed over and crusty, with grossly swollen jaws and eyes squinting through puffed-out mounds that glistened wetly. Its large udder stood out starkly between its thighs, bright pink and soft-looking, like some inflated dirigible.

It turned its black-water eyes on the boy and froze him where he stood. It came to life then and began to beat a savage din against its breast with one and then another pounding hoof-fist. The sound that it emitted was an awful mix of mewling and hoarse lowing. Each blow resounded loudly within the claustrophobic room, and young Billy was acutely aware of the force contained in the thing's curled fists, in its immense legs like tree trunks knotted with thick veins, underground blood streams pumping beneath its leathery skin as it kicked furiously at the dirt. With a grunting effort doing little to disguise its natural grace, the beast rose from its hunched position and towered over the shaking boy.

It was at that precise moment, while enshrouded within its great shadow, that young Billy realized he was looking at a goddess.

A true goddess, a strange and special thing, like some creature of myth come to life. A beautiful and remarkable being unlike any other living creature that the regular world of men and women and the weapons they fashioned could possibly contain. He knew in that instant that it would remain the most awesome sight he would ever lay his eyes on in his life.

Then: the knocking rattle of thick chains from the opposite side of the room, the squealing of straining door hinges, the echo of boots along the stone staircase, and the grotesque shadow thrown against the wavering torch-lit walls. And Billy's father, with malevolent and woeful eyes, was standing at the base of the stairs, hands sheathed in cement blocks that reached to his forearms. Lifting one monstrous fist on the air, beckoning his son forward.

The roar of the bovine thing filling up the chamber at the sight of him, dropping stones from the raw ceiling in a tapping rain all around, shaking its cross-hatched framework of wooden support boards. Billy scuttling beetle-like to his father's side, cowering beneath the shadow of him with his new hands.

His father looked down on him with strange and distant gaze, unreadable. Then he spoke.

I discovered the thing myself, son. Roaming the ranges. Stealing chickens and goats and grazing on farmers's crops all around. I found it in the night, covered in moonlight, a demon in the corn rows. Eating entire ears whole, stalk and all. Watching me with its black eyes. The look of evil, son, watched me that night.

210

Billy shivered at his father's story voice. Detached-sounding, and different from his regular coarse speech, yet matching his miles-away gaze.

It loped off, disappearing in the fields. I waited for it every night with my rifle and ropes and, eventually, it returned. Months later, on a full moon night. A Devil's night. Some say that a farmer's cow birthed it. A freak of nature, a freak among God's creatures that should have been put out of its misery. A skull filled with lead, son. That farmer made the foolhardy mistake of not shooting it that night, if that story is to be believed. But I believe something different. Most people here do, son. This is a small county, and a good place, with good people. That thing was birthed somewhere else altogether. That abomination comes from Below.

Here his father pointed toward the earth with one gigantic fist. Seeing his son's wide-eyed appraisal of the block, he nodded. *Beautiful, aren't they?* He hefted it up closer to Billy's face and the boy shrank away from it. *You're ready to know about them now, son. I made them myself. After I saw it murder a man. And that man was my own father, ten years ago. Waiting up with me night after night. Waiting for it to return the way we knew it would, and then finally standing up to it bravely.* He paused a moment, rubbing the enormous fists together with a sharp scraping sound. Then, *The Devil's hooves must be combated with strong weapons, son. Your mother wears her cross well, and I fight with my hands. Like my father fought before me.*

Billy shuddered at the awful import of his father's words. He saw the distant glimmer in his eyes, like a man only barely present in the room with him while his thoughts drifted in far places. A madman's eyes, burning weirdly in the torch glare. And when he swept the room with that gaze, Billy shook all the more, noting the hateful look which fell upon the captive cow goddess, chained pitifully among her refuse of feces and blood, displaced from her rightful place overlooking the small doings of men and kept in a tomb of torment ten years long.

Billy couldn't suppress the sudden flood of tears at his father's words. The way he hurled them spitefully at the stricken bovine deity huddled pitifully into herself, shrinking from the sight of the rock fists gesturing in her direction.

We feed it, son. We feed it hog slop and chicken bones and rotten vegetables, and it takes them all. It longs to eat our children, but we deny its awful hunger. We feed it and keep it alive so that the Devil knows to keep his hauntings away from our town. This is a place of good people, who fight back against the meanness and evil in the world. We have a warning chained up and ready for any comer who wishes to haunt us again.

His father approached the cow goddess warily. Billy, watching the two confront one another, realized the small size of his father in relation to the thing before which he stood. His father was a large man, tall and lean and muscular, and yet the deity towered over him. Billy noted also the new attitude in her posture, a resigned kind of fearlessness as she gathered herself for this next fight in her seemingly endless existence of combat with cruel and hateful madmen. She flared her nostrils, set her giant hooves into the dirt, curling and uncurling her hoof-fists threateningly, the guttural growl she emitted raising the hair along Billy's arms and at the nape of his neck.

Billy's father wavered at this bristling fury, glowering in the thing's wild eyes. He faltered, took one and then another step backwards. Billy wondered at the great fear he glimpsed in his father's eyes in that instant, something which he'd never seen there before. Muttering under his breath, like a curse of his own vacillating courage, *The Devil is a dangerous evil, son. We must make certain to be cautious in our dealings with Him. In numbers we must find our strength. We cannot be lured, deceived, into the Devil's hands.*

With great reverence, his father removed the fists and placed them, side by side, on the earth. He squeezed Billy's shoulder roughly, said, *The boys are in the fields. We will be gathered here shortly. Wait here, son. The time has come for you to see and understand. The Devil has finally tried to lure you into His clutches, too. You're old enough to understand now. We will protect you and make you understand.*

And he turned and ascended the stairs towards the light above, leaving Billy alone with the goddess once again. He turned to her, saw her tense posture loosen, her muscles relax. He sensed her instinctive trust of him and watched her helplessly. A moment later she was sunk once more to the dirt floor, cradling her head in her hoof-hands. A low, quiet burbling drifted to Billy's ears.

212

He ached for the goddess. He wished earnestly to be able to take her pain away and bury it in the earth. His ears rang with the song of her mournful crying. He felt it gather somewhere inside him and tug away there. An unrelenting pressure, a powerful force threatening to unravel him in that moment.

The deity raised her watery eyes to him then, and a moment later dropped her gaze to the giant cement blocks resting on the ground at his feet. She turned to him again, and then again looked to the fists, and she began another percussive beating of her hooves upon her chest. A dull sound, of bone beating upon meat. Forlorn and hopeless. Pitiful and horrendous. A sound to break a boy's heart.

Acting on instinct, Billy lunged for the cement fists.

It took all of his strength, and though his arms grew numb with the effort he succeeded in dragging the weapons along the floor and toward the shackled cow goddess. Unlike her violent eruption at the sight of Billy's father, though, she only raised her head curiously at the boy's slow, effortful approach. Her eyes widened in excitement or wonder when she saw the boy edge one enormous stone slab and then its companion close to where she lay huddled against the wall.

Eventually, a light of understanding shone in her black-pool eyes. She reached her hoof-hands to one of the blocks. She hefted it high on the air and brought it down heavily onto the loop of chain trapping her neck to the wall. She repeated the action several times, sweat lathering her bruised face as she went about her difficult work. Soon enough, the loop lay severed at her feet. Again, she repeated her efforts on the chains connecting her ankles to the wall brackets, and then on one of the two chains shackling her wrists. Billy trembled as the goddess freed herself of her remaining bond, ripping the chain from the wall bracket with a single violent wrenching of her two powerful arms. He cowered as she loomed over him hugely, brandishing the ends of the chains in her hoof-fists. He wet himself in his sudden terror as the savage strength of the goddess returned into her massive frame.

But she only lingered there over him, snuffling and snorting on the air, smelling her new scent of freedom, offering occasional raps of her hooves against her breast while her black eyes watched him fixedly. Waiting, even as Billy gathered his courage and rose to his feet, and scrambled toward the staircase, thinking

213

madly about the good or bad thing he had done. When he reached the base of the stairs, he dared to cast a wide-eyed look to the goddess and was startled by the immense dull wallops of first one and then the other of the two cement fists crashing into the dirt near to him. His eyes locked tremblingly with the deity's. She bowed her massive head to him in several short motions, accompanied with a swinging gesture of her hooves toward the discarded blocks.

Billy understood, and took hold of the giant cement fists by their worn leather straps and, as quickly and quietly as he was able, began dragging them up the stone staircase.

Behind him, he noticed the heavy silence in the secret room: no more cracking of iron fetters. No exerted gruntings of the goddess freeing herself from her bonds. And the sad, percussive dirge of minutes earlier had ceased its beating, too.

Silence had descended in the room like the anxious calm before a great storm, as the freed goddess awaited her final bout in the arena.

Young Billy emerged from his hiding-place in the kitchen cupboard, shaking with revulsion after sharing the claustrophobic space with the cement fists. He'd dragged them in after himself and lain hiding in the darkness with them pressed against him, waiting for whatever was going to happen to happen. He only crawled out when the screaming began, and he was certain that the great fight had begun.

Through the open window, he could see farm animals rushing panicked and headlong from the barn, whinnying and squealing and lowing. The screech of splintering wooden beams carried loudly across the yard, and the sizzling sputter of wood on fire. And the screams of men in rage and in pain. And the roar of a goddess bellowing in all of her long-held fury as she fought back against her captors, unchained in her combat for the first time. Free.

And, over all, a newly risen wind roaring furiously, tenaciously.

Billy would never learn exactly how the great fire began. Perhaps during the violence of the fray in the secret chamber, a torch was jostled from its sconce and set fire to a wooden support beam. Perhaps the battle had simply made its way up into the

214

hold of the barn itself, where hay bales were plentiful and a dropped torch spread quickly into unquenchable, uncontainable fire. Or maybe some divine power witnessed the battle from on high and let loose one or more jagged arms of redemptive lightning to strike at the barn, scorching to the ground the terrible prison it had represented for one wondrous and unearthly creature. The great wind had surely helped to spread its fury and had perhaps aided in the collapse of the roof as well. Whether any men survived the great conflagration, Billy didn't know. Nor did he ever hear whispered stories of strange and incredible animals glimpsed in the fields or roaming the ranges on star-lit nights.

He would never know the truth behind the incident, or what happened in its aftermath, but would take turns considering each scenario many times during the coming years. And though he spent many years away from the county of his youth—drifting and learning about the world and growing finally into a man—in his dreams he often saw her, bathed in a nimbus of supernal light, striding boldly in the night, cutting swathes through cornfields as though those fields belonged to her and no other.

He stands at the base of the stone staircase, looking out into the rubble of wooden boards and dirt mounds. The cement fists lie on the step beside him.

Peering closer, he spotlights a section of dirt floor with his flashlight beam. He nudges a wan white object with his toe, turning it out of its half-buried position in the dirt. He's uncovered a bone, and judges from its size that it had belonged to a man. Somewhere below this dirt, he knows, lies a small silver cross which belonged to his mother. Someday, people will return to this land, when expansion drives its way through the rural county. Police will be called, and they will come here and disinter the buried, though never will they solve the mystery buried here.

He reaches behind him, hefts the stone fists by their worn leather straps. He holds them swinging heavily in his hands a moment, looking out into the rubble. Then, together, he rocks them backwards and forwards in his hands, his swings gaining great momentum and breadth, and he lets go and they soar and drop with a hushed thud into the dirt of the secret room. He

215

exhales heavily at the labour and with relief at the grisly drama completed at last. A final burial, of a shameful piece of the past.

Billy sees his father coloured in torchlight, raising high fists of his own sculpting. He sees his father's misguided blows inside a room like an arena or grave below the earth, and he cries for him, and for what transpired those many years ago.

He turns away, gathers his flashlight, and ascends the stairs.

He crosses quickly through the barn, and marches without hesitation to the gasoline tank he'd discovered in the yard earlier. Uncapping it, he returns to the barn, making a meticulous circuit of its far rubble-strewn corners while emptying the tank. Making sure to douse the ancient hay bale lumps and wooden walls, the wooden stall gates and the hay-littered floor. He marvels at the amount of gasoline it contains, an anomalous wellspring in the evaporative temperature of this desolate county, considering again the seemingly preordained nature of his having found it among these ruins.

When the tank is emptied, he drops it onto the ground. He stares around him, gathering himself. He wishes silently for the barn spiders's and mice's forgiveness, for he is not one to harm any living creature, great or small. And he strikes a match and lets it fall into the gas-soaked hay.

Billy steps into the dusty yard and takes some time to admire the fury of the burning barn.

Then, he turns away from the flames and walks in the direction of his car. The tears lingering in his eyes make a wash of the sky, and everywhere he looks is a fiery grandeur.

DYING DAYS OF TREASURE SPIDERS EVERYWHERE

For my last two years of high school, I lived in the poverty-filled projects that proliferate like a contagion in the depths of Windsor's west-side ghetto. Townhouses filled with cockroaches and mice, and a low-income surrounding neighborhood where residents, unable to afford air conditioning, would spend the summer months draped like sweaty clothes all over the identical tiny concrete porches that jutted from the house fronts like calcified, mocking tongues, smoking cigarettes and drinking beer and dozing. Children would play in the communal central park, shooting hoops at the rusty mesh-less basketball net or climbing the paint-stripped jungle gym.

This is the setting for this story. The boy in it might have been me, if I'd been around this age while living here. (As I said, I was a little older, a teenager at the time). This was where my certainty about one thing was confirmed: there was indeed magic in the world, if you had the eyes to find it among the everyday squalor and sadness. My mother passed away the year after I wrote this story, but there is a scene in which a character recollects a terrible moment inside a hospital that was a strangely prescient description of my own experiences in a hospital setting in the year ahead. I get a tight feeling in my chest whenever I look at that passage.

The story was originally published in Structo Magazine, *in an issue that featured a cover story and interview with the great Richard Adams. It was a huge honour for me to have my fiction appear in an issue with Mr. Adams, because I've always been a huge fan of his books,* Watership Down, Shardik, *and* The Girl in a Swing *being my favourites. There's also an audio recording of this story, published in the online journal* Birkensnake. *One of the* Structo *editors, Euan Monaghan, read the story, and he did a fantastic job.*

Keep your eyes open. Peer through the cracks in the grime and rust: the world is full of treasure.

The projects burned before them: children hung like listless simians from the rusted skeleton of the decrepit jungle gym in the communal park; the black and white trash tenants of the townhouses haunted their porches languorously, drinking bottled beer and smoking cigarettes while watching the street with despondent eyes; the occasional car rattled past trailing exhaust and adding a chemical stink to the already pungent reek of late-staying mayflies that stippled the house fronts and streets and sidewalks.

The familiar scene filled the boy's chest with a thick kind of anxiety. He inhaled the awful air hungrily but felt as if something blocked its passage inside him.

His grandfather's voice was husky, as if from disuse, but the boy knew that this was only the natural sound of his old-man voice, the sound of sand granules crunching deep down in the moist darkness of his throat. "How is your collection of spiders these torrid days of August, my boy? They're well, I imagine? They're used to the sultry weather, I'd say." His grandfather always sounded as if he were reciting poetry from books, which always calmed the boy when he was upset about something in the same way that reading books made him feel better, too.

Now, though, the boy only nodded mechanically. Eager to obey his grandfather's wishes, though feeling physically depleted and as though any movement was beyond his capabilities just then, he leaned from the porch overlooking the dirt garden abutting the left side of the cement. He retrieved the large, sun-warmed glass marmalade jar embedded in the soil and held it aloft between his small hands for the old man to see.

Squinting into the sun-flashing jar, his grandfather examined the creatures within. "Oh my, what colourful friends you keep, my boy. Vivid! Bright as flowers! What is *his* name?" and he cocked a trembling crooked finger toward the immense yellow banana spider owning the upper portion of the jar, its prodigious leg-span covering completely the breadth of the lid's underside.

"Sunny," the boy answered. "Like the *sun* sunny."

"Ah," and his grandfather was nodding, the hint of a smile playing at the corners of his mouth. "A fitting name, surely. He is a splendid specimen, that's clear. Just look at him! The size of him! His grace hanging in his jar sky! His pride, evident in how he overlooks his glass kingdom." And, turning to his grandson, he added, "You, my boy, are a daring child, to brave such a king and transplant him to this kingdom of your own making. I can't imagine where you found friends such as these, in what high tree-places you had to climb, and into what dense, green brambles and bushes you had to crawl and search."

The boy, with some effort, succeeded in smiling for his grandfather. The old man, seated beside him with a glass of lemonade in his liver-spotted hand, saw clearly the strained nature suffusing the gesture, as well as his grandson's overall discomfiture. He sipped from his lemonade, savouring the tang of its aftertaste on his lips, and murmured, "Remember this lesson, son, and for your sake remember it well: there will never be days like these again, no matter their good or bad ingredients. Live them like there's no tomorrow and you'll be making the most of what you have."

Of course, the boy, despite trying hard to take his grandfather's wisdoms to heart (as he sought to take all of his advices to heart) was unable for his huge grief, and only stood nodding his head falsely where he stood before him like a quietly respectful knight before his king. The porch was coloured with sunset's burnt orange fire, though a murky tinge hung in the air too, as if heralding the arrival of inclement weather. The boy toed the concrete at the foot of his grandfather's tattered lawn chair, making sure to avoid crushing the lone ant winding its way across the burning concrete square.

"I know, I know, my boy," the old man murmured, wincing in the glare and scrutinizing the boy. "It's a harsh lesson, in its way, and disheartening. But take heart in this, son: know that the lesson is also filled with huge joy, once you've grown to fully appreciate it, that is."

The boy cradled the jar in his arms. He examined each of his spiders carefully. The two small specimens skittering among the loose grass blades along the glass bottom like revellers among fallen confetti; a larger arachnid perched on the tip of the narrow oak branch, his body black with bright emerald markings; its twin hiding among the grass beneath, its design the same but its colour scheme one of black paired with blood-red; and, of course, the massive banana spider suspended over the rest like a ruler overseeing his subjects.

After a time, the boy, frowning, said, "They must be too hot in there. I put holes in the lid but still I bet it's too hot in there for them."

The old man said nothing, only continued watching his grandson carefully.

The boy removed the jar's lid and placed the container delicately on its side in the stubby lawn grass. He and the old man watched as the spiders within made their collective way cautiously to the jar's rim and convened briefly on the grass before its mouth as if jointly plotting their next move before making off in all directions, the sun finding their brilliant skins like reflections from a collection of marbles dropped into the grass.

"The day thanks you, my boy," the boy's grandfather said, a proud glimmer in his eyes. "You've enriched its fabric plentifully."

A moment passed in silence between them. The old man sipped his lemonade and offered his glass to the boy, who only shook his head and stared into the street or sky while pacing the small expanse of the concrete patio. Eventually, he sat down upon the brick stoop protruding beneath the front door, not so much relishing (as he usually relished) the sun scalding his bare arms and legs but bearing its relentless touch. He wanted to shun this too-bright smoggy world and retreat indoors, to the safe blue shadows of his curtained bedroom, where he might immerse himself in comic books and the colourful tales they held. But he remained with his grandfather, because this is what they did each night after supper while the boy's parents cleaned up inside, and to abandon the old man felt wrong, and in a world where incredibly wrongful things happened too often the thought of committing another such deed made the boy feel sick. So, he shared the hot silence with his grandfather, following the determined progress of red and black ants wending their ways across the cement or among the grass, laden with leaf bits like backpackers on the march. He sent flashes of lambent sunlight reflecting from the glass watch-face on his wrist out across the street, to dance erratic patterns along the siding of the townhouses there. He picked with a cautious hand at the scabs owning each of his knees, relishing the stinging pain he awoke with his probing fingers. Finally, he sought interesting and wondrous pictures among the cumulus, but clouds were few and far between in the pure blue sky, and those that did float there were wispy and small and difficult to imagine with, which only left the boy with his own troubled reflections. The sun hung relentlessly overhead but its light seemed dimmed to the boy's eyes, a waning circle, as if partially obscured by clouds or swallowed by an eclipse, or else simply sinking in the near-dusk hour towards its temporary death beneath the horizon.

The boy and his grandfather sat and sat in the baking silence.

A nearly imperceptible cracking disturbed the gargantuan stillness. The distant song of cicadas buzzing from the trees ceased, as if grown hushed at the small but great noise, too. The jungle gym children ceased their chattering in the hazy distance, possibly likewise awed by the startling, somehow unearthly disturbance. The boy and his grandfather, startled from their pensive somnolence, followed the direction of the noise, looking to the concrete floor of the porch. Directly between them, a small fissure had appeared, and peeking forth from the aperture was a narrow green stalk, as of a flower. Peering closer they saw its bulbous tip, where fragile petals grew upwards and came together into a teardrop-shaped bud holding ensconced within its embrace some hidden beauty—its flower, of course—with the potential to brighten the milky-aired, dusking day.

"Perhaps the world of old is at last come to reclaim itself from us," said the old man, sounding especially wise to the boy. "Perhaps our little green friend is repayment for your gift to the

221

day." And here he nodded out towards the lawn before them, with its hidden arachnid jewels, and concluded, "Perhaps there's a lesson in this, too."

The boy looked to his grandfather, awed, and again to the fragile looking but mighty green stalk. He stared at it for a minute, imagining or actually perceiving its subtle perfume of peaches on the muggy air.

He returned his gaze to his grandfather when the old man grew suddenly rigid in his chair. He'd left the lemonade glass lifted midway to his waiting mouth, his eyes straining into the distance. A moment passed and he lowered the glass to his bony knee and exhaled deeply, sounding to the boy's ears as if he'd just returned from a very long and wearying journey. Then, his voice hushed, "Look, son. Over there and up there. In the trees in the park, past the projects shimmering in the haze of the east. There's something there. Something strange and special. I can sense it but I can no longer see it. That's your special gift, while you have your good and young age, and eyes less clouded than mine. For now, for these lucky days of your huge fortune, you're able to see it among those sun-fired branches, while some of us can only feel it. Look, look."

The boy looked. He stood from the stoop and drifted to the edge of the patio, the tips of his grass-stained sneakers hanging past its concrete lip and making him feel distantly as if he was a sailor, a captain of a ship and standing in its prow while searching the water horizon stretching endlessly before him. He cocked his head one side to another, squinting in the burnt air. He sought to conjure something wondrous and happy among the sun-limned trees but saw only his grandmother as he'd last seen her: heaped like a collection of bones in the hospital bed underneath the stark sterile lights, more a skeleton than the plump woman she'd been, the roses vanished from her cheeks, gaunt and deflated from their former roundness like shrivelled apples gone bad; her bald head gleaming alarmingly through her remaining wisps of snowy hair; cloudy yellow eyes staring at the ceiling, utterly vacant of the person once living there; while the transparent plastic nebuliser mask suctioned to her mouth and nose added a fantastically horrific aspect to the scene, as if she were the unwitting subject in some mad surgeon's experiment gone terribly, terribly awry. It had been weeks since that haunting and endless morning in the cemetery—the sad look of everyone

222

dressed in black, making their faces appear more pale than he knew them to be; the charged air, as if the day itself was in mourning like everyone gathered among the headstones beneath the milky sky; the dull, hollow clamour of dirt clods being shovelled overtop the casket embedded inside the gaping earth following him into his dreams that night and most subsequent nights, too, a terrible percussion that awakened him with heart thundering and breathing ragged and tears never very far behind the well of his wakening eyes.

"I know, son," the grandfather said, crumpling further into his raggedy chair and soothing the boy a little merely with his reliable ability to read his murky thoughts. "I know it, too: it's hard. A very hard thing, to truly, truly bury those things passed away from us."

And he wept, long, agonized sobs that made the boy fidget and scan the house fronts on the opposite side of the streets with increased determination, as if he were seeking some very particular thing among the blank tarnished facades only to find dejected-looking project denizens like himself, unmoving in the meagre shade of their porches, sleepy from the heat or weary from the strange, indefinable darkness hidden among the deceiving bright air.

The old man stabbed the sky with his quivering finger. "I feel it now, son, more than ever. Oh, it's a strong feeling, and one worth investigating for a boy with the eyes for it." Following the gesture, heart thumping, the boy looked from the house fronts and with renewed determination to the trees of the park abutting the nearby parking lot.

Something took form from the oven air. A vague shape coalesced among the emerald leaves and tiny crab apples like sapphires decorating the trees like a holiday celebration of the summer. He watched it materialize, details embellishing themselves and growing more pronounced with each passing second that he held it within his steadfast gaze.

The boy smiled. He laughed a moment later, laughter free and hearty, the laughter his grandfather had once owned before he'd grown old and been confined to creaking thrones unfit to bear his bent but regal frame. The boy looked avidly now among the leaves of the trees. He turned his attention then with an earnest enthusiasm into the air over the trees. He looked where the dropping sun—bright and blazing now and freed suddenly from its stifling eclipse—limned the crumbling projects in fire.

And he saw.

He *saw*.

"Do you see?" his grandfather asked the boy, eagerness infusing his voice, desperate and brimming with a hopeful joy. "Do you see her? You do, don't you? You do."

The boy nodded. His grandfather smiled and wiped at the tears suddenly returned in his eyes. "Good, my boy," he murmured. "Very, very good. The young colt hasn't grown into a new skin and run away on me just yet." And his large, weathered hand patted a gentle melody of camaraderie and thanks on his grandson's back.

From the lawn before them a jewel flashed, and then another and then another: brilliant yellow and emerald lights reflecting the sun's final moments of that day as it sank and sank beyond the houses, freed monarchs reclaiming their kingdom among the grass and trees. In the distance, laughter sounded, free and joyous and drifting like a song on the humid air. A car horn barked somewhere like a cry of celebration or fanfare documenting the scene.

The boy continued nodding, seeing all of these things, examining the world as he knew it—faltering, tenuous, yet filled with the potential for secret worlds gathering their strength beneath the streets and of familiar floating faces among the summer leaves—through his stinging, clearing eyes.

WE ARE ALL LIGHTLESS INSIDE

My mother was diagnosed with terminal cancer just before Christmas, 2011. A few months later, she was gone. This story came out of my hatred of the disease that took her and my desire to see it manifested in front of me so that I could do to it exactly what it deserves. Looking back on it, it's sort of a mix of SF, horror, Weird, pulp, medieval romance, and maybe something else, though I'm not sure what. In any case, I was ecstatic when editor Trevor Denyer accepted the story for the first issue of the re-launched Midnight Street Magazine.

My mom, incidentally, was a wonderful woman, who always supported and encouraged my creative endeavours whatever form they took. Case in point: all throughout my childhood, I was notorious for missing school in both elementary and high school. The supposed reason was that I was ill. This was rarely the case. Actually, I simply preferred staying at home where my debilitating social anxiety was kept at bay. My mom, allowing me the freedom to play hooky almost whenever I needed, made two stipulations about which she was very adamant: I had to keep up with all the schoolwork I missed (no problem), and as long as I stayed home from school I was obligated to do something creative: read a book, write a story, draw a comic book, make something.

I read and wrote a lot of stories while my classmates were slogging through spelling dictation and math quizzes. Thanks mom—you were the very best mom a troubled

225

little boy could have had, and that rarest of people who did, in fact, have a light inside of them.

I: THE NEW CRUSADES

The containment tanks were full again.

This knowledge—dark and festering in his thoughts—hounded him even in the midst of his passion. It transformed it, made it violent and efficient, a survival gesture getting him from one moment (tense, lustful) to the promise of another (transient peace). He fucked her briefly and without gentleness. Afterwards, lying there together in the gloom and quiet disturbed by the whirring ceiling fan, she commented on it.

"What was that, Phil? Are you... okay?"

Sybil's words hung on the dank air of his compartment and seemed immediately swept away by the ceiling fan. She felt foolish, like she'd exposed some girlish, juvenile weakness to him. As if she'd revealed that she wasn't true technician material like she was supposed to be.

"I'm a summoner," Philip said by way of explanation, eyes as lost in grimness as she'd ever seen them. And it was all he had to say.

She understood, and forgave him, and stroked his scar-mottled chest and gleaming silver mechanical arm until he closed his eyes and turned away from her, feigning sleep that he'd known all along wouldn't come that night.

Lieutenant Philip Jackman glowered at the readout in the computer screen, focusing past the excited chatter of the techs at their stations echoing throughout the Cure Room's control centre; past the deep humming of energy in the cables plugged into his temples, their channels open and linked to the sub-e plane.

The containment tanks were indeed full again—fit to burst, in fact—which meant the purging was mandatory and needed to be done immediately. He was looking forward to the looming violence of the great eradication but was disheartened by the resiliency of the many Diseases they'd captured to spawn more of their children elsewhere in the world, and at such a relentlessly quick pace. And, of course, this meant that their time studying this batch was at an end.

"The statistics have been good, sir," Sybil said, trying to infuse her words with enthusiasm. "They show an undeniable decrease of certain—"

"Shut up, Tech Elling," he said, remaining turned away from her, staring at the monitor, though he was grateful as he said it. "Let's flush them and make room for the next batch for study. Dee-Dee's infiltrating the barrier wall and invading thousands of people this very minute, so let's get to it."

Sybil Elling was a seasoned technician, having worked as part of Jackman's team for nearly seven years. She was used to his brusque manner and efficient methods. Most summoners were like this, and forgiving them for their callousness and social shortcomings went with the territory. Their duties were hard: being the conduits for the magic that lured the enemy into the boundary zone that borders on our own plane, while the scientists located and fixed their coordinates; and then together, working to pull them into the containment tanks from the sub-ethereal realm.

This, in layman's terms, was the basic system by which the Group operated. But no system was flawless, of course, and even when the Group gained ground or found some new small success, always it was forced to take steps back as the enemy retaliated; and retaliate it always did, because the enemy was a formidable one, having existed since as far back as humankind walked the Earth. Yes, theirs was a stressful line of work.

"Yes, sir," Elling said and punched in the commands, feeling as she did the ruthless excitement all Group personnel felt when taking part in a cleansing. The Group had lost many of its members to Dee-Dee, but the losses of the world at large dwarfed their own personal hurts because Disease, they well knew, ate its fill everywhere. In short, they were doing some good, however small in the greater scheme of things, and being a part of the effort made each of them proud.

All around them the voice of the labyrinthine underground station awoke. A great and deep humming that seemed to rise up and up from the heart of the Earth. A sound of power gathering.

As always, it filled them—summoners, scientists, techs, and everyone else involved on any level in the Group's efforts—with an emotion as close to comfort as they could know in their line of work. The Group, made up of roughly equal numbers of summoners and scientists, didn't always function smoothly. Its internal politics—the theologically-constructed framework of the former and the empirical-minded approach of the latter—proved difficult barriers for some to see past, though their common goal kept its members united. And witnessing the execution of a batch of entities inevitably brought them together in an unspoken comradeship.

"Flush has begun, sir," Elling confirmed.

Lieutenant Jackman said nothing. He watched with burning intensity the radiation bombardment taking place behind the observation room glass. The Cure Room was filled to brimming and as each Disease was burned to oblivion more were jettisoned into the room via vacuum tubes from the adjacent containment tanks. The sound of Dee-Dee's agony was unlike the sound of men in pain. No creature on Earth sounded like it, and though the high-frequency keening and wailing went on unabated for hours, every Group member in attendance—the lab techs operating the atomic armaments and containment tank-Cure Room transport; the assistants; the military personnel of all ranks, from heavily suited and armed grunts awaiting emergency combat duties to generals overseeing this latest purging operation; to the summoners and scientists who'd entered and navigated the sub-ether and captured this latest crop of Diseases—each and every one of them felt no pity at the annihilation taking place at their hands, only a savage satisfaction that kept their attention fixed firmly on the spectacle of death.

Jackman watched the carnage closely, waiting for its conclusion and the commencement of the next pull, when he would push himself to physical, mental, spiritual exhaustion harnessing all the power he had in luring the next batch of entities into the tanks.

II: FOR MOTHERLIGHT

"I'm almost twenty years your senior and you look shittier these days than I do."

Dougherty had a way about him that Jackman couldn't help liking. He was direct. He was honest. He talked like a soldier despite his fanatical dedication to the science behind their efforts. He meant well and, looking up at the glass he held out to him, Jackman was grateful to call him a friend.

"Thanks, old man," he said, taking the glass and knocking it back in one gulp. It burned going down. He shook his head. "Maybe I am getting old—whiskey used to go down smooth as O.J."

They were in one of the rec rooms, empty but for themselves, Jackman seated at a small card table and Dougherty leaning against the bar. The ancient jukebox stood silent in the corner, its screen of song selections from by-gone eras dark. Overhead, the sodium light from the long rectangular bulbs flickered nervously.

Dougherty chuckled. "You're not old. You just look old. Haggard and thin, and those bags under your eyes add some years to the picture." He swallowed his own drink, then refilled their glasses. "Anything you care to discuss?" he said. "Recent thoughts? Concerns? Your health? Your love life?"

Jackman cast a suspicious eye at him. "No," he said. "I'm okay." He flexed the fingers of his mechanical hand thoughtfully, forcing down the urge to wince at the pain he felt, and had been noticing more and more often, where steel met his body in a tangle of raw nerve endings and wires. Amputations were common among summoners—even the most superficial of wounds from Dee-Dee usually resulted in a deep-rooted onset of disease—but the sensation of ghost-limbs never went away no matter how long one had been mechanized. "I'm okay," he repeated, mostly in an effort to convince himself rather than his friend.

"You're not," Dougherty said. "You're not and we both know it."

"It's nothing," said Jackman, swallowing his whiskey.

"It's the job," said Dougherty. "It's a job with a weight to it unlike other jobs. Sometimes we all need a break from it, or we run the risk of getting broken by it." He pointed to the ceiling, said, "That last pull was a huge one. Go up top and get some sun. A week's vacation will do wonders. It must be months since you've been above-ground."

"You know I can't do that."

"I know you won't do that."

The Group worked in secrecy for fear that the arcane powers they harnessed in their work—both ancient magic and experimental science—would awaken too much Old World fear as people recollected the War; though knowledge of the Group had leaked so that over the years a kind of mass awareness of it existed throughout the world, though not everyone acknowledged it, treating it like an urban myth or the stuff of fantastic conspiracy theory rather than a reality. To most, the Group was a spectral bogeyman so shadowed in government-hushed secrecy that it instilled as much fear and paranoia as support for its efforts. And to most Group members, going above-ground became increasingly difficult the longer they did what they did. Most veteran members had forsaken the world above completely, living solely for the pursuit of their work. Those who'd been with the Group since its inception twenty years before seemed to have forgotten that any other world might exist at all.

They left their glasses on the card table and passed the bottle back and forth, drinking silently. The muted sound of footsteps came through the wall, grew louder, and then faded: a troop of soldiers marching past en route to a different part of the underground facility.

Jackman said, "How's your research going?" He was sure he wouldn't like the answer.

"The same," Dougherty said. "The fucking same. The Barrier is the barrier. Even if we could penetrate the wall, we simply couldn't exist on the other side. And, of course, we still have no way of knowing what it's really like there, or how great the population of Dee-Dee might be."

"It's Hell," Jackman said. "Whatever your belief system, whatever your interpretation of the crisis and war, we have common ground in this case: Hell is on the other side."

Dougherty said, "I try to see it in more tangible terms. Otherwise, what hope I have for our success dims quickly."

Jackman understood all too well. "Maybe someday you'll let yourself be guided by the light."

230

Dougherty cocked an eyebrow, smiling wryly. "What light is that, Phil? God's light? You forget who you're talking to."

Jackman lowered his eyes, feeling exposed and weak with talk like this; and thinking, of course, of his mother.

Dougherty, guessing what his friend meant, and with a pained expression suffusing his features, said, "We are all lightless inside, Phil. Maybe that's why Dee-Dee feels so at home inside of us." He'd said it gently, but the truth of the words carried their own heaviness. Talk of these things couldn't be softened.

The two men held each other's tragic gazes a moment, feeling caught in the tangling fibres of the old debate and quandary. Much of the Group's iconography—the perennial cross and related heraldry citing its religious foundation, particularly its prominent use of the pine tree symbolizing a simultaneous acceptance of death and rebirth into eternal life after—was actively rejected by the scientists, who tolerated it insofar as it didn't affect their work in any way. Belief, though, was another matter entirely.

They continued passing the bottle back and forth. Dougherty took a pull from it and, eyeing the digital wall clock over the door, sighed. "Duty calls."

Jackman eyed him, forcing a smile. "You're one to talk, Don—maybe you need some top-time, stat. Or maybe you just need to hear the word of the good Lord."

Dougherty's cynical smile looked gloomy in the dimly-lit rec room. "I'm a better drinker than you are. My escape's in the lordly bottle, and the bottle, my friend, is never very far away." He placed it on the bar top and said, "My gift to you. With my blessing."

He left Jackman in the silent rec room.

Jackman remained sitting there, nursing his drink and considering Dougherty and his place in the Group. As head of the Science Research Division, he held a great deal of sway. Despite his personal motivations—his wife, a fellow physicist, had been killed by a manifestation leak, when the escaped Dee-Dee in question, a minor tumour, had torn through a weakened portion of the transport tubing between the Summoning Room and the Cure Room and entered her laboratory via a ventilation shaft. She'd been devoured instantly. Her assistant Janet, a pretty Japanese girl barely out of her teens, was also killed before the soldiers arrived and exterminated the Disease. What was good for the Group was too often un-good for its individual members. Before the incident, Dougherty had been a dedicated scientist; afterwards he'd become a man possessed. His newfound fanaticism found no foothold in religious doctrine, despite science's limited ability to define the nature of Dee-Dee and the sub-ethereal realm from which it came. Jackman found himself wondering more and more whether there might be something to the secular perspective, because what kind of a God could allow—or possibly have created—a world in which such monstrous invasions happened, and so often. And were occurring more and more every day passing.

Statistically, they were still losing the struggle but gaining infinitesimal ground every day. And this, of course, was reason to continue. It was a war without end, for always the enemy was reborn somewhere in the world—in some dark corner of a person's molecular structure, some hereditary trace of the enemy lingering on at the cellular level, its wicked, demonic seed churning in the toxic winds of the ever more polluted world—but still the Group had made progress. Still the Group struggled onward in the face of it, confronting its own dark heart every day.

Of course, many members were personally invested in the Group's efforts. Some had lost loved ones to sickness; others were sick themselves; while still others worked from fear of their own mortality living in the world they did, where pollutants ruined the land, sea, and air. Living was difficult, but dying could be so much worse. The war went on.

Musings like these left a bad taste in one's mouth, and Jackman felt the oppressive weight of things wrap around him once more, suffocating him.

The incoming communication startled him, but the voice in the wall speaker made everything better:

"Sir."

It was Sybil, unmistakeable despite the static and fuzz muddling her voice inside the intercom. Sybil, short and dark-haired and curvy and tough, but for her give-away eyes, where her ghosts lived and could be seen as clearly as an animal on display in a zoo habitat. "Our team summoned a Sickness this morning, during a routine sweep of the sub-ether. We... We found it. Finally, we found it, and in the peripheral zone, not even in too deep. We have it here, locked up in C.R. It's... Sir, this

Dee..." Her excitement made her stumble over her words, and Tech Elling never stumbled over her words.

"Tell me," said Jackman, sensing the momentousness in the static-fuzzed noise of the connection.

Forgetting protocol, she addressed him informally. "Phil, it's the largest and most sentient manifestation yet. We've captured an extremely high A-level form of *Cancer*. And it's *tagged*, sir. This is it. *It's the same Dee-Dee from six years ago.*"

Silence, only the fuzz and crackle in the intercom between them.

Elling went on, excited and nervous. "It's grown since last time. Like I said, it's by far the biggest manifestation we've wrangled, ever. It's a fucking beast, and for this type especially it's by far the largest and most virile strain—"

"Show me." His voice was distant. He felt excited but unprepared for a success like this. In his line of work, every day was a day of confrontations, but this confrontation would be altogether different.

"We're ready when you are, sir," she said.

Philip clicked off, staring at the intercom, the glass forgotten in his hand.

He was in the elevator descending to the observation deck before he allowed himself to exhale the breath he'd been holding inside his lungs like the final hope of a drowning man.

The room became hushed when he entered. A silence of respect and anticipation.

He saw that the shielding that covered the observation room window had been kept closed. He stared at it for a long time, envisioning the manifestation within the Cure Room beyond. A minute passed. He said, "Give it everything—*everything*—we've got, but nice and slow. And then get me my suit and weapons. Old World weapons only. Clear my schedule. I want forever with it."

Elling turned to him, wide-eyed. "Only Old World? Sir, maybe you should look at that thing—"

"I remember it well, and you heard me, *technician*." He always emphasized the rank of those under him when he was in it deep and good and had no time to dilly-dally with bullshit. She made no more objections, knowing the futility of it. She'd seen his eyes and the fury there. This battle was personal on a level that made her feel uncomfortable witnessing. But, of course, she'd stand by his side and be ready if he needed her. Everyone gathered there in the observation room would stand with him. "Yes, sir," she said through the icy lump constricting her throat and keyed the bombardment start-up sequence into the console before her.

"And leave the window closed until I'm inside with it," he said. He wanted to meet it eye to eye with no barrier between them. That would be the first and last time it saw its vanquisher and the avenger of humankind into whose clutches it had fallen after its many years of hunting and rampaging through the world.

The internal clamour of the station's armaments going online sounded inside the walls, that familiar sound of near comfort and great exultation. Several minutes later the room was ready. A thundering and groaning echoed from the walls: the thing trapped within the Cure Room trying to free itself. They could all sense the malignant intelligence behind the window barrier, could feel its immense loathing and endless hunger.

"We're good to go, sir," Elling said.

Philip hadn't looked away from the observation window's protective steel barrier. He'd waited so long to have it here, captured, his to do with as he pleased, as it deserved. "Good," he said, addressing Elling and Meyer, the assistant containment operator. "Blast it slowly. Start it at a low level and then slowly bring it up. Nice and slowly and make it last as long as possible. Soak it. Make it roast. I want to torture it. I want to torture it for days before I get to it myself."

Meyer, ashen-faced, nodded in understanding. "Of course, sir."

Dougherty, who'd heard the news and had slipped inside to stand to the rear of the room, cleared his throat. "Phil, I have to interject here and—"

"You have to shut your mouth, Don," Jackman said. Passing by him, though, he pressed a hand to his old friend's arm and squeezed it. He said, quieter, though everyone heard, "You understand, Don. I have to do this."

Dougherty nodded, his worn face wearing a pained expression. This mission was personal. It had to be, of course. Everyone in the room knew this. This mission was a vendetta. This mission was less a mission than a simple, greater, and

234

overarching duty Jackman felt both to the line of his family, and to the greater species of humanity. It was a duty to which he was committed and from which nothing could sway him: he was going to depose the greatest rebellion against humanity that had ever risen from the muck and mire of Hell.

III: ST. GEORGE AND THE DRAGON

He stood before the scoop-tube in full combat gear.

The Group had decided in its early days that a suit inspired by traditional garb would be most appropriate in close-quarters encounters, something that signified long-standing nobility and honour, something that carried history. The Group had adopted a hierarchy modeled largely after the modern military machine but infused with a code of chivalry and honour dating back to the medieval period, and they had modelled their standard combat suit after twelfth century knight's armour, though of course adhering to the highest standards of modern craftsmanship, durability, and functionality. Each suit came equipped with both advanced armaments of machine gun, high-powered rifle, and revolver, as well as traditional period weapons: sword, knife, mace, and shield. Soldiers carried electric lances as well, a hybrid of traditional weaponry with modern technology, the tips of the weapons emitting electrical charges of extreme magnitude. Grunts and summoners—and the occasional scientists who chose to face a manifestation in person—always opted for the former and only used traditional weaponry as an emergency measure, at which point they were usually rescued from whatever predicament they found themselves in by their comrades watching the encounter from the observation rooms. Mostly, the Old World arms were ceremonial and ornamental in nature, a nod to the chivalric tradition of knighthood.

Elling had accompanied him without an objection from anyone present in the observation room. Their secret relationship was no secret and everyone turned a blind eye. In her best attempt at a formal farewell, she said, "Good luck, sir. Give it Hell."

Uncharacteristically for him (it surprised even himself), Jackman said, "Thanks, Sybil. Don't worry about me. I'll be back." And his gloved hand found the cross emblazoned on the chest of his suit of armour, touching it, drawing strength and comfort from it.

Elling was about to say what she'd really wanted to say, but just then the doors whispered open. He lowered his visor and stepped inside without looking at her again. The doors closed and he was lifted via the scoop-tube to a wide atrium. Beyond this, in a straight line, stretched an expansive hall. As he walked down it, the deep roars of the captured Dee shuddered the walls around him, muffling the echoes of his booted steps in the great space. Its keening was unnervingly loud, and even through the earplugs he wore his eardrums ached.

He arrived at the doors of the Cure Room. These doors— immense, double-gated doors, reinforced with a dozen layers of tantalum and steel—began creaking open a moment later. He was tightly suited but wondered how long he had before the radiation they'd been pouring into the thing for the past 24 hours seeped its way through and into his own body. He should be quick about this, but if he was then he wouldn't be able to relish his time with Dee-Dee.

Jackman stepped into the Cure Room. He stood beholding the manifestation.

The Disease was titanic. It was a mountain towering over him. The Cure Room was immense, a veritable underground cavern of reinforced steel, but it barely contained the thing. Long, black tendrils shivered and spasmed along the floor. Millions of immense tumours enveloped its body like glistening, hairy meteors. Its million sightless eyes glared at him; the million blackened teeth of its countless slavering mouths jutting in every direction gnashed hungrily on the scorched air; its stink of ancient death fought to pierce his suit and strangulate him. It was in great pain, its hulking form blistered and bloated with radiation, but still it lived and would try to kill him, the same way it had stalked and killed so many millions before him. Eyeing the thing now, Jackman understood how very capable of killing him it still was.

This was the great and terrible rebellion against the human being, conjured from the collective pain of everyone whom it had touched in some way over the thousands of years, pulled from its infernal sub-ethereal realm and manifested in the Cure Room with him.

236

"I've got you right where I want you, you wicked piece of shit. Now it's you and me, demon. Just you and me."

It droned with a tenacious horrid vitality, despite the atomic attack it had suffered; black effluvium dripped from its haphazard orifices; its wet appendages shuddered in excitement as he stepped fully away from the door's threshold and into the room with it. Its death-stink was like a tangible pressure against his airtight-sealed steel suit, a thick aura of putrescent soup through which he waded.

He felt the eyes of the many Group members watching from the windows of the observation rooms that lined the upper portion of the circular chamber's walls but didn't make eye contact with any of them.

He kept his attention focused on the thing in the room, bloated and black and deadly. He unsheathed the broadsword from the scabbard at his hip, hefted it high in his gloved hand, fingers relishing the feel of the tape-wound wooden handle, his eyes savouring the sight of the besieged Disease. He held his shield protectively along his left side, knowing that a direct strike from the thing would tear the shield to splinters.

But even as he raised the gleaming sword for the first blow and let it arc downwards with all the strength and fury and grief in his heart—even then, he felt the defeat in the gesture, the utter hopelessness when he remembered the placid green gaze he would never ever feel touching him again. His mother had been a dichotomy: the gentlest and strongest woman he'd ever known. She was the only person to have loved him without reservation, no matter how foolish and terrible a man he'd been over the years. She'd been a forgiving woman, and a pure soul, and she'd deserved so much more than her final, fruitless weeks-long battle with the merciless murderer that had blackened her pancreas and liver and devoured her from the inside out, swallowing the light that had burned in her like in no other person he'd ever known.

All the more horrific for Jackman was that the onset of her sickness was almost certainly related to the Group's unsuccessful attempt to destroy the manifestation in question once they'd managed to lure it from the sub-ether; wounding it, torturing it with radiation before it managed to destroy the Cure Room and escape back through a tear into the sub-e from which it had been dragged, leaving in its wake a mass contagion—an epidemic of

237

disease—that razed the population of the Group's headquarters in the months following; all those seed-children spawned of itself left like a black curse to scourge the people who'd dared try to vanquish it.

Jackman's mother, Molly Rose Jackman, retired from her career as a professor of biology, had been a volunteer with the Group, and had been present in the headquarters at the time of the catastrophe. She'd returned home that night not feeling like herself, and by the following morning was displaying symptoms associated with advanced stage cancer: extreme weight loss, fatigue, loss of appetite, vomiting, diarrhea, and severe, debilitating abdominal pain. She was admitted for tests that day, which revealed a mass profusion of tumours that had devastated her pancreas and surrounding organs. Radiation treatments proved futile and she was dead within weeks, another random casualty of Dee-Dee, like so many before and after her but like no other, of course, to Jackman.

And so, Jackman took heart in knowing that every blow he landed was a few million lives prolonged and, more than this, that the pain and death he was delivering the thing was honouring and avenging something dear and precious that deserved to be honoured in this way. He took great satisfaction from the braying, keening wails of agony that emanated from the obscenity with each cut and stab he made. Black ichor and thick blood sprayed everywhere. Slabs of rotting tumour-flesh fell about his booted feet. He drove his sword—which he'd long ago christened Molly Rose—into the thing again and again and again and again and again. His sword-arm ached and grew numb and he attacked it still. The thing's tendrils and appendages flailed about, battering at his shield, cracking it asunder, and sending bolts of white pain shooting into his body where mechanical arm met flesh.

"I'm a summoner and I've summoned you, demon," he seethed. "Let Christ guide my sword."

He was seeing his mother's golden smile, her cherub's face, her eyes of kindness and unconditional love; and with the strength these images gave him, he spat at the vile blackness locked in the room with him and raised the gore-drenched sword high on the air.

● ● ●

Lieutenant Philip Jackman died in the Cure Room that day.

The manifestation of Cancer suffered tremendously at his hands but, in the end, its counterattacks got the best of him. His artificial arm seized up after the thing delivered a blow that shattered the shield he'd been wearing, and a moment later one of its mouths had champed down on the limb and ripped it from his body. The blood loss had been severe, and the trauma from the wound, as well as the several other bites and stings it delivered him while he was lying helpless had wrecked his body beyond repair. The radiation exposure as a result of his ruptured suit would have proven fatal besides. He'd lived and he'd died the only way he'd wanted to: a summoner, fighting for the memory of one dear to him, and for the good of all.

His comrades had, of course, tried to intervene, grunts and officers alike bursting into the Cure Room and beating off the Cancer with electric lances and dragging him to the emergency surgery, his armour ragged, his limbs broken and disfigured. They'd then proceeded to blast the trapped manifestation into nothingness with every last bit of atomic power they had at their disposal. It was the longest concentrated attack on any Disease entity pulled into the Cure Room, a necessity both because of the thing's tremendous size as well as the avenging nature of the barrage. The satisfaction this gave the Group was ruined, of course, both by Jackman's death and by the appearances of new Cancers throughout the world, reports of which sprang up immediately in the wake of the encounter. It was almost as if the collective Disease consciousness had been informed of the death of one of its supreme entities, and gathered its strength in a vengeful counterassault, the severity of which the Group had never before witnessed.

The Devil had planted many seeds, and they were bearing black fruit in many places.

IV: THE NEW FESTERING

The Secret War went on.

Small victories for the Group continued mounting in the years following Lieutenant Jackman's death and were met with renewed strains of Disease throughout the globe. It was the same perpetual stalemate and eternal conflict they'd known from the beginning, marked with recurring peaks of hopefulness and valleys of despair.

In the Summoning Room, recently appointed summoner Lieutenant Sybil Elling cast a worried glance at her partner manning the console beside her. She felt the unsettling sensation of her ghost-limb stirring anxiously at what she saw on-screen. She reflexively touched the leg, thinking as she so often did of Jackman and his scarred, beautiful body, absently massaging the steel limb as if it hadn't been lost to the Cancer conjured in this very room over one year before.

She thought frequently of that fateful bite from one of its million carrion-stinking mouths when Dee-Dee had escaped the Cure Room and punctured the wall to attack her in a pain-maddened fury that nearly cost her much more than her left leg; its crooked teeth puncturing the leg clean through with a splintering like dry wood, before her men rushed to her side, fighting the thing off and dragging her to the surgery. Her leg, infected and blackened with disease cells, had, of course, been impossible to save, and she'd been lucky to return from the encounter with her life. It had been just another Cancer demon vanquished. Who knew how many more were being born that very moment?

She narrowed her eyes, seeing beyond these memories to the current moment. "What is it?" She glanced to Meyer, his face pinched and pale in the blue-lit room, and could tell he was close to unravelling. She'd seen this same look in the eyes of many other Group personnel—the things they saw every day did this, of course, and the ghosts they lived with, too—but rarely had she seen Meyer succumb to it, hardened veteran that he was. The swirling cloud of smoke and gas filling the chamber behind the observation glass was dissipating slowly, revealing the amorphous shape of the summoned Disease.

"I don't know, sir. I've never seen anything pulled through from the sub-e like this before. My readings don't... they make no sense, sir. No sense at all. What is it?" He turned to cast his wide, haunted eyes on her.

Elling examined the screens. She turned and looked through the observation window amid the clearing gases, seeing the horror within take shape. It was so different from the hulking black and grey Disease manifestations, with their nauseating, amorphous hair- and teeth-sprouting bodies, their sucking and biting mouths and stingers. This entity's body was long and narrow like a giant stalk of corn, and it was the sickly yellow of vomit. It trailed millions of hideous filaments from the head and bottom of its body like vast, spasmodically shuddering nerve endings. An unsettling, high-frequency buzzing, like the sound of electricity in a shorted circuit, was being emitted from somewhere within it, clearly discernible through the thick glass.

The gases continued to evaporate until the manifestation was revealed in all its horror. An icy stabbing erupted in Elling's chest. Her stomach lurched with revulsion, loathing. She said distantly, "I haven't seen this before either."

But she had. Her younger sister, Penelope, had been committed to Higher Hopes, an acute-level Toronto psychiatric facility, while Sybil had still been in grad school. This had been ten years earlier, but Sybil remembered it clearly. Penelope had remained a resident there ever since, her condition worsening considerably each year passing, so that her level of functionality was now mostly catatonic but marked with regular, un-triggered episodes of extreme violent behaviour. *Paranoid schizophrenia, with symptoms of dissociative identity disorder, in which one alter, or personality, is markedly more violent and aggressive than the patient's other two personalities*. This had been the team of doctors's unequivocal and unanimous diagnosis, a particularly severe and incurable disease of the mind.

The look in her sister's eyes the last time Sybil left her at Higher Hopes—that distinctly otherworldly combination of vapidity on the cusp of violence, unsettlingly dead with something savage and inhuman lurking just beneath the tranquil surface—this expression she would never forget. And she unmistakeably saw it in the dozen immense, black, wet orbs watching her hungrily through the observation window's glass.

Suddenly, a new enemy had entered the conflict, and the war had become more personal than ever.

"Meyer," she said. "Dump it into the Cure Room and soak it good. Then get me my suit and sword."

ELOPERS TO SIRIUS

A brother and sister finding sanctuary in each other, because they have no one else in the world to whom to turn for help against the evil that terrorizes their shared life.

And then they find a saviour.

It makes sense to me that so many people find haven in something as extreme as fringe religious fanaticism. It makes sense that some people pledge devotion to suicide cults's promises and systems of salvation, something that most outside observers see as the darkest, most twisted places.

Maybe they get pushed. Maybe they get pushed hard.

For the sake of those who endure profound suffering in order to reach their Paradise, I hope the visions of the prophets they devote themselves to are true. Amen.

If there exists a paradise
it lies in the dust of his doorstep,
where we have
our eternal abode.

—*Hunting the Hunter*
Kamal-od-Din Khajoo Kermani

Do I wish my time with the Sirius Group
had ended differently? Yes, I do. I've seen
the sky give birth, and yes, I do.

—Dennis Murray
from his book *Away from Night and Into
Light: The Ascension of the Sirius Group*

The day was golden-aired. Its light poured into the cabin
through the open windows and doors, touching them both where
they stood close to one another in the baking stillness. The
pungent scent of vegetation hung on the sultry air: the distant
jungle's perfume, a thick and intoxicating brew of banana and
elephant grass and wildflowers that seemed to have seeped into
the bamboo walls surrounding them, the light silk bedding, their
clothes, their pores, so that even their breath exited as an exotic
zephyr as they spoke in hushed voices, heads bowed together.

"Are you scared?" His voice was electric with his own fear and
excitement at the imminence of the great event looming before
them. He was kneading her small shoulders gently by way of
reassurance, smiling fondly at her doe eyes and anxious
expression.

She turned to the window and the brilliant day it held. She
smiled. "Not really. Not *really*. Not as long as I'm with you. As
long as we're together..."

"Always. We've always been, we'll always be."

"I know. I know."

He saw her fear plainly. But he sensed her looming joy, could
envision it changing her, if she only allowed herself to accept it,
embellishing her features with a new brightness, the kind he
hadn't seen there for too long. He smiled broadly. He whispered
it: "We're here. Finally, we *made it here*. We're one step from
Paradise."

Speaking of it aloud—something which they hadn't done
since waking hours before, as if consciously avoiding discussions
of the momentousness of the day—now urged excited and
relieved laughter from them both.

Together, they went to the cabin's long window. The field
beyond, cropped low, was exuberantly lush, the yellow
Heliconias dotting the landscape glowing like gold in the bright

afternoon light. The perimeter was lined with wooden cabins like their own, small and efficiently sparse inside, creating a great enclosed field between themselves. In the centre of the space stood a flagpole, its flag hanging limply in the windless air, though the symbol adorning it remained partially visible: the silver hexagon containing a pair of overlapping gold circles like some enigmatic Venn diagram. In the heat-hazed distance they saw the forest shimmering: the solid wall of palm trees, with the shadows of occasional monkeys traveling among their verdant reaches like manic acrobats; the bright parrots like fire among the leaves calling from the tropical depths and creating through their wild song the illusion of being transplanted to another world.

It was difficult to believe, he reflected, but true nonetheless: only days before they'd been merely another couple of teenagers living a downtrodden white trash townhouse life in a drab, forgettable little Southwestern Ontario town where few good things happened and badness abounded, where the days dragged one into the next with no end to their monotony and despair in sight. The black oaks and spruces of that former world filled only with everyday sparrows and crows. No trees sang as vibrantly in the place they came from. No gold fire burned in the fields they'd known all their lives.

Awed by the might of the island music, humbled by the unbridled wildness and beauty offered up by this mysterious land floating in the middle of the Pacific Ocean, he was inspired to murmur, dazed-sounding, "It's like a dream. Every minute we're here, the sense of it only gets stronger. Here, it's... It's almost like we're already there. You know? It's like we've already found Paradise. What more can there be?"

The thought—the mystery it hinted at—caused him to smile, warm in the sun-filled window. She sighed a luxurious sigh. She squeezed his hand. Watching the bright day, she said, "You know, now that we're here, I... It's like only now, after we got away from them... After we finally got away from him, it's like I realize only now how tired I am. I must have been so tired all the time, but just didn't know it. I feel like since we got here, I've finally been catching up on the sleep I missed the past million years."

He smiled sympathetically. He ran a hand across her sun-warm cheek. "Me, too. I was so tired, too. Maybe we were just too busy making up reasons to stay away from the house, and always hiding in all our hideout-places, and trying to not think about everything... Maybe we were scared of getting tired, because if you're awake and ready to run then bad things might not get you..." He could speak freely of these things in this place: the realization filled him with joy.

"Kiss me," she whispered tremulously.

Smiling, he leaned to her.

Sun-warmed lips on lips: it conjured their first kiss. It was an easy and painless recollection in the burning midday, safe with miles and miles and miles from the old world and the wickedness of those days.

Home alone, a brother and sister freed. Best friends from the beginning, warding off the dual attention and neglect of the demons hounding their shared home life. Friends crossing an inconsequential boundary to celebrate an escape in one another, all while coloured in late day sunlight slanting in through his bedroom window's shutters while their parents were away on a rare daytrip together. All of the years's worth of restraint let unbound on that special day, as if perhaps the secret burden they shared at last offered them compelling enough reason to forge forward as they both desired, in an effort to leave behind these very secrets through their new union. Lips to lips and arms wound about each other, timidly at first but then more forcefully as the old clock mounted on the wall over the bed continued its staggeringly loud ticking, as if measuring the seconds passing with a more vigorous movement of its hands, as if serving as reminder that they must, as always, make the very most of their rare moments of peace. Entwined in the room's centre and moving eventually into the walk-in closet to close themselves within its safe, congested darkness. The musty smell of the closet enclosing them, of leather and cardboard boxes and old clothing. Slipping out of their summer clothes—his faded denim shorts and sky-blue t-shirt, her white and orange summer dress—and once more into one another's sweaty embrace. Even then, in the madness of the moment, they'd both understood it for what it was: their first true step towards the purest happiness they'd known and could ever know.

They leaned from each other now. Their lingering kiss burned their mouths. The molten-aired cabin made them sleepy. The scent of exotic wildflowers hung heavily in the room. Feeling

246

romantic in the dream-like atmosphere, he reached a hand through the open window and retrieved a bright white lily from its vine crawling across the exterior cabin wall. He curled the lily's stem behind her ear so that the flower rested amid her hair at the side of her head.

Remembering something he'd read long ago, he said, "People in ancient times said that lilies were really stars that fell to Earth."

"That's so... That's perfect," she said. She watched him a moment without words, then, "You're the only family I've ever needed," a teardrop appearing in the corner of her eye and rolling down her cheek. She'd been saying maudlin things like this to him since they'd arrived here, flown in with a dozen or so others days before. The island seemed to summon the words from her, as if its elements of sultry climate and burning white-sanded beaches and dense jungle and endless rolling waters and delicious remoteness—a seeming lifetime of distance from the world they'd left—came together like an uncanny spell that allowed her to revel in emotions she'd never been able to fully relinquish herself to.

He held her tightly. He kissed her earlobe. He nuzzled her sun-burning cheek. She sighed and felt it anew: like a wave, the surge of happiness, the likes of which she'd known for the first time in their secret stolen bedroom moment years before.

A moment passed. They continued to hold each other, unmoving at first where they stood but slowly bending to the lazy but charged rhythm of the day and moving a slow side-to-side dance that creaked the wooden floorboards.

"We're here," he whispered in her ear. "We made it."

As they danced, the memory arrived for them both, like a snippet of dream, hazy and luxurious: the day the path, unexpected, had been revealed to them.

A deceiving day for its same-old beginnings: seeking sanctuary in the wilds of fields beyond their townhouse neighbourhood. Wandering among the tall grass and cattails waving in the November wind, shivering in their coats and toques. A chance or fateful encounter on the balding trail cutting a circuitous design through the tangle of woods: a young man, a teenager not much younger than themselves, stopping them where he stood staring with a look of expectation through the patchy ceiling of tree branches into the cloudy sky. Something in the boy's face—a strain in his eyes, maybe, some furtive thing like a shadow seeking to hide a secret knowledge or bleakness but revealing it instead to those accustomed to such shadows—gave them cause to stop and hear him out, to accept what he offered them: a pamphlet from the bag of pamphlets he carried.

They unfolded it, examining the words within while he inexpertly explained its contents, stumbling over his words in his haste, jumbling his meaning and having to start again before skipping along to his next imprecisely made point. Maybe it was the earnestness with which he spoke, or the desperation in his eyes. Something in the boy they recognized and sympathized with. Thanking him for the pamphlet, and promising to consider the information it contained, they'd left the boy on the trail, sky watching earnestly again.

They'd spent the next hour or so sitting along the break wall overlooking the grey river, reading the pamphlet together, again and again.

At some point, it became understood between them that the words on its pages made sense, and that the gift of the pamphlet was a special one, and that finally, after all the years and all of the pain, there was suddenly a path opened before them: an escape from the clutches of their shared life.

She'd turned to him, excitement brimming in her hushed voice: "Sirius... I don't... I can't say why exactly, but... but it makes sense. It *feels* right... Doesn't it? *Doesn't* it?"

He turned to his sister. The smile he smiled told her that, as ever, they were caught in this adventure together.

His voice came softly, stirring her from her drowsy reveries. "Everyone's arriving now. It's time to go."

She followed his gaze through the window. From everywhere they'd appeared, making the unreality of the moment that much more profound: the lines of people drifting from the cabins identical to theirs, from the abutting forest paths, from the white-sanded beach like an immense strip of ivory in the distance, individually and in pairs and in families of three and four and more, and all convening in the great field. They looked like ants, arranged in their neat lines, she thought. Seeing them, her heart

248

beat faster. She smiled, prepared to enter the dream-picture stirring outdoors.

They crossed to the threshold of the open door. The pulse of the forest had risen into the air like a song of celebration. Looking into the bright day—sky cloud-free, blue and pure from east to west—they sensed the stars beyond trembling in the rapture of the moment, and in anticipation of what lied ahead.

A small wooden platform had been erected to one side of the field, flanked by a pair of battered speakers mounted high in steel brackets. A lectern stood in its centre, looking regal despite its rather flimsy construction; its imperial quality stemming from the narrow blue satin curtain draped the length of the podium's front, adorned with the emblem familiar to all those gathered before it: the pair of gold circles filling a large, silver-limned hexagon. Resting upon the podium was a small silver microphone which flashed in the sunlight.

A great hush descended upon the people when the man appeared in the distance behind the platform. He emerged from one of the small cabins, crossed the lawn, and mounted the steps, moving to a place before the lectern. His white hair belied his ruddy, youthful features, his eager blue eyes surveying them all. His smile was broad, benevolent. A moment of palpable anticipation passed as the man cleared his throat into the microphone, testing the reach of his voice across the fields. A brief surge of feedback split the air, and then silence. He looked over the gathered with gentle eyes, smiling eyes, joyous eyes. Michael Boreal had arrived, and in the great hush of his arrival even the distant parrots and monkeys seemed to have ceased their banter to listen to his words.

The kind-eyed man spoke. "Greetings, brothers and sisters, and thank you for being here with me on this day." His voice was sweet and soft but sure. A yet more profound hush descended upon the fields. Those gathered there—the man's family of four hundred-plus children—hung on his every word, breath, fluctuation of emotion, and subtlety of gesture: the creasing of the crow's-feet limning his eyes as he smiled benevolently upon them; the gentle but assured way with which his fingers held the microphone stand, as if he were long accustomed to addressing multitudes through this technological medium, a performer and

249

man of prestige and renown but without the pomp and arrogance of men in similar roles. Strands of his snow-white hair gusted in the ocean-salt wind, revealing a high forehead and a somehow aristocratic quality.

"Fifteen years ago, nearly to the very day, a vision materialized before me. In the midst of my old life. A life immoral and without law. And then this vision. Giving me purpose. Giving to me a reason to find you, all of you, in time. To find you and bring all of us together as I have. Here, to this place of wild splendours, unsullied by those who inhabit the places from which we all come. This vision showed me this place. This vision showed me the treasures of this place, treasures beyond its wild beauty, its serenity away from the old, noisy world we've known. Here, on this island, lies the gate to the better place. Here, today, on this island, is the day that this gate will open—for a brief piece of time only—and allow the chosen and privileged admittance to that place."

Here the man paused, gathering his breath, his strength, as if summoning the courage and faith of his children and disciples listening raptly before him. And,

"Sirius. Twins beautiful and powerful and glowing in the eastern quadrant, like a beacon for the souls of the good, the benevolent, the marked, the privileged. I know not *why* Sirius, but only that Sirius it is. I am but a humble vessel through which a greater voice speaks. I direct you, my beloved and chosen ones, by these unseen means, and it is a voice to which I have listened for fifteen long years, and a voice which has likewise spoken to you. My children. My friends. My family. My *family*."

At this, several cries rang out. A portly woman, weeping with joyful abandon, raised her arms skywards, tears streaming from her eyes. Towards the front of the crowd, a middle-aged man, grey-haired and square-chinned and rapturous, likewise lifted his hands high on the steaming air and proclaimed his love for the father-speaker. "I love you, father!" he cried, weeping, his voice cracking in his ecstasy while his adulation was echoed emphatically by those around him.

The man's new-father smiled. He clutched his hand to his breast, showing the man below, and everyone there, that this love was reciprocated. He went on, his voice faltering for the strength of his emotions.

"We each of us wear a mark. It may rest upon the physical shell of some of us, but it most certainly lies in the deepest parts of each of us. It binds us, this mark. Throughout our lives we have loathed it, feared it, wept over its eternal presence haunting us like the most tenacious of ghosts. But it is also that which has brought us together at this end, and this beginning. You all have your reasons for being here today. For exiting your life before and ridding yourselves of its shackles, and traveling from afar to arrive here, in this great moment now. Let us leave it behind. All of it. The rage. The pain. The despair. The hatred. The pain. The filth. The vulgarity. The pain. The *pain*. The pain of all kinds and sizes and agonies. The memories of these things. Let us leave those dark places forever to rot in their own cesspool of turmoil and unrest. Because now—finally—everything will be made right. All that is behind us now. We were alone, and are now together, and will have no end, together. Today, everything is okay. Today, the pain dies."

Those gathered in the field echoed their new-father's smile of freedom, relief, ecstasy. They each of them remembered the day not so long past when they had set out on their great odyssey, leaving behind their old life and traveling far from their corner of the globe so that they could be here in the sunlight of a different place: a middle-aged wife weary of the years of her vindictive husband's relentless attentions; another woman, older and frailer, tired of wearing bruises and burns from the boyfriend with whom she shared her woeful existence; a boy grown into the semblance of a man but hiding merely the boy within the shell, petrified in his place of youth by the ghost of his uncle's secret meetings with him; another man dying inside, too, but his progressive killer the cancer blackening his pancreas and gnawing the life from him each day passing, hoping, this man, to beat his untimely murderer; a former adolescent prostitute grown old and angry and no longer able to live and work in the world and to lay his trust in any of its chameleon-coloured people; a veteran of too many tours of duty whose napalm-fired jungle-dreams have banished sleep and peace from his life; and a brother and sister, thinking back to the day that felt a lifetime ago, when they were children and not the people who now, for the first time, felt like adults when they'd stood huddled close together at the bus station, tickets clutched in hands, hearts storming inside of them, the air March-dark with rain misting the

251

street and chilling them in their jackets as they embarked on a desperate trek across the world, and then further by far than this meagre opening leg of the journey.

A storm cloud stirred suddenly in Michael Boreal's eyes. Suspicion and mounting fury grew there. Grabbing the microphone from its stand, he stalked the small wooden platform like a hunting animal. His burning eyes scoured the crowd ravenously. The people stirred. His children grew frightened, looking about themselves for the cause of their new-father's unrest. They had never seen the man in such a state. They'd believed they were on the cusp of Paradise, and now this transformation, as if everything they dreamed for was set to fall to ruins. They continued to eye each other. They murmured nervously. When the father-speaker's voice came again, all fell right away into a listening silence.

"I sense... I sense a... There is an intruder among us today, my children."

At this, a greater anxious murmuring arose. Suspicious gazes flew about. People stepped further apart, setting in disarray the close-knit formation they'd been holding.

"Wait, my children," the man implored the roiling host. "Wait, and let me see... Let me find this intruder among us..." Michael Boreal continued to roam the platform, looking and looking into the ranks of the people, eyes wide and wild. A moment later he stopped mid-stride, his frantically roving gaze discerning something amiss. Then, his expression livid, he stabbed a finger toward the front of the group. "There! He is *there!*"

Perhaps it was his being detected by the prescient speaker that caused the man to remove the small camera from where he'd held it unseen within the sleeve of his shirt and raise his hands into the air in a seeming display of admission or surrender. Sunlight flashed angrily from its polished grey skin. He continued to hold the camera in his trembling hand, as if the man was reluctant to cease documenting the father-speaker. A great cry arose, of alarm and fury and indignation. The man did not move. Fear or resignation held him in his place before the stage, traitorous camera held ineffectually in his hand, eyes stunned, awaiting his fate.

This fate was determined by the father-speaker's children. A desperate hand swung from near the man, batting the camera from his hand. It became lost among a tangle of feet, crushed in the ensuing stampede to seize him. Hands pulled the man to the grass, while others found his throat and squeezed.

Seeing the swarming throngs of his disciples, Michael Boreal implored them, "My children, wait! Apprehend this impostor among us peaceful worshippers, but harm him not! Leave him his life or else we become as those from the old world from which we escape on this day!"

The people heard their new-father through the clamour of their fury. And when the crowd parted, it was a young man and woman who stepped finally from the prostrate, bloodied, though still living man. These two looked to the blood on their hands, and then to each other. The strange gauze of madness lifted from their eyes as they found one another. They collapsed into each other's arms. A sympathetic murmur arose around them. Gentle hands touched their shoulders, backs, arms, reassuring them that they were in a safe place. Those close to the couple heard their words of lament: "I never meant to hurt this man. I don't even know him." "I know, darling. Of course, I know." "I never wanted to be like *him*." "No. You're not. Not ever. Not in any way." "Oh, I never want to be like dad." "Never. Not ever. We're free of him. We're free."

The father-speaker's eyes twinkled in the bright air. A tear beaded from each of them, glimmering like jewels as he looked upon his followers. He flew a hand to his breast and held it over his heart. His words wavered with his great emotion, but everyone heard him plainly: "Thank you, my children. Oh, thank you. Now, please, someone, will someone please remove this sorrowful intruder from our midst? Will someone restrain him so that he can't interfere again with our destiny this beautiful afternoon?"

Several of those gathered hurried the dazed man to the shade of a nearby cabin, where they bound his wrists with a stout rope, and fastened these bonds to the sturdy wood of the porch railing. From his place on the porch the man had an uninterrupted view of the clearing.

Michael Boreal looked to his wrist. Sunlight flashed from his silver watch. He checked the position of the sun overhead. He cocked an ear, as if listening to a secret telemetrical voice in the golden air, in the subtle zephyr breeze, among the whispering leaves of the forest across the fields. And his smile broadened. It

253

grew and became huge and it seeped its way into his eyes, and the father-speaker said in an exultant voice,

"Now: the door lies open. They're coming for us. The moment has arrived, but for a brief sliver of time only. Drink, my children. Drink the energy of a new life, and follow me on our long walk to the better place!"

An immense bird lifted from the trees and arced across the blue sky behind the father-speaker, as if signalling the journey's commencement.

As one, he and his children looked upward to where the stars frosted behind the clear blue afternoon sky, and they tipped the slender silver cylinders they'd been clutching to their lips.

Amanda looked to Dillon beside her: still, brother and sister wept with abandon. They held each other's hands tightly. They were prepared to leave. The world had given them nothing. They'd fought to find each other. A brother and sister bound in the deepest ways. Together, now, in their new family, they were prepared to leave behind the endless blackness they'd known for as long as they'd known each other. He whispered earnestly: "Will you marry me?"

The tears running from her eyes; the smile on her face; the urgency with which she clasped his hands: these things told him her answer.

The sun shone fiercely. Wildlife sang jubilantly from the wilderness to the north, south, and west, as if celebrating the moment, too. In the east, the water shone with a dazzling fire.

Beneath it all, and over it all, and all through the serene fabric of the sun-washed afternoon, a voice of great energy grew and grew, until it roared; shaking the monkeys and parrots from the trees like confetti and filling the air with a rhythm born of a cosmic scale: a song of power, joy, celebration, triumph.

In the years following what came to be known as the Magahatti Massacre, speculation abounded as to the various unexplained circumstances surrounding the event. Myriad books documenting the known events which took place on the island of Magahatti in the Pacific Ocean were rushed into publication in the early days following the mass suicide, while a slew of authors returned to examine and reinterpret the subject in the years after. The event continues to enthral many, holding a morbid fascination for some and a point of intense scholarly interest for those working within the disciplines of sociological behaviour and group psychology.

The most popular view of the incident considers eccentric millionaire and Sirius Group founder Michael Boreal to epitomize the supreme cult leader: charismatic and convincing, seemingly benevolent and purportedly prophetic, and owning the necessary monetary capital required to fund and maintain the illusion of the haven he'd created for his devotees. His fifteen year-long crusade of recruiting members for his group and nurturing the farflung ideas which made up the core tenets of the Sirius Group's modus operandi were made possible through both his obsessive devotion to the project as well as the unlimited resources at his disposal. Egocentric and sociopathic, his mastery of group dynamics allowed him to manipulate his followers in the most extreme of ways, fulfilling his religious zealot's mission of mass suicide and promised ascension to the paradisiacal place of his own invention; the fabricated celestial haven for his troubled disciples supposedly having been a location within the binary star Sirius, outside of our own Milky Way galaxy.

Others cast doubt on this popular skeptical perspective of the Magahatti Massacre, positing that the mysterious circumstances surrounding the case of the Sirius Group suggest some authentic basis in the reality perceived by the group itself. Most notable among the devotees to this school of thought was Dennis Murray, the sole survivor and witness of the Massacre. It was Murray who, acting in a freelance capacity as reporter to Ontario-based newspaper periodical *The Toronto Sun*, had infiltrated the group but been discovered via inexplicable circumstances during its final moments, and been restrained within sight of the events he would later describe to be both "beyond explanation and beyond belief, but absolutely true" as documented in his best-selling book, *Away From Night and Into Light: The Ascension of the Sirius Group*.

The author's most astounding claims include the arrival from the sky of hundreds of immense silver egg-shaped objects, coinciding with the group's mass ingestion of cyanide; the enigmatic loitering of these objects for several minutes among the throngs of recently deceased suicide victims; and their eventual return into the afternoon sky, leaving behind the bodies of the newly dead.

Dennis Murray committed suicide a little over six months following the publication of his book, likewise by cyanide ingestion, and likewise on the island of Magahatti, in the vicinity of the site of the cult suicide. He left no suicide note, leaving his final thoughts and specific motivations unknown.

A second group inspired by the tenets built and ultimate deeds nurtured by cult leader Michael Boreal is known to exist, with adherents from around the globe. Known as Sirius II, the potential danger (though some argue nature of salvation) posed by this secret society to its members, as well as the danger to those who stand in opposition of its doctrines, remains open to speculation.

THE PRISON HULK

I'd been doing research for a freelance book project when the idea for this story came to me. The project in question was a children's history book about the explorer Marco Polo. I'd been working through the second draft and reading a lot about the different types of ships of that period and their development throughout subsequent eras.

I came across some fascinating (and horrifying) information related to the late-nineteenth century British practice of incarcerating criminals on unused ships left anchored in the Thames. I jotted down the words "The Prison Hulk" on a scrap of paper and turned back to my freelance work while continuing to write a story in my head: a tale of a group of criminals imprisoned inside just such a ship of horrors. Hanging over this scenario was a question I wanted to answer: given such a plight, what hope could men like these have?

As soon as I'd finished the freelance project, I wrote this story in a single late-night burst and came up with a dark period tale examining a low point in human history, filtered through a tentatively optimistic speculative fiction lens that gave my criminals the only vision of hope I could imagine for them.

The story was first published in a 2006 issue of Revelation *magazine. What more fitting home for a tale based on such real-life horror and annihilation than a publication devoted to literature of the apocalypse?*

With its narrow slat-cracks and portholes like sad vacant eyes, our floating house of pain stares forlornly at the night sky reflected in Thames waters. Peering through a gap in the hull, I watch the stars suspended there, shifting in the dim depths like a wavering dream-picture. The liquid mirror rivets, engages my eyes when I should try for sleep.

Behind me, a man groans, and then another, and the dull, hollow thudding of bodies maneuvering for some scrap of space. The clank of chains, heavy and like a knocking from some place far, far below our feet.

But only fishes sail there, in the unseen depths. Bass and eel. Salmon and countless nameless swimmers.

Lucky, free.

Poverty plagues our dear girl England these days. So many of her children penniless for years, it seems. The result, a sad one: a class of destitute criminals stealing through her streets, bread loaves tucked inside coats, biscuits held anxiously beneath petticoats while the roar of policemen in pursuit grows to raucous dins. One hundred years of our dear girl ridding her shores of these criminals, sailing them away like waste removals to Australian or New World colonies. North America, with its great promise of incarceration.

I'd heard of their distant American rebellion. Independence, and they no more stood for our dumping of prisoners like garbage upon their shores. So what was she to do, our dear, lovely girl, with starving convicts gathering into the arms of police like confetti on some grand day of punishment? With the gaols and bridewells filled to brimming with the land's new breed of petty yet unforgivable criminal?

I was hungry, too. Like so many others I knew and know now, and with whom I share these conditions of squalor. My crime had been simple and atrocious. The loaf of bread for the children and a snuff box for my wife, filched from the general store countertop when all eyes were elsewhere. Until the hand of authority upon my shoulder, as if a shop-owner's tall, stocky son should ever wield such power; and then a quick descent into this life of iron fetters and mouldy biscuits and rats nibbling my toes in the darkness.

258

England gave her answer, and her thieving children shuddered at the portent it held: convert those silent old merchantmen, those relic naval vessels from their disuse since past times of war on the water. Transform them, and give them new loads to bear while the world continues on its daily course. When New World colonies have no further desire for them, confine those lawbreakers in the bellies of boats and anchor them firmly in our harbours and rivers.

Floating dungeons. Prisons-at-anchor. Deplorable prison-houses which have come to be known as the Hulks, wearing inappropriate names like glorious celebrations of past victories and pageantry:

Warrior.
Retribution.
Discovery.
Success.

Names that carry great weight and suggest vastness of vision and high hopes of achievement. Hollow titles in our buoyant prison town, where cries or curses to God and death-moans are the language of necessity. And my own hell's name: *Justitia.* As if inside this humanity cramped corpse-boat any brand of justice is meted out to its crew of skeleton men.

I listen, chilled, as a soft splashing sounds where a man rolls onto his side. The water has gathered in the bilge once again, a new hole which might be patched in several days's time but then perhaps might not. If the red coats can be bothered from their stations above. If we don't wake with dirty water in our mouths and eyes and then the torturous fate of drowning in darkness.

The thought steals into my mind, seamlessly gliding into my awareness as it always does. As though it's never very far away at all: 1841, the hungry year of my criminal act. The first day of my new, unimaginable life. And how long has it been now? And how much of my time on this Earth has slipped away from me?

From the shore, the hulks bobbing in the river seem a derelict shantytown, and we broken men file toward them like ghosts returning to inhabit their hollow, rotten bellies.

Another endless day behind us. Non-life in the Woolwich Warren, that awful labyrinth of warehouses and workshops. Toil in the machine shops, many of us in the foundries and dredging along the river. Twelve-hour days stretched to an interminable length amid the fire and racket and sweat and tears. The guards drift by on all sides, alert with cutlasses drawn and aimed toward our dragging ranks, as though any of us possessed any scrap of strength after the punishing labour behind us. As always, with the sun sinking in the sky and setting the opposite shoreline on fire, the great weight settles upon us. The despair from which not one man among us has ever been able to try for his break toward freedom. A weight of mountains.

The mere sight of her drifting idly in the dark waters off-shore. Her wood paneling old and decaying. Her loathsome mass of groaning boards and limp, soiled sail, with rats scampering through her rotten gut among our waste and refuse. Our hell, our *Justitia*.

I hate her. I dream of burning her into the river. Sending her boards helter skelter to the river bottom for fish to drift among and wonder over.

And we're guided across the narrow wood plank and ushered inside of her stinking carcass once more. Stooping, we enter the thick atmosphere, our heads brushing the ceiling only four feet from the floor, midget's quarters for grown men. We collapse because we can stand no more, vying for what little space we can secure. Soon enough, we are all gathered here once more, our strange, silent, aching family. Three hundred half-starved, unwashed men living skin on skin, among their disease and shit and piss. Our stink suffocates us and is a rank, fetid presence along the shoreline for miles.

Minutes pass like days and then another mouthful of mouldy biscuits and my supper is done. I drift soon, only dimly aware of the sound beside me, the man urinating where he sits against the wall. His warm flood reaches me, envelops my thigh, and stirs me from my almost-slumber. A reminder, and I let myself go, too, enjoying the small relief of pressure in my bladder. We don't speak of such things any longer. We are one among all this refuse and degradation.

I awake in the deep morning to the roar of a new agony.

Two fools have tried for escape, and their cries from the shore are anguished, almost inhuman sounding. Some of us peer through portholes and spy the scene in its gruesome unfolding: netted like a pair of fish, our brothers flop amid the reeds while the uniformed men beat downwards into the tangle of ropes and limbs with their short wooden clubs. Dull thuds and wallops without echo. Flat and moist the racket, amid the grunts and screams of the would-be escapees.

I watch as if mesmerized until the pair is dragged off, still entangled in the fishermen's netting, surrounded by men with cutlasses gleaming in the moon glow and rifles in hand, too. Toward the gallows, where another kind of rope awaits them. And I think of how it might feel, that tight grip around my own throat while my body swings wildly to and fro, and I wonder whether our captured brother fish are lucky in this way. Free, at least, from the anguish of the Hulks.

The year, and time at large, elude me in this place.

Perhaps September 15, 1841 had only transpired one week or one month before, with all its fateful events. Maybe the bread loaf I once held trembling beneath my coat is still edible, and an officer somewhere is now buttering a slice cut from its plump body. Maybe he pinches sprinkles of snuff from the ornamental box I once held nervously in my pocket, while visions of my darling's eyes alight with surprise and joy washed over me. Maybe very little time has elapsed and my wife and children still weep freely over my fate as they did the day they came to see me. The dark day of sentencing. The final day before this life inside terrible, terrible *Justitia*.

Many of my brothers think him mad. The Mad Pirate Prophet, they laugh scornfully, an old sailor and merchant with wild white hair, a smile empty of teeth, and a history of illegal trafficking behind him. He's sailed among whales and seen the distant shores of the world and where has it got him? Always promising us cataclysmic salvation, this has become his self-proclaimed duty among our clan. Another day of toil and then our forthcoming night of reward. One final night and then we will be allowed rest once and for all. If only, if only.

I feel a kinship with this man who others curse in the dark and spit on each time we're taken ashore. We are of similar temperament, and something in his vigorous soliloquies reaches some deep part of me every time he rails in his darkly comical

261

way. Arms outstretched, always wagging his hands in the air, toward the shadowed roof of the *Justitia* when we're huddled together in her hold or thrust toward the early morning moon and stars fading from the sky as we're herded into a new day of labour; beseeching us all to listen and hear him out in his prophesying.

Ours is a simple friendship: he rages, and I listen, his sole audience.

There must be an end to this. Some day, brothers. There must be an end. Man should not be made to endure this purgatory. The apocalypse nears. And what awaits us afterwards?

I make no answer, only give him the gift of my attention while curses fly from the cabin darkness.

Shut up, old man.

Mad Hatter, I'll be watching you at the foundry come tomorrow, with the hot tongs in my hands.

You'll meet your end soon enough, my word on it.

We are not all friends, nor are we one another's enemy. Simply family, with its own particular hatreds and occasional camaraderie while enduring the same misery day after day after day. The old man is grateful to me and offers me his toothless smiles and surreptitious winks from beneath bushy eyebrows like two caterpillars keeping guard over his eyes and the prophetic visions they see. We are silent allies in this claustrophobic prison of wrecked men.

Usually, we lie anchored alongside the southern shore, and the dreary sight of the factory district close at hand keeps our eyes away from the cracks in the hull and the few small portholes. The din from the machine shops drifting to us, and the picture of those other unfortunates like us, rests before our eyes. The great river holds many Hulks, each with her own cargo of skeletal corpse-men, slaving differing shifts in the deathly foundries.

But tonight, we lie anchored along the northern shore, with the murk of the Essex marshes ominous before us. Mist hangs over the shoreline, and the intermittent cries of waterfowl or tree owls sound grotesque in the uncertain light. This is where our Hulk has been towed, and upon this shore, among the wild grass and reeds, our punishment meted out.

It is a very long night, for there are many of us. We are chained together, released one man at a time to meet our punishment in front of the rest. The cat-o'-nine-tails licks the backs of each of us in turn, and two dozen of our number especially severely, those with the loudest voices of courageous or foolhardy protest. The whips make a meaty racket that send icy sweat drizzling down my back. I fear their scorpion-sting in the moon-lit darkness along the shoreline. In the dark, everything is worse. Our punishment for two of us fools who've tried for a futile escape into the dreary maze of the Warren and the slums beyond. And the *Justitia* serves out her justice.

When it's my turn, the rags are torn from around my body and my feet kicked out from beneath me. Grass blades scratch my face as I topple to earth and the lashing begins. From beside me, through the tumult of my cries and my pain and the jeers of the guardsmen delivering the agony, I glimpse him watching as if entranced and hear fragments of his newest prophecy:

Worry not... The end nears... These old bones feel it... The end nears and salvation will be ours... Apocalypse will save you.

Apocalypse will save you.

When it's his turn, the beating lasts exceptionally longer than for the rest of us. Poor, mad, brave Pirate Prophet, railing and wailing and finally silent among the reeds in the silver moonlight. Invisible frogs croak their throaty night calls from their secret nooks, sounding loudly and like some strange dirge for the dead.

The stars flicker like nervous eyes, he whispers to me through grossly swollen lips. *Something stirs there.*

The Pirate's trembling finger, like a twisted birch branch, points through the crack in the wood toward the moon and her celestial children frosting in the black. I follow his gesture but the vastness of the sky taunts, its immense free stretches where I wish to be able to fly away, lucky bird-man with Pegasus-wings. And so I cast my gaze to him, frowning at his anxious eyes, wilder-looking than usual in the moonlight slashing through the miniscule hull cracks and portholes; surrounded by ugly, dark bruises where the guards's sticks and lashes found him soft and unprotected. He has become a friend to me, among our ragged clan, and so I hush him softly when his voice strains too loud, stirring sleeping men with their own bruises to nurse. But even

263

they leave our Mad Pirate Prophet alone this night, having witnessed his flogging on the shore. The atmosphere this night holds a humbled silence, amid the usual congestion of hopelessness.

I nod at his words, touch my fingers gingerly to my split and swollen cheek where the cat-o'-nine-tails struck me despite my cowering with hands over my face. I hurt, but then this is nothing new. His words, as always, are a comfort. Escape, from the endlessness of this existence. A glimmer of movement between constellations. Hope, even if frail and tenuous. Even if he is indeed mad, and the visions he sees no more certain than other men's desperate attempts to escape hell.

And he turns to me and the silver beads rolling down his cheeks are his tears, and his whisper is coarse and despairing and truly frightening to hear. *Friend, I can't continue like this. It must end. It must! The pain...*

He trails off, pathetic and small. Stunned, I let him sob gently into my embrace. I've never seen the Prophet this broken, so reduced from his usual vigour and passion. A man undone, unraveling in my inadequate arms.

We hold each other and drift to fitful sleep, bone-weary and without hope, our ankle-shackles entwined like our bodies.

I awake and the sound has followed me up from my fitful dreaming: a hissing, as of some great burning thing.

The pain in my shoulder is the vice-grip of his fingers, and as I stare bewildered from my place curled on the planks, I see that the Prophet's face of old has returned. Set ablaze, a crimson glow flickering over his wizened features, he says, *The time is here*, and turns his intense gaze to the porthole before him and stares fervently into the night.

His words are strange to me, and like a magnetic force draw me into their mystery:

There are lightning birds in the clouds. An angel army circling.

Slowly I grow conscious of the scene about me, of the others wakeful and anxious on all sides, straining their eyes to other windows or tiny apertures in the walls and the deep crimson glow permeating the entire drab hold of our prison. And the fiery hiss, again and again, of an unknown spectacle my mind can't begin to imagine without witnessing it myself.

264

Unfurling my numbed limbs from the floor, my joints stiff and muscles sore as I stretch, I pull myself to my feet along the rough paneling of the wall. The old man shuffles aside so that I may take a turn at his spyhole, his eyes alive, toothless smile ecstatic and coloured in the light. Anxiously, I place my eye to the circle of window, and I see.

The sky on fire.

Crimson shapes descend in wide arcs against the illuminated cloud cover, trailing fiery beards in their wake. The great river is violent with its new reflection of fire. My mind makes harried attempts at rationalization and I nearly whisper the question aloud: are we under attack, are we witnessing cannon balls shooting across the water, the British and French meeting once again? But my eyes digest the wondrous and terrifying picture as they can and admit to me that these are no cannon balls. No man-made missiles fire the sky over the Thames, quaking us in our filthy dungeon. The scene mesmerizes, awes with its power and calamity and strangeness.

I dreamt this, or something like this, I tell him, amazed as my senses drink their fill of the spectacle. He turns to me briefly, and with a twinkle in his glaring eyes tells me that perhaps our brothers have been wrong all along, and maybe it is I who is the prophet among us.

Our brothers are watching, too, riveted, taking turns at windows so all may see it. Some cry out like children, cowed by the violence and immensity of the scene. Prayers howled to God, they cup dirty hands across their mouths and let their eyes flood. *Dinner plates,* swears one man like an oath torn from his throat, noting the odd saucer-like shape of certain of the descending fires. *And we the feast. And we the feast!* And his descent into gibbering sends him amid the rats skittering nervously along the tops of our feet in the bottom of the boat.

The lightning birds. Angels above.

And the Pirate Prophet's finger paints an invisible circle in the clouds for the benefit of my frantic eyes. I look and see them: shapes among the clouds, nimble and fleet as they dart about behind the cumulus. A flock of enormous shadows illuminated through the blazing luminescence of the fire plumes plummeting all around. More of the arcing fires appear, and these other moving objects, as well, seemingly ordered—*intelligent?*—amid the chaos of sight and sound.

A cacophonous noise, part explosion, part rush of water deafens us momentarily. A fire-object striking into the river close at hand. We scramble for a clearer vantage and I'm in time to see the geyser of Thames water spout into the air in aftermath ricochet. I hear the creaking racket of dozens of men who have begun tearing freely at the boards along the southern side of the hold, dismissing any thought of the guardsmen above. I can hear the Red Coats's cries of alarm, the loud stamp of their boots as they dash panicked to and fro throughout the cabins. *You scurry now, too, like we down here with the rats*: I think this, relishing our captors's terror, despite the astonishing scene unfolding before me.

Another explosion and we're thrown helter skelter as the river rocks violently. We clutch at one another, crying in terror, a tangle of sweaty limbs and sodden rags. The creaking at the opposite end of the room erupting into a final screaming of splintering wood, and the men have succeeded in pushing through a single long panel in the hull. Water splashes in where the Hulk lurches in the wake of the last concussive collision of fire-object and river, shocking me with its icy touch.

Look! Someone's voice rises over the din. *To the Warren!*

And we fight each other for a glimpse, those fortunate enough to see letting the rest of us know with their booming cries like shouts of victory. *The fires have struck in the Warren! The foundries burn!*

I smile at the joy in the speaker's voice. His words fill me with satisfaction. I'm suddenly inspired or brave or foolish, and without thought lash out with my fist against the wall before me. The wood is firm and cracks my knuckles, and though I wince at the stabbing pain I strike again, and then again. The Pirate Prophet begins to help me, wordlessly, squeezing his ancient fingers into the aperture in the wall that I've helped to widen and tugging with what strength he has. Together, we pry a strip of boarding loose while the floor quakes and groans beneath our feet. Water licks at our ankles and the crimson sky-glow colours us violently.

Peering through this new window into the night, we see the sky, painted crimson in its criss-crossing of flaming lines. To the east of us, another Hulk burns, casting thick black smoke columns into the air. The *Retribution*, and I relish the feeling filling my heart as my lips curl in a grim smile while I watch the

266

frantic, Red-Coated forms dotting its deck. Vindication, even if one or two or three hundred helpless men must die like rats in their below-decks dungeon. And I look away only when the sight of men on fire becomes too grotesque for my already churning stomach.

The northern shore is close at hand, its mass of treacherous foliage and swampy terrain illuminated vividly. *Witch lights*, breathes a man close to my ear, his body hot and moist where he's pressed up closely, while others whisper of will-o'-the-wisps smoking and shimmering over the mysterious marshland. I stare a moment, hearing the weak attempt at rationalization in their words, when any eye can clearly discern the foreignness of the thing we're witnessing.

And we recoil instinctively at the sudden flare of light which casts our tight, claustrophobic space into clarity as the fire plume drops from overhead and directly into the swamps. Like a mountain plummeting from the sky and into the wilderness, the roar deafens. The concussive tremor ripples forth from the mists, throwing us to the floor once more, sending river water into the hold in waves. A small flailing thing in my lap is a fish sent inside with the water, its scales glimmering silver-pink in the violence of the fiery light. Instinctively, clumsily, I wrap my shaking fingers about its narrow body and hurl it from me back through the gaping space in the wall and into the churning river. I consider following, but something halts me where I crouch, feet set wide apart in the gathering water, knees buckling in strain and fatigue and terror.

His hand is returned to my side, gripping my fingers tremblingly. His words are soft but loud at my ear. *They are sailors from afar. Just look at them, in their glory. Who knows where they might come from? Just look at them burning. Burning so brightly. Nothing ever burned so brightly. And the stars of Heaven fall unto the Earth...*

I make no answer to my friend the Pirate Prophet and can only stare at the spectacle of the night sky, the burning lights shooting over the river. The water burns where the fires drop like enormous blazing stones. Fire on the water. Fire against the stars. As if the constellations had descended and lit up our existence in our filthy prison squalor. As though the stars have fallen to offer us respite from our miserable lives, through a mass incineration of our fetters and chains, and the hulking monstrosities which box us up tightly and without hope.

What a fireworks display, shouts a man beside me in a gust of fetid breath, his stench of sweat pungent. *What a glorious fireworks night!* he cries. *The best I'll ever see!* And though he shambles past me, making for the space in the hull, he halts at its threshold as I have, letting the water engulf him up to his knees.

And the Pirate Prophet at my side, clutching my hand tightly, whispers, *If this be the final night, if the end looks so pretty to my eyes, then I welcome it, brother. Oh, I welcome it.*

Hearing his words, I think of astronomers and their riddles in relation to the stars and the things beyond our world. The Greeks with their tales of meteors like mountain ranges hurtling through the void, and comets traveling the universe on journeys much longer than our small lives. And then I ponder the shapes of the flyers behind the clouds, and the inexplicable nature of the destruction—this utterly beautiful destruction—raining down on the Earth. And I wonder what these scholars might say of the picture before me now.

No, I tell my brother the Mad Pirate Prophet with a hard knocking of my bloodied knuckles against the wood planking. *No. Maybe this is the apocalypse. Maybe the* Justitia *is the name given to the end of man. Because look at us. Look at us here in her stomach. We're not even men. And maybe they—*and I point towards the beauteous sight of the lights shooting arcs across the sky, and I am lost for words.

A new beginning, finishes the Pirate Prophet for me, his words a rush of warmth against my cheek.

I nod, turning once more to the sky and its incredible vision of fiery comets, or meteors, or unknowable harbingers of God's will sailing in their divine ships like a host from the heart of Heaven itself. Burning the swamp before our eyes. Burning the Warren maze with its horrible foundries and barracks. Burning the Hulks and setting the guilty or un-guilty free.

Maybe we of the *Justitia* will be free come tomorrow and begin our new life together among the smouldering remains of the land beyond these walls. Sharing the world with the flame birds. Burning away our terrible memories of where we've been and the things we've seen. Or maybe our own fiery meteor awaits us yet, and we'll burn this night too. Because we the sullied might no longer belong here in a new, cleansed world.

A tremendous groaning begins, tensing us all, and we know that the *Justitia* is reeling. The river is filling up her belly. Fish swim with us everywhere. A canoe-full of Red Coats paddling away from her close by is engulfed in a fiery wave, their screams cut short beneath the torrents of burning water. The river rocks us violently in its chaos of electrified waves and foam. I press my palm against the *Justitia's* wood wall, feel her trembling beneath my touch. Once she'd been a lady of war, but no more. Gone are her days of warrior-prowess, leaving her a derelict relic fit only as a cage for us criminals. I watch dozens and dozens of my brothers scramble through the gaping maws in the hull, disappearing instantly in the foam and waves. Their faces as they stumble past me and into the churning river are pale masks of energized terror, and I silently wish them luck in their escape.

Time passes while others scramble to freedom from the rocking Hulk, blind shambling forms diving into the roar of river and light. Gradually, I sense the queer calm settle around me. The remaining men cease their tearing at boards, their kicking in of walls. Laboured breathing becomes even, mellow. As if we have grown resigned to whichever fate is destined to be ours. As if we are too enthralled with the great clamour and chaos to stir any longer. A humbled family gathered together for a viewing of some great and significant thing beyond our comprehension. Falling into silence, we several hundred free men watch the night from our trembling prison queen, like awed revelers on an eve of great fireworks and celebration.

I wonder, as I occasionally do, as to the passage of time. When is it? 1842, perhaps? And a hope for rebirth? 1850, maybe. A new, free world.

The morning dawns and we stir and peer eagerly through the cracks in *Justitia's* hull. The swamp horizon smoulders, blackened tree stumps against a sky of spoiled milk and grim clouds. Not a thing stirs on the far shore. No man, convict or Red Coat, in the grass, nor bird in the sky. The foundries are silent and no racket issues from the machine shops to the south, where only smoke billows like black forlorn ropes leading languidly into the sky. There is only the knocking sound against our hull where drifting pieces of trees and nautical flotsam bump gently in the mild current.

We've stayed here through the night. Several hundred emaciated survivors of we might never know exactly what. Of a night of retribution. A night of fiery warriors wreaking havoc and offering freedom. A night of beautiful fires.

I realized when his fingers began to grow stiff and cold where I clenched them between my own. He'd died in the wee hours, silently and at peace. His expression conveys it, his serene eyes staring upwards, lips parted casually, revealing the faintest of toothless smiles. His weight comforts me still, and I'm glad of the circumstances surrounding his end. A peaceful departure, into a freedom he well deserved.

Maybe it will stay this way forever, I think. A silent world, but for the energetic noise of men freeing one another from leg-fetters with the banging of sharp stones against iron loops. Maybe no guards will return and bring us forth from this sinking, skeletal Hulk and into another form of darkness. Maybe we are accidental survivors of the Great Sky Fire, the missed, who should never even have been allowed the chance to see this first morning in the reborn world. Maybe the *Justitia* is at last truly dead, and we must only pry apart her remaining boards and flee into the new day while she flounders and falls in the great Thames, bringing all of her chains and other evidence of pain and barbarism with her.

But none of us stir. Despite the icy river waist-deep in the Hulk with us. Despite the fish swimming freely between our tightly-wedged bodies. Not a man remaining of our giant, strange family stirs from his scrap of space, although the way lies open through the disassembled hull, and the swampy shoreline beckons beyond.

I wonder what might lie there, over the singed horizon-line of treetops to the north, and I shudder. Because I can't fathom that spectacle at all.

And so we stay, our remaining rags drifting languidly in the current, fish tails making small splashes among us. As though waiting for a sign. Some word of direction. Some utterance, from somewhere, of absolution, or the asking of our forgiveness for a wicked life delivered upon us. Maybe a troop of red-coated guards with down turned eyes and apologies in their words. Maybe our families with incredible and good news explaining the science or divinity of the thing we witnessed in the night. Maybe the peering through the clouds of the dawn sun, like a signal of a new day or year.

A new age, good for living.

Although initially only developed as a temporary system of incarceration, England's deplorable Prison Hulk penal system lasted 80 years. It was finally abolished in the year 1857.

"What ghosts walk these paths?"

—Unknown Hulk prisoner
c. 1840

LOVE IN UNCERTAIN TIMES

This story's hopeful note, amid the myriad fantastical and frightening and unknown scenarios it presents, made it the only choice for the final story of my third collection, Blacker Against the Deep Dark, *and a nice parallel to the joyful turns of my life around the time the story was written.*

These welcome turns, coming after a long period of bereavement, mourning, and depression, included some pretty significant and all-around wonderful milestones: the simultaneous publication in 2014 of my second fiction collection, Songs for the Lost, *and its companion volume, the poetry and essay collection* Ballads to the Burning Twins: The Complete Song Lyrics of the Deathray Bradburys; *completing the education program and related field placements at the University of Windsor, something that, due to my social anxiety and general shyness, represented quite the personal triumph; and, of course, marrying my best friend and partner in adventure, Elizabeth, on Pelee Island, Ontario on Halloween 2015.*

The times are uncertain. We all need our moons to watch for in the sky, hope flooding our hearts.

"Then the LORD said, 'My Spirit will not contend with man forever, for he is mortal; his days will be a hundred and twenty years.'"

—Genesis 6:1–4

"Henry, honey, watch your sister now, and stay where I can see you both from the kitchen window, okay? Dinner'll be ready in half an hour."

Henry's mother's voice drifted through the open window and adjacent screen door to where her son stood on the backyard patio, comic book tucked beneath one arm, the latest issue of *Time* tucked beneath the other, her desiccated hanging ferns sagging over the lips of their plastic pots in the heat. He nodded disconsolately. Seeing his slumped shoulders, his mother frowned, said, "After supper maybe we can walk over to the Twisty Treat for some ice cream cones, okay?"

He nodded again, shading his eyes with a hand, unmoving in his place on the burning cement. His mother worried at his dismay, and in that moment felt an indescribable desire to ensure her son's and daughter's safeguarding and a deep loathing of anyone who might ever do them harm of any kind. "Okay, don't wander, honey." She returned to her cooking, distracted. Her frown of worry remained.

Outside, Henry continued to loiter in his place on the patio. He looked from his sister playing contentedly in the dirt to the copy of *Fantastic Four* in his right hand to the issue of *Time* in his left. He found the burning circle of the sun overhead. He looked for some sign of the moon, but it was nowhere to be found the way some afternoons revealed it hanging ghostly and half-formed in the blue sky. He knew not what to do with himself. There were more important things to think about than ice cream cones and superheroes and fathers always absent from dinner tables.

He sat down on the burning cement and, acting without thinking, placed the comic book on the ground beside him and opened the magazine across his lap.

SIGNS ABOVE, BELOW, AND WITHIN:
SEARCHING FOR MEANING IN OUR WORLD TODAY

By David Chilton, Professor of Astronomy, Harvard University

The news is running riot these days. But then how could it be otherwise? We are living in the Age of the Great Discoveries, the magnitude of which lead only to more questions and a deepening of the overall mystery. The latest of these extraordinary events completes a triumvirate of Discoveries. The question now—the most important question among the many—is what happens next?

I.

The world was stunned and left in a turmoil of excitement and fear when the Great Discovery was announced seven years ago. The finding changed everything. *It proved science to be in its infancy. Religions the globe over had become unreliable purveyors of folklore, the Holy Bible an unfinished collection of magical parables. Some called for a great mass penitence and prophesied salvation for those who were worthy, the humbled and virtuous and pure of heart. Others waited for doom. The new believers and doomsayers are still waiting, along with the rest of us.*

It was on December 1, 2013 that a 9.2 magnitude earthquake and subsequent avalanche in the Cordillera Blanca mountain range of the Andes in Peru revealed the most shocking and indisputably important discovery in the annals of recorded history. The avalanche occurred within the mountain peak, Alpamayo, near the village of Caraz, and initially unearthed a single being, perfectly preserved deep within the mountain's igneous core in an immense chamber that palaeontologists determined to be carved from the mountain itself. The rock is estimated to be over 300 million years old, placing the being's interment to a time approximately 70 million years before the first dinosaur roamed the Earth. The being itself is entirely encased and perfectly preserved in a substance physically resembling amber, but whose composition has never been encountered in science.

Preservation in the amber-like substance leaves the being— who is entirely naked—clearly visible, revealing male sexual

reproductive organs and a physiognomy similar to that of human beings, but with notable differences. Its most distinguishing traits are a significantly elongated forehead and round, extremely large eyes in proportion to the face. The most startling aspect of the being—besides the astonishing fact of its existence, undetected throughout history until modern times—is its size: from foot to head, it measures a mindboggling five kilometres (or three miles), the equivalent length of approximately fourteen modern aircraft carriers lined up front to back. A true giant, who might have once used mountains as thrones just as readily as tombs.

Further archaeological digs unearthed several more beings in the immediate vicinity: one female, shorter in stature by approximately one head's-length, placing her at a little over two-and-a-half miles tall; and two smaller beings, reaching an average in height between one half-mile and one full mile: children, both male. Each being lies entombed within a different, neighbouring mountain—Jancarunish, Tayapampa, and Quitaraju, respectively—as if they were interred in their own individual stone mausoleums.

Some refer to them as the Nephilim, after the Biblical giants said to be a product of the union between the sons of God and the daughters of men, as noted in Genesis 6:4. Others, who fancy themselves of the new, progressive-minded, consider them true Gods who were here long ago and for reasons unknown left us this Earth we share—the ancient astronauts theorized by bold (and once ridiculed) thinkers such as Harold T. Wilkins and Erich von Daniken. Whatever one believes, the undeniable consensus remains that today we are all that much less certain that we, as a species, are the omnipotent and all-knowing rulers of this world as we once believed ourselves to be.

Today, it seems as if everyone is watching the sky, or listening to the ground beneath their feet, or simply looking into each other's eyes with a new way of seeing the world: questioning, awed, changed. And excited*: people have noted this too, the way we all seem to share a more youthful eagerness, as if some mass remembrance of once-lost childhood wonder has swept the world. And there is fear underlying the great excitement, too, because the unknown is always a catalyst for it, and never before have we been faced with a mystery so vast, so seemingly impenetrable.*

Popular culture's need for claiming ownership has garnered the giants the saccharine but fitting nickname, birthed in the Western world and now acknowledged globally: the Big Family. Pilgrimages to the site in the Andes have become commonplace, a new Mecca for those seeking to absolve themselves of sin or to give themselves over to a greater power. New religions have sprung up revolving around the worship of the beings, and old religions have rewritten themselves to make room for them. The effects of the discovery on the worlds of art, literature, and film have likewise been profound, serving as the inspiration for countless documentaries, feature-length films, and both non-fiction and fiction books. Our world history is now rightfully defined as being pre- or post-Discovery.

"People everywhere are crying, we are all like children again," exclaimed one emotion-seized newscaster live on-air the day the first giant was found—Adam Chamberlain, based in Birmingham, England—his impassioned monologue instantly going viral and standing as one of the defining public reactions to the Discovery. He went on: "Yes, let us be humbled by the unknown revealing itself to us, and let us be overjoyed, too, because maybe someone or something believes that we're finally ready to learn this new knowledge, and that we'll be wiser for having learned it, and that we'll do good with it. Please, let us do good with it."

But it was the words written by an anonymous and death-defying hand and marking the South Tower of the Golden Gate Bridge in San Francisco, California, spray-painted in enormous letters worthy of the subject they speak of that have become the mantra of the times, because they say what is in all our newfound poets's hearts:

Tomorrow is a new kingdom.

II.

Seven years to the day of the unprecedented discovery of the Big Family, the second monumental discovery of the modern age was made, adding to the great puzzle of our times.

When communication with an unmanned NASA robotic front-hauler stationed on the moon was inexplicably severed, a robot probe was sent to investigate. The front-hauler, which had been strip-mining for regolith throughout the moon's marias, or seas, was found wrecked at the bottom of a deep fissure that had evidently opened in the surface of Mara Serenitatis (the Sea of Tranquility), near to the moon's North pole. The robot, equipped to repair the crippled hauler, stumbled on the enigma.

A 100-foot-long blue whale was found entombed a quarter kilometre beneath the moon's surface, perfectly preserved in what appeared to be an amber-like substance visually similar to the one encasing the Big Family. The gargantuan animal lay embedded within a 150-foot-long chamber seemingly carved from the surrounding rock. Analysis of the photographs sent back to Earth has shown the walls of the tomb in great detail, revealing their surface to be etched with arcane symbols: a language, foreign to anywhere in our world.

"There is a complex pattern woven among the tapestry of the universe. And each of us is a star sewn into it. Now the time has come for us to step back and see the constellations we have formed together." These words, spoken by renowned Polish physicist Nikolas Pieczonka in a moving televised address among fellow members of the European Research Council, we have come to understand and accept, not least because of its unspoken message: there is more to be revealed.

III.

At the time of this publication, even as investigations into the new Moon Mystery and study of the Big Family continue, a third Discovery is upon us. The finding occurred exactly seven years to the day of the second Discovery, and exactly fourteen years following the First.

Researchers have responded to an extraordinary geographic anomaly located in the Weddell Sea approximately five miles from the Antarctic coast. There, several hundred passengers and crew on the polar cruise ship Gallant were the first to witness an unexplainable ray of white light, one mile in width, which shone with startling brightness and intensity from beneath the water's surface and directly into the sky for as far as the eye could see. The manifestation of this light was followed by the formation of an immense tidal pool that the ship barely escaped. The disturbance dissipated, although the anomalous light-ray remains, shining like a colossal beacon and drawing the attention of the world.

Adding to the mystery is the large number of sea creatures that have begun gathering at the site, as if somehow drawn by the spectacle. This includes a wide variety of species, both those native to the region, such as the Weddell seal, as well as those ranging from neighbouring water regions as far away as the Atlantic Ocean. The phenomenon has drawn comparisons to man's own spiritual pilgrimage to the Andes site. The National Oceanographic Institute, which had been undergoing preparations for the deep penetration of the sea near this area of the coastline, has now refocused its mission as an imperative exploratory dive seeking to determine the cause of the anomaly, for which no scientific explanation can be given at the time of this writing.

The romantic nature of the mission to solve the mystery of the Divine-Light Anomaly, as it has become known—all while following in the wake of the two other Great Discoveries of our times—has earned it the official title of the Diving for Humankind Expedition.

A triumvirate of Discoveries is here. Will there be more? What will we learn, about our world, and ourselves, and the greater cosmos of which we're but a small part?

Life goes on, the same as before but changed in every way.

The world waits.

Henry eyed the sky, ignoring his silly sister messing with grasshoppers and red ants in the dirt beside the patio where he sat burning in the July air. His issue of *Fantastic Four* was abandoned on the cement beside him, its paper hot to the touch, its staples shining in the molten light. The issue of *Time* lay across his lap, opened to the final page of the article, waiting for him to finish it.

He was thinking, like most people those days, of big things. Things he'd heard his schoolteacher, Mr. Dixon, say during class in recent days flitted through his reveries. "There were giants here. Maybe we're the giants now." These things sounded wise and frightening to him. The neighbourhood beyond the backyard seemed too quiet and ordinary a place to exist in the same world as these other, much bigger happenings. He looked to the place in the fence, partially obscured by a rosebush at the rear of the yard, where a loose board provided a secret means of escaping the property and felt the old stirring inside him that he often felt while lying sleepless in bed after midnight and dreaming of the world, mysterious and unexplored, outside the walls of his home.

"Look, Henry," his sister said, trying to show him something, but Henry had eyes only for the fence-gateway, and the treetops, and sky beyond. The day seemed suddenly hushed, the cicadas's electric voice from the trees stopped, the buzz of bluebells absent, and a graveyard silence from the streets beyond as well, empty of the chugging murmur of cars, the occasional barking of a bicycle horn. When he continued to ignore her, her pleading voice disturbed the stillness: "Henreeeee."

He grew annoyed with her, as he often did. He seethed, "Shut up already, Jackie. Don't you even care? They discovered a family of giant people someplace, and now there's a whale on the moon. Who knows what they'll find under the ocean."

Then, through his burning anger, he saw:

His sister Jacqueline was smiling, unhurt by his anger, squinting in the bright light and waiting patiently for him to see what she'd found in the dirt, proudly displayed in the palm of her dusty hand: a family of five potato bugs, searching tentatively among the folds of her grimy little hand, hesitantly probing the cage of her stubby fingers. Seeing that her older brother had finally tuned in to the treasure she held, she pointed into her palm and said, "That one loves that one loves that one loves that one loves that one."

Henry smiled for her. "That's great, Jackie. Keep on looking, and show me what you get, okay?"

She happily obeyed her older brother, gently replacing the insects in the dirt before grabbing her bright red plastic shovel from the cement. Henry looked into the sky again and found the moon emerged in the blueness like a ghost.

There you are, he thought, watching it earnestly a moment before turning back to the magazine opened in his lap.

The afternoon wore on, as endless afternoons in the heart of burning Julys—good for pondering big things—always, always did.

IV.

A relevant statistic has emerged: The rates of violent crime throughout the world—including those in even the most violent cities on Earth, such as Ciudad Juarez, Mexico; San Pedro Sula, Honduras; Sao Paulo, Brazil; Cape Town, South Africa; and Detroit, Michigan, U.S.A., each notorious for excessive rates of murder, rape, armed assault, drug trade-, gang-, and in some cases military-related fatalities—have declined a record 44% since the discovery of the Big Family.

YOUR BONE SPIDER WILL FIND YOU

Open a newspaper. Turn on the evening news. Scroll through an online news feed. Peruse the True Crime and History sections of your local bookshop.

It's heartbreaking when you consider some of what goes on in the world every day.

Thank God for escape routes. Thank God for inner strength. Thank God for vengeance.

She fingered the keen blade extending from the finger-smudged plastic base of the pocketknife. Its edge, caught in the moon's light, flashed a silvery smear through her tears. She pressed the blade against the throat of the snow-white kitten pinioned between her knees, wincing as she did this but resolute in her action. She paused there, though, unable to go on. The animal's plaintive, mournful meowing shook her. Its soft emerald gaze seemed to implore her. She closed her eyes on the moon-coloured picture of her great fury and cowardice.

A moment passed. A wind from off the river gusted through the great desolate yard, chilling her in her denim jacket. She shivered, her bangs annoying her eyes and her cheap plastic earrings jangling loudly as she trembled. With as steady a hand and determined a mind as she could muster, she pressed the blade into the kitten's scrawny throat.

Her wrist was caught in an unyielding grip. She tried turning about to confront her assailant but, thrown off-balance, only toppled onto her side amid the tufts of wild grass. These spiked into her face from where they shot up through the time-shattered cement, momentarily blinded her. She felt the knife pried from her fingers, discerned through the pounding rush of blood like a river in her ears the heavy breathing of the man behind her and the renewed frightened yipping clamour of the kitten from somewhere near at hand.

She ceased her futile struggles, allowing her arm to grow limp in his grasp. She waited, heart hammering, until the kitten's saviour released her. Cowering, she peered over her shoulder. Gradually, her vision cleared, and the man coalesced from the star field against which he stood silhouetted. His eyes were hard but solemn. They burned in their appraisal of her. She couldn't help but look away from them, to examine her hands in her lap, the frayed cuffs of her jeans, her fingernails bitten down low and the grime wedged behind them. She took her first impression of him with her, though, and saw his dishevelled hair, unshaven features, wan skin, filthy sweatshirt and jeans as if he lived in the streets, or perhaps in this very lot behind the derelict warehouse.

She looked to him after a prolonged moment had passed in silence, found him looking into the middle of the vacant lot with his intense stare. She peered there, too, saw the snowy kitten padding through the wild grass, away from her and her knife. When next she looked to the man his eyes were beholding her, accusatory but curiously sympathetic, compelling her against her will to look to her hands again. They looked small, she thought distantly, thin-fingered and too weak to wield knives efficiently.

She saw from the corner of her eye as he raised an arm. She followed his hand gesturing in the direction of the river somewhere in the night. More specifically, she understood, he pointed towards the skeleton of the warehouse before them. Its belly had long ago been eaten by fire. Its roof, she saw, had collapsed inwards. Long, fire-blackened wooden and steel support beams spiked outwards from the rubble like an enormous, splintered ribcage. The structure's aura of death and abandonment had called to her when she'd wandered through the lot thirty minutes earlier and found the kitten pawing at a spot in the grass, looking startled at her presence, shaking in the crisp wind, utterly lost in the night.

284

Suddenly the man's hand was beside her face, palm out as if offering her to take hold and be guided from the lot by him. He turned his gaze to the warehouse and then again to her, beckoning still with his hand.

A ball of fear unfurled itself in her stomach at this invitation.

"I'm not going with you," she said indignantly. "Fuck you, man."

The man's voice sounded younger than his weathered features appeared, his tone firm but its timbre un-coarse, un-ravaged by time. "Oh, yes, you will."

The man's striking incongruity startled her, the combination of his calm demeanour and grave gaze unsettling. She watched him with a hard, angry stare. She considered her proximity to the street beyond the empty warehouse towering between her and freedom. She considered her small voice in this large, unfrequented lot near to the river past midnight on an icy Fall night when most sensible, untroubled people were indoors and sleeping and wandering in their good or bad dreams. She watched his tranquil but uncompromising eyes a moment longer without words and then finally she spat at him, audaciousness in her voice and a seething look of disdain in her gaze, "I'm not scared of you. Fuck you. Let's go then. Come on."

She stood and led the way towards the shell of the warehouse hulking at the periphery of the weed-choked lot.

She felt the man watching her and then heard him following in her fuming wake like a thunderstorm blowing across the cement and into the black mouth of the derelict building.

The place smelled of rotten wood and old fire. The floor was filmed in ash and dust and debris. Shadows ruled the immense room despite the moonlight pouring through the hole where the roof had once been and illuminating the central portion of the space.

She walked brazenly into this moonlit area, feeling immediately as though the shadows surrounding her had begun to encroach into the lunar light. Once there, she turned about, extending her arms defiantly. "I'm here. Okay. Now what, man?"

The man watched her without words and then only nodded sympathetically, a gesture which infuriated the girl further. "Well, what the fuck, man? What do you want? Eh? What do you want from me? Have I got something you want, man?"

His voice was soft following hers, a caress from the shadows pooled before her. "This is a lesson for you. To not do things like you tried tonight. To not add to the darkness and foulness in the world, when it's not in you to do. How... How old are you?"

She grew silent at this. Dark suspicion returned as she sought to appraise his indistinct form. Her mouth moved as if to speak but no words came. Emotions played across her features, naked in the lunar light for the man to examine as closely as he wished: her tell-tale emotions, along with the added weakness of her general unattractiveness; speckled around her mouth with tenacious acne whose presence haunted her no matter how diligently she scrubbed her face with soap-lathered washcloth each night before bed and upon waking every morning; the hint of purple lingering among her brown chin-length hair from when she'd dyed it herself several days before, the only way she could afford, with grape-flavoured Kool-Aid, so that teachers would look at her disapprovingly and certain boys with interest; her thin lips and makeup-less cheeks and eyes as un-feminine as a boy's. Grown discomfited by this unexpected turn in their strange exchange, the girl fidgeted in her place but remained standing helplessly beneath the man's scrutiny, waiting.

Then, as if he'd extracted something from her that he'd wished to learn, the man said with a solemn, teacherly tone, "There."

His hand stabbed from the shadows and was pointing with a grubby finger into the darkness beyond her. He stepped forward a step and she saw his feral eyes devouring her, as if he gained strength from her great unease. "Look!" he seethed with greater vehemence until she turned in her place and followed where he looked.

When it became evident that she discerned nothing in the shadows he placed his hands on her small shoulders and edged her forward, step by incremental step. Her instinctual resistance to his pushing her forward ceased, and she allowed him to move her easily. Then, when they were bathed in the shadows beyond the perimeter of the moon-washed central space, his whisper guided her: "There, in the heap of rock and wood. In with the bones, those pale sticks rising from the debris in the centre. It's moving there."

286

She wondered if the wan timbers rising from the heap were indeed bones, felt an instant queer thrill and revulsion at the thought. They watched silently. Then, there, amid the blackened wood and soot-smudged bricks and bones, she saw long, slender, skeletal legs unfolding.

She held her breath reflexively. She placed a hand across her mouth as if she might cry out, though no sound issued from her. She looked with incredulity at the great grey- and white-furred spider and the bones over which it traveled. She sought to fathom the weird spectacle of it floating in the dilapidated warehouse remains like some malign spectre or scavenger. Its size was staggering—both her hands placed beside one another would be dwarfed by it. It wove a strange pattern with its nimble legs, making a soft but clear percussion in the huge quiet, a sound of sticks rattling across the rubble. She remained standing in her place though her revulsion of the thing urged her to hasten away. She shuddered, no longer discerning the man's hands where they remained resting—gently now—on her narrow shoulders.

"I first found it ten or more years ago," his foul-breath whisper came in her ear. "Crawling on a homeless man laying dead in a room of rubble. The man's skin was like ash, grey, powdery. He looked like his life had been drained from him. His neck, though, was dark, black with bruises. Like he'd been choked to death. It was perched on his chest. It seemed to be... watching me walk toward them through the room. It didn't move, just sat there on the hobo like it owned him. I guess it did."

She murmured, feeling as if too-long after he'd fallen into silence, "What... What is it? I've never seen a spider so big. Not even in books."

He eyed her curiously. A tender expression came over him, as if he suddenly realized the age of the girl he was observing. "A spider? Is that what you see?"

She nodded, noting absently the strange nature of the man's question. Turning to him, feeling suddenly greatly afraid, she whispered, "What do *you* see? I mean—what is it?"

But he only watched her with his new eyes of unsettling sympathy and then turned to observe the gargantuan thing once more.

They watched it a while and then he told her, "I see a great... hand. I see a large, strong hand. Masculine and muscular. Fingers long, hard. With long, dirty nails. That's what I see. It's...

It belongs to the homeless man, the hand. It's the hobo's hand I see."

He paused and she heard him swallow deep in his throat, and this silence before he next spoke seemed to her to be one in which he gathered himself. Then, "It's the hobo who stole me when I was around your age, with a knife at my throat in the lot behind the convenience store behind the house where I lived with my parents in the neighbourhood just beyond this lot. He was younger then. Quick and strong. His hands were quick and strong. And awful. When I saw him next, he was dead, in this warehouse. I come here to... to see it. I come here to see it and give my thanks. It's always here. Here and elsewhere, too. I've seen it throughout the city. In overgrown fields, on the hoods of cars in driveways after dark. Once inside a locker in the change room at the downtown gym, stuffed into the bottom of the locker like a grey baseball mitt. Once it was on the porch of a well-to-do house on the south side, a giant hand spread open in the middle of one of the two chairs sitting there, facing each other at midnight." He paused, and swallowed audibly again, and making his voice gentle said, "I see it often hanging from bars in jungle gyms, in schoolyards around the city. Half-buried in sandboxes and among the steel-and-wood skeletons of bleachers, and scuttling through moonlit school parking lots. I've looked inside dusty old school buses parked there and found it on the leather seats, waiting.

"For me, though, it's always here, in this place. This place is the place I see it without fail. I know this place. I know this place well. It's good that... It's good that you see it, too."

Her breath had been stolen by his revelation. She felt tendrils of cold snake all along her body beneath her denim jacket and t-shirt and jeans. Her heart crashed behind her chest. She turned to the spider, saw its hackle-like forest of pale grey and white fur spiking from its rotund body, its baleful grey eyes beholding them coldly, its long, needle-like legs perched delicately in its place atop the mountain of rubble. She felt the words rising up from her like vomit, unbidden and unwanted, bitter and shameful.

She said, in the quietest of whispers, though it sounded like thunder in her ears, "I woke up yesterday. In the middle of the morning. He... He was... He was *raping* me. *Raping* me. Oh God..." And she wept softly and shook violently.

In the bated silence they felt acutely the thing watching them with its cold avid gaze, unmoving in its perch, as if estimating their intent, weighing their sin or innocence.

After a moment, the man spoke, softly, too. "Then it'll find him, too. It finds everyone, I think. They wake up one day, they look up one day, and they're face to face with themselves, like they've never been before. I hope it finds him soon. I'm... I'm sorry I frightened you."

She nodded. She wept harder, hugging her thin arms about herself.

The man said, "I mean that. I am sorry, but I saw you, young and angry and foolish with a knife in your hand. I saw your future, of regret, and, and... I wanted you to know. I saw your eyes, and I wanted you to know about... this."

He let her have another moment of silence and grief.

Then, she murmured, "I didn't mean to want to hurt the kitten. I've never done anything like that before..." Trailing off, dismal and small.

"I know," the man said to her. "I know."

He let her cry. He wept, too, as he did on nights such as this. And all the while the pale thing remained there with them, unmoving but watching, silvered in a shaft of moonlight and kingly in its throne of debris and dilapidation, like a protector of that place, and perhaps the two of them as well, convened within its kingdom.

When the girl's crying ceased, the man murmured, "Here."

She looked to his hand extended toward her. In the centre of his palm lay her pocketknife, its blade folded into its rounded plastic shell. She stared at it. She shook her head, denying the idea of it. He dropped it among the dust and stones at their feet.

Eyeing the thing on the summit of ruins, she said to the man, "Are there... Are there really bones there in all that rock and wood?" The thought of someone, anyone, having died here, their remains undiscovered in this neglected shell of a building in the heart of a ghetto—it saddened her.

"There are bones everywhere," he said, watching the rubble with her. "The city's filled with them." Then he turned to her. "Goodbye. I have to go home now."

She eyed him curiously. She wondered, for the first time, about the man's home, his life outside of the night and this place of shadows and moonlight and memories. She wondered about those things which interested the man, his hobbies and passions, the everyday activities in which he engaged, and the people—the friends or family—with whom he shared his days. He watched her with a peaceful gaze over his shoulder as he trudged through the toppled warehouse.

He left her like this, in the dust and ashes. A great fear stabbed its way into her heart in her new aloneness. She shivered and cast huge eyes around the chaos of shadows surrounding her. Her nostrils seemed filled with the acrid aftermath-stink of fire. She considered the thing before her and the man's description of what he saw when he looked at it, like an amputated appendage belonging somehow to the city. She wondered about its other forms, in the lost, weeping eyes of others like herself and the haunted man who brought her here to this place. She wondered what other awful representations of human beings ghosted the streets and alleys and empty lots and fields, and she shuddered a long deep shudder. And though she was cold in the chill air she shook from a deeper cold that had been awakened in her: a new knowledge about the world and the dark things happening in its secret folds, everywhere.

She eyed the crooked landscape of wood and stone and bone. To the spider she said, in a loud, clear voice, "His name's Frank. Just so you know. His name's Frank and he stinks like sweat, and his breath stinks like vinegar. He's hairy all over. Thick grey hair all on his back and arms and chest like a big tarantula. I hate him more than anything in the world."

The spider, watching her, placed two of its long legs together before itself as if in prayer.

She turned from it and its kingdom of rubble and bones and fled the shadowed place.

Moonlight drenched her anew when she arrived in the vacant lot. The air tasted cleaner somehow than before as she sucked it into herself despite it being the same city air of smog and foundry fumes she knew every day. She relished its faintly acrid tinge but with the subtle suggestion of the nearby river permeating it, too, icy and aquatic, the perennial smell of the docks, where old boats lay tethered, bobbing in the current, where dirty ducks occasionally were to be found, too, misplaced in the chemical waters with their pretty emerald plumage and innocent passage.

And to the night, quite like a fervently uttered prayer, she seethed, "Just you wait. Just you wait." And she felt relieved, expelling that fury from herself with the words, and the great burden of it like all the concrete and stink and badness of the city filling her up and blown out like smoke into the air.

She turned eastwards and began her fearful and brave walk home. And, strangely, the longer she walked, the cleaner the air tasted, the cleaner her thoughts seemed to become, unsullied with dreams of blood and vengeance that had never really been her dreams at all.

AN ANGELA
NAMED VENGEANCE

This is the story of Angela... and Angela.
"A lot can happen on a dark road at night."
Indeed.

"Did you know he brought the apocalypse? It's true. Just like that: the end of the world. It's true, and so is this: I'm bringing it right back to him. I'm going to carry it in my hands and drop it at his door. Tonight, he's going to understand what he did. He's not answering his phone but I know where he's at. If you talk to him, could you tell him this for me? I'm going to bring it to his door. Tell him to wait for it. It's coming."

The tinny voice inside the receiver implored her: "Miss, calm down. Can you tell me why you've called 911? Is there an emergency? Can you tell me where you are? Are you confused? What's wrong? Miss? Are you still there?"

Angela sought to replace the telephone receiver in its cradle but it fell and battered against the plastic wall of the booth. She watched it swing by its thick steel cord as if mesmerized. The tinny voice exiting the mouthpiece sounded robotic and unnerving. She went to leave the booth but found it difficult to navigate its dual doorway. She barreled her way through angrily and arrived in the cool, nocturnal air, refreshing following the congestion of the booth. Into the silence of the early morning fields to the north and nearby forest to the south, a voice:

"Are you finished?"

She followed the thread of the words. Like a fish on a lure she felt her eyes drawn across the uneven asphalt of the gas station's lot, overrun with weeds rising through the countless cracks; through the alcohol-haze fucking her vision to the immense bulk of the man rooted tree-like at the small lot's periphery. In the moonless dark, she could just discern a suggestion of his leering yellow grin and intimate appraisal. Mostly only the immensity of him reared from the shadows, limned in starlight: his swollen belly draped over his belt like a great whale carcass, his thighs like tree trunks, his stout ankles thrusting from his brown leather shoes, his large, womanly breasts and shuddering jowls.

She smiled, and nodded, and staggered a wavering line towards the voice.

She'd found him at neither of the three county trash bars she'd visited that night, where she'd looked foolishly for men to wield like knives; this man she'd found, as if preordained, thumbing his way down a little-frequented farm road past 4:00 A.M., a mile or so from her home at the precise moment when she'd resigned herself to a fate of aloneness following her night of flirting with every trucker and biker and farmer she'd come across without a lick of success.

In him, she'd found something much more powerful, speaking in terms of weaponry. The distinct sensation filtered through the fog of her inebriation that she'd pulled this one from some deep place, like a figment of childhood nightmare, to fill her night of unabated misery and bitter fury with his sheer size and potential.

She'd pulled the car onto the gravel and watched in the mirror as he lumbered forward. Moving less like a grossly obese man than a great bear, shaking all over, flesh swaying in all directions at once. Clambering in, his weight groaning the vehicle. She'd seen his eyes clearly then: black and narrow and slicing through the dark with their keen intelligence. He was everything she'd wanted to find that night, and much more, too, she realized. Before the man could speak, she'd said, "Do you want to come to my house? I'm lonely."

His beady eyes had widened, revealing yellow spots like pustules sunken in the white. Realization seeped into them, and

294

then a devilish exhilaration: maybe he'd understood his own great fortune in that moment, too.

Turning from an examination of the camera on its tripod where it stood before the bed, he murmured in his voice of gravel, "You're a dirty one, aren't you?"

"Yes," she told him from her place seated on the edge of the mattress, unbuttoning her shirt and tossing it to one side. Her bra and pants and underwear followed.

He appraised her from top to bottom.

She saw the saliva bubbles forming in the corners of his mouth. "You like kinky," he grated matter-of-factly, and finished with a confidence and excitement which caused his voice to rise, "I got kinky for you."

He tore the shirt from himself with a hand like an old baseball mitt, scattering its buttons across the floor. He unzipped himself and let his pants drift like a massive tarpaulin about his feet. He turned around so that his immense ass was level with her eyes. Beneath the tautly-drawn silk of his powder blue underwear she watched the undulating mass first with revulsion and fear, and then with a sickening determination rising up inside her. He peeled the underwear from himself with measured theatricality and his tail lay revealed. It was stout. It was fish-belly pale. It was pimple-covered. Its root was forested with thick, greasy pubic curls. It curled and lapped on the air like a thirsty tongue. She saw with equal parts revulsion and titillation that it glistened with a sexual moisture in the dim light. She was revolted. She salivated. She hated her Bobby, who was no longer her Bobby, nor would he nor could he ever be hers again—a god of her own naïve and optimistic invention become an everyday whore and traitor.

She watched the tail stir on the air, mesmerized by the undulating patterns it wove. She hadn't even entertained that such a weapon might exist for her.

"I'm Angela. What's your name?" she asked distantly.

"Well, sometimes they call me Mister Filth, baby. Sometimes they call me the Big Old Big Dick. I'm always the Cheapest Trash Available If A Woman Needs It Bad Enough. I got an eternity of names, sugar-tits. What do you want to call me tonight, honey?"

He licked his swollen, smiling lips.

295

She told him without thinking about it at all.

"Revenge. You're my Revenge."

He turned about and faced her. His man-breasts swayed at the motion. His nipples had hardened and jutted towards her longingly like long brown bullets. The stink of him wafted from his immense cock and permeated her airspace. She reeled within its pungency. His testicles, bloated and shiny beneath their villous covering of ginger hair, appeared fit to burst. He proceeded to fall onto all fours. He shook himself in a queer, canine-like manner. He rippled everywhere. She examined his stout toes, yellow-nailed and hoof-like. Unlike his gauzy-haired pubis, prodigious back-hair carpeted him from shoulders down to buttocks. His wet tail wove an ever more excited language in the air.

Looking up at her from where his chin nearly grazed her bedroom carpet, he grinned his yellow grin.

His voice was eager, its pitch higher than ever. "Angela. In case you want to know the truth. My name's Angela, too. I got teased in school for it, but I'll prove I'm no sissy, honey. See? *See?* We're the same, you and me. We're so lucky to have found each other. A lot can happen on a dark road at night. We're so lucky we found each other."

Bile rose up in the first Angela's stomach. Her senses swooned. Through her revulsion the anger rose, parting it and making clear the path before her. Her nipples hardened. Her stomach turned. Her resilience hardened, too. She slipped a hand between her thighs, testing her wetness. She rose from the edge of the bed and went to the other Angela. He knelt closer to the carpet, draping his fat tongue across her calf. She clambered onto his back, sighed as he straightened himself and she was lifted from the carpet. The other Angela—snorting and bellowing like a great bull—pranced about the small bedroom with the first Angela straddling his bulk.

The first Angela felt a moist touch coil across her bare buttocks. She lifted herself from the other Angela's back, allowing the barbed-tipped tail to slip beneath her. She let herself settle on top of it. The tail explored her. It found her wetness. It slipped inside and settled deep inside her. The first Angela groaned. She cried aloud, louder than she used to permit herself during sex with her former lover of five years cut short. She screamed and howled like the animal without restraint she'd always been hesitant in allowing herself to become.

"Oh, Revenge... you feel good..."

The other Angela craned his neck and found the first Angela's eyes rapturously watching him. They locked feral glares and held on, and on, and on.

Bobby, seeing her handwriting on the large envelope he'd discovered tucked inside his mailbox, felt hope seize him. Perhaps Angela had found it in herself to forgive his callous, foolish ways. His apology—heartfelt and written in a flurry of desperation the day before—maybe, just perhaps, had found her heart of hearts and swayed her initial fury with him for his transgression and betrayal. Maybe she'd see him again. Maybe she could—one day—forget all of this.

He tore open the envelope and seated himself on the bed, his heart crashing madly.

He leafed frantically through the dozens of photographs of the hideous fat man fucking his once-girlfriend. Positions he and she had never tried, though he'd wanted to (asked her fervently on many occasions, in fact, but, frustratingly, never been able to cajole her beyond her bashfulness).

He realized then, while examining with revulsion the final photograph of the collection, just how beautiful she was, and had always, always been: his girlfriend of a half a decade crushed beneath the bulk of the grotesque red serpent, her mouth filled with its tail as if she were a link in some perverse ouroboros, her eyes angry and defiant and staring directly into the camera lens with the beast's black, forked tongue flicking beneath her eye as if emphasizing her resolve. Her hard, volcanic stare, utterly lucid as she looked out from the unfathomable grotesquery, in this way showing that she remained miraculously untouched by the blasphemy crawling on her but was ruined utterly inside by him and the crime he'd committed upon her.

Bobby replaced the photographs in the envelope and left it on the bed. He sat for several minutes in stunned silence. He thought about the different kinds of evil and wrongfulness living in the cracks of the world and sought to rank himself among them. He stood and crossed the room. He slipped into the bathroom and removed a naked razor blade from an old plastic shaver. He laid down in the bathtub and filled it with his blood.

Somewhere, a woman—broken but remade a queen—knew the truest and mightiest of closures while looking out from her new kingdom.

THROUGH FOGS DEEP AND FIRES LONG

People seeking refuge from profound personal trauma: this to me is not only a subject worth writing about but important to write about. I realized just how personally important it was when I was compiling Songs for the Lost, *whose fabric is sewn together with this thematic thread.*

Can we truly transcend to a better place through joining ourselves—emotionally, mentally, sexually, spiritually—with another human being? This story says yes. But there's a price to be paid for true *transcendence, and the toll here is not for everyone.*

Is this a love story? Is it a horror story? Is it both? Is it something else? Does it matter?

Here's to all of us getting away from the bad crying.

They'd met at an outdoors music festival in the sweaty heart of summer, noticing one another standing alone at the parking lot's periphery while the throngs of people watched the stage and the band on it. She looked small and shy and cute, her summer dress clutching at her body in the humid night air. He was looking tall and gangly and more than a little drunk, staggering a weaving line toward her as she observed him with her small, dark eyes.

Their initial conversation easy, as if they'd known each other many years. Tipsy and wishing to impress her with his intelligence and quirky sense of romance, he'd told her, "Let's hang out tonight. Maybe we'll stumble on an empyrean." Explaining to her his definition of empyrean while she'd smiled at him with an amused patience: a good place for them to be together without anyone else there to intrude on their conversation and peace.

They'd spent the night together, killing the long hours in late night coffee shops and on parking blocks overlooking vacant, moon-washed lots long after the shops had closed for the morning and the loud, drunken bar-goers had stumbled homewards.

With the sun rising they'd retreated indoors to his nearby apartment and a platonic sleep holding one another gently while the day breathed at the tightly shuttered windows.

It was on their second night together, while seated in her van in a lonely lot overlooking the Detroit River shimmering with the moon in its current, that they'd first kissed. He'd been gentlemanly about it and simply asked her permission: "I want to kiss you right now. May I do that?"

He'd never been kissed like it before: desperation lived in the gesture, her lips clutched to his own as if they were long-lost lovers reunited after many years apart. Again, they'd returned to his apartment, beating the dawn and spending the hours before noon making love in his darkened bedroom.

A week later she cut him.

She'd drawn the knife from beneath the pillow where she'd hidden it while waiting anxiously for him to enter the bedroom, surprising him not long after he'd slipped inside her. Blood trickled over its keen edge. His throat bled more and more. It was an epiphany. Something in them awoke in the blood and heat of the moment. It made him fuck her harder. Sex had been good throughout their few days together but this was something entirely new. Nearing climax, she lunged forward and bit into the

300

wound she'd opened. She tore at it with her teeth. Blood spurted. The taste of iron filled her mouth. They screamed together, revelling in their inhuman harmony. They came at the same time.

Soon afterwards she was driving him to the hospital, the towel he clutched to his neck heavy with his blood.

In this way, through a cut and a bite, began Daniel and Ellen's ascent to better places.

"It doesn't look so bad," he called from the bathroom where he examined his neck wound in the mirror over the sink. Its raw edges had scabbed over in the week following, and the surrounding purpled bruising had faded to a sickly blue and lighter green-ish tinge beyond this.

He saw her reflection appear in the doorway behind him, earnest-eyed. She said, "It looks beautiful."

They watched each other's reflection. Wordlessly, they retreated to the bedroom to stretch the night hours.

Their relationship deepened. Their nights stretched interminably and within their eternal folds the secret things they did grew in number and extremity. Often, she led the way and, emboldened by her courageous madness, he would follow her into new places.

She beat him. He beat her. Open-handed and fisted. He dislocated her jaw once, and she broke his aquiline nose on several particularly primal occasions. They took to using tools with which to pleasure each other, initially ordinary household implements because they were too sheepish to enter a sex shop let alone purchase any of its products. She liked being whipped across the back and shoulders and buttocks (first they used leather belts and electrical cables, later an actual tasselled leather whip); and he relished when she burned his neck and chest and genitals (eventually substituting the run-of-the-mill butane lighter for candle wax, which she thought added significantly more romance to the act). Knives for cutting and stabbing and pliers for pinching and twisting and rope for binding: all these implements and others played their roles in fairly equal measures, too. More often than not, they returned to the simplicity of using their hands: choking each other, pinching, scratching zigzag patterns into each other's flesh like mysterious hieroglyphs for them to decode afterward, and biting until blood was drawn into the bed with them, their perennial partner in the night. Every so often they would need to rush to the emergency in the middle of the morning, making creative excuses for spurting neck injuries or gaping stab wounds in thigh or ribcage or her left nipple cloven in two.

They grew to admire the scars they gave each other. Like art, they considered them pieces worthy of scrutiny, to revisit and reinterpret often. She'd given words to themselves in this way, one night while watching him towel off after a shower:

"You're like an art gallery."

Smiling, he told her that she was one, too.

Their evening escapes grew to invade their daytime duties to work and academia. Distraction plagued her while seated behind her desk, the computer screen all but forgotten before her and the payroll spreadsheets unfinished as visions of her and Daniel's previous night together haunted her.

Likewise, it became increasingly difficult for Daniel to concentrate in class, his professors's lecture voices dwindling into inconsequential background noise as startlingly vivid scenes of Ellen distracted him: her lips wrapped around his cock; her welt-lined buttocks quivering as he attacked them with the belt in his fist; her plaintive, primal cries bouncing from the bedroom walls as he fucked her from behind while gauging her back with the thumbtack gripped between his fingers. Then, stirring as if from a profoundly deep dream to find himself back in the lecture hall, the students around him oblivious of his most recent journey as well as the erection throbbing between his thighs.

The manifestations began making their appearances in these early days of their relationship.

She'd see them over Daniel's shoulder while he was fucking her, floating above the bed. He'd see them coalesce from the dark wet tangle of her pubic hair while he gave her cunnilingus.

Vague, half-formed, hallucinatory spectres born during the long hours of their fucking. Amorphous and ethereal, obeying a sensual, sentient choreography as they mimicked the writhing figures entangled beneath them. Silently moving through the air, something in their fluid movements beckoning to Daniel and Ellen, as if they were meant to follow the lights to whichever place they disappeared each night.

In the aftermath of the sex-visitations neither Daniel nor Ellen questioned what they'd witnessed. Neither did they rationalize the experience, chalking it up to imaginations running wild with frenzied lust. They knew: their love was mightier than a definition so small. They knew: there was a reason they'd been shown this gateway. And they knew: they were meant to understand this mystery, somehow, to fathom it and embrace it, somehow.

Once, while laying sweaty and weary and bruised beside each other after sex, they watched a pair of the spectral presences drift along the ceiling over their heads. They coiled about each other, their pale luminescence glowing a sexually-charged crimson wherever they touched. The lights disappeared within the ceiling, trailing tapering appendages, as if urging them to follow.

"I want to go," she whispered, fighting tears she felt rising without warning. "So badly, Daniel, I want us to go, too."

He said, watching the afterglow of the amorphous lights fade and disappear and leave them in blackness, "We weren't built for this world, darling. We have to do something, darling." He knew the truth of what he'd said: the only time he felt right, safe, like himself, was when they were together.

In the wake of his confirmation of her own despair, she allowed herself to cry. He did, too. Together, Daniel and Ellen remade the nature of their tears, as was their way. They clutched one another tightly until they were ready to fuck again.

Occasionally—very, very occasionally—the outside world trickled into their shared bubble of escape.

Something had stopped her hand and the knife it gripped, its moon-glimmering blade ghosting his cheek as he stared up at her straddling him in his bed. Concern and a lucidity entirely removed from her earlier mania shone in her eyes when she whispered, pleadingly, "Why do we like to... Why do we *need* to do these things?"

His answer was simple and so brazen with revelatory truth that it elicited a startled cry from her and pulled her headlong into her frenzied passion once again: "Something awful happened to me, too, and I've been living with it every day since it happened. I... I was really young when it happened."

She kissed-bit his lips. He bit her back harder. She wept through it while slicing patterns across his back with the butcher knife in her trembling fist. Above them, the spectral lights mirrored their fucking, wrapped about each other in an intimate, hungry air-dance. Feral and violent, Daniel and Ellen stayed entwined until the sun rose in the bedroom window, deposing the moon and the silver ghosts it had painted across the bedroom walls.

As the months passed, they began exchanging letters via postal mail, a romantic mode of communication in a fast-paced virtual world in which they felt completely misplaced.

Having used the key Daniel had given her to enter his apartment, Ellen made her way directly to the bedroom closet. There, she retrieved the extra-large bubble envelope from where it lay resting conspicuously on the top shelf. It was marked with a single word, in her neat cursive: *Daniellen.* She spread its contents across the bed: their collected correspondence, letters dog-eared from much rereading, some stuffed in envelopes, others loose and folded neatly. She liked that they'd decided to keep them together in one place: one day they planned on making an album of them, each letter framed behind cellophane like the pieces of art they were, like documented proof of the places they both came from and the place they'd found in each other.

She placed a hand among them, drew a handful randomly from the pile. Opening the first of these, she read:

Daniel,

> *You said you thought about me a lot when you arrived home last night!*
> *So, let me ask you: what do you think about, specifically, when you think about me?*

Am I taking this in a very naughty direction? I think I am! You know *I am...*

I blame Cosmo.

Love,
Ellen

Smiling at her playfulness and boldness (and silliness—she loathed *Cosmo*, and every other magazine like it), she replaced her initial letter in its tattered envelope and retrieved the next, remembering from the red paper on which Daniel had written it that it was his answering letter. Always more like prose than mere personal communication, always brimming with a fiery kinetic energy she relished, his letters never failed to arouse her.

Ellen,

Don't blame Cosmo: *the culprit is you, and only you...*
...I think of kissing you, and how your lips and tongue taste. I think of all the incredible wild sounds you make when I'm touching you, and putting my fingers inside you, and moving my tongue inside you. I think of how your voice changes when I'm doing these things to you and takes on a primal high timbre that makes me crazy. I think of how you smile sometimes when I'm touching you, a very specific smile of ecstasy and release that I've only ever seen from you while we're in bed together. I think of how amazing you feel when I'm doing these things, and how amazing you taste and smell when my tongue is moving around inside you in search of the secret madness I always want to awake. I think of how wet I make you. I think of how much I love squeezing and licking and kissing and pinching and scratching and biting and burning and sucking on your nipples. I think of how much I love gently running my fingers across your inner thighs, and then squeezing them as roughly as I can, and then kissing them and biting them and leaving the scars of my bites deep inside your skin. I think of how much I love it when I'm in

305

your mouth, and of how the anticipation of exploding in your mouth while you're sucking me builds and builds until I think I'm going to lose myself in the moment and never return. I think of your tongue and what it does to me. I think of how much I worship the sweaty, burning little temple of your body, and how much I love turning you around on my bed and filling your cunt from behind and just fucking you forever, until the sun replaces the moon in the sky and still I can't stop fucking you. I think of how amazing it is when I'm standing behind you and filling you up completely while you're bent over our bed, as if we're worshipping the bed for the holy place it is. I think of you on top of me, riding me hard and fast while I bite your swollen, bleeding nipples and bite your neck and wrap my fingers around your throat and squeeze and squeeze and tell you how much I want to put my tongue inside you again and climb on top of you and hold you by your ankles while I fuck you until you've lost your mind in the fucking. I think of scratching you with my nails and carving messages into you with my knife and leaving a new belt of welts across your hips from candle wax dripped across your skin. I think of your spit hot on my face and your blood burning on my hands and your hair tangled in my mouth while I'm making you scream like an animal. I think of you telling me you're coming while I'm fucking you and fingering you, moving your hips and legs around in my bed like you're possessed by a demon, and how incredible this serpentine writhing is to behold—frantic and helpless with head thrown back and toes splayed and eyes crying and fingers clutching your perfect scarred breasts—and so madness-inducing that I'll never be able to properly articulate to you. I think of the cigarette between your fingers burning circles into my chest and the smell of my charred skin mixing with the smell of our sex on the air. I think of the knife in your trembling little fist threatening my jugular while I'm growing harder and longer inside you, and your feral eyes watching me and waiting for what will happen next. I think of becoming so enraptured in the moment and each other that we feel as if we're close to losing what shred of control we have remaining and just devouring each other with the most incredible lust we've ever known, so that when we're finished and laying beside each other, sweaty and tired and bloody and scalded and spent, it feels as though we just returned from the longest and most mind-alteringly miraculous trip with each other, from a place far and far and so far away. I think of how amazing it is that I'm able to elicit a reaction from you like crying while we're in bed together, and how that in our rare case it's a positive and purging and desirable emotion, and you feel incredibly good while experiencing it. And I think about how I want to make you feel this good, and much, much better, every time we're together, in bed and out.

I promise you, Ellen: I will take the tears from inside you, from whichever deep well they exist, and drink them all away until that well is dry and you have nothing but happiness filling you. I will drink away all the badness of memories and fill you with new memories: us, together through all the darkness the world throws at us, together through it and stronger than it by far. And we'll pity the darkness its weakness when faced by the burning light of us fucking and loving and loving and fucking forever...

...Thank you, Ellen, for always being there when I come back from bad days, and reminding me how lucky I am to have found you. Some people claim they've found God. I found you. My goddess.

Daniel

Ellen stared at the words covering the paper, remembering her initial reaction to it. Heart hammering, lust reawakened in her, she let the paper drift onto the bed and hurriedly opened the next letter.

Daniel,

Last night was the only good crying I've ever done in my life. Thank you.

Yours,

El

Looking among the chaos of letters strewn on the bed she knew exactly which answered the one she'd just read, recognizing it for the marks of semen like a series of continents etched into its crumpled, battered surface. She recalled how he'd fucked her on that particular night, clutching her calves while thrusting into her, pausing from time to time to glide the knife blade across her stomach while she dug her nails into his forearms; and later filling her mouth; and the prodigious amount of his ejaculate she'd swallowed while he'd drawn a bloody map across her back. She recalled this night and this letter with them in bed, crushed beneath their entangled bodies, sodden with their sweat and come and blood, marked with their bodily fluids like a signature of their passion and loving violence.

El,

All day long, I kept remembering in the most uncannily vivid way how it felt when we were sitting up in my bed last night, kissing and biting and licking each other for that prolonged period of time before fucking. I've been experiencing the amazing ghost-sensation of your breath on my face, and your lips brushing mine, and your tongue in my mouth, and the feel of your neck and shoulders and nipples between my teeth as I'm biting you and making you gasp and cry out and shiver and writhe in the incredibly entrancing way you do. I want to bite you and kiss you and ravage and scar every inch of your perfect body right now. I want to sign my name in your skin with the knife in my hand. I want to trace your new scars with my tongue, exploring the intricate map of you again, and again, and again.

You open a gate for me, to a place beyond definition. Its ingredients are fire and blood and come and sweat and more love than the world could ever contain.

Tonight:

I am going to devour every part of you: hands, arms, neck, mouth, tongue, breasts, thighs, calves, feet, and then finish by devoting myself to consuming the amazing and transporting portal of your cunt until the light that burns inside of you lies revealed for me to swallow.

I will cannibalize and drink every inch of you, and then breathe you out like fire to burn away this sad, desolate, hateful world.

Yours,
Daniel

In her eagerness to read more she neglected to replace the letter in its envelope. Instead, she dropped it beside her and snatched another from the pile.

Daniel,

I was thinking about you today. The day after we spend the night together, I always find myself zoning out and thinking about the night before.

You have no idea how much you mean to me, and I wish that there was some way that I could show you, and you would believe me, but I don't know that there is.

All I can say is that I'm yours, always.

Love,
El

Finally, she reached among the papers fanned open before her and came away with a single sheet of paper which she recognized for its bent corners, its tattered evidence of having been read and read time and again. Unfolding it, she read his words to her, written in the aftermath of the night that, wholly devoted to their shared moment of fucklust and bloodlust, she'd given him the gift of a first cut and then drowned his chest with candle wax and touched him with naked fire. Chest still smoking, he'd sat at the foot of the bed and written the words:

Momma, the world was bright and kind
You were all I ever knew
Then in a great darkness a man was born
And inside a night he brought it to me too

Momma, I cannot jump away
Momma, this dark is spun too tight
O you, you are the one I hate
O you, you are the one I hate
But you don't have to worry, momma
You don't have to worry about your boy:
I found the temple
And together she and I make a new world

The letters inspired her to masturbate. She removed all of her clothes, laid in his bed amid the letters, on her stomach with her pelvis raised, touching herself. When she was nearing climax, the thought occurred to her. Snatching the telephone from its cradle on the night table beside the bed, she called him at school.

She could tell by the officious way he answered that he had someone in his office with him, an undergraduate student disputing a poor mark on a term paper, a professor meeting with him about this or that. In a playful but firm voice she told him:

"Daniel, I'd like for you to come home to me right now, and cut me, and burn me, and shock me, and hit me, and fuck me, and punish me for making you feel uncomfortable right now. I need you to be the demon possessing me. I need to be consumed by you. I need to be completely *consumed* by you right now. I'll be waiting."

She clicked off the phone and lay with it pressed to her breast. She was waiting for him like this when, thirty minutes later and his office hours cut short and forgotten behind him, Daniel burst through the door, pulling at his clothes as he came to her.

Their city was mid-sized and considered a blue-collar lunch-bucket town for its many automobile factories and trash bars. Daniel and Ellen were drinking at such a bar, only because of its close proximity to his apartment. As always, they felt out of place there, on this night especially, being that the long holiday weekend just passed had seen them indulge in their secret deeds with even greater fervour than usual: without co-workers and classmates from whom to conceal the various evidences of their nights together, they'd felt even less inhibited than usual. But their scars were on the mend, for the most part, and they wore their coat collars up around their necks, and they huddled closely together over the little wooden table, and so they remained invisible to the other bar patrons and content within the usually impregnable bubble they created between themselves. They were talking quietly about their respective days, discussing with excitement their forthcoming anniversary and the ways they would celebrate.

There were nights, though, when against all odds the outside world succeeded in invading their fortress.

A couple entered the small, dingy room. It was clear from the way they loitered in the entrance and examined their surroundings—furtively but with eyes looking into every corner at once, as if they didn't wish to appear as the newcomers they were—that it was their first time in the bar. It took Daniel and Ellen a moment to recognize them as Daniel's neighbours, who from time to time would bang on the bedroom wall in condemnation of the sex noises keeping them awake. The woman's gaze passed over Daniel and Ellen huddled at the small table alongside one wall, did a quick double-take, and found them again. Her eyes widened with something like horror, drawing her partner's attention. They looked Daniel and Ellen up and down with a blatantly critical and disdainful eye, examining openly the scar-mottled flesh where their necks showed above their collars, the bruises and welts around their eyes, the fine blading-scratches etched across their cheeks.

The couple whispered between themselves and appeared ready to leave when the man turned back and called out over his shoulder towards Daniel: "So, when can we get our turn with her? You'd both like that, right? You sick fucks." Shaking his head, he spat with theatrical disdain onto the tiles. Together, they exited the now-hushed venue, indignant, contemptuous, and with no small amount of discomfiture showing in their faces, in the telling manner with which they hurried on their way.

She was stunned. Her initial shock quickly turned to anger. She resented this unwarranted derision from people who neither knew them nor wished to know them. She felt exposed and ostracized, suffering ambush in the middle of an otherwise tranquil night. A shuddering grew up in her, encompassing all of these emotions vying for ownership of her—in its wake she felt depleted, defeated.

They sat quietly, holding hands on the tabletop as conversation in the bar resumed.

311

His wisdom came in a gentle voice, though his eyes were troubled. "Every inch of the world is so covered in fog that no one can see anything but the tiny space of their own life around them. Let people live there. We're like fogcutters, you and me. Right? We sail through the thick of it. We chart open waters."

Daniel and Ellen took solace in each other, as ever, clinking their bottled beer in a toast to themselves. "To navigating the misty streets together," he said, and they smiled at the romantic flavour of the words.

They watched through the window after the departing couple walking down the sidewalk. They might go elsewhere for a drink, this man and woman, and then home, possibly have sex later that night—good or bad but non-transporting in any case. They might split up before long, or continue plodding through their same-old lives, wholly content or wholly dissatisfied, but either way with their vision of the world dimmed by what they deemed aberrant and forbidden. Daniel and Ellen, though, bonded by blood and love and a secret cache of shared memories, would endure. They'd beaten much with an initial cut, bite, and revelatory bloodletting. Friends, if they'd had any besides each other, and family, if any knew what it was their children had discovered in each other, would have envied them their finding. He was right, Ellen knew: in a world of loneliness and wickedness, they'd found a solace known to few people, a feat all the more miraculous given their misanthropic ways.

And yet something in her continued its persistent gnawing, and it was the selfsame ache she saw in his eyes every so often, once the rabidity of their lust had gone to sleep in conjunction with the ghost-lights disappearing into the walls and he lay beside her staring at nothing, looking troubled. She witnessed this transformation overtake him then, while he sipped his beer and stared off into the smoky air of the bar with eyes miles and miles away, making her wonder, making her anxious, making her fearful: without him anchoring her, she could feel herself drifting into old and deadly places. She clutched his hand, and though he squeezed her tightly in return, still the fear continued to constrict her, a forbidding touch the likes of which she knew she couldn't endure alone.

Much later on, in the deepness of the A.M., long after they'd made love and fallen asleep to the swirling tangle of phantom-figures weaving patterns in the air over the bed, Daniel woke to

312

find Ellen missing from beside him. He followed the faint illumination in the hall to the bathroom door and listened to the sound of her crying within. Among her weeping he discerned the words, muffled through the door:

I hate you. I hate you so much. Why won't you finally fuck off and die?

His heart ached: it was the sound of her old despair, a world removed from the good crying.

The day had arrived—their true anniversary, marking a full year from the night they'd discovered their true nature and bond—and Daniel vowed to make good on his promise to Ellen.

"My gift to you... You'll love it. It's the most I could ever give you. I've been waiting for this night to give it to you." He said this while helping her from her clothes and handcuffing her to the bed; both wrists to the sturdy oak headboard and her ankles to either side of the footboard so that her legs were held parted wide. He repeated the words while running fingers between her breasts, down her belly, among the curls of her pubic hair and across her cunt, along her inner thighs and tracing a path the length of her scarred calves to her small feet.

She trembled. A shiver snaked its way the length of her spine. She exhaled a wavering breath. She smiled. "I can't wait for it," she told him.

He smiled at her spread before him, his own gift that special night. He pinched her disfigured nipple. He leaned to her. They kissed. He ran his tongue from her lips to her small round chin, down her quivering, bruised and blood-blistered throat to her collarbone, where he bit her gently but not so gently.

Standing from her, still smiling a feral smile, he said, "One moment, my darling."

When he returned to the room several minutes later, he was naked and stroking a massive erection. She smiled when she saw him, her Adonis, her beautiful and mighty conqueror.

He climbed expertly on top of her. She was wet. He slipped his cock into her. She groaned, tingling with the expectation of what was to come. He shook, too. He told her he loved her cunt. He explained how much he loved her but admitted he could never define his love with mere words, only through the medium of his cock filling her, his tongue filling her, his fingers filling her,

313

his lust filling her up until it swallowed the outside world and pulled her into ecstasy with him again.

This was the poetry she deserved from him. She wondered excitedly what pleasure-pain he was going to give her on this, their special celebratory night, and watched entranced as he revealed two more pairs of handcuffs encircling his wrists and with which he bound himself to the headboard alongside her own bonds.

She watched with a start as he reached as far upwards as he could with his handcuffed hand and dropped the key to their bonds through the ajar window and into the night. Her eyes widened with alarm. She smiled then, whispered in a voice tinged with excitement and fear, "Oh, my. Now what are we going to do? We'll be trapped here forever." Knowing, of course, that she was safe in the throes of his mad plans.

He shared the secret with her, in a whisper like a scream into her ear that reached her heart with a vicious and beautiful stabbing of epiphany:

"Do you smell it, El? I've always loved the smell of gasoline. I drenched the apartment with it. A sea of gasoline everywhere. I dropped a match into it before joining you here. I've set the place on fire. We're burning down right now, as we speak. The door is locked and bolted. The building alarms will go off anytime now and warn everyone, but no one will get to us in time. Happy anniversary, darling."

Her eyes widened further. Her jaw dropped. She breathed, "We'll never get out."

He felt her heartbeat against his chest pressed tight against her: mighty and frantically fast. He nodded, smiling as he leaned to her and clenched her upper lip between his teeth, biting her hard enough to draw blood. He grew harder inside her. Her nipples, crushed against his scar-mottled chest, grew harder, too. He began moving around inside her. Her wetness had grown, an ocean of warmth for his cock to move through.

Minutes stretched past languidly. The fire's glow seeped into the bedroom from the apartment beyond, red and wavering like some living, agitated thing. The temperature had risen sometime during their fucking. The bedroom had grown hot. Sweat beaded their faces and bodies. They shone with it like melting wax figures. The excited crackle of flames devouring wood and

314

wallpaper came to their ears and, a moment later, the distant wailing of the building's main fire alarm.

In the air over the bed, they appeared: the orgy of phantasmagorical figures, a dozen or more of them tangled in an elegant but excited air-dance, sending red tendrils of their light towards Daniel and Ellen entwined in the bed and other appendages ceilingward, urging the lovers to follow in their wake.

She gasped the words into his ear, the epiphany like a sun exploding inside her: "Oh, sweetheart... They'll never hurt us again... No one will ever hurt us again..."

He whispered into her face: "Oh, darling, now—finally—I'm going to fuck you *forever*..."

She smiled. He did, too. He thrust into her with greater violence. She moaned. She screamed. He did, too. The fury of the fire grew, devouring the door and eating its fill of the room. Wallpaper curled away in strips and plaster fell away in charred, jagged pieces that clung sizzling to their naked flesh. The heat rose and rose and scalded their bodies while smoke darkened the air. In the great conflagration she screamed; he screamed; and the flames themselves roared with a voice like all the agony in the world pushed to its threshold and—breaking through the difficult barriers of sin and death—became something else entirely.

Through the suffocating, scalding fireful of pain:

Happiness.

Ecstasy.

Peace.

They woke, as if from the longest of lives and into the gentlest, most cradling of dreams. They struggled to see but the strength of the light blinded them. It seemed to flow all about them in a saturnalia of perpetual movement, caressing them gently everywhere. Tears flowed from their eyes as they thought back to the night behind them, of fire and fucking. It seemed distant and like a dream, too. It had been no dream, they understood, sensing the potency of the alien atmosphere surrounding them. The light touching them was warm, and stirred against their skin, like a million burning kisses, like the kiss of a naked flame, like a tropical sun. The scent of flowers was heavy on the air—heliotropes, roses, magnolias, and countless others merged into a heady brew—dizzying them further. A

315

sound of music around them, too: the song of a million birds nesting and rejoicing among trees. The thousand gentle ghost-touches continued to caress them, coddle them, soothe them.

They sat up, the ground beneath them soft and thick: the lushness of grass, the velvety touch of flower petals. They clutched each other, anchors, as ever, for one another. Their eyes cleared. They made certain that they were the first thing they saw. From the brightness they materialized. Their scars were vivid against their pale complexions, blatant and regal like insignias of honour, marks of valour from a time when they'd needed to be courageous. Light seemed to shimmer in wavering prismatic lines from these scars, as it encircled, halo-like, their bodies, too. They smiled. Together, they'd reached their empyrean.

They stood on trembling legs, still staring into each other's watering eyes. Inside, they felt a great missing thing. They understood then that they were unburdened.

Then, as one, they turned and faced their Paradise.

A VALLEY
FOR DOROTHY

A story about a bounty hunter hired to hunt another man's demon and learning that the demon family tree is a complex, many-rooted one. This is a very dark story, and it wound up being sort of a combination of weird western and dark fantasy and outright horror. It deals with the extreme evils we're capable of, as well as the ways we're able to find redemption for those sins.

Oh, and pardon me my cussin', but word is that there's a vile motherfucker of a monster nestled deep in the dark stinkin' heart of it, too, all coiled up and waitin' for you to read it awake from its restless slumber.

Tread carefully, partners.

The days were long for the toil filling them, but the nights, oh, the nights: an eternity growing up each dusk and stretching long and long until the dawn sun scalded the mountains of the east like a great malefic fire to cleanse the world of all the sorrow it carried within its endless miles and eternal hours; though of course the sun, great deceiver that it was, gave no such mercy. For the nights always returned to hound Henry Barber, who hadn't slept a good sleep in forty years and more. They stretched a worse and wicked length and even darker depths, laden with all of the pain he'd known in his days, and pain he'd known much of.

And so it was that another eternal night had set upon Henry Barber: he put his hands on the air to examine them by the young lunar light. All of the old scars and the stories they told, and the new scars and their stories, too, those mounds of flesh paled by the years or raw and red and new, criss-crossing his hands and arms; and the dirt, as well, always dirt like a perpetual second layer of skin cloaking him, and working with the scars to make his hands unsightly; always the dirt dusting his skin, caked beneath his cracked fingernails like a permanent part of the battered man he was. Though he could not see inside himself, he knew his heart was similarly battered where it hung thumping within the lightless shell of him, for it ached and burned beyond measure then as it had every night since the days of his youth, days he only ever recalled as if through the densest of fogs; a vague golden-aired time, a half-remembered oasis before the light was put out of the world and all of the darkness he came to know so well was ushered in.

He stared down into the hole he'd dug in the earth. It gaped at him like an immense, black, toothless mouth. He shuddered, despite having faced countless such mouths.

"Sleep forever," he said to the blue-skinned, bloated woman he'd dropped into the earth-mouth minutes earlier. Her crime unknown, her violent demise known intimately to Henry Barber. The sound of her corpulent corpse thudding its way like a feed-laden sack along the rough-hewn grave into the darkness haunted the nocturnal air.

And Henry Barber slammed his spade into the earth and hefted the first mound of the woman's burial dirt over her in the tomb darkness below.

The milky semi-light of pre-dawn filtered through the grime-encrusted window to illuminate the small work shack. Henry Barber's employer, a portly, apple-jowled, greasy-haired scumbag named Huxtable Crocker, eyed him shrewdly with a beady black gaze from where he sat squeezed behind the small wooden desk and looking to Henry's eyes like some fat fish beached and doomed outside of its water hole.

"Barber," he growled through a mouthful of tobacco bulging his shiny red cheek like a balloon. "I got a job for you, but a job the kind you ain't gonna want to have no part in digging. I need

318

you to dig me a hole, but not like any of the usual holes. This hole's gotta be deep and deep, and deeper than any hole ever dug, by you or any other killer and gravedigger this world ever seen."

Henry Barber nodded. A job was a job. He'd dug holes for hundreds of dead men and dead women, and plenty for men and women not dead yet but with their fates preordained for them by vengeful minds and the dark and bad mediums of their doom: bullets and daggers, cups of poison and suffocating piano wire and choking hands. He'd dig this hole and fill it and buy himself supper and some beers with its depth. He'd dig any hole he had to if it would keep him alive, though he wasn't very much content to be alive. The only thought more distressing to him was his death, and what might lie waiting for him then. His employer could stress the importance of this latest of countless holes for digging and he'd treat it like any other: a job to work to help get from this day to the next. A job he'd do well, because he owed his employer for the many jobs he'd given him in the past, and he owed him for more besides.

The boss lowered his gravely voice and, with chary sidewise glances to left and right, grated, "You gonna dig me a hole for to bury a demon."

Henry Barber thought on this a moment. He nodded, still pondering the words and their possible meaning. A shivering began its creeping along his spine and among the thick hairs along his forearms, and this uncanny shiver he didn't like at all.

As if seeing this invisible reaction in him, Huxtable Crocker narrowed his vulpine eyes more shrewdly still, and whispered, "She'll try to deceive you, for she's a deceiver through and through."

Henry Barber thought the boss was referring to his wife. Possibly he'd caught her with another roughneck and this roughneck proved to be the final straw for her. Maybe he'd just grown weary of her dark eyes flashing at every cock and balls strutting the muddy streets of their oil town.

"Yeah, I'll bury your demon."

The boss smiled a vicious smile. He laughed grimly. "Barber, you a strange fella. And you got courage in you. But don't you for a second be believing this special hole's waiting for my wife, or some tart with my bastard child growing in her belly, or some roughneck I caught deceiving me in secret. This demon is the

319

genuine article, Barber. Maybe you got trouble understanding it. Maybe you don't care much for the Holy Book and the things it say—maybe that Book's some kind of bane of your days like it is for some kinds of us men—but I ain't lying to you one word."

Barber matched the boss's narrowed eyes with his own. His voice was frosty: "I don't know no banes, Crock, and I ain't much for reading. But I'm gonna dig for you again, like I told you."

Huxtable Crocker's sardonic, grotesque grin creased his features. "You a man with honour in you, Henry. That's why I'm asking you. I'd never give this job to no one else. I'd rather try it myself and have it murder me, what with my age eating my bones. Some say a man can't ever bury no demon, but I got faith in your skills and your grit. How much you think I'm offering you for it?"

Henry Barber sucked on his cigar. Its burning sounded in the A.M. stillness like the crisping of autumn leaves. He said calmly, "I'm thinking it's a lot heftier than the measly nothing I get paid for busting my balls in your fields and keeping quiet about all the holes you need dug in this world."

The boss chuckled again. "I appreciate your candour, man. I always did, did you know? I got respect for you, and that's saying something because there ain't many I respect in this shit world of wicked and gormless men."

He spit brown, stringy phlegm onto the mud-caked wooden floorboards and finished: "I'm giving you retirement money, Henry. Money enough to keep you fed and without worry for the rest of your years. You been my steadiest hand for how many years, I can't recall no more. You always clock the most hours in the fields. The best digger I ever saw, and by digger you, of course, know my meaning. You work the shittiest of shit jobs and work them better than the rest. You never bitched a word about none of it. You deserve this."

Henry Barber ruminated on this a minute before answering. "Alright. Maybe I do. So, okay: I'm gonna dig your hole."

The deal with Henry Barber's job as hole-digger was that he dug the holes, filled them with their occupants, and, most importantly, took those occupants out of the waking, living world.

"Henry," Huxtable Crocker said, leaning towards him, his belly rolling onto the desktop like a hideous toadstool. "Are you a believer?"

"I believe in some things."

"Well, whether you believe or no, what you're gonna see might bend you. It might bend you near to breaking, and might do just that. You need to know this, so you ready for it, even though ready ain't something a man can be in a bad situation like this."

Henry Barber wasn't in the habit of asking his employer unnecessary questions pertaining to his jobs. Now, though, something compelled him. "I got one question: where did you find your demon?"

"Oh, no, Barber. It ain't that way at all. My demon found *me*, though my resources found me its nesting place." He smiled a smile tainted with regret. "I ain't lived a saintly life, like you might know. This cursed thing was heading my way for years on end. Maybe you can be like my guardian angel, Barber. Or my angel of vengeance. Stranger sights this world's seen, maybe."

Henry Barber thought on this. It made sense to him. He nodded, watching Huxtable Crocker unfurl the creased and time-yellowed scroll of parchment and spread it across the desk. Pinning it open with a pair of rocks, he leaned back in his wooden chair, screeching its frame with his weight. His voice was grim: "You gotta look and look good, and put it all in your memory, Henry. In case you don't make this one, I got to have these directions to show the next brave or mad man."

Henry Barber leaned over the map, examining its faded lines etched into the ancient, flaking paper. A rough, black circle marked a place among the tangle of crags several miles south of town, beyond the county line among the baddest of the Badlands—difficult country, barren and lifeless but for roaming coyote packs with the hunt on their mind. He knew the area, having buried many a man and woman thereabouts. He could find the thing's nest easily enough.

Henry Barber glanced up at the slippery sound as Huxtable Crocker slid the leather satchel across the desktop toward him. He took it from the desk. Untying it, he glanced within. He sought to betray no emotion or reaction but wasn't certain if he'd succeeded. His toad-like employer, sinner and scumbag and wicked man deserving of his hauntings, had made good on his word.

Henry Barber touched thumb and finger to his hat's brim and tipped his head to the ashen, fear-eyed man behind the desk.

Turning, he strode from the work shack and stepped into the wakening day.

The sun was lost to the badness of the day. The tenebrous sky glowered, oppressive clouds devouring the daylight as the wind lashed the clothes against him like a punishment. The muted caliginous light upon his face as he trudged across the mud-puddled fields felt angry, spiteful, burning him with an uncanny touch he'd only ever known the moon to scald him with during its eternal vigils. This was different: this was a different day than he was accustomed to, and it made him wonder how long and deep a wicked night lay waiting for him.

The way was long, and so he traveled by horseback from the outskirts of the town, across the county's fields of waving wild grass and marigold while the invisible sun crept the sky from the far east to emerge from the clouds in the bleeding west; until the path became too perilous for the beast, all jagged granite crags and tricky, unnavigable slopes and arroyos rising and plunging from the plains like ancient, monolithic citadels. There he tied his mount to a small gimp of a tree bending in the gusting breeze, seeking to calm its braying whinnies with a palmful of sugar cubes.

He was set to go when some instinct told him he was being watched. Sure enough, in plain sight on top of a nearby hill stood a line of Indians. He wasn't sure which tribe they belonged to, though he raised a hand toward them, both to show he had no quarrel with them and also that he had no fear of them, neither. Without a word or sign in return, though, the men turned and disappeared from wherever they'd whispered from, like they didn't want anything to do with him, though Henry knew it was really the place that done kept him safe from their arrows. His employer wasn't the only man with tales of spooks and other terrible things making their homes in this ugly country.

The moon was risen and red when he entered the maze of the crags, winding his way upwards with cautious steps, rising steadily to a dizzying height above the plain far, far below.

●　　●　　●

A stench of offal on the wind told him: it was near.

He grew faint, his stomach sought to revolt, though he succeeded in steadying his reeling senses and keeping his breakfast in his belly. Another quarter hour of crawling a precarious path through the brambles and thorn-bush dotting the jagged slopes and, peering through the skeletal arms of a massive blackened and leafless bush, he saw the great maw of the cave. It was black, its granite lips scalded and scorched with an ashen dusting.

The hairs on his neck stirred looking upon it. His balls shrivelled up inside of his sack as if bitterest winter blew its breath upon him. His heart grew cold and cold. What felt like a great sickness clutched at him, constricting the breathing in his windpipe and stabbing daggers into his temples.

Still, though, Henry Barber stepped one and another step forward, determined to see his job through to its grisly end. He un-slung his rifle from where it hung across his back and clutched it in a fist. In his other he held the looped rope, wound through with the stout chain of iron which he'd felt compelled to reinforce it with before setting out at dawn that day. The daggers hanging on either hip were heavy with the ghost-blood of countless men and women but somehow offered little reassurance. Still, crouching low to the ground, a hunter's gait, Henry Barber slinked his brave way into the stinking stygian mouth open before him.

The queer thought arrived and nipped at his courage as he slipped into the blackness: he knew this blackness. He knew its taste, its kiss and bite and touch. And it knew him, too, he sensed, like no other knew his mystery.

As he edged forth, Henry Barber held his small lantern high, though he wasn't very grateful for its illumination: the wavering orange light crawled over the granite walls with their design of deep gauges and scratches, as if the claws of some great rabid bear razed them regularly; and he was forced to sidestep the mounds of bones littering the passage at irregular intervals, soaked in something like yellow bile or vomit, for fear of sending their rattling din echoing into the heart of this mountain-bound kingdom. He grimaced as he stooped to examine a cache of such bones: a frail skeleton sleeping upon the muck-heavy ground, its

323

small skull cracked in twain. Henry Barber wondered how old the boy or girl had been when their doom had arrived to steal their life. He stood a moment later and, scowling into the darkness, continued on his hunterly way.

Yes, he was near to its vile nest.

He crept forth, descending step after descending step, for the ground began a deep sloping downward. He walked for so long that he grew to wonder whether his progress had taken him beneath the floor of the plain, and if so, exactly how far below. He sweat in the infernal heat emanating from below. It felt like a great hot breath blowing on his skin. It burned his cheeks and sizzled his hair, and the stench of carrion grew more potent as he crept on his wary way.

Without warning, Henry Barber stepped from the passage and into a room. This room was furnished, and furnished in a startlingly familiar way: a small wooden bureau he knew, and a window he knew holding a gibbous moon he knew, too, and with a bed he knew well owning a familiar, shadowy corner. And there, beside the bed, two lines of absent floorboards revealing the black mouths of a pair of holes: the first holes he'd ever dug in a long life of digging. This familiarity bewildered him, shocking him into immobility while his dazed senses sought to give a name to his surroundings or reject them from the dank, deceiving underworld into which his job had taken him.

Henry Barber's heart shook, for he realized that even then he faced the thing. It lay upon the tiny bed, creaking its wooden frame with its great bulk overflowing the small confines, bulging the wool blankets, soaking the wooden floorboards with the mucus and urine dripping from its orifices, drenching the mattress. As if sensing his awareness of it, it clambered from the bed in a spasming of its many limbs, splintering the frame and rearing to its full height, scraping the ceiling with plate, horn, tentacle, and spine. Its diseased shadow blanketed him like night putting out day, its bedlam of voices howling and barking and growling and bleating and lowing and screeching and gibbering at him all at once.

Peering closer among the gigantic ruin of the thing, he saw her: a swarm of distended, rotting cocks undulated about the young girl's head like an abominable Medusa's headdress, caressing her neck and cheeks with a moist clamour. A hissing escaped their holes among squirts of jizzum and piss and blood.

Their fetid stench reeled the senses, and beneath their reek Henry Barber felt his knees buckle. Shafts of hair-covered appendages—a grotesque orgy of bruised and bloodied and tumoured arms and legs and canine and lupine paws and tails—shot upwards and flailed towards the moon orbiting in the bedroom window as if in rapt worship of its numinous silver light while random groups of immense, nictitating eyes watched him hungrily from among the tangles of limbs, bloody and bulging.

Acting instinctually, he brought the rifle to his shoulder and fired into the seething mass before him. Its huge weight buckled beneath the blast. A great and perverse shudder rippled through its swollen, festering body, a prolonged groaning issued from it. A colony of pustules convened upon one of its immense, sagging, dirigible-like bosoms burst, and their acidic effluvium squirted like semen over Henry Barber's shaking hands, burning his skin. He remained resolutely in his place, aimed carefully, and let fire another bullet. The blast was greeted with another sexual spasming and a high-pitched crying like the excited laughter of a blood-maddened hyena pack cornering a kill.

Henry Barber, having succeeded in crippling the demon, lay his rifle beside him and looped the rope-chain in his hand, whirling it about his head. He let it fly expertly despite the terror gnawing at his insides, the open noose of it finding purchase among the undulating cocks and swollen sacs, and finally slipping and tightening about the narrow neck of the girl nearly hidden among the saturnalia of appendages.

The abomination spoke then, in a condemning rasp of voices curdled with blood and phlegm and semen bubbling in the corners of its million cock-mouths and from the blasphemed mouth of the girl, too:

"Here I am, daddy. Here I am, daddy. Here I am, daddy. Here I am, your wicked love."

Henry Barber tasted a sea of salt. It flooded from his eyes at the words and ran like rivers into his mouth. It couldn't be helped. He was a tough one, and a bad one, but a man still, with a beating heart within himself. Through the monstrous bedlam of the many-voices he discerned her former voice, angelic and pristine and unsullied. Through the torrent of his emotions and through the stinking gale wind of the girl-demon's condemning diatribe, he grated his answer like a judge likewise delivering his own sentence, while tightening his grip on the chain-rope.

325

"I'm burying you now. Darling, sweetheart, I been trying to bury you for years, Dorothy, but tonight the night is finally come for it. Every hole I ever dug I dug for you but never none of them took you away from my mind. But I got to finally bury the big pain of it all. I *got to*, darling. This is my one and only shot at it, maybe. Maybe this is my one shot at burying the Devil that got inside me and owned me for one night. Forgive me for my terrible sin... In you go."

He accepted then that it was his daughter whom he faced, upon the stage of her bedroom on the night she last lived in the awful shit world that was awful and shit enough to birth a man as wicked as himself: the first hole Henry Barber had ever dug, after waking from the blasphemous frenzy that had gripped him one deep Winter's night while the world outside was banked in rolling snow-hills and the world indoors burned with a malevolent heat, and seeing her lying upon the wooden floorboards of their home: bedraggled and bleeding and shrieking a weeping lament that would forever haunt him; her agonized caterwauling litany that needed to be silenced there and then, for if it wasn't his sanity would splinter in the tidal roar of it; and reaching for her again but this time with a different violence burning in his desperate hands as he squeezed and squeezed and squeezed and choked the life from her little pale throat before reaching for the rifle leaning against the wall and likewise silencing the howling woman with flailing hands seeking to halt his madness—his wife, whom he'd cherished before his transient madness stole his reason—and blowing a hole clean through her stomach with a single close-range blast from the gun's angry mouth.

Two holes dug in the deep hours of the first eternal night Henry Barber had lived.

And with these visions before his eyes yet again, in the deep dank hell-nest beneath the crags and inside the earth, Henry Barber pulled tremendously on the fraying-rusted rope-chain encircling the thing's brawny, swollen shoulders and diminutive, vulnerable neck. It fought hard to remain in the world. Their struggle was vicious and long. They grunted, and sweat, and clawed, and scratched, and bled, and howled in their efforts.

In the end, though, the long-tormented man won this battle and succeeded in dragging the bloody, maimed demon into the hole he'd made for it many and many years before. Its masculine

326

hands and lupine paws scrabbled for purchase on the floorboards but Henry Barber beat the thing downwards into its hole with the butt of his rifle, splintering its wood so that he was made to resort to bashing the thing with his iron fists, bruising and bloodying and cracking them, too. Stomping upon its jagged fingertips and slithering, frenzied cocks with his boots, he watched it plummet toward the small, dark bed of the familiar pinewood coffin embedded in the earth.

The thing's immense size, he saw, wouldn't be contained in the child-sized box, so he pulled both daggers from his hips and dropped down like a stone into the earth. There, Henry Barber hacked and hacked with his blades, severing tentacles and stingers, clawed fingers and gushing cocks, uprooting curving horns and sharp black teeth, slitting throats of snakes and other creatures that looked like no natural animals he'd ever seen or heard tell of before. Not soon enough, the grisly deed was done, and he held the amputated demon-child pinioned with a bloody boot in its belly, and a moment later slammed the coffin's lid down upon it. For nails he made do with his daggers, plunging them in at top and bottom of the box, which he then turned upright so that he could lasso it from above.

Henry Barber left the room and descended the black granite corridors, pulling the child-sized coffin that weighed more than a mountain upon his shoulders, down and down and down, to finish the final job of his too-long career.

He sang as he worked, which was strange for Henry Barber, who'd never been good at carrying a tune and who'd never had an ear for melody. A wordless tune but with an increasingly purposeful, mournful melody, as though the song's words were close to becoming birthed within the blood and relief of the funereal moment. It echoed its way through the dark, labyrinthine tunnels and into the dark fields above to hush the nocturnal birds and field mice in their foraging and to stir county dwellers from their slumbers to scratch their heads and wonder, uneasily, as to the haunted quality of their dreams.

And all through the night and morning Henry Barber dug, and he dug, and then Henry Barber dug deeper into the earth still, guiding his spade's tip until its steel grew twisted and bent and brittle with the tenacity of his work. And when the battered tip was sundered from its wooden shaft, Henry Barber dug with the wooden pole alone, until it too splintered in his fists and stabbed his flesh in a dozen places; and then he clawed away at the earth with his bare scarred hands, bloodying them and adding a new story to the countless tales of blood and murder and vengeance already collected there. And all throughout this endless digging into the earth, Henry Barber hauled the small coffin, with its brokenly-wounded but undying horror that he'd tracked in those dark pathways scratched into the earth, and that he'd felled in the dream-room above, drawing it ever closer to the molten land where it belonged.

He wept, of course, while he worked, long into those morning hours, salting the earth upon which the burial pit ran, and then finally upon the very grave site itself in the deep bowels inside the world, upon a spot where the rock was impregnable and the fiery heat had grown too great for even a man such as he, gritty, driven, possessed in his mission. There he interred the maimed thing in its coffin, beneath wood and rock and rubble, in this way burying the child who'd owned his heart from the moment he'd beheld her infant's eyes like blue jewels watching him openly and unafraid, and too innocent to exist in a world that loosed men such as him to wander its lands.

Up from the heart of the earth, the perverted child-beast's voice echoed its judgement of him: "I'm with you always, your wicked love..."

To the echoes he said, "Sleep forever."

He felt it in that moment of burial: the black seed within him, ever breathing with an eternal life, never to be interred deeply enough, the Devil's rape-seed left to fester forever, or else one man's own inherent wickedness grown up like some black flower from his dark, poisonous heart.

And then Henry Barber, humming his unexpected, wordless song, began his long, slow climb upward toward the light, heaping armfuls of soil and bone and jagged stone over his shoulders as he went, filling in the deepest and final hole he would ever dig.

In the years following, an anomaly of the county's geography was discovered. A group of farmers seeking to locate tillable land in the little explored southernmost miles were amazed when they stumbled upon a cave which opened onto an expansive underground cave system and ravine which cut beneath the flat county landscape. Of prodigious depth, and several miles wide, geographers and cartographers at the time defined it as an underground valley and named it thusly after the leader of the party of farmers who discovered it and mapped the vast majority of its labyrinthine trails and corridors: Barber's Valley, after Henry Barber.

To this day, nearly thirty years after the discovery of the site, Barber remains one of the few locals to inhabit the land upon which the hidden valley exists. A retiree, his property consists of a lovely house with accompanying garage and barn, and more than fifteen acres of verdant land, as well as a variety of farm animals. His home is located within sight of the original cave, marking the boundary between the county and the increasingly inhospitable terrain of the southern badlands. Barber has grown over the years into something of a local legend and is known as much for his predilection for song as he is for his saturnine temperament and preferred life of solitude. It is said by those who visit the area around Barber's Valley that an old guitar's sombre chords haunt the air there, and a grizzled old man croaks his song—copied many times and sung now by younger voices the county over—in his distinctive bullfrog's croon:

O little darling, the world is bright and kind
You are all I ever knew
Then in a great darkness a man was born
And inside a night-time it was brought to me, too
O little baby, it wasn't Richard Bane cut you with his knife
The papers was wrong about him through and through
He hung and he swung un-guilty
And the demon, he slithered free
O sweet girl, I seen me choke you all night
Darling, I can't jump away
Darling, this dark is spun too tight
O me, you are the one I hate
O me, you are the one I hate
I'm so weary from all the days
But I had me just one more hole to dig
But I had me just one more hole to dig

Now there's a fire in the valley that no wind ever quiets
For I had me one final hole I dug
And now I live only to tend the hole I dug
I deserve this fire
I deserve this fire
It's my lover, forever

And the children of the county bordering the badlands—and the roughnecks and farmers, too, though they laugh it off to flaunt their manhood and hide their fear—tremble at the words and recall them in some deep and primal place within them while laying sleepless in their beds after midnight.

Another popular story concerning the old man Henry Barber speaks of the ghastly clamour arising from his home or thereabouts in the nights and bottomless mornings: a banshee's caterwauling that silences the coyotes in the fields and shakes the people in their homes fringing the area of the secret valley. A tortured song, of deepest anguish and suffering that some say contributes to keeping the land a mostly uninhabited place, despite its lovely wildflowers and picturesque woods and sweeping vistas, making it very much like a tainted Paradise known to few.

ANOTHER LIGHT CALLED 1-47

I will always wait for you, 1-47.

—AL-X Z
Age 6

The following story is a love letter to NASA, from the universe-obsessed little boy who grew into this adult author with his head still in the stars. I'm happy the dream never went away.

The summer of 1-47 proved to be one of peace and gallantry, and particularly so in the small but historically significant town of Spring's Grove, Ontario. Boys held doors open for the girls they crushed on and for those whom they'd never dreamed of at all, too. Police officers saved careless children from the turbulent river and rescued stranded cats from trees and apprehended the very occasional villains who held up confectionaries before midnight struck and shop doors were closed for the night. Bullies were rare that summer, too, either hiding indoors and out of sight or else electing instead to revel in the chivalry of those days and simply join the ranks of their former victims.

Over the years that summer grew to be remembered as one of fairy tale splendour and good will among people everywhere, though, of course, nowhere in the world was this more true than in the small town that lay at the heart of the summer's most wondrous ingredient. *Oh, the Summer of 1-47*—an incomplete phrase, yet containing all of the indescribable emotion born that momentous July night, to be spoken with wistful and nostalgic fondness for years and years to come.

1-47 was a handsome model, and would remain so, even in the eyes of future generations accustomed to norms of increasingly streamlined design as well as technologically and structurally advanced capabilities. 1-47 represented a utilitarian and efficient beacon of hope for anyone who dreamed, and in the summer of 1-47, who didn't dream? It was these qualities, in fact, which remained wholly inherent to 1-47 alone, to the exclusion of all of its brethren. Some would reason that this was due to its being the first successfully completed model of its kind, and the first to be sent away on the quest for which it—and its many failed predecessors and future brothers and sisters—were created.

Some—perhaps the more romantic of heart—claimed 1-47's nostalgic favour stemmed from its golden voice, like the very pulse and heartbeat of summer. Indeed, poetical descriptions of 1-47 abounded in those days, likening its voice to everything from a million cicadas singing their electric song to the sound of moonlight paling hillsides and rooftops to stars trembling in their constellation-bodies, and countless others.

1-47 was—at its most fundamental element—a promise made to all people everywhere, ensuring them that the future awaited them, and that its sunrises and sunsets would rival those of even that most idyllic of summers.

Ten-year-old Angela Samson was present that day on the sward on the town's outskirts, several miles from the government facility where 1-47 was born. There, among the majority of the townsfolk and many visiting people who'd traveled from afar to witness the milestone event, and the indelible spectacle that it was, and the bright light of hope that it represented. She'd stood with her mother and father and younger sister Abby, who was too young to fully understand the portent of the event they'd gathered to witness but was more interested in the ice cream cone she was licking, dripping fat chocolate drops across the front of her orange-and-white polka-dot summer dress. Angela also had an ice cream cone that afternoon, but she rolled her tongue across hers with less gusto than her sister because her eyes were riveted the whole while on the colossal needle spiking from the field and stabbing towards the dusking sky.

A simple parting from 1-47, delivered in its golden sunlight's voice. "Goodbye, friends. We will see each other again." And the politest of waves to the gathered—returned by all, with tears running freely across the cheeks of many—and 1-47 entered its gargantuan needle, disappearing from sight.

"Goodbye, 1-47." Angela found her voice cracking with emotion, and though she said no more because she feared she might burst into tears like some of the people standing near to where she and her family stood, she thought, *Please come back, please come back, please come back.* Only when she was older would Angela realize the innate fear she'd felt for 1-47, though she never fully decided what it was that she feared.

The silver needle spitting fire and smoke and roaring a roar felt for years to come in the souls of all the watchers. And the needle lifting and lifting from earth, and then shooting into the starfield overhead, merging with its countless distant shimmering points. And the long wait was begun, while life sought to return to a semblance of normalcy, as if the world hadn't been witness to all of its collective hope shot into the ominous eternity of the heavens.

And little Angela Samson cried that night, too, despite all her efforts to remain visibly unmoved. Her tears washed the celestial scene into an oblique, silvery smear, and she would forever associate this image—this saddened portrait of evening skies— with feelings of fearful hope.

A blackened carcass arrived from the sky some thirty years later. A husk, charred and broken, and though its beauty was ruined and its once healthy heart lay cold and inert in its chest, the name emblazoned thereon remained, if only barely visible beneath the scabbed, scarred steel skin:

1-47.

It fell to Earth with neither grace nor dignity, a careening wreck spouting fire and smoke like a red and filthy beard in its wake. Like some dark comet, an ill augury for all those witnessing the furious descent across the skies. The site from which the remnants of 1-47 were recovered was near to but not precisely

333

upon the site of its original departure—the wounded needle having nearly plummeted it into close-by Lake Molnar—a clear indication that its trajectory had been severely tampered with by unknown means. Little else could be learned from the remains, despite the arduous study devoted them in the years to come.

People fretted everywhere. Some called for doom soon to fall from the heavens while others prayed for salvation. But neither doom nor salvation arrived, only the same day-to-day joys and sadness as always.

Angela Samson was then a forty-year-old widow, childless and though not quite destitute—what with her husband's life insurance preserving her—she wasn't altogether financially secure. She had her pets: two terriers named Luke and Bernard and a tabby she called either Hunter or Sleepy depending on its mood. These animals were her only true friends. She'd never left Spring's Grove and, until her husband's passing, believed that she didn't want to. In the days afterward, she felt a distant tugging inside her, but by that point felt too tired and old to follow its voice anywhere but through the same day-to-day ennui and menial work drudgery to which she'd been a slave for the past twenty years.

The day she'd heard the news she was sitting before the television in the kitchen, alone, a cigarette in her fingers and a half-eaten T.V. dinner grown cold in its foil tray before her. She watched the television and cried. When she could bear no more of this same news on every channel she came to, she shut the television off, and she went to her room.

There, sitting on the edge of the bed she'd shared with her husband for twenty good years before he'd died suddenly of a bad heart, she held the naked razor blade she'd popped from the plastic shaver in quivering fingers. She fingered its sleek edge, pressed it first to one wrist and then the other. She drew blood, a dribble from the line she scratched across her left wrist, and the itchy, stinging pain it aroused caused her to abandon her efforts, too afraid to continue. Even in this instinctual act of self-preservation she wasn't able to gain any sliver of confidence or optimism, thinking instead only of her younger sister, who three years before had taken herself from her own downtrodden futile life with a razor much like the one she so ineffectually wielded. Even her kid sister had shown more courage and determination than she could muster.

334

Things had not turned out for her the way she'd dreamed the future days would unfold. Life was far more dismal and discouraging than she'd foreseen, or even believed possible when she'd occasionally considered the worst possible scenarios that might lie waiting. Little money and an assortment of tedious jobs following a failed tenure in the local community college, and her eventual resignation to the fact that she'd never be the writer of children's stories that she'd aspired to become during her more sanguine academic years; and her husband, faithful and loving toward her but eternally unhappy in his own work, doomed to toil long, bone-wearying shifts in the local foundry until his untimely passing.

 She went to bed and slept only fitfully and dreamt of her husband, but her husband as the boy she'd fallen in love with when she'd first grown to know him, in the distant summer of their shared youth, at an age before most girls and boys fell in love with each other but maybe only felt the nascent, strange pull toward each other that would one day blossom into true love.

She saw, recurring throughout that hopeless night, his child's eyes, wide and blue and sparkling and filled with all the potential she'd needed in order to imbue her vibrant young world with contentment.

After many years, the ravaged husk of 1-47 was inducted into the Museum of World Wonders and served as a dual reminder to those who traveled to look on it of the lofty pursuits humankind is famous for, and the fragility of our dreams.

Severe and debilitating arthritis came to gnaw Angela Samson's joints in the ensuing years. She grew crooked and became imprisoned in the confines of a wheelchair, thereby joining the ranks—in her mind—of the near-useless citizenry of society, no longer able even to engage in the day-to-day activities that had made her who she was. No more pottery sculpting at the kiln, and gone were the days of her being able to stand for long hours before canvases and paint the abstract blobs and swirls and eddies which gave her such joy, even in the face of the bewildered reviews given her work by her neighbours and few acquaintances; and even her pastry recipes—famed throughout the old neighbourhood—seemed to have lost their indefinable magic, tasting less flavourful and much more flat and dull than

335

she, or anyone, recalled them tasting. The future had brought with it technologies capable of placing men's dreams into the furthest corners of the sky, but still she was destined to wheel her way through her remaining days as an invalid. Her dogs and cat had passed on, too, like all of her family and those few of her acquaintances whom she'd considered even remotely close. She'd never felt so alone in all of her life, and she often fingered the old naked razor blades and toyed with ideas of the salvation they might provide her if only she could muster the courage for the simple but difficult cutting act the way her sister had mastered it years and years before.

It was then, nearly sixty years after the day the little girl she'd once been had watched in rapture as a giant silver needle spiked into the heavens, that an answer came from the sky.

A light descended.

It hung in the sky for eleven days—as if ruminating on the fates of all those watching it raptly—before falling, on the twelfth day, to earth. It had hung over the small but important town of Spring's Grove, and that's where it fell early in the evening. People came from near and far to live the event, of course, awakening Spring's Grove from its decades-long somnolence, like a ripple through a placid pond.

No needle landed upon the sward that night. The sliver of bright light descended slowly and, with a ginger grace uncanny to behold, settled itself softly upon the grass. The luminescence seemed to hum a hum felt by everyone gathered there, like a familiar voice touching their hearts. It stirred the people to whisper among themselves and ponder the course of their lives over the past sixty years.

It was, wondrously—almost *magically*—a renewed 1-47 that strode forth from the shard of light.

Its skin was pristine, new and lustrous, yet undoubtedly encasing the 1-47 of old. It seemed to reflect each of the gathered people's faces of wonder and awe—many of whom were old and grey and had seen this sight before, on a night imprinted upon them forever—as well as the stars trembling in the sky. Its steps were sure and measured and fluid. Its gaze as it surveyed all those people convened in the field held vitality. It radiated this

336

vigour in a way unmatched by any of its successors throughout the years. Fleet, graceful, mighty and reassuring.

Of a sudden, a pair of arched tents unfolded from its shoulders and the masses stared in wonder at 1-47's silver wings, which hadn't ridden there those many long years ago. They fanned the balmy air, stirred the hair on the watchers's heads and mosquitoes into more excited heights.

A pervasive hush fell over the throng.

"Hello," it said into this great and expectant quiet, and its voice was exactly as golden as that long-distant dusk nearly sixty years past. "I have a long and strange story to tell you all, about where I have been and of the things that I have seen and learned. I have a message for you. I have for you a story dark with death and bright with birth. Will you listen to my story, which is also your story?"

1-47, sixty years on, was just as polite and respectful of people as in the far past.

A collective sigh escaped the thousands gathered. No one stirred. The night birds had grown hushed in the surrounding trees. The crickets's evening serenades were paused. The world listened. Overhead, dusk had descended in its full celestial glory. The sky was clear and cloudless in all directions, and the earliest stars, it seemed, had begun their frostings with a greater insistence than usual, pulsing, pulsing, as if eager to transmit some of their ancient light into the scene unfolding on this very important night in history.

And Angela Samson, hunkered down inside of her rickety steel and rubber wheelchair, felt the old crone she'd become straighten its crooked skeleton; felt the blood flow more freely through her withering veins and stiffening arteries; and she remembered the little girl she'd lost through the long hard years, along with so many other friends; and she felt that girl's heart becoming a slow, sure, steady pulsing behind her frail chest, suddenly filling her with something she'd believed long lost. Excitement. Strength. Hope.

She placed her feet from the steel chair's footrest and onto the lush lawn. The thousand tiny pricklings of grass blades reached her numb, callused and bunioned soles and toes through her threadbare slippers. She gripped the sides of her chair with fingers suddenly stronger and stood; so that she could gain better vantage of the drama unfolding; to hear better the words being told; to feel like she once had, long before when she'd stood with shoulders straight and head held high.

"Well, listen then, friends," sang the golden voice, having received its answer from the tears flowing all around. "And listen well."

And the tears that ran from her eyes as she listened to the story told by 1-47 watered the July grass below her new feet, a small rain of renewal while everyone remained huddled close together in the night, hushed, in rapture, and—for the first time in a very long time—wholly at peace with one another and the world held enthralled all around.

THE HOMES WE DESERVE

This story was originally published in a limited edition mini-collection chapbook called A Test Tube Family *that accompanied pre-orders of my third full-length collection,* Blacker Against the Deep Dark. *The volume is currently out of print, and of the five stories it contains, this one is my favourite. This seemed like a good opportunity to unearth it and share it again.*

The setting here is the Second World War, somewhere in the Pacific Theatre, within sight of a nameless island where something truly terrible has happened—an event seemingly tied to another inexplicable occurrence. These two incidents give the soldiers who witness them reason to question things about the world and themselves.

Put your compasses away. They won't do you any good here.

They'd counted forty dead—sixteen their own and the rest the enemy. The stink of death and smoke was heavy on the still, sweltering air. The jungle droned loudly, its eager night-voice building up as the sun burned beneath the treetops in the west.

Garrety removed a cigarette from the pocket of his shirt, lighted it, and sucked on it disconsolately before offering it to McVries beside him. They passed it back and forth, oblivious to the corpses drawing thick clouds of flies, the radio resting on the grass between them waiting for their call to base to be made so that a dust-off would be sent to rescue them. They made no move to call base yet, though. They only stood smoking and silently recalling the past several hours, so unreal-seeming now. First, the battle on the trail winding along the coastal plateau with the ceaseless voice of the Pacific murmuring to the south, this now-still place where their friends had been cut to pieces in the grass: Olson with his chest bullet-riddled and torn to shit; Parker with his face blown off, his fine blonde hair grotesquely untouched and brilliant in the gloomy air under the dense canopy of the trees; their Colonel, Stebbins, destroyed, belly spilling his intestines into the grass as he sought fruitlessly to crawl to cover while holding his guts inside himself with one hand, like a butcher handling a bundle of sausages; and all the rest too, all dead after an unexpected encounter with a Jap patrol just as startled as they'd been when they'd collided on the footpath curving the plateau's scenic rim and, now, just as dead as their friends.

Mostly, though, their attention was riveted by the evidence of that other unfathomable happening of that strange, strange day: the giant cloud darkening the view of the open ocean before them. Immense and mushroom-shaped, it appeared suspended in motionlessness over the tiny, distant island, plunging it into deepest shadow, as if somehow paused against the sky for them to study and glean some meaning from.

McVries, staring at it, seeing ghost-armies swirling in its depths, said, "What was it?"

Garrety remembered the great silent flash of hours before, and then the concussive thunder that followed, so colossal it defied a man's ability to articulate. He said, "It was a bomb."

"But—it—I know—but... *look* at it."

"Yeah. I know."

"Was it a... test? They do tests like that, I heard."

"Maybe."

"Do people live on that island?"

"Nothing lives there now."

They digested the words.

They were silent. The excited buzz of flies surrounded them, the distant lapping of waves.

Then McVries said, "We don't belong here, brother."

Garrety said, "Where can we go?"

They continued smoking and watching the cloud, thinking of the blinding flash and the visible ripple of the water pushed before it to slam onto the rocks at the base of the cliff on which they stood and the gargantuan plume of fire and smoke rising upward from the tiny island to obliterate the daylight. They thought about these things, ignoring the strewn dead and the radio between them, and then each began to weep quietly while giving the other the respect of not looking at him, offering a false but necessary privacy with their sorrow. They were men, after all, and more than this they were soldiers with a duty to stay strong in this place, and if they needed a moment to pay their respects to their friends, and to nameless islands burned to oblivion, this was acceptable.

Minutes passed. The jungle's night-voice grew louder. Monkeys brayed like lunatics in the green gulfs of the interior. Birds screamed, their voices like mockery from the trees. Deeper darkness crept in to steal away the remnants of the day. The giant cloud continued to hang in the sky, terrifying and fiery and darker than all.

The men turned to the Japanese soldier, the sole enemy survivor of the firefight whom they'd found crawling desperately among the elephant grass, bleeding violently from the bullet that had decimated his thigh. They stood looking down at him where they'd tied him to the base of the tree, mouth stuffed with a bloody rag, awaiting their attentions with hateful, dignified eyes. They'd forgotten about him after the flash and the thunder and the fire and the waves and the monstrous cloud.

McVries pulled the knife from the scabbard at his hip.

Garrety, observing the fury and dignity in the captive's eyes, said it again to McVries, to himself, to the captive man before them, to the jungle watching them in their great desolation beneath the shadow of the mushroom-cloud. "Where can we go?"

They looked from the Jap to the radio resting on the grass like a relic from another time and its bankrupt promise of salvation. Maybe they were finished altogether with youthful notions like those. Maybe their long trek to base had been compromised long before they'd even set out that morning. They were only men, after all, trying to walk through a world that gave birth to calamities large enough to blot out the sun and moon.

Garrety unslung his machine gun, aimed it at the radio, and let off a short burst that blew it to pieces.

McVries stared at the smouldering wreckage, unmoved. Then he knelt behind the captive Jap and sliced through the rope binding his hands. He stood and said to the man, "It doesn't matter. We'll meet again soon. Go."

The man spit the dirty rag from his mouth, struggled to his feet, crumpled a moment later with a groan, and then crawled off down the trail, watching them apprehensively over his shoulder until he reached the bend in the path that led off among the denser trees of the interior. The trail of blood he left in his wake gleamed in the dying light. It glistened through the torn fabric of his pants as he crouched on the trail, unmoving.

Garrety and McVries passed the cigarette back and forth, watching him curiously. They observed him for several minutes. The man's posture was peculiar, kneeling on the trail and staring upward at something that was invisible from where they stood, especially since he'd hastened from them with such eagerness to be free again. Only when the sound of his frantic whispering drifted to them did the two men exchange worried expressions and, raising their weapons, slink forward to investigate.

What they found took them a moment to comprehend.

The ladder was a brilliant gold, inlaid with silver particles like celestial dust that glimmered in the moonlight.

They looked up its length, saw that it disappeared high among the canopy of trees, though inexplicably—*impossibly*—it wasn't leaning on any tree trunk that they could see. Rather, it was held firmly in place in the soil, at a perfectly vertical angle. Where it had come from, they didn't know. It certainly hadn't been there during the firefight. And its colour? Its brilliant gold and silver-frosted colour, so misplaced in that stinking jungle?

Garrety slung his gun over a shoulder and removed the binoculars from his pack. He placed the lenses to his eyes and, leaning back as far as he was able, peered upwards along the length of the ladder. He made small adjustments in his position, stepping this way and that to see beyond the obstacle of branches scratching out the sky. When he returned a ways along the path, he found a good vantage on the plateau, where the trees were sparser, and saw that the ladder rose clear of the trees and continued upward, ascending as far as his telescopic eye could see. Literally, the impossible ladder disappeared out of sight into the moon-limned clouds miles overhead.

"Where's it go?"

McVries sounded upset. Indeed, glancing to him, Garrety saw the fear in his friend's face. He felt that fear, too. The element of ever-present danger that surrounded them when they were in the bush was one thing—it represented a *known* unknown. They expected it, lived in obeisance to it in order to preserve their lives as they slunk and sweated and fought and bled in the jungle every day. But the ladder was an unknowable thing, beyond logic, beyond understanding. And it had appeared in the wake of the abominable explosion that had engulfed the nearby island—almost, Garrety thought, as if in answer to it, though how or why that could be he couldn't begin to guess.

Garrety could only hand McVries the binoculars and motion for him to stand just so, boots planted there and there. Because how do you explain a thing like that to a man?

He waited, as McVries looked, and gasped, and swore, and began speaking and stopping several times before, finally, lowering the binoculars to stare at Garrety with haunted eyes.

"I don't know," Garrety said.

McVries looked to the Japanese soldier, as if hoping to find an answer to the mystery in the enemy. The Jap only stared upward in total absorption and incredulity, unmoving, seemingly oblivious of the two Canadian soldiers.

Garrety motioned for McVries to give the binoculars to the Japanese soldier. He did. The man, torn from his rabid observation of the incongruous ladder, stared at the proffered binoculars as if he'd never seen something as alien in his entire life. Then, suddenly, meaning arrived, and with it a hungry look in his eyes as the man nodded vigorously and snatched up the binoculars. He looked into the sky. When he turned to the Canadians, he was weeping.

He handed the binoculars back to McVries with a shuddering hand. He pointed up, and made a motion as of climbing, hand over hand. The look of entreaty on his sweaty features was impossible to not understand.

Garrety nodded.

McVries also nodded.

Tears continued to stream from the Jap's eyes. He placed trembling hands on the golden-silver rungs directly before his face and pulled himself upward. He used his good leg to leverage himself up to the next rung, though a grunt showed his discomfort. Blood drops pattered from his thigh onto the ground beneath him. Once he'd attained fifteen feet along the ladder, he looked over his shoulder at the Canadians watching his progress. He carefully removed a hand from where it gripped a rung and made a questioning motion toward himself: *are you coming, too?* They were no longer enemies, he and the Canadians. How could they be, after finding the ladder together and witnessing its mystery?

Garrety shook his head. McVries looked away to stare into the shadows of the jungle. He walked off, and Garrety followed, raising a hand in farewell to the enemy soldier clinging to the shimmering rungs above the steaming jungle floor. The man watched them go with troubled eyes.

The friends walked in silence, sharing another cigarette, listening to the sounds of the night surround them. After a time, they turned at a voice coming from the path behind them, instinctively raising their weapons. They weren't particularly surprised to find the wounded Japanese soldier crawling in the path, a hand raised in greeting as he picked them out among the shadows.

They waited as he crawled to where they stood. No one spoke, except the great voice of the wilderness all around them. Then they set out together, still wordless, going slowly to maintain the crippled pace of the crawling man. They walked together for hours until they came to a crossroads. There the Japanese soldier turned to crawl along an even narrower path that sloped down steeply into a frond-shrouded ravine. The two Canadians kept to the original path, looking for their own place in the darkness.

THE BLOODMILK PEOPLE

Part body-horror, part Bizarro, part black comedy, part apocalyptic tale with a healthy dose of anti-natalism embedded in its centre: this one's weird as hell, and I enjoyed the hell out of writing it on a rainy, windswept morning in March a few years ago.

And yes: I have the distinct feeling that the Bloodmilk People are among us. If you'd seen what I found in the public washroom at the bookshop the other day, you'd believe it, too...

He vowed silently to never ever, under any circumstances *ever*, allow another customer to use the store washroom. Though he was repulsed—horrified—by the sight, he couldn't stop looking into the toilet.

The bowl was filled with blood. What water had been there to begin with was tinted a deep red and the level of the liquid in the bowl was alarmingly higher than it was after even the longest piss he'd ever taken. Red drops spattered the sides and rim and plastic underside of the raised seat. Droplets splashed the floor directly before the toilet as well. If there was urine mixed in with it, it wasn't visible amid the red.

He shook his head, revolted and perplexed. The customer in question—the only one he'd allowed to use the washroom this dreary, rain-swept morning, when even the regulars chose to stay at home rather than indulge their passion for books—was a young man, thirty at the oldest, and from all outward appearances in good health. He was tall, trim, athletic-looking. A varsity man at St. Clair College, possibly, active in sports. He'd been amiable enough both before and after using the facilities, and God knows if he had faced the same blood-filled toilet bowl this morning he would have been hysterical and promptly en route to admitting himself at the downtown emergency.

It became more awkward still when, after hurriedly wiping the exterior of the bowl clean with a wad of tissue paper and flushing the whole red mess into the sewers, he exited the small bathroom and nearly collided with the same young man in the narrow hall outside. He'd mentioned hunting for a book he was looking for upstairs—in the room devoted to the western, science fiction, fantasy, and horror genres—but the employee, lost in thought, hadn't heard him making his way back down the rickety stairs.

"I'm sorry," the young man said. "Didn't mean to startle you. I found the book I was looking for though." He was smiling triumphantly as he held up the slim volume.

The employee was too discomfited by what he'd just witnessed in the toilet to notice which book it was, or to make small talk about it. "Oh, good, that's good to hear. I can, uh, ring you up now if you like?"

The customer watched him a moment too long, his expression unnervingly penetrating, before answering. "That would be great, thanks."

The employee led the way the length of the hall and down the short flight of stairs to the main floor. He winced at the awkwardness of their exchange, at his own tell-tale discomfiture, and was all too aware of the salient absence of music playing in the bookshop. (He'd arrived that morning with a headache and, preferring silence, left the CD player off.)

It was while they waited in tense silence for the debit transaction to go through that the customer spoke what was on both their minds.

"I'm sorry, I... I should have said something. About the blood I left in the bathroom."

346

The employee looked up, startled. To have this young man openly address the situation was shocking enough. But then the fact hit home, that he'd apparently done what he'd done... on purpose.

Before the employee could say anything, the customer said, "Just so you know, it's nothing personal. I do it everywhere."

The employee stared, dumfounded. "What... do you mean?"

"My blood," he said. "I leave it in as many places as possible. Toilets mainly, because then people know where it came from. It makes more sense than on a tree somewhere, or in an alley, where no one would see it or, if they did, they might just think it was something else. Juice, say, or pop."

They stared at one another, the employee flabbergasted, the customer cheerfully patient.

The employee looked to where the debit machine had spit out the customer's receipt. Absently, feeling very distant, he tore the receipt from the mouth of the machine and bookmarked the paperback with it. Around them the stunned quiet of the shop hung like a fog.

Then, "Why... do you leave it in the toilet?" He tried to keep the disgust and horror he felt from his voice but wasn't sure he succeeded.

The customer was quick to answer. "Because maybe you should know about it. And by *you* I mean the world at large. Maybe the world should know what we sacrifice every day just so that we can keep on living. It's almost like we *are* the world, you know? With all the violence going on out there, all the bleeding going on, more and more every day. Maybe we're like a reminder of how the world is."

"We? Who's *we*? Are you... sick?"

The customer laughed. "My girlfriend and I. And no, not sick exactly. Sickened by the world infecting us with its mean-spirited bullshit every day that passes more and more, yes. But sick in the traditional sense, no."

"Then what..." He trailed off, watching the customer across the desk wonderingly.

"My whole life, since I was born, I've had the ability—and the bodily need—to expel blood from my body. If I don't, I start to feel nauseous, but it's tricky because if I expel too much, I of course start to feel faint too. Because my body needs time to produce more blood. It's there every time I urinate. It's strange, I know. I can't explain it. Neither can any of the thousand doctors I've seen since I was a kid."

"And if you didn't expel it?"

"It hurts. A lot." The man placed a hand on his middle to emphasize the degree of the resulting pain. "Here, and everywhere. Strange, I know."

The employee, buoyed a little by the subject being spoken of so frankly, said, "It seems to me even more strange that you feel the need, as you said, to let others know about it? By leaving the evidence in public toilets?"

He shrugged. "What can I say? I've always felt a bit like I've been cursed. Like, the same way women call their time of the month *the curse*." The customer ran a finger thoughtfully along the paperback's cover, tracing the line of its title font, and said, "Except I live with it every day of every month of every year, and I have to be careful all the time. So, it seems that if people knew about it they might realize how good they've got it, all things considered. So maybe I'm doing a public service by letting them know. Like I said, maybe we're a reminder of how the world is." He laughed.

"I'm... I'm sorry."

"Don't be," he said, cheerfully as ever. "It's all good. It's who... It's what I am. My girlfriend doesn't mind, and she of all people is closer to it than anyone, in more ways than one."

The employee stared at him a moment, processing this new potentiality to the already awesomely grotesque and shocking equation.

The young man laughed. "You got it, my man. I come blood too. We're not weird about it or anything. It's not like a turn-on or anything weird like that. It just is what it is. But, of course, she's okay with it, because she's the same way as me. A blood expeller, and blood-ingester, whatever you want to call it. It's like a cycle we've got going between us, which is great. We're so happy we found each other, as I'm sure you could guess."

I don't want to call it *anything*, the employee thought, doing his best to keep an undisturbed expression on his face. *I don't want to think about this or ever recall this conversation again.*

The young man went on with a chuckle. "It's how Rebecca and I met. When you're this—" he searched for the word a moment—"when you're this *unique*, well, you tend to be drawn to people who are like you. Sometimes we think that maybe it's totally normal—that maybe we're just the next step, in evolution or whatever." The young man paused, and a frown of concern creased his smooth features. He said, in a more subdued voice, "We're a little worried about the baby, though. We've both had bad dreams about it. Recurring dreams. Beck woke up last night and told me her dream. In it, we'd had a demon." He laughed, said, "Wouldn't that be fitting, considering what you've learned today about the world, and the weird things that go on in it?"

Yes, oh God yes, thought the employee. For some reason, the vision of the world inhabited by inexplicable, blood-gushing beings seemed just about right. The world, after all, could be a very cruel and punishing place, a fact corroborated every time he perused the shop's History and True Crime sections. It was a place that could make you *bleed*.

"No, of course not," the employee said, feeling numb with revulsion all over again, and hearing his voice as if from a great distance. "The demon will be fine—I mean," he caught himself, shaking his head and laughing awkwardly. "I'm sorry. *He* or *she* will be fine. Sorry, I'm just slow to process everything you're telling me, I guess."

The customer smiled warmly. "Okay, thanks man. I appreciate that. And no more talk about my sex life, I promise."

They chatted a while about other random things, though small talk came cumbersomely following their blood-talk—the Leafs on a rare winning streak heading into the New Year; the mom-and-pop greasy spoon across the street and how damn fine their western omelette was; the Philip K. Dick paperback the customer had bought, *A Maze of Death*, and how underrated it was among the author's canon, and how they both considered it one of their favourites of his.

Then, following a brief pause during which it seemed to the employee that the man was finally—finally!—prepared to leave the shop, the customer said, "Hey, man, I'm so sorry to have to ask, considering the weirdness of our previous chat, but, since I've got to go catch a bus and head all the way across town, I was wondering... Could I use your bathroom again? I promise to flush this time." He placed a hand over his stomach, offering a sheepish and apologetic expression.

The employee, amazed that he was even having this utterly insane exchange on this otherwise same-old dreary day, laughed, said, "Sure. Knock yourself out."

The customer left his book on the counter and walked toward the back of the shop, calling over his shoulder. "Yeah, I'll *definitely* be sure to flush this time... Especially since something's not sitting well in here. Maybe it's that omelette from across the street."

He disappeared amid the stacks and a moment later the employee heard the sound of the bathroom door thudding closed. He shook his head, bewildered, grossed out at the vision of a bloody, shit-filled toilet possibly in the process of being created at that very moment. Then he chuckled, thinking the notion ludicrous—different bodily systems and all of that. A ridiculous, fantastic idea, even in light of the fantastic things the man had told him already. He laughed even more, banishing the vision.

He busied himself by stacking the remaining paperbacks that needed to be filed in alphabetical order along one side of the counter. Then he replaced both the ink cartridge in the printer and the roll of receipt paper in the debit machine. Then he finished the chocolate chip cookie he'd picked up at the doughnut shop next door on his walk to work that morning and washed it down with some coffee while peeking through the blinds at the rain-soaked sidewalk outside the window. Then he stood there in the quiet shop, listening to the distant murmur of traffic drifting from the main drag down the way, the sleepy hum of the heat inside the vent behind the counter, the patient, relentless ticking of the wall clock over the place where he stood, counting down the minutes until his work day was done.

Then his skin broke out in gooseflesh, a shiver snaking along his spine as he spilled his coffee and recoiled from the sound coming from behind the bathroom door at the rear of the shop:

A baby crying.

LET THE FIREFLY MEN REMIND YOU

One thing that always makes me excited to sit down and write is a particular atmosphere that I want to convey and to permeate whatever it is I'm working on at that time. That was certainly the case with this story. I wanted to live inside this story before it even existed, while it was still a nascent idea percolating at the back of my mind. And so I wrote it, and I'm in it, somewhere, maybe just past the edge of the firelight where the shadows are plentiful, maybe a ways inside the distant tree-line, watching the dark, wondrous event at the tale's centre unfold.

It's about a group of casual friends, and one deeper friendship within this strung-together group, and their shared experience of something completely beyond comprehension; and about the ways that it affects them in both the short term of a very strange summer and the long term beyond. It touches on an idea that recurs in other stories of mine that deal with similar Fortean subjects, namely that when we experience something beyond our ability to define—something we can only interpret as being either alien or divine—it changes our lives in both good and terrible ways, and that we're never the same afterward. Because how could we be?

Reading this story now, I found myself wondering what happens to these characters after the story ends. We know that they're different people than they were at the story's beginning, but questions remain. Where are they each going? What will they do once they get there? Will they try to explain what they saw to friends, family? What will they do if it becomes clear that nobody could possibly understand, or sympathize, except those with whom they'd shared the experience? What will they do differently from now on, given what they've witnessed? What will their dreams be when they fall asleep that night?

If this seems like a lot of questions to inundate you with before you've even read the story, don't worry, because just like I know the answers, you'll have yours. They'll come fairly easily, I promise. Because you're in the story, too.

Nothing lasts.

Endless summers fade away with all their strange and wondrous ingredients. And only their ghosts linger. And even though we all knew the truth in those words, that summer still felt eternal, like the most magical and painful summers of your life tend to fool you.

We were like hippies, so crazed from the acid frying our sizzling minds that we could never claim the truth about the things we'd seen to anyone but ourselves. But we knew it, because the mornings following such hauntings found us all pale and cold and contemplative, and we didn't talk as freely throughout that strange summer as in other, less significant years past.

So that was us, day in and out, afternoons drifting by the river behind Natalie's farmhouse in Comber County while her parents were away in distant Windsor; and the nights were bonfires and pointing out fairy spirits amid the clusters of sparks shooting into the air. In twos, we'd sneak off and kiss our partner behind the first thin wall of trees bordering the deep, dark bush where we feared demons roamed with the deer and rabbits. But we were young and crazy with fire between our legs and the bark of trees scratched at our backs where our shirts were lifted up and over our heads while we were kissed hard into the trunks, disturbing spiders and caterpillars in their crawling, nocturnal quests.

352

Gary was my man most of that summer and we were lost in each other's touches and whispers when the Big Burning happened. He was thin and wore his hair long, and his beard, too, all twisted and pubic-looking and so sexy with river water drenching it like some wet animal. We were good together and the funniest thing about us was the knowledge we shared that we'd never last past that summer. I pictured him moving away somewhere else, which he eventually did, to Toronto, I think it was, and I knew it then and know it now, that he didn't take my number with him when he went. Just like I erased his name and number from their place penciled into the headboard of my bed back in Belle River, where I'd lived with my parents.

Maybe it was the sole thing that kept all of us so happy those hot months: our awareness of the transience of all things leading into tomorrow. We never once entertained the idea that we could possibly repeat the grandeur and mystery of those days, and so we weren't too upset knowing we'd never even give ourselves the chance to try. We lived in the very instant of each moment and never considered the existence of time outside of that safe neutral bubble.

Natalie was the same as me, my twin sister it had always seemed in the way she thought exactly as I did, who loved her man's presence beside her every night while the fire crackled and spit wheeling sparks like fireflies around us. But it was only the presence of him she cherished, never any warmth beyond the simple physical tangibility of him being there that summer. We were content enough having another hot body to hold us and to clutch to us when we felt like sharing something good of ourselves.

My man Gary Texo spoke like a preacher and swore to me that he was a real child of God. The real McCoy, in his own words, with his own carefully wrought set of beliefs which allowed him to indulge in any excess he chose while still flaunting the silver cross on its silver chain around his neck. *If you love God, He won't reject you because of your lifestyle, He's bigger than that.* I liked his eyes. They were always looking inwards at himself, as if he were dreaming about himself, and I suppose I really only thought that he was rather self-absorbed and pretty, but I never cared. He knew how to nip at my neck like a vampire and make the skin all along my shoulders ripple into goose flesh. He knew how to remove my bra quickly, he never

353

fumbled with the clasps like so many novices I've known. When he kissed me, he was absorbed totally in the moment, and at least during times like those I knew for certain that he was mine.

Natalie was a wondrous child, silently wise about the things she saw around her, and so I think she knew it, too, felt it in her petite bones: everything that summer was fleeting, despite the daily slow-poking way we went about the things we did. As if we had all the time in the world left to us. The days tasted too good. The night air was too perfect, a constant temperature of neither too chilly nor too muggy. The mosquitoes were out, of course, but never in droves, and our long-sleeve shirts were adequate enough armour to thwart their needle-kisses.

We were always commenting on geography. It was all around us, a kind of wild, sprawling magnificence. We'd all visited Natalie's farmhouse before, when her parents were away in Windsor, where they went often on business as well as socially to visit their many friends. But it was different then. The tree line rippled better against settling dusk every early evening. The fireflies among the thick, twisted trees were more celebratory in their bobbings and flutterings than in previous Julys and Augusts. They'd always been pretty but never quite magical like they were then. And the sound of the river was calmer, the best and most soothing music that stretch of corn country had ever produced. What a soundtrack. What a time. And the sounds of insects moving through the stalks and brittle husks never carried so sweetly on the air.

But then there were other things at work those days, too.

Oddities, peculiarities among the everyday laze and summery haze which ruined our good cheer and brought us down from our drunken, spinning reveries. Incidents and happenings we only ever seemed brave enough to acknowledge once the wine had been poured and the acid delivered onto our tongues. The bizarreness of things which always brought us down to lucidity, and that instilled an unsettling ingredient into the days and nights. Which stretched their fabric so that the time from dusk through to the following dawn felt eerie and endless, until another grand yet haunted day was suddenly upon us.

●   ●   ●

I'd found the burning animal at the edge of the woods.

I'd been drawn to the flicker of flames from where I stood on the backyard deck and trudged across the field to investigate. It was still twitching about in its final death-agonies, croaking horribly. Disfigured from the heat, smoke sizzling from its black, lumpy body, its remnants of fur twisted and scorched. Several patches of the thing's misshapen body were still smouldering angrily by the time I'd reached it, little plumes of fire crackling grotesquely in the bright light.

I never did discover exactly what species of animal it had been. A small dog, maybe, or a raccoon. Foxes were plentiful in those woods. Perhaps one had wandered into the hands of— what exactly? According to Natalie, there weren't very many children or teenagers in the area, the next farm being located several miles to the east. We'd buried it, Natalie and I, at her request and without mention of it to our friends. They had their own stories to shudder along to without benefit of ours.

One of the summer couples, Maria and Franklin, returning from a trip to the forest with a strange artefact to silence us all and bring our barbecue merriment to a standstill. As they unfurled the dirty woollen blanket they'd used for lying down together among the trees, we gasped and didn't say very much at the sight of the cargo it contained. It smouldered, too, the mass of snakes burnt and congealed into a single web-like organism. Black and awful, suffocating us with the stink of its broiled flesh. Scales peeling off and pocking the blanket all over, the stiff calcified tongues black and pitiful on the noon hour air. Maria and Franklin with stunned eyes all over the grass, as if too frightened to show us their faces, or maybe only embarrassed that they'd felt the overwhelming need to share the horror of their discovery with us so that we might offer them some sliver of comfort.

These odd fires and their ashen remains, and the evening occasions of pointing out strange sky-fires to one another, too. The flashes in the air over the treetops, and the pulsing from deep inside the heart of the thicket in the distance, which most of us witnessed at some point during those weeks and attributed half-heartedly to fire bugs or teenagers's bonfires. Like some visual code flickering to us where we reclined in lawn chairs or lolled on grass-stained blankets. Eerie messages we never could decipher, and only wondered over, awed and anxious, and were occasionally curious or brave or high enough to venture towards with our summer partners in tow.

Strange, strange summer.

Terrifying, but we relished its beauties, too.

Once, while I was staring into the fire with the combination of cough syrup I'd been drinking and Gary's kisses on my neck making me simultaneously drowsy and excited, I noticed Natalie watching me. Her own man, Ted Hansen, was smelling her hair and running his hands across her chest overtop her tank top. I smiled, thinking it funny that we were talking without words, as we often did, while our boyfriends were oblivious and lost in us. I'll never forget what she said to me then, without words, and it was the most perfect and most defining thing about the whole situation that she could possibly have imparted.

She smiled and put her fingers to her mouth and kissed their tips and then blew me the kiss, on the air and sailing invisibly towards me. I motioned like I caught it, and I held it a second, her kiss hot in my hand, and rubbed it into my chest. A secret communication of our own when we needed it most. A reassurance in the uncertainty of the night.

Then we turned to our men and lost ourselves in good places where less powerful kisses lived.

Neat-O pranced before us and we laughed, such frantically elegant behaviour for a hog.

She was enormous, her round belly nearly scraping the straw-littered floor of the barn and spotted all over with dark circles on her white-pink skin. *You look like an inverted night sky,* Natalie said, and I watched her as she knelt in the hay and scratched the pig under her bristly chin. I wondered at her words about the inverted night sky. Always like her to say things that didn't quite make sense when you looked at them carefully, but which sounded pretty and felt endearingly genuine in their intention to define the moment.

I nodded and bent down and tugged on one of Neat-O's drooping ears. I held it aloft on the air, liking the warm look of sunlight burning through the thin cartilage. *You're beautiful, Neat-O,* I told her and let her ear flop back down, and I could have sworn that she smiled up at me with her pig mouth and tiny eyes. *You named her perfect,* I told Natalie, and we were watching

356

Neat-O retreat toward her section of stable, side-stepping expertly the piles of manure in the hay. *The neatest creature in the world*, she laughed, and we joked about poor Neat-O's stressful family life, living daily in a perpetual pig sty with her many filthy brothers and sisters.

We had the radio in with us, resting among farm tools on a narrow shelf set into the wall. The batteries were running out of juice. Black Sabbath droned a little slower than on most days. Natalie bobbed her head in time with the tune and brought my attention to the lyric. *It's a symptom of the universe*, she sang along in pretty accompaniment to Ozzy Osbourne. *A love that never dies*. Then she said how it sounded dreadful, the way he made the words sound, as if something as ephemeral as love might be capable of doing harm.

I laughed and said something about the amounts of acid the band probably dropped while recording the album, but I thought about it a long while afterwards. One of many subtle little hauntings making the days nervous beneath their perpetual laze and haze. I thought of my Gary and Natalie's Ted and how neither of us really cared if we woke up alone the following morning. We hung some wildflowers from a hook set over Neat-O's stall—I think Natalie said they were gardenias—and they smelled vibrant in the gloom of the barn. They lit the air up, and we were sure the world's tidiest beast would enjoy their perfume among all the shit and slop.

We left the barn to grab a couple of iced teas from the house and I asked Natalie as we walked whether she was happy. She said: *Yes, I'm happy*. The days were lazy and the nights drowsy and what more could we ask for. I wanted to ask her if she wanted it to last forever, but the thought had arrived in my head so unexpectedly that it worried me slightly and I only nodded and started talking about how the setting sun turned the fields bloody and savage-looking. Like a horizon-long fire. Like a Frank Frazetta painting. She'd graduated from art school the year before and loved the look of powerfully feminine and masculine things, so she knew what I meant and squeezed my hand to show it. She only said one word about it, too: *Primordial*. And once again, it was just her way to be completely right in the way she described the world before her.

Rounding the corner of her parent's house, Natalie tugged on my shirt sleeve, halting me in my tracks. I followed her wide-eyed look and shuddered at the sight: the plump raccoon barring our way, teeth bared ferociously where it stood before the ruin of another of its tribe: a brother, maybe, or sister or mate. A charred obscenity frying in the warm air and drawing clouds of agitated flies. The stink of burnt meat on the breeze was potent, violent even, watering our eyes and gagging us while we gulped ineffectually for clean air.

Backing away fearfully, we gave the animal the courtesy of solitude with its deceased companion. *Did you notice?* Natalie whispered urgently in my ear once we were a safe distance away, as though we were sharing secrets. *The flies? None of them were crawling on the dead raccoon. Only buzzing around in the air. They wouldn't touch the thing.*

We were doubling back in the direction we'd come from and turned at the noise behind us: there it was, the mourning raccoon, lumbering frantically away from the site of its stricken friend. We watched it lope hurriedly through the field and toward the distant woods, scrabbling over dirt clods and rocks as if it was in some great hurry to be away from the scene.

We stood a while in the warm shade of the house, amid the drone of drifting hornets and bumblebees wandering from flower to flower. It was the unsettling aftermath of a sighting, the jarring post-fire awe and humbled silence. In that moment, Natalie and I were reminded all over again of their presence, the great mysteries of the summer, having been offered another glimpse of the season's strange and immeasurable depth.

But after a moment of quiet between us, it was Natalie who saved us with her usual odd observations like unexpected offerings of wisdom. Pointing toward the rows of corn husks burning in the afternoon glare near to us, she murmured, *Corn. Sombre. Comber.* I followed her gaze and saw it immediately, the morose posture of the heat-ravaged stalks leaning toward the soil, a glum, static sea of greenery shot through with sun-paled yellow kernels like failed attempts at brightness. I shook my head in wonder, wondering why it was that her words made me feel better, but soon giving up on any kind of scrutiny. It's best to take some gifts as they come to you, without question and with gratitude. I worried at the somewhat unhappy gleam in her pensive eyes and squeezed her hand and reminded her how much we loved this county of dirt and sun and corn rows and won a smile from her that warmed me more pleasantly than August sunlight could ever.

Eventually, we remembered our big thirst and continued on our way, passing out of the comforting house-shade and making certain to avoid the dead animal. The sun put tears in our eyes, and we winced the entire time. I thought as we walked about the beginnings of pictures like the one in front of us, all sun fire and bloody land. The beginnings of big things. But the thought weighed too much and I set my sights on the relief of iced tea moving down my parched throat, and I found that it made me content enough.

They looked good shirtless, both our men, and we leaned back against the hay bales to watch them while we smoked.

Ted Hansen lobbed a warbling spiral toss of the football skywards, his back glistening with sweat or sun tan oil, we couldn't tell which. Gary Texo, my man in dusty jeans and bare feet, pounding across the grass with arms outstretched, running, running, wincing into the glare of late afternoon sunlight. He nearly tripped over the rake hidden in the tall grass but made the catch successfully. We listened to them whoop and cheer like they'd won an important game but were too tired to applaud their efforts ourselves, and only exchanged weary looks while smiles tugged at the corners of our mouths.

We sat awhile, listening to the dry scratching noises of mice tunnelling in the hay beneath us, at our backs. The air was a little cooler, early evening air, and our cigarettes tasted good then, just right in anticipation of the big supper the men were barbecuing for us. The potent smell of hot dogs drifted to us and we joked about how poor Neat-O must feel smelling that meaty breeze, poor, frightened, nervous hog.

It was an uncanny ability of Natalie's to name my thoughts before I ever even realized that I was thinking them. I'd convinced myself that I was feeling fine, looking forward to a greasy meal and getting stoned and hopefully laid afterwards. But then her words were there between us and I woke up from my stupor.

Do you feel scared right now?

I watched her watching me and was nodding my head before I realized with any certainty what I felt. It struck me then: all day

I'd been uneasy, tripping over things in and around the house, farm tools, clods of dirt, my own feet, jumping at hog squealings and cursing at the crows squawking down at me from the barn roof and making me edgier. I'd nearly gotten tangled up in the garter snake that crossed my path in the morning outside of the barn, a long specimen zipping madly across the gravel, a frantic blur of movement at my feet, difficult to follow against the earth the colour of its skin. A constant, pounding pulse of anxiousness in my temples all day, threatening me with imminent headache pain and nausea. Peering outdoors with eyes squinted in anticipation of some new smouldering vision, another animal roasting in the grass, or a torch of flame dropping like a stone through the air as a burning crow fell from the clouds.

I watched our men cavorting in the grass like they were superstar athletes or children, their jubilant cries small with distance, and I hoped they were careful where they walked. Because there were snakes aplenty in Comber County grasses, hidden among the emerald stretches and wildflower colonies. In the grass where things sometimes burned like strange sacrificial fires, ruining the good smell of gardenias on the air.

Her voice was a whisper. A chill on the air. *Me, too. I'm scared, too.*

It was all she said, and we dragged on our cigarettes and listened to the furtive travels of mice around us. A slight breeze picked up, carrying the smell of manure from the stables and mixing it with the scent of cooking meat. I was watching the sky when she told me what I was thinking about that picture, and maybe the bigger picture of everything else, too.

But the sky's gorgeous today.

And she was done speaking, resting her head on my shoulder while I only kept looking upward, admiring the purity of the blue, unmarred by clouds, except in the far west, where the hint of a distant storm brewed. We finished our cigarettes and sat a while longer in our admiration. Even when the v of crows flew into view and coincidentally crossed the path of another which a moment earlier had taken flight from the barn roof, and for a miraculous instant they'd formed a cross in the air, scratching out the blue and making us frown.

● ● ●

It began as just another night of fairy dances in the fire and the electricity of cricket song in the tall grass.

We in our regular positions doing our usual things, the tribe convened once more about its fire and revelling in bliss: there was Lawrence, like a hippy with his tympani drum on the grass between his legs, its battered skin thin and warped in its centre from weeks of his pounding palms, his eyes glazed with drink and marijuana and staring at shooting bonfire flecks; ignoring Julie beside him, it's where she always was although he only ever paid her very little attention, except for when he noticed her ample breasts through his fog of being stoned; Julie from Belle River, with her quiet way and fragile voice, too timid to remind Lawrence what he was missing most of the time, her nice smile and nice legs and nice way of overlooking his rude blindness, too meek to do anything other than wait for him to notice her at all. Beside them, Madeleine huddled into her wool blanket, keeping the mosquitoes and her man Tony at bay because she was tired of their stings during the night, his especially; always chiding her for eating too much and smoking too little, barbecue goes straight to your thighs, Maddy, didn't you notice, here, have a toke, you'll love it. Stupider words from him than usual, of course, because who didn't crave leftovers like crazy while they were high. She was from Windsor. We'd met at school two years before and become close friends seemingly overnight, amazed at our similar tastes in movies and music and cruel men. And Tony himself, tall and lanky and scruffy with a week's stubble, staring at her and wanting her despite the barbecue in her thighs, too sluggish from marijuana to try sidling closer to her or under the blanket with her, too thoughtless besides to offer an ineffectual apology for his usual brusque ways. Across from them, Maria and Franklin were a single animal illuminated by bonfire glow as they pawed and licked each other unabashedly. They'd met for the first time that very week and had mutually decided to live their summer like the lyrics from a rock and roll song, carefree and with abandon. Her long blonde hair spilled over him and he wore his hair the same length, and because it was almost the same colour we often joked about it while watching them make out: where does one begin and the other end, and in the end we'd only chuckle and return, inspired, to kissing each other.

I watched them all with lazy eyes, old friends some, others only acquaintances who I knew I'd never see again after our holiday was finished, yet all fitting the moment just right: everyone in their place, and the crickets in the grass around us sounded so amazing, too. I sighed luxuriously, Gary's hand resting on my thigh and edging higher, slipping underneath my summer dress, and the bonfire reflected in his narrowed eyes like miniature smouldering suns, the way I liked his eyes best, volcanic and self-indulgent.

We were on fire, too, and so it took a moment for us both to tune into the startled cries of our friends around us. Our mouths were pressed together and our tongues searching each other out, our cough syrup breath hot and ready. There we paused, lips to lips, tongue on tongue, suddenly aware that bigger things lived around us, outside of the easy splendour of losing ourselves in each other and in a sleepy moment so slow that minutes seemed to stop entirely.

It was Lawrence, I think, who murmured it through a cloud of pot smoke: *Those aren't fairies, guys.*

I followed the direction of his huge white eyes and saw the line of figures approaching from the edge of the forest. I stared and stared, trying ineffectually to determine exactly how it was that they were illuminated. Where was the light source which lit them in green fire like horrific storybook illustrations? I looked for lanterns or flashlights around us to help illuminate the scene but saw none, only the hazy forms provided light as they seemed to shimmer toward us like wavering projector images.

Lawrence spoke again, a volley of speech infused with mounting panic: *Those aren't fairies, guys, holy God, man.*

They weren't fairies, and it was poor, unravelling Lawrence who started our sudden and instinctive retreat toward the farm house. Our bottles we left behind on rocks and lawn chairs and overturned milk crates. Some of us left sandals and jackets, too, in our mad flight through the suddenly moonless night. There was no sound except for our laboured huffing and clumsy steps and the occasional hushed curse from one of us as we stumbled in the darkness. We never discussed or debated our retreat. We only felt a most pervasive nameless dread at the sight of those green lights like fiery men walking from the forest. I couldn't rid myself of it no matter how I tried, refuting my own inadequate attempts at logic as I fled. They weren't will-o'-the-wisps or some other gaseous phenomenon, because gases don't move with purpose, and the sight of another sliver of wondrous county

362

geography would only make us sigh in wonder and admiration rather than hurl us scrambling over each other as we ran for our lives. Because something primal in each of us awoke at that moment, instinctually assuring us of danger. A threat to our peace, our lives. Compelling us to flight like no ordinary summer ingredient could possibly move us.

So, we scurried like mice in the night, until we were gathered panting in the darkness of Natalie's kitchen. Jostling for a glimpse through the window and into the changed night outside. I think it was Maria who whispered with hot whiskey-breath at my ear: *Oh, dear God*. And I reached behind me and took her hand in mine and squeezed her tightly. Because I was watching the burning figures gathering in the yard, too. Their march hadn't ceased. They hadn't winked out of existence simply because we'd turned our eyes from them during our brief dash into the house. They weren't figments of mescaline-tripping or cough syrup-conjuring. They were setting the night alight. Burning silently like enormous torches or mysterious beacons. They were closer now—so very, very much closer—and still moving resolutely toward us.

How are they moving, for Christ's sake? It's not fucking normal. I think it was Gary, poor quivering Gary with his silver cross of Christ hanging among his chest hair, and all his well-pondered beliefs shaken and reeling.

None of us answered him. I could only let the breath whistle out between my clenched teeth as we stood and stared helplessly. I didn't know Maria as well as our other friends did but gripped her hand as tightly as I could. Because we were there in the kitchen darkness together. Sharing its depth and tension and numbing expectation. Watching in silence a scene which we could never possibly understand. I trembled at the realization of the sentience we were witnessing in the distinctly purposeful progress of the flaming men, walking or gliding toward us where we stood shaking in the blackness. Hovering like some strange species of giant phosphorescent insect awakened from their secret nests in the forest.

Maybe I shouldn't have said it, but I was terrified, too, and things just happen that way during times of confusion like those. And so, the words slipped out, in a whisper that everyone heard and that made us tremble even more.

I said: *They look like giant fireflies.*

And they did, with their bobbing gait and the way that they shone, eerie but beautiful too, pushing back the darkness around them. And therein lay our real terror: because we couldn't look away from those bodies of light, so undeniably gorgeous in their burnings, even in the face of the dread they put inside us. Frosty yet fiery. Savage and beautiful. Intoxicatingly violent. Mesmerizing and blinding, a collective of dark burning things spell-weaving us to rapt attention. Another summer ingredient blasphemed.

Oh Jesus Christ, look. What are they doing? It was Madeleine beside me, her hand covering her face, eyes wide moons peering through her fingers. I'd never seen her frightened before and shuddered at her new face: she looked like a ghost beside me, pale and insubstantial, a spooked moth that threatened to flutter away at any moment.

We watched, riveted. The firefly men had formed a wobbly circle outside of the yard housing the pigs. We could make out the animals's rotund bodies through the crooked fence slats, and then their high shrieks and squeals sounded as they scrambled away from those burning lights. *They better not hurt the pigs,* swore Madeleine, which I'd later think was a sweet thing for her to have said, to have cared for Natalie's animals while we shook and cried ourselves. And I thought of the world's best-groomed pig and I feared for her deeply, wishing she was there with us in the shadows of the house.

Then I realized. And I whispered her name: *Natalie. Where are you, Natalie?*

No answer from the kitchen darkness.

Oh, God. It was Gary talking to God again, and I saw him in the light cast by the figures outside as he gripped his glistening chain tightly in his fingers, tears like silver paint trails down his cheeks. *Oh, God, oh, God,* and we had to tell him with raised voices to calm himself and be quiet. We were just as helpless as those pigs if those lights heard us and got into the house.

But we felt it, too, a desperate terror for our friends: poor Natalie, and her man that summer, both snuck off into the woods to have one another among the spiders and fireflies, as they'd done half a dozen times already those few weeks, as we'd all done some time or another with our August partners. There was no question in our minds that they'd met up with the burning men among the trees. It was something we knew with certainty. And I

364

still feel a pang of shame at the memory, but in that instant, I suddenly found myself wishing I could trade one for the other: my Gary, a fleeting and miniscule sliver of my summer, for our Natalie, so much like me in how she looked at the world and understood song lyrics and how to stroke pigs under their chins to make them grunt and burble in pleasure. A wrongful malice toward him swept through me, and then the vision, of me hurling him through the kitchen door in the same unthinking way he might have lobbed a football skywards.

I began to cry around this time and I felt my friends's hands touch me gently in different places. Instinctive caresses in the darkness, because they were there with me, too, in our shared moment of staring into the unfathomable, the burning unknown lighting the night terribly, like no handfuls of sparklers or fireworks had ever done. Waiting for meaning or the touch of fire, or maybe these things were one and the same on a summer night when county forests unveiled their smouldering and inexplicable secrets.

Someone else began crying behind me somewhere, the sound disembodied and ethereal. A ghost-moth, fragile and lost in the night. Julie, I think it was, and it was Tony whispering for her to be quiet, soothingly at first because he was terrified, too, but then very heatedly because her sobbing wouldn't stop and it was a very unnerving presence there in the dark. Beside me, Maria was swearing softly, a terrified kind of litany in conjunction with the sound of Julie's sobbing underlying all of her words: *Oh, God, oh, no, oh, God, oh, no,* and she was squeezing my hand so severely that soon all I could feel through the numbness was the stabbing of tiny needles in my finger joints.

What was going to happen to us: the pervasive worry engulfing my mind and certainly consuming the others as well. And then through blurry eyes I saw: among the strange figures, in the centre of their circle in the dusty yard with the hogs shrieking madly in chorus, two motionless forms. I think some of us exclaimed in horror and grief, maybe I did myself, though I can't be certain.

They were our friends, that pair of unmoving bodies: Natalie and her summer man, Ted Hansen from Comber. They were naked. I could make out the large birth mark on her calf that she felt so self-conscious of, and his lanky limbs looked less wiry, less taut with muscle than I remembered them. Bathed in light, they looked small and fragile and helpless in the openness of the yard. Trapped and in the clutches of we didn't understand what, in the midst of the ring of glowing, weirdly lit figures. Like hapless pawns in a ritual beyond our fathoming. Like meat pieces in the heart of a fire. Like a doomed scene from a Frazetta painting.

And I thought helplessly of our conversation of the day before: primordial, this picture, too, or maybe an illustration of some un-guessable next step in all our lives.

Then:

One after another in quick succession, as fast as a family of fleas leaping from one region of human skin to another, the malevolent figures jumped away into the night air, shooting like silent rockets at light speed up toward the stars. Like that, a flash of hyper-movement, and they were gone, trailing wispy comet tails in their wake.

And they'd taken our friends with them.

An aftermath glow remained briefly and we watched terrified and hatefully as it faded, until normal moonlight peered through the cloud cover and coloured the lonely, molested yard forlornly.

We stayed in the kitchen the entire night, staring out into the blackness with wide eyes and hammering hearts. We huddled close and knelt on the cool tiles and whispered half-hearted encouragements to one another while we wept: *Ssh. Don't worry. We're safe. It'll be light soon. Don't think about it.* It might have been when we cared most about each other, our time together crying in the dark.

When the sun burned bloody over the trees we were there still, until mid-morning when we were all too tired to let fear keep us from collapsing over one another and finding sleep wherever we could, some of us on the living room couches and the rest of us remaining on the cold linoleum tiles. A commune of confused, frightened children dreaming fitfully, dreaming dark dreams.

Nothing lasts.

Yet the first thing I recalled when I woke up to the nervous, subdued chatter of my friends, and the thing I would recall for the rest of my years, was Natalie's ghost-voice telling me how she felt about it all, summer and its bitter-sweetness.

The days were lazy and the nights drowsy. What else could we ask for?

Yes, she'd been happy. We'd all been, those few strange weeks.

But the forests held walking lights like men on fire, and the skies said the same thing over and over again when they sucked those figures up and swallowed them and made them into stars winking overhead: it wasn't that simple. The picture of the world wasn't nearly so simple. Savage and bloody, like a painting, like a sunset dipping the fields in the colour of carnage, yes. But simple. No. Not simple. Very difficult. Profoundly intricate and impenetrable, a design bottomless with potential.

We lacked courage and so we escaped from the farm and spoke with one another only infrequently in the years to come, making certain to choose our subjects carefully. As a group, we were essentially no more because this was the simplest solution. Eyes mirroring each other's memory of a standstill moment of chaos rending our lazy peace apart: these weren't places any of us wished to look again. Natalie's parents's fruitless initiation of a missing person's search left us hollower and more terrified still, and the only answer we could possibly offer them or the methodical inquiries of the police: *We don't know. We don't know where our friends are now.* And the meticulous sweeps of the surrounding woods and fields by uniformed officers and volunteer farmers's families yielding nothing but spooked local wildlife and occasional inexplicable remains of mutilated animals. Raccoons and dogs, crows and cows, charred and ruined and scattered like blackened obscenities in the countryside. Raising only more speculation, and instilling an aura of even darker mystery over the horrible event.

I stood in the dust that final afternoon, watching the line of their cars filing away down the winding drive that led to the road a half mile to the east. It looked grim, a gloomy funeral procession traveling at high speed to distance themselves from the memory of their recent woe and terror.

Before I got into my own car, though, I said goodbye to Neat-O, who had remained fortuitously unscathed during the bedlam of the night. I found her rooting about in the hay for some stray food nuggets and I rubbed her under the chin, and when she swung her head sideways in approval, I liked the pricking of her bristles on my palm. It's a sloppy world, I wanted to tell her, but only sniffed the withering gardenias and felt sad because I knew I didn't have time to pick her fresh flowers.

I had to leave quickly because time felt suddenly against me, an enemy threatening my every moment, and yet even in my hurry I was the last of us to drive from the farm. There was no sign of my friends's cars in the distance, and I felt alone in the world, and the irony, I guess, was that I'd never known so fiercely that I wasn't alone. I scanned the hulking forest which loomed like a threat on the western horizon as I turned from the winding driveway and onto the road. Pebbles ticked loudly along the underside of my car as I sped along, trailing dust clouds. I continued glancing uneasily into the rear-view mirror, catching the forest's reflection and wondering what else I might at any moment see there. I felt unreal, divorced from my body somehow, but knew that I'd be crying soon once again. For Natalie, and her man, and for all of us.

It was early in the day and I was glad that the remnants of night sky were no longer visible. No faint star-shimmers or pale, hanging ghost-moon like a hint of the larger universe reeling behind the summer-blue atmosphere. I slipped on my sunglasses because of the glare but removed them a moment later because I wanted to feel water welling in my eyes, an illusion of my grief when I otherwise only felt a hollowness filled with fear. The sunlight, the daytime, was welcome: I couldn't bear the thought of seeing all the stars above me and wondering which of the million twinkling dots might hold our friends. An inverted sky, and once again her words were perfect, if a little enigmatic. But I drove fast besides, over a hundred, even on the narrow winding back roads, because Belle River was a ways away and I was running on empty with no gas station in sight. And the next night of my life was fast approaching. And I wasn't sure what it might hold for me.

I slipped a tape into the cassette player and listened anxiously to the strained whirring of the machine's internal guts as it readied it for play. The tape hadn't been marked, a blank, filled with what songs I didn't yet know. But I knew I'd listen to it all the way through and soak it all up, because I wanted nothing more right then than to make the most of my drive through the fiery-hot day.

THIS
LUSTFUL EARTH

You didn't think I'd let you get this close to the end of a compendium of my stuff without giving you one of the most depraved stories I've ever written, did you?

Yes, this is a nutty story. It's probably not quite as nutty as some of my other stories (say, "The Animals Have Seized the Diamond Sea Kingdom" from my first collection, or my Long Dirty Night Trilogy *of novellas, which at the time of this writing is forthcoming from Somniatis Press in an extremely limited edition boxset—the award for Most Fucked-Up Story Zelenyj Ever Wrote might have to go to one of those two), but it's definitely up there on the nutty meter. It depicts perversity and depravity and brutality. But then, it's based on very real and true events, and so its ultimate moral position is justified, I'd like to think.*

Human beings make war, and during war they often do unspeakable things. Tell me I'm wrong. I dare you. And if wartime crimes were to be observed by a divine force or forces, what would they have to say about it? Whoever tells the story, as awful as it is to tell, it's going to be dark and difficult if it's being truthful, but nowhere near as dark and difficult as the real-life atrocities our inadequate re-tellings can ever hope to capture. Peace is better. A-fucking-men.

The echoes of their voices bounced from the walls, melding into a single primal roar that boomed throughout the shell of the desolate church.

The Czechs and Poles were lined up along one wall, the splintered pews piled haphazardly along the opposite wall. From this long line of captives, the Wehrmacht pulled the women and girls—seven of the former and four of the latter—and drove them violently into the room's centre. The men and boys who protested were bludgeoned with stout clubs and rifle butts. One man—an old man and father to one of the women, grandfather to her child—was stabbed through the stomach with a bayonet. He was left to writhe screaming in the debris of statue-work and broken pews, reddening the dust in which he thrashed.

The Germans—the remnants of the 61st Battalion—had made the church their temporary headquarters after leaving the front several miles to the east. They'd tended to their wounded and were set to decamp when the survivors of the evacuated Czech village had passed through the town in which the Germans had stationed themselves, looking like some lost gypsy caravan that had traveled a lifetime through the harshest of geographies. They'd killed the majority of the men immediately and brought the rest to their isolated camp, where they'd remained for weeks afterwards, hidden and seemingly forgotten by time amid the chaos of the war.

At a sign from a soldier, another man dropped a phonograph's needle onto a record. A traditional song began crackling through the speakers mounted on either side of the doorway. Through this archway a group of officers entered the chamber in ceremonial fashion: one after another in a neat line, marching in military step to the music. They were naked but for the officers's caps on their heads and the boots on their feet and, clutching their erections, made their way to the women gathered in a circle of terror between them.

A soldier announced in a strident voice:

"Czechs and other lesser animals who bow beneath the great German strength: this is what your women are good for, and this only barely. Once you've witnessed this good use, you will be shot where you stand."

It was only another instance of liberty indulged in a world of rampant, insane freedoms.

The Wehrmacht watching the spectacle joined in with the song coming through the speakers. Their manic voices rose into the domed reaches of the chamber, merging with the chaos of screams echoing there. Another man, a tall Pole, seeing the women being sodomized by the officers, broke from the ranks of the prisoners and rushed to their defence. He was systematically beaten to death by a pair of Gestapo wielding clubs. His cracked skull bled its brains onto the dusty floor while his darkening eyes watched the spectacle transpiring in the centre of the desecrated room.

From the distance came the renewed concussive thunder of explosions pummelling the earth at the Front. It echoed inside the cathedral, shuddering the remnants of stained glass from their ornate window frames and sounding like a distant storm blowing closer, closer, closer, if only they could have heard through the ecstatic din they made.

"You are all such a curious, curious history in the universe," He declared and, laughing ruefully, slowly lowered His smiting fist to retrieve the great goblet where He reclined on His ivory throne among the churning cosmic debris. He sipped from it, shaking His head in wonder, a pensive look troubling His eyes.

A moment passed and, still following the events taking place through the hole in the air, He blew hard into a great conch held to His lips by an angel. It produced a weird, mournful cry that carried far and far across the air, deep and deep into the Earth far below.

A moment later and the Other appeared in the palatial throne room, amid a plume of red and black smoke and the stink of a charnel house: the red-furred Beastman, His fat, black, pythonian tongue flicking restlessly from His black-lipped mouth, immense crimson nipples and dripping phalluses jutting from His cheeks, His high regal forehead.

"I'm here," He vomited, yellow and red curds frothing from His lips. "This better be worth My time in this cold place."

He began a slow, prolonged, wet, lazy, sewage-stinking flatulence that caused the silver-haired One to chuckle, despite Himself. "You and Your vulgar toilet humour. Does nothing change?" Then, attention drawn back to the scene unfurling

371

before Them, He said, "Watch, just watch!" He pointed through the rent in the air, eagerly leaning forward in His ivory throne.

They watched a moment together. The scene—chaotic with shadows and blood and semen and tiny, shouting men and tiny, screaming women—prompted the Beast to nod approvingly and inquire, "How much have You dictated the scene?"

"Ha! That's the beauty of it, friend. Not at all! This is pure fate or folly, ill or grand madness to exist at all! Truthfully, I thought I'd detected Your hand in this!" He gestured to an angel who wordlessly presented the Beastman with a twin goblet to His own and began filling it from a large ewer.

The nipple- and cock-faced Beast laughed, spilling some of the glittering juice over His cloven fist. "No, no, though I admit to its savage, clumsy, stupid beauty. Just look at them slaughter each other with cock and bullet and knife!"

"Truly!" said the One, shaking His head in grave wonder. "Shall We throw in, perhaps, some bears, or a great mastodon, for more gladiatorial sport? Why not?"

"No, no, these creatures You name are pure of soul and know no evil in their hearts! Perhaps a battalion of Panzers plucked from the heart of number One instead!"

"Yes! Yes, *indeed!* And a squadron of Spitfires for good measure! They are good at making war machines. Why let them go to waste, after all?"

"Ah, yes," said the Beastman, a wistful tone in His voice, eyes distant with remembering. "From their very start they were adept at making war, and making war greater and crueller as their intellect grew." The cocks on His face were growing harder, standing erect as if drawn to or saluting the scene in the sky-hole.

"You are correct." The One was nodding thoughtfully. "Perhaps then We would do better to inject the scene with a tribe of Cro-Magnons, strong with their war clubs and great fear of the unknown and all of this loud commotion! Perhaps this would serve as a lesson—evidence of the meagre distance they've crawled since their primordial beginnings? Perhaps this would awaken these strong and wise men to the nightmare of their small world?!"

"No, no," said the Other. "I think not! They are much too young and much too broken for such understanding!" Two of the phalluses adorning His head squirted excited geysers of steaming, bloody semen across His shoulders, spattering the

372

stone floor and the virgin robes of the angel standing sentinel closest to Him. He began languidly stroking another, from which a head of flame licked feverishly. "Oh, My, look at that! They've killed nearly everyone, men and women alike. Only the children remain! But how long can they possibly last? Shall We place wagers?"

"What strange and voracious passions they have. At which point did they turn down this road? At which point did the sickness of hatred manifest itself in their hearts? Oh, but it's like a plague rampant among them."

The scene in the sky-hole continued to mesmerize Them: a young boy fighting to save his sister bludgeoned to death with the butt of a German rifle; a woman shot in the back of her head by the officer still fucking her; a young German soldier holding the small white kitten he'd discovered somewhere on the church grounds, distractedly stroking the terrified animal while watching the saturnalia in the middle of the room in all of its bewitching, vile, never-ending splendour with vacant eyes, as if searching for meaning.

The One and the Other roared with mirth and horror and wonder, spilling the star-juice from the goblets in Their hands.

A shrewd expression came into the Beast's blood-filled eyes. "Let Us refrain from interfering. Let Us instead wait and see what they make with the fire they have between them," He suggested, whooping with His hyena's laughter and slapping a burning hoof upon His knee. "Though, perhaps some day they may learn something different than they know today, that day is certainly a long ways away."

"Yours is a good plan, My Adversary, a good, good plan," the One conceded with a heavy sigh, wiping a silver tear from His eye. "They are not ready for learning, and for now the dark entertainment they provide is truly mesmerizing, though it awakens a pity in My heart and a blight upon the old hope I've long held for them. Indeed, the grand finale they write themselves will likely be more blood-drenched, epically shameful, all-around fucked-*up*, and apocalyptic than any You or I could ever hope to author!"

The echoes of the screaming voices and the roaring guns continued to rebound like thunder from the walls of the great chamber.

THE DEMON TAKEOVER OF WINDSOR, ONTARIO

I have little recollection of writing this story. Until now, it has never appeared in a book, but it certainly does have a place in my heart for a couple of different reasons. For one, it was one of three stories accepted simultaneously by Fourth Horseman Press editors Brian A. Dixon and Adam Chamberlain—and the first published—in Revelation, the Magazine of Apocalyptic Art and Literature, *back in 2004. This represented the beginning of a long and fruitful creative relationship between myself and Fourth Horseman Press, who would go on to publish many of my stories in numerous places: various issues of* Revelation *magazine, a variety of anthologies, as well as my first book, the short novel* Black Sunshine... *and, of course, the book in your hands right now.*

Secondly, "The Demon Takeover of Windsor, Ontario" struck a chord with Brian who, in his eloquent foreword to my second collection, Songs for the Lost, *cited the story as being thematically representative of my work generally, and commented favourably on its examination of our culture's descent into an apocalyptic darkness. I'm extremely grateful that my stories were received as favourably as they were, as my work with Fourth Horseman over the years has yielded a prolific run of fiction of which I'm very proud and, more importantly, resulted in a long-time friendship with said editors, two gentlemen whose writing I admire and whose wisdoms I cherish. So, the story's inclusion here (including a new scene absent in its original version) is in tribute to Brian A. Dixon and Adam Chamberlain, who saw something more in it than I initially saw, which is why I decided ultimately to excise it from my first story collection,* Experiments At 3 Billion A.M., *in which it was originally set to appear.*

Thank you, Brian and Adam. I hope you enjoy revisiting this little story about an infinite darkness.

The voice in the plastic receiver at my ear had died along with the lights in the small convenience store. And my mother's ghost-voice has lingered in my thoughts ever since, her words stranger than any she's ever spoken to me:

Harlan, they're inside the lights, and the lights are everywhere. We don't know where to go. They're everywhere. It's happening, Harlan. We love you. We love you so much. We don't—"

Silence in the receiver.

Over two hours ago, that strangest of midnight calls.

I sit here now, on the cool tile floor of my father's convenience store, graveyard-shifting near the city's outskirts as I've never done before, my back to the magazine and comic book racks, the girl sitting across from me in the darkness. She's been quiet for most of the two hours she's been here with me. She'd stumbled in shortly after my mother's voice in the dying phone, wide-eyed and blubbering something about seeing a burning man in a field. That's all she's said about it, but that black stare tells me there's more. Now she won't say anything at all, and she only toys with the snack-size bag of Doritos she pulled from the shelf behind her one hour before. The way she'd done it, quickly and anxiously, it seemed like she only did it so that she could have something in her hands, something tangible to keep her hands occupied, and maybe help keep her thoughts off of whatever she kept seeing in her head. But what do I know?

I know it's dark. There's no moon out even. And that's really dark. And the immortal family of late-summer fireflies that haunts the storefront windows has blinked off for the night, I suppose, because I don't see them hovering in the air, as

376

comforting to watch as a Christmas tree when you're a little boy. I found a flashlight and a pack of batteries behind the counter, but I haven't turned it on since the girl screamed at me to put out the light, recoiling from it as if I was holding something dangerous in my hand. I don't want it on either. I saw her eyes, caught for a split second in that spotlight. She had black eyes. She looked so *scared*. She looked so *sad*. I don't want to put the light on ever again. I can hear tiny footsteps around us, because the mice are always brave in the dark, but I don't mind. I feel scared now, too, like the girl. There should be someone brave in this room now, at least. And somehow, like her, I also feel safer hidden in the darkness.

I locked the door a long time ago. Once, maybe an hour ago, we heard someone trying to open it. At first, I thought it might be my father come down from the city to save me, but something stopped me from going to the door. Maybe because there'd been no sound of a car turning into the small gravel lot. But as I listened, whoever was at the door was fumbling at the lock for a long time, and then it sounded as if they were scratching at the glass. They did that for a while, but they made no other sound. My father wouldn't have done that, of course. And though it might only have been my agitated imagination, it seemed as if a weird glow, one that I hadn't even been aware of, had faded with whoever had been at the door. Not a flashlight beam or car headlight, but... a *different* kind of light, that I'd noticed only with its sudden absence.

We only sat huddled here in the middle of the store through it all, out of sight of the windows. I felt safe here, and I could tell the girl did, too, because she wasn't crying anymore by then. Maybe our comfort comes from the heavy iron anti-burglary bars across the windows and door. Probably it comes from the darkness, where no one can see us.

I've been wondering about my mother's voice in the phone, about the sound of it. The strangeness of what she'd said, too, but mostly the *sound*. I've never heard that kind of a sound in her voice. Not fear. *Terror*. That scared me most of all, maybe. I can't stop wondering what's going on out there, back in the city, back home. We're so far away from the city out here, out here where there's nothing but tall-grass fields of swishing corn and lonely back roads and only one or two cars every two thousand years. And there hasn't been a car all night. No visitor at all, except for the one an hour past, the one who scratched at the glass in silence and then walked off into nothing but corn fields and night everywhere.

Home, Windsor, is so far away in the night.

At least I have the mice. Friends are amazing to have with you when the lights are out and fear is with you and sleep is nights and nights away. And the girl. I have her, too, I suppose. I can hear her breathing near me, and when she stretched her leg out a minute ago her toe nudged the cardboard display beside me and sent a package of ear plugs dropping to the tiles. It was a soft sound, but the mice were quiet for a few seconds after that little bomb fell. It's best to be cautious, I suppose. That's always best, I suppose.

I wonder what's falling outside these cramped walls. Are there deadly fireworks raining down onto my cozy neighbourhood at this very moment, burning down my row of town homes and the houses of my friends all around? Is my battered old Louisville Slugger safe from fire nestled in the deep green grass of my front lawn in the heart of Forest Grove where I'd left him at noon today, or is he just another victim in whatever this is? Is my mother safe, in her old powder blue slippers and out-of-fashion Bea Arthur permanent? And my strong, take-charge father? Is he safe, or is this—whatever it is—too much for even his strength to defeat? And is the hairy spider I keep nervously as pet behind the toilet in my bathroom safe in his shadowed web, or are even the little creatures not spared from this thing?

I recall my misadventure of earlier, not long after I'd locked us safely inside the store. Despite my unease from my mother's unsettling call and the girl seeking haven in the store, I'd tried to assume the role of adult, of leader. "Wait here," I'd told the girl with false confidence, thinking that if my father could see me then he'd be proud. Then I hurried into the stockroom, where I fumbled my way until I pulled down the old rusty ladder that gave entry to the building's roof, from where I hoped to see evidence of something hopeful: lights among the distant farmhouses, maybe, or car lights speeding down a road far away. Up I went, unlatching the metal door in the ceiling and clambering without grace up onto the flat surface. Kneeling there, heart racing, I looked westward—the only direction, I knew, in which my immediate view wasn't blocked by trees.

378

There were fires in the fields. Large, person-sized. Strangely bright, as if they were the only light for miles, yet in and of themselves not bright at all but *dark*, somehow. The longer I looked, the less sure I was of exactly what I was seeing. Stranger still, some of the fires were moving, slowly but surely drifting through the fields in all directions. Other fires only smouldered motionlessly, but with a fitful fury I would come to recognize.

It wasn't the weird fires that sent me rushing back down the ladder so quickly and clumsily that I nearly slipped and fell into the lightless stockroom below. Something had compelled me to turn my eyes directly upward, just as I'd started on my way down the metal rungs. I only looked for a brief moment before scurrying back down into the safety of the store below, but I'd seen: the sky seemingly cloudless, but completely empty of stars and moon. A darkness so black it looked solid, extending everywhere I could see until I clamped my eyes shut and hurried back into the safe little space of the store.

I hear her crying again from in the shadows, shaking me from my thoughts.

There's nothing I can do. Nothing at all.

But I say: "Do you want a Kit Kat and a Cosmic Blue Kool-Aid?" The juice boxes are actually very near to us, getting warm in the aisle, still packed behind cellophane, waiting for the distant, cold salvation of the freezer. And Kit Kats, they're good anytime. Any occasion's a good occasion for a Kit Kat, if the TV ads are to be believed. "They're my favourite late-night snack," I add, lamely.

She doesn't answer me, and we sit in silence again.

I've always hated the sound of people crying—people in pain—and I realize now that they're always worse in the dark, those kinds of sounds. The potential of the comfort I've been feeling hiding here in the darkness being taken away, made un-good, scares me.

What's going on out there, in the world?

The mice answer me, from the shadows, but they make only furtive, padding footsteps, and they don't know a single thing.

I reach beside me and fumble for the edge of the candy bar shelves. I search blindly with my fingers, secure a Kit Kat for myself. It's easy to tell them apart from the other candy bars, with their distinct flat, rectangular shape. I eat in silence, wondering if this might be my last taste of something grand. Is everything black and sour and like the bitter taste of sadness from here on? I don't know. But the soft chocolate is delicious in my mouth, and if everything good that I've known perishes tonight at least I'll have its sweet aftertaste in my mouth and wedged brown and creamy between my teeth. A simple joy, but something, at least, to have, and to cling to.

I stop mid-bite. I'm rigid and the girl is frozen, too. I can tell because I can't hear her low breathing anymore. We listen intently to be certain, and our ears tell us: our visitor has returned, or maybe it's another, and fingers again scratch at the glass of the door. And with the noise, a slowly growing light. This time I pay close attention and I'm certain it's there, but it's one that I know instinctively doesn't belong to a policeman's flashlight as he checks on a local business during a power outage in the night, or to the car of a late-night traveler looking to buy a pack of cigarettes. This light is somehow... *dark*. Menacing, the way it shudders and shakes and crawls across the walls and the tops of the shelves. The same kind of light I'd seen from the roof earlier, burning in the distant fields, only so much more frightening now because it's right here with me, a dark fire as close as the width of a windowpane.

A moment later and the scratching stretches the length of the small store to the front display window. The light continues to flare and shake violently, like a living thing filled with excitement or hunger. We sit tense and silent, knowing neither of us would even remotely consider opening the door and letting in anything from the night, and in so doing we forge something between us. I feel like a little boy again, sealing pacts under the cover of nightfall.

We listen and hear footsteps shuffle off into the night.

With the receding steps, the strange darklight dissipates, too.

Everything is quiet again, and we breathe again, and our invisible friends in the shadows take tiny steps again. This world of chocolate bars and penny candy and sodas and heroes dancing deadly old dances with their oldest arch-villains across comic book pages is returned to normal again. Everything in the world is as good as it has been since the lights winked out and our frightened faces disappeared in blackness.

And then her timing is suddenly somehow perfect, because as I give in and let the black terror that's been damming up behind my flimsy wall of calm finally spill over, she saves me.

380

"I once read a story called 'The Demon Takeover of Earth.' It wasn't any good. It was kind of stupid, I guess, and I don't remember anything about it, really. Mostly just the title stuck in my head. It was in some old magazine my little brother had. Like a sci-fi magazine, filled with short stories and pictures of rockets. I remember it smelled amazing though."

I sit stunned and amazed, and I forget the milk chocolate and wafer like some heavenly body melting in my mouth. Eventually, I catch up with the passing of time in the dark store and I ask, "The story smelled amazing?" My voice is so hopeful I might have blushed in the dark after I'd said it. Maybe I need proof of magic's existence, good and strong in the same world I live in now, shaking and scared and uncertain.

"The newsprint paper. I've always loved the smell of newsprint paper. It's... I love it." Her eyes in the dark are watching me, I can tell. I think she might sense something like a fading glimmer in my face. But her voice, I suddenly notice, is soft, and soft things are soothing, especially at night.

"Who wrote it?" I ask, truly needing to know. Maybe I'd recognize the author's name. A connection to the world I knew outside these walls.

"I don't know. I never knew. Who cares?"

I nod, reluctantly, holding my silence.

She says, "Besides, maybe the world's ending as we speak. So who cares?"

I wonder about this girl I don't know and of the things she may have seen outside in the night, and of dying fireflies and of the ugly kind of picture stars winked forever out of the sky would make. And I think of something important to ask her. I say, "What do you care about?"

She takes a while before answering. When she does, her voice is even quieter than before in the silent room. I doubt she's sure of what she's saying. She says, "Well, my parents. And my house. And my room, especially. And my friends. And my boyfriend. We... We've been together for almost six months. He has blonde hair and... He has blonde hair and a nice smile."

I nod for my own benefit in the dark room. I can tell she's uncomfortable now, and she doesn't know what to think anymore, about me, about herself. About all the strange things burning outside these walls, out there in the dark in the fields and dusty roads and the city filthy and familiar beyond. She kneels forward, and I hear her groping amid the dozens of candy bars on the shelves. When she sits back in her place, I know she's found herself a Kit Kat in the dark. I just know. The snack size bag of Doritos is still cradled like a baby in her lap. I can hear it when she makes any slight movement.

And I think of my mother, my favourite woman in the world, and I think of the terror I'd heard tonight in her straining voice, and I say to the girl before me, because it's very important to say: "I hope you can find that magazine somewhere in your brother's room. I hope you find it when you look tomorrow."

And here we sit on the floor of my father's convenience store, in the blackness of night without electricity, with no more words between us, waiting: waiting for good things, bad things, any kind of things at all. And though our thoughts wander, to many places, not all of which are cozy and good-tasting with memory like Kit Kat melting on our tongues and made smoother with delicious Cosmic Blue juices, we feel safe.

Our friends walk in the darkness around us, tiny steps, stealthy and reassuring.

Mighty little steps.

POPPY, THE GIRL OF MY DREAMS, AND THE ALIEN INVASION I CAN DETECT LIKE RADAR THROUGH MY BRACES

This is the story of mine that feels the most special to me. It was the first story I ever had published, way back in 1999—twenty years ago. It appeared in the second issue of Front & Centre Magazine, *a joint Canadian/UK publication, one of whose editors was Canadian author and Black Bile Press founder Matthew Firth. It remains the only story I've had published under the abbreviated version of my given name, "Alex." It was later republished in* Revelation *as well as in my first collection. I wrote it in one long summer afternoon stretch, which is pretty much all I remember about the writing process. It's a simple story: a young love tale set against the backdrop of the imminent apocalypse. It's short and sweet and full of youthful innocence and courage as onrushing doom hangs like a curtain set to drop over everything.*

The motif of blackness, or lightlessness, representing the end times is something I've returned to often, most obviously in my short novel Black Sunshine. *But its first appearance is here. The two main characters—our young couple—are good kids. Those are the kind of people we need more of in the world. Long may they live despite the devouring darkness.*

━━━━━━━━━━━━━━━━━━━━━━━━━

"We can't read this," protested Poppy, wanting to.

Jill looked from the sheaf of dog-eared papers her friend was clutching and rolled her brown eyes skywards.

"What?!" exclaimed Poppy anxiously, her grip on the papers unrelenting.

"You want to—you *have* to read it," persisted Jill.

"It's too mean! Evil, even! If Raymond found out—"

"He worships you! Read it!"

"But he—"

"READ IT!"

A pause of perhaps one second, then, "Okay."

The two friends hollered in combination mirth and excitement and their two heads came together to peruse the papers simultaneously.

The bunch of papers was a diary of sorts. It belonged to the boy next door, Raymond Hoop, who had no clue that his two friends were reading it with wide eyes. And if he did know that they were reading the sheaf of papers, with his secret thoughts made out into words, he would have to make certain that he died right there on the spot, for sure.

The title he'd given the diary or mess of dog-eared papers summed up why, and concisely.

"Poppy, the Girl of My Dreams, and the Alien Invasion I Can Detect Like Radar Through My Braces," read Jill aloud. She swivelled her curly head to look at Poppy, whose eyes continued to burn holes into the cover page between them.

Folding this initial page back over the rest of the manuscript, Jill took in with awe the blotch of blue ink that covered the paper. "That's a *lot* of writing."

Then, starting at the top, the two girls began to read.

One hour and a half later, they were finished.

384

"Holy cow," murmured Poppy.

"Yeah," nodded Jill in agreement. Then, "Um, Pop? Like, do you think Raymond's a psychotic?" A tiny smile accompanied her query.

Poppy shook her head no.

"No?" cautiously.

"No," affirmed Poppy. "Raymond is not insane. Well, he is, but you know. He's a fun insane, not like, you know, a psychopath insane."

"Yeah," said Jill very tentatively. "But you realize he does think he can hear aliens from another dimension talking across the, uh, airwaves of space or whatever, and that he says here that they're planning to invade Earth by tonight at three after midnight?"

Poppy was silent a moment. Then, thoughtfully, she looked up at the pure blue of the afternoon sky.

"Why not?" she said. "He said he could catch a radio station through his braces last summer. He'd hear baseball games and oldies music."

"Poppy. Poppy... A radio station, aliens from another dimension. Do you see a difference?"

Poppy looked strangely at the diary, which lay pinioned to the hot cement of the driveway by a white rock. "He said he loves me in there."

At this, Jill grew less anxious. "Yeah. He says it all the time, Poppy."

Poppy smiled. Picking up the papers and shuffling through them, she came to the page she sought. Picking it out, she handed it to her friend. "Read the third paragraph."

Jill looked at the designated string of words.

Her eyes are like stars tossed in a milkshake and all shook up, and that's all I need to know.

"Wow," nodded Jill. "You're lucky."

"Yeah?"

"Yeah."

"Yeah."

Jill leaned back and stretched herself out on the driveway. The blue blanket above them stretched on cloudlessly as far as they could see. "It's beautiful," she sighed. "Why would anyone want to ruin that?"

Poppy followed her friend's gaze. "Maybe they don't plan on ruining it. Maybe they're just jealous and want it for themselves."

"Jealousy hurts."

"For sure."

A minute passed as the friends stared into the blue.

"Raymond's more in love with you than anything. Wanna know how I know that?"

"How, Jilly?"

"Because somewhere on, I think, page three or four, he said that you're better than a sparkler lying on the grass in July."

Poppy wanted to smile but felt pleasantly too tired and so she just lay there, warm.

"And somewhere else on that page, he described the aliens as looking like a big dark cloud coming out of space and making all the stars wink out of existence in their wake. Or something."

"Yeah."

"And then he said that although he's not sure why, he has a feeling that they're a few feet taller than the average Earth man and that they're blue-skinned with orange and brown spots and that they're going to exterminate the entire human race with laser rays."

The two friends dwelt on this a moment, then chuckled quietly. Peacefully.

"And he's right, you know?" murmured Jill, her eyes all over the sky.

"About which?"

"You're better than a sparkler lying on the grass in July."

Poppy felt warm there on the driveway, and she smiled.

Poppy had just finished apologizing to the boy she loved, Raymond, for reading his diary that they'd stumbled across in his garage earlier that afternoon.

"Do you hate me?" asked Raymond as he stood there on Poppy's porch, all elbows and knees.

Poppy smiled. "You make me happy."

They stood there, in the fading afternoon light.

"Meet me on my roof tonight around eleven-thirty?"

Poppy nodded yes and turned to retreat into the cool blue of her house.

Raymond was just unlocking the gate that led into his backyard when Poppy stopped him. "Raymond."

"Yeah, Pop?"

"Do your braces hurt nowadays?"

"No," Raymond answered, a crooked-toothed smile upon his face.

The stars were everything.

They were a spiralling, cascading rain that gave promises you knew they could keep. If you chose a direction and were vigilant, you might see yourself any way you liked to. Better, stronger, or the way you once were, but always, always against the twinkling backdrop of the strange universe.

"Holy cow," whispered Poppy in Raymond's ear.

He craned his neck and looked down into her eyes, which reflected the sky about them.

Silently agreeing with what she'd said, he squeezed her shoulder gently.

"You know, you're a pretty good writer, Raymond."

He shook his head. "My journal's non-fiction. It's not that hard."

Poppy breathed in deeply. She reached to Raymond's side and drew his arm about her small shoulders. He loved the way her ugly green sweater felt to his touch there on his roof in the cool fall night. Underneath the emerald weavings he felt the warmth of everything he ever loved to think about.

Casting his eyes upwards was difficult, but he managed. Raising his left arm, he gestured that-away and said, "Hey, Pop. Watch that spot over there."

Poppy followed his peter-pointer with her smaller hand atop his. She saw.

A wonderfully bright and dense swirl of stars were the object of the friends's scrutiny.

"Name it," said Raymond, indicating the constellation.

"Name it?" laughed Poppy. "I can't. I... I don't have the right to name it."

"Actually, you do," nodded Raymond assuredly. "You really do."

Poppy thought for a quick moment, and then announced, "Q-Tip."

Raymond laughed, and Poppy joined in. "Q-Tip! That's great. I love it."

Poppy had her blue-painted lips apart to say something, but she stopped herself as her panning eyes discerned something in the blackness above.

"Look," she breathed, pointing to Q-Tip, although she didn't have to point at all.

Raymond knew what he'd be seeing before his eyes located the spot. There, in the middle of the gorgeous constellation Poppy had just named, lights were winking out. Where a billion stars like Christmas lights had shone their joyful and sorrowful radiance mere moments ago, darkness now reigned. Where there had been many somethings to gaze into and wonder about was now a steadily growing nothing.

"Well, here we go," whispered Raymond, eyes fixed on the spot.

"Void," said Poppy, and she repeated it. "Void." It was a word she'd never used before. She didn't even remember where she'd heard it. But it fit what she saw happening perfectly. She shuddered.

Raymond held her tightly in his frail arms.

Then, suddenly, that entire portion of sky was gone. Gone and that was it, except in the two friends's memories, where it would linger.

"Goodbye, Q-Tip," whispered Poppy solemnly.

Raymond echoed her with the grief in his eyes. The oncoming blackness was resolute. Lights winked out of existence, here, there.

Poppy felt cold, even beneath the might of her ugly green sweater, so she turned to Raymond. "Raymond," she spoke softly. "Do your braces hurt right now?"

"No," he answered Poppy with a flawless smile and accompanied it with a kiss on her cheek.

The blackness came on, turning off the sky in its wake.

SONGS FOR THE LOST

This is one of my personal favorite stories of mine. I remember very little about writing it, only sitting down at the computer one late night and then, many, many hours later, looking up feeling exhausted and a little dazed, knowing that I'd written something that I was really excited about having written.

It was first published in a great Fourth Horseman Press anthology called Way Out West. *It couldn't have found a better home. A few years later, I would think it was a perfect summation of the themes and ideas presented in my second collection, which is why I made it the title piece of the book. In fact, the story was written years before the majority of the other stories were written, and although briefly considered for inclusion in* Experiments at 3 Billion A.M., *I had the foresight and restraint to wait and save it for my next book.*

There is *a place, just like this story says, and I feel there's a glimpse of it right here in these pages.*

"Songs for the Lost" seemed a fitting way to end a retrospective compendium of my published fiction of the past twenty years, because its cast of damaged characters is bidding goodbye to their pasts while looking into the future, with all of its fears, uncertainties, and hopes.

Aren't we all?

In an outer rim galaxy of frontier violence and sin, a legend is whispered, making the rounds of the lawless worlds and dusty spaceports. It tells the tale of a temple in a cave in a town in a valley in a planet just as alien and dangerous as any, but with something special and impossible and nearly unfathomable existing in abundance at its core, for those lucky or worthy enough to find it.

Peace.

I: THE CURSED

LASSO THE SUN

"Trying to talk sense to her was like trying to teach your peter to piss up a rope, son."

The boy, hearing his father's words, thought of his mother and fought the tears that threatened to well into his eyes. He focused his vision on the vastness of the sun-bathed plain before them, its few wispy skeleton-trees stark against the earth, its sharp granite outcroppings like bizarre sculptures formed by the tenacious wind. He sought to make-believe some of these into something more: to the south, a herd of bison pounding over the ground! To the north, a gigantic valley serpent reared from the plain! But his game of old didn't entertain him that hot morning. He was unable to conjure beasts from the earth. This day he could only ache bitterly and wince at the stinging in his eyes, the dust and tears itching and scratching and making him wish the world wasn't so mean.

They stood in silence. The father spit into the dirt. The boy saw and spit too, like his father. Together they continued to watch the scene burning before them. In the distance, the boy saw a shape, a scratch against the crimson sky. It circled high in the air, its progress slow. It was graceful, the way it dipped groundward and then swept back up toward the outline of the rising sun's rim in a long arc like some gargantuan and majestic bird. But, of course, the boy knew it was no bird, and, of course, he would never dare talk of its grace to his father. For fear of his

390

father's hard hands curling into fists and finding his cheeks and arms, adding to his collection of bruises. For fear of sounding like some kind of a traitor, to his mother's memory, to his father still alive, though he seemed more like a statue of late, hard and quiet and sitting unmoving for hours at a time. The boy was only eager to point out the flying speck to his father, proof that his eyes were sharper than they'd been the day before, and much keener than they'd been one week before that.

But his father spoke up first. "There's one, son. Ruining the sunrise with its wicked shape." And he spat into the dirt again and added with venom, "I *hate* them. Those Varkoom scum. Blood-skinned cocksuckers. *We* hate them, don't we, son?"

The boy nodded, re-focusing his squinting gaze on the dark shape making arcs in the stifling air. Focusing what hate he had on that single mote in the sky, sagging his shoulders with the effort, feeling small and weak in the act.

The father followed the flying shape with scowling features and aching grey eyes. He recalled the clouds on the day his wife left him forever, their heavy grey look overhead as he regretted for the first time his terrible ways toward her every day that they'd lived together. Every long day of her serving triple duties of toiling in the fields and tending to his needs and, of course, raising their son, dutifully, admirably, honourably. A strong woman, to have borne his ways for so long, and the equally wicked ways of life in the Colonies.

"But still," murmured the father, "She was a great woman, your mother. And strong. Fiery like this picture burning out there. Piss and vinegar and tough as nails through and through." His voice grew unsteady as he finished. "Your mother, son, she... she was like this here sunrise, when you put it all together and look at it long and hard. Sunlight, bright and fiery."

And he made a sweeping gesture before them with his good hand, his left hand, which still owned all of its fingers. And the boy nodded, thinking of his mother wearing her own bruises like badges of courage around her troubled eyes and frowning lips.

"Yup. Like fire," said the boy, thinking he might impress his wise father with the conviction he put into his words.

"But don't forget, son," the father said, the hardness returned into his voice, shrinking his son a little more in the shoulders, deflating his chest where he'd tried to swell it out like a rooster owning the chicken coop. "It's also the colour of blood that we're looking at. And always remember it, son. *Always* remember the colour of blood."

The boy thought he understood, and together they nodded their heads in the shimmering air. They stared into the bloody sky until the father raised the battered silver stick in his hands, awkward work since his right hand had been mauled in the attack weeks past, along with his knee; sighted along its ancient telescopic lens and searched through a film of scratches and nicks the air one mile in the distance. A moment of panning the instrument from east to west and west back to east, and then the magnified flare in the crimson, a darker image of fire against the blistering sky.

The boy tensed when he sensed his father become taut beside him. He wanted to raise his hands and plug his ears with his fingers but wished to appear tough, hardy, ready for anything. Unafraid of loud noises like men are unafraid of such things. Still, he jerked against his will when the loud report cracked from the old gun, knocking his father back a half-step with its force, clapping his ears like two invisible hands smashing down on either side of his head.

Through watering eyes, father and son surveyed the sky in the west, saw the black speck dropping like a stone through the air.

Satisfied, the father cleared his throat, spit once more into the dust. "Got him. Got the cocksucker like he deserved it." And he paused with the Old World rifle slung over his shoulder, still smoking its grey wisp of smoke from its nose, and he turned his eyes down on his son, and said, "*We* got him."

The boy looked to his father's ruined right hand extended toward him, missing three of its stout fingers, making it look crab-like and alien. He felt proud as he took it in his own smaller hand, pumping it up and down vigorously as though it didn't feel grotesque, nodding his head in unison with the motion. His father's skin felt boiling-hot, a burning touch gathering all the fire of the morning sun in its leathery landscape and transmitting it to him through the binding gesture of their handshake.

They took a moment to look over the farm spread out before them, forlorn and quiet with its machines shut down, its animals set to pasture, never to return again. The whirring ceased in the old moisture sheds. The air filters silenced and baking in the light. The electrified fence surrounding the property on all sides and above, too, in order to prevent attack from the sky, silenced from its regular quiet buzzing. The sparse grass unmoving in the oven air, the twittering of triceedas from the dry corn husks bordering their property on the east and west sounding somehow nervous, frenzied in their calls.

The father said, "There is a place." And it was all that he said.

And, wordlessly, they stepped into the space bubble resting like a gleaming silver egg in the weeds and dust along the periphery of the yard, prepared to leave memories of blood and fighting forever, and find Paradise.

BLACK CHARM, BLACK HEX

Harry Dalmar felt the coarse bite of the hangman's noose sink into his throat through the thin fabric of the black hood, circling his oxygen and constricting its progress. He imagined his throat as a shrinking pin-hole through which the final moments of his life were fast bleeding. The courtyard air was still, boiling, and the murmurs of the rabble grew as the moment neared its grisly climax. His hands were being bound with the same coarseness of rope. He felt its biting touch as the executioner fiddled there roughly. Harry Dalmar wore the hood of the dead man, and in the darkness of its shroud, saw her like a mirage amid his despair:

Hair red like her lips like the wild roses that grew along the river bank behind her owner's plantation home. Lily-pale skin and her body's beautiful shape, long and strong and sleeker than a canyon cat in its prime. Her pair of slender tails curling around her leg, their red tips lapping on the air like thirsty tongues. Her slave-name as ordinary as she was alien, exotic: Jane Smithsa, though he'd always call her the universe's gift to him, unlike any Dalbidian ever cursed to live in man's New Frontier.

Something hit him, a heavy object smashing across his back and shoulders and ripping him from his reverie. He staggered unsteadily atop the trapdoor set into the creaking wooden execution platform, just as something else crashed down onto the top of his head. He crumpled to his knees, stars exploding inside the claustrophobic world of his death-hood. He knelt there, head reeling, amid a commotion of movement all around him: boots stomping on his hands, bodies colliding with him. As he swam toward full consciousness again, he discerned it: a *different* touch, oily and close upon his neck-skin, a slithering movement pressing against his throat.

Piercing screams erupted from below as those come to witness his death bore witness to some new horror; and his executioners, too, and the priests and his enemies standing attentive all around, seemingly all crying out in terror or revulsion, and the knocking of their boots upon the wood of the death-platform as they scrambled madly to escape whatever thing this was. The heavy sound of falling objects striking about him intensified, a loud thumping in the dirt below and the deep hollow knocking from the rickety floorboards.

Harry Dalmar managed to fight his way to his feet, uncoiling himself from the frail grasp of the half-knotted ropes. Tearing the hood from his head, he marvelled at the necklace he wore—the black snake, its skin slick and its obsidian eyes deadly. Its forked tongue darted into the boiling air and quivered something inside of him.

Frozen with horror, he stared about himself and watched the rain of snakes.

Specimens of every length, infant snakes like long dark worms, and adult serpents like immense coiling whips arcing down from the sky like some dark judgment, all the same tar-black colour as the serpent he wore about his neck. Something told him to leave the creature be, to not try and rid himself of it, for it and its many brothers had been his salvation on his doomsday. His gut told him this, and some other, even deeper place of instinct.

As if in answer to his thoughts, the serpent hissed in his ear, and in its sibilant voice Harry Dalmar heard the impossible, the miraculous, the unmistakable: a word.

Peacccccccccce.

Maybe he was a madman, after all, like the people said, like the law declared. Maybe his place *was* strangled and swinging in the hangman's noose and—

He stumbled back a step when he felt fingers clutch his ankle, looked aghast at the purple-faced priest at his feet, with his new black collar of slippery scales, thrashing wildly while the snake squeezed his life from him. Harry Dalmar turned to the bedlam of the courtyard below and everywhere it was the same: here, a massive serpent sinking its fangs into the face of a woman around

394

which it was wound; there, a screaming child nearly invisible beneath the tangle of black coils; everywhere, panic and death.

Screams followed him as he wove through the men crowding the execution platform, stumbling on quivering legs down the squealing steps and into the chaos of the street. A dust-storm billowed upward from the commotion of fleeing and struggling people, putting dust in his eyes and slowing his progress. Around him, the horrific deluge continued, the sound of the serpents striking the earth reminding Harry Dalmar of some dark, tribal drum dirge signalling ominous things. The sheer number of snakes seemed to cast a shroud over the daylight, or perhaps it was only the dust billowing around him that caused this darkness.

He fled amid terrified and pleading cries to Heaven and bullets and heat rays singing through the boiling air. The serpent clung tenaciously to him, and with it whispering its miraculous message in his ears he scrambled through the filthy alleys of the ramshackle town, crying fearfully every step of his terrible journey. But though he wept miserably, that inner voice kept telling him to leave the serpent alone, for it was his saviour. And so he ran on and on, until he came across the lone honji tethered to the rear of the dive tavern, an ancient pre-Frontier Era tune drifting languidly through the ajar window.

He rode his sturdy little mount to death in the Black Santiago steppes bordering the town, and then he ran his boots to tatters among the cacti and horned Lecki lizards beyond, and then he crawled until his knees bled into the dust and attracted giant grass spiders with the sticky taste of iron. Throughout his long trek, he'd worn his serpent like a grotesque ornament about his neck, like a black charm or hex, and all the while it whispered and whispered in his ear:

Peacccccccccce.

Only when, hours and hours later, he felt that it hung less tenaciously against his flesh, did he finally let it slide from him and into the dirt. He stared at it, shaken and awed, and when he saw what it told him—its final, dying message—he remembered an old legend he'd heard whispered in space bars and cattle yards and jail cells countless times since the days of his youth.

As though possessed by some dogged demonic spirit, the serpent's body was stretched tautly in two distinctly opposing directions: its tail still quivering in its dying throes and pointing into the sun-dropping northwest, while its black-eyed bullet-head trembled due northeast; its tough-skinned body cracked sharply midway through its stout bulk, creating a horrid base of grotesquely bunched, cracked, and flaking scales that marked a distinct 'V' in the dust, a single gruesome letter trembling terribly in the heat haze like an oracle.

And he thought of his own hand scratching this same symbol with knives or rocks into the wood of fences and tabletops long ago, the only smattering of writing he'd ever learned how to set down.

V.

V, for Valley. V for the Valley of Green.

The silent planet too far from the sun to grow any lush greenery and forests but defying science and logic in every way, or so the tales said. Amisam, with its deep, green valley and impossible supply of contentment. Paradise, in the wildness of the Big Black's nethermost reaches. Impossible and miraculous. Like a dream warm and beautiful in the icy reaches between stars. An old legend or myth for young and old alike. Whispered hopefully after a father's harsh beating left his son petulant and resentful of the world while confined to his bedroom; or muttered like a prayer to the setting sun during a prisoner's recollection of less difficult days as he lay shivering in his cold grey cell; or wished for by anyone thinking back to the time before the Great Expansion brought war and hunger to the New Worlds, and to so many of the Frontiersmen who were supposed to have been revelling in their promised glory long, long ago.

And Harry Dalmar blinked sweat from his eyes and watched the salty beads drop down onto the serpent-oracle blistering in the weeds. And he stared and stared until the snake became a crumbling mound of skin-husk and scales. And gathering these remains to himself, because this suddenly seemed the right thing to do, he draped them over his shoulders once more, where they clung despite their limp, ruined state, as if with some lingering shred of life. And then he slunk several miles more into the bloody setting sun, into the back roads and alleys of some unnamed mining settlement in the far west. Into the dark corners of a dusty market square, hidden in shadows where lawmen were too afraid to look. It was here that he strangled a merchantman with the silky kerchief he'd worn, directly beneath his stall's filthy striped canopy, and then emptied the man's pockets for their gold coins and his small tin box of eclectic multi-world coins, too, kept in the safety and shade beneath his tables all day long, away from the eyes of furtive cutpurses and murderers like himself.

Harry Dalmar thought about very important things as he choked the man's life from his slumping body. He thought about how he wanted judgment for his wicked ways. He wanted answers for why he was allowed to live and walk among men being as cold and unfeeling as he was. He wanted to know just who or what he was, Devil or awful man of unforgivable sins, or whether these things in the end were one and the same. He wanted to shed his snakeskin hide and reveal his heart to someone who might understand him and explain him to himself so that he might see what he was all about, and whether he existed for any reason other than to be hurtful and wear snakes like witchy charms around his neck. He wanted to rest his aching heart and tired thoughts the way he'd needed to for far too many years but never been allowed by the ways of the universe.

And Harry Dalmar bought himself a junk ship that couldn't get the best pilot on any world to any place at all, and with hope hammering and smashing inside his chest like he'd never ever felt it there before, he rocketed out of that lawless dust-bowl settlement and into an evening sky filled with a billion stars. And among them all, he searched with a frantic eye until he found the brightest-glowing, and this was the same one that whispered to him across the gulfs of blackness, like a serpent in his ear. And toward this glowing, emerald speck he steered his rickety ship, and sailed off quickly, straight as an arrow and just as surely.

BLOOD SKIN

The Varkoom were savage and soulless, all fang and fire-skin and arcane, primeval rituals.

Untamed and primitive, they were a race of cruel warriors who devoured the young and set fire to the land. The atrocities they committed upon humans and their children were the stuff of hushed campfire tales, to scamper children off to bed when mothers and fathers wished to be rid of their naggings and complaints. The Varkoom were archaic and stupid and the deadliest obstacle the Colonizers had met in their sweeping expansion throughout the Rim, obstinate and determined to not bend to the will and wise ways of their superior man.

These things men called them.

The Varkoom were in fact the only strong race of the Fringe, resilient and proud. Rebels in the face of the pioneering poison spreading across the worlds: Man, and his hunger for expansion, his penchant for slaughter where slaughter furthered his greedy goals.

These thoughts Helma-Rar pondered as he held the shrieking human baby in his enormous hands. The creature's skin against his own both repulsed and attracted him—its wan hue, its softness, such a fragile-looking creature. He thought the thing might simply burn up inside of his red-skinned grasp. But the infant wailed on and on relentlessly, chilling him somehow, a nervous racket that unnerved him the longer it went on. He'd eaten them before, the human children abducted from Colony towns during skirmishes. It was a taste that had only ever sickened him, bringing to mind aftermath battlefields of corpses burning in the sun, rotting in their atmospheres of ecstatically-buzzing flies and twitching maggots.

He turned at his comrade's roar beside him where he owned the attention of their fellow warriors gathered in the grassy compound.

"The would-be Colonizers brand us wicked, while acting out their own wicked deeds upon us. They feed our young and old alike into the mouths of their ovens on the Extermination Worlds and preach against our sinful ways of wishing peace between all." Here the Varkoom soldier raised a human infant high into the air, carelessly, violently, as if it were a sack of feed. "Then let us fall in place among the honourable white raiders and feast as they feast."

And the Varkoom soldier brought the mewling infant to his mouth, placed it between his immense jaws, and champed down viciously.

An awful crunching sounded throughout the compound outside of the barracks, accompanied by a piercing shriek from the child and a celebratory roar of his comrades that shook the earth. It was in the wake of this old, terrible song of blood and vengeance that Helma-Rar thought, very unexpectedly in that moment, of a place he'd heard tell of long, long ago. The young whispered of it, and the elderly cackled of it, too, while only

398

occasionally those of the in-between ages acknowledged the potential reality behind the mystery or legend. Amid the screams of babies being murdered and the exultant roars of his brothers-in-arms, the gentle touch of the name fell upon his ears like a gift of softness in the war field.

Hamisamrah and the caves of peace.

In that moment of blood and death, Helma-Rar wished like he'd never wished before in his many, many years, for the chance to rest his weary bones in this place. The only place where true peace could be found, if the fables were true. The caves and caverns like a great metropolis beneath the green valley, tended by an ancient and peaceful people much like his own, secluded and safe in their impregnable retreat. For unnamed dangers barred the path to Hamisamrah's warm heart, littering the world above with the skeletal remains of those unworthy who sought egress into this wondrous sanctuary.

It was the potency of the suddenly arrived need to discover this truth that urged Helma-Rar to do what he did that fateful day, guiding his hands as he set the infant down in its steel tub, tearing free his weapon from its scabbard at his hip with a quick whisper of steel slicing leather.

Turning upon his brothers and with his gruesome gun letting fire. And his six brothers falling dead before they even realized the great betrayal, in vivid pools of blood and bone, the shells detonating their cargoes of steel spikes within them, splitting skulls and chests and abdomens wide, drenching the grass. He watched the fallen warriors only until he was certain none had survived and re-sheathed his weapon with a pain in his heart.

Without thinking, he scooped the screaming infant from its steel tub and with one giant hand deposited it inside the warmth and shelter of his belly-pouch. And with a sound like the popping of springs and groaning of tarpaulin, Helma-Rar spread his long, powerful wings from where they were tucked along the length of his back and he drifted upward like a bloody beacon into the star-filled sky.

SUN ON THE RUN

In the instant of the Big Death, she'd given up all that her father's preaching had committed her to over the years.

Just like that, in the unreality of that moment of blood and bullets, and she'd forsaken her beliefs like snakeskin shed and discarded in the dust of a derelict town where only ghosts roamed. Like the sun put out, and from then onwards a life living in shadows and uncertainty.

Darla was the heaviest little girl in the universe. Her father had told her this as if it was something to be proud of, to stick up in the face of anyone who might use the same words but in a way that would try to make her feel very small and weak. Like a bug in the dirt, easy to be crushed into dust under a tough man's boot-heels. She kept her thoughts to herself, like secrets, especially those that concerned her embarrassed feelings about the way she looked. She only shared her secrets with one friend, and it was the only friend she'd ever made in her life: Lucky Lecki, her tiny and old Lecki lizard that she'd saved from the steel jaws of a canyon cat trap where he'd wandered by accident and got his tail snagged. She'd cried as she pried open the rusty steel trap-teeth and the little emerald Lecki wriggled and spasmed in silent pain in the grass.

She'd taken him home hidden inside the pocket of her apron, and when she plucked him out in her bedroom less than one hour later, it was the first magical thing she'd ever seen in her life: her Lecki had sprouted a new tail, healthy and nimble as he flicked the air with it cheerfully. "You're my good luck charm, Lucky," she'd whispered to the creature as she helped nurse it back to health with a steady supply of live field flies and baby grass spiders appropriated while her father and mother were looking elsewhere.

There wasn't very much lucky about the Death Day, though, not really, not for anyone except maybe her, and for her only a very little bit. None of those big, eager men had expected her to be packing something more than her rolls of skin and giant sagging breasts beneath her faded print dress, like an enormous flag wrapped around her immenseness. The Old World shotgun fitted like a secret toothpick between her folds, under her big sweeping dress, it was a surprise when it snuck out in her pudgy fists and shot up the little room and all of the dirty-thinking men getting in line to take their turns with her like they'd probably taken turns with her momma and sisters in the other rooms. Those dirty, filthy pioneers, revolting like her father had always predicted they would if the innocent killings got to be too many and the people sick of it all. Killing and raping the wrong side of the war, this is what conflict will achieve in the end. He'd predicted and been right about it all, as she eventually saw with her own terrified eyes.

Big Darla loved the red look of the men's faces when she set off that big ruckus. Like a bunch of Varkoom taking over the faces of those ugly, dirty men, red everywhere, and wasn't that just perfect, wasn't that just right. And she only cried about it a long time afterward, once she'd escaped from the room and the town and the planet aboard the little single-pilot ship she barely squeezed herself into. Only when she was already among the stars and they twinkled on every side and she felt how utterly alone she was in the universe—only then did she finally let herself behave like a little girl.

Big Darla looked at the red and brown smeared all over her fat hands. She saw the dirt under her nails and caked on her big body where her dress had been torn during all the fighting and shooting and running away. She remembered finding her momma and little sisters, big Windy nearly as big as she was, and tiny Maria, only a little baby and with such pretty eyes like two green-watered ponds—all dead with bullets cracking their heads, their dresses gone and thrown around the room, unholy and awful. Leaning in close to baby Maria, Darla had heard it, clear as day—the tiniest of voices, whisper-quiet and frail but unmistakable, the impossible words it spoke:

"In the Valley in the Cave, we'll be together again, sister."

Babies didn't talk, Big Darla knew, and she took it as the final sign from a God that had otherwise abandoned her to the awful and cold embrace of the universe. At least Lucky Lecki hadn't left her, she reasoned while considering the icy ways of every world in the Rim. He'd remain her truest friend, until the end.

Amid the stars, Big Darla cried and let go of God, but not before vowing to seek Him out if He existed at all. Because she had some questions that only He could answer for her. He might have forsaken her forever, as though all the warmth of the sun had gone away and left her cold and alone, but she aimed to find

401

Him so that she could get to the bottom of some very big things. And with all the sadness and rage she'd felt throughout her life burning her up inside, Big Darla, feeling very tiny and hugely guilty, guided her ship toward the brightest star in the field before her—a green and green star pulsing in the dark miles—and flew and flew and flew.

II: LOST IN THE CROSSROADS

The man and his son left their silver bubble nestled among a small grove of trees that bordered the great desert. Looking over his shoulder, the boy marvelled at the heat waves shimmering the distant horizon line, magically. He waited to see whether a castle or fort would appear there, but soon he grew tired and turned his eyes back to the path he and his father followed. It was in that instant he realized that the oasis lay before them and not behind.

His father had shouldered through the overhanging arms of tree-branches, holding them aside for his son to see: in the distance, a valley, its sides steeped in the most lush of green trees and tall grasses, dipping down and down, with a promise of deep forests at its mist-shrouded bottom, and all the mysteries and answers they might hold in their leafy reaches. A strange animal scampered into the greenery at the commotion, its silvery fur dappled in sunlight filtering through the treetops. The boy risked a bit of childish excitement and asked his father, "The caves, Papa? The caves are down in there someplace, huh?"

The man laid his ruined hand on the boy's shoulder, firmly, warmly, murmured, "Hush now, boy. We got some walking ahead of us still."

The boy nodded and walked onward, silently exhilarated with the new smell on the air: like perfume, something sweet and exotic which he'd never smelled before, and then he noticed the pretty pale flowers dotting the path everywhere. He breathed deeply of their scent, heavy and juicy, and different too from any of the wildflowers he'd smelled back home, or those cultivated by the farmers. A small flash of crimson blurred the air, coming to rest on the fragile branch of a sapling sprouting from the earth near to him. He looked, marvelling at the wondrous creature,

402

bird-like yet nearly completely globular in shape, its butterfly-like wings spread open on the warm air like a pretty scarlet fan. It fluttered off a moment later, a whizzing bulbous blur of red, and the boy watched amazed as it disappeared among the branches over their heads.

A worry-thought wrinkled his brow for a moment and he asked his father, "Papa, what about our silver egg? We left it behind, at the edge of the desert."

The man shook his head, muttering, "We're done with that egg, Son. Hopefully, we're finished with all of that from now on."

And they walked on, silently, along the slowly dipping trail.

It seemed for a moment as though the old ways had returned to haunt the father and his son.

The scene in the glade, of the gigantic Varkoom towering over the obese girl like some immense, bloody obscenity, chilled them both. An instant later and he saw the pale-skinned baby nestled in the crook of the thing's arm, and ice stabbed at his heart. Tearing free the gun from where it lay slung over his shoulder, the man hollered for the woman to take cover.

The girl and the Varkoom started at the commotion, she instinctively raising her hands on the air and the creature stooping into a threatening posture, fingers rolled into square fists, legs spread wide in battle-ready stance. Its wings opened like vegetable chutes in some sort of incredibly accelerated growth spurt, whipping the long grass with a strong gust of wind, bobbing the fruit in the branches of the trees all around them. The man's finger tensed on the trigger of his weapon as the girl's frantic cries broke through his awareness, halting him only barely.

"No! Don't shoot! Please, stop! We're friends!"

The incongruous sight of the Varkoom passing the tiny infant to the woman, one-handed, gently, daintily, puzzled him. The man ceased sighting along the tip of the gun but didn't lower it from its place trained on the Varkoom. His ears heard and his mind reeled as he processed what the girl had said, matching her strange words to the incredible scene of her standing fearlessly alongside the horrid creature, arms thrown up in its defence. It shivered him all over his body, and when at last he found his voice, he croaked, "What place is this, where girls walk with Varkoom on their arm?"

The Varkoom stood to its full height, grazing the branches with the top of its fiery-plumed head. Its eyes smouldered, but its voice was gentle when it murmured, "I've a feeling that you know what kind of place this is. We are here for much the same reason, I gather."

"Please, sir," said the big girl, hands still raised in the air, eyes pleading. "Please put down your gun. My name is Darla, and you got nothing to be scared of from us, I promise you. We were just talking about the place we're going to, in the valley, and that we'll be able to get some milk for the little one there, I'm sure of it."

She'd followed the song of baby's burbling, she explained, and found them curled together at the base of a tree, the infant and her strange guardian. She implored the man and his son to believe her words, that the Varkoom was gentle and kind, to just look into his eyes and they'd see for themselves.

The man's expression remained ashen as he tried with great difficulty to suppress the hatred trembling his body as he looked at the red-skinned monster before him. He looked into its crimson eyes and saw his wife's face of terror being ripped from him forever. He saw the thing's massive wings and fists like square blocks of molten rock and imagined his wife being flown into Hell and touched all over by the hands of demons.

He simmered and trembled but managed, "Okay, Darla. Okay... You... You're with this Varkoom, and we're all here for the same reason. I'll give you that, and so I won't do right now what I know should be done, on God's own will." And his knuckles twitched white along the stalk of his rifle. And he raised his wild eyes to Helma-Rar and whispered hoarsely, "But I want you to know something, Varkoom. I want you to know that I won't ever trust you. I know what you are, and I've got my eye on you. I'll always be watching you close, and I'm waiting for the chance to kill you good, demon."

And he turned and drifted away from them, stopping to peer over his shoulder at his son, a small, wide-eyed owl, more curious than fearful, distractedly stroking the gregarious Lecki lizard in his palms and staring with unabashed awe at the Varkoom warrior towering over him like a scarlet mountain.

And the man's anger was swept away by the deluge of sorrow which then gripped him, putting tears in his eyes, and he could

404

only turn away from the blasphemous sight and hide among the bushes and flowers with his huge shame and grief.

Big Darla's voice was soft in the stillness. "She's adorable. Just so gorgeous. I had a little sister once."

Helma-Rar looked up at her words, sensing the sorrow filling them up and making them significant. He only grunted and turned back to the pink infant he cradled in his lap, her eyes serene blue jewels as she drifted in his embrace.

"Don't worry, I'm sure he'll come around," she added, meaning the angry man, and she gave the boy a gentle look where he sat close to them, entranced by the alien warrior in the grass.

The Varkoom said simply, "I could kill you all, very easily. Right at this moment. Eat you and have my supper. Sharpen my teeth with your bones, like so many of you think we do. But I like this grass more than thoughts like those." He stirred a wildflower with a gigantic hand and then he added, almost as an afterthought, "I am Varkoom in blood. I am Varkoom in spirit. I've come to be set free from all that I've seen my brothers do." He cocked his head at the small gurgling sound falling from the infant's moist mouth, said, "What is her name, I wonder?"

Big Darla smiled at him, blushing because of her secret thoughts: how she would make a good girl for the warrior in the grass, a big girl like herself. A girl of rolling hills to his hard mountain range physique. She said, "Her name can be whatever you want it to be. She's starting over here."

Helma-Rar wrinkled his brow in thought. Soon, he murmured, "Pomma." And when he saw Big Darla's eyes smile at the sound, he revealed, "In Varkoom, this means 'soft.' Because she is so soft." And he stroked the child's round cheek with a huge, callused thumb, marvelling at her texture.

The boy barely heard Helma-Rar's words, only continued to stare, awed, at his massive limbs, shining in the bright light. Corded heavily, his arms were red tree trunks rooted to a body of prodigious mass. He rippled all over with muscle like steel springs beneath his skin. Sitting in the grass, stooped and with sunken shoulders, he was still much taller than his father, who was a big man among most men and the tallest of their family. The boy eyed the Varkoom's enormous tusks with awe and fear, the bright bones like ivory glistening where they protruded from his immense mouth. His single tuft of red hair drifted in the breeze, a crimson plume like a banner of war from some far-past time.

Because it sounded like the right thing to say just then, the boy said, in a small voice, "I don't know nothing about you, Varkoom."

And Helma-Rar answered, "No one knows, but the Varkoom."

The boy noted Helma-Rar's sad eyes but said no more for fear of angering his father once again, who he knew might be able to overhear where he sat cleaning his rifle several feet away. The boy's eyes continued to be drawn, however, to the strange trinket, carved from steel, which dangled from the massive creature's hip and made little tapping noises whenever he moved any which way. A carven image, of a Varkoom, it seemed, vivid crimson in colour and shiny and glittering in the sunlight. Only its shape was less sleek, less taut and wiry and immense and dangerous than all the Varkoom the boy had seen in pictures, as well as this one sitting beside him in the tall grass. A baby Varkoom. A child alien conqueror, although something about those words put together in such a way sounded strange and not right to the boy.

Helma-Rar saw where he looked and only said, "It was a gift from my mother. She is dead now."

The boy looked into the grass, mulling this over and twirling an emerald grass blade between his fingers, pretending it was a magical pen and that he scripted secret invisible words on the air, which were really his secret thoughts that only the truly good-at-heart would be able to decipher. But no one said anything about the things he wrote, though he reasoned that it might only have been because he'd been to school for a few years and probably nobody else among their party had done that.

But the Varkoom watched the progress of his air-writing and seemed to understand. His livid eyes softened, and he cupped a huge hand over the boy's, gently, briefly, before returning to fiddling among the tiny flowers stirring in the breeze. And when a gentle dusk breeze blew through the branches, he unfurled his mighty wings and curled himself beneath their canopy, like a living tent to shelter the softness of his adopted child through the coming night.

406

●   ●   ●

Helma-Rar thought of his mother as he'd last seen her, on the final night before he'd embarked on his quest, during his brief visit to her house. Her eyes like water, sad and mercurial and unseeing, her thick fingers clutching in her death-grip his last letter to her, in which he'd confessed to her his war-time sins with tears running freely from his eyes: he'd partaken of the human flesh-feast and eaten babies with his warrior-brother brethren; he'd heard the tiny creatures's high shrieking screams as his tusks ripped and crunched into their flailing little forms.

He explained his reasoning to his dead mother, quoting his own letter-words: "I saw them, mother. I saw the humans spearing our children in the villages and waystations. I saw them slaughter our little ones so easily. I understood my comrades's thoughts, to eat through their ranks, too. But still the taste was awful, so very awful in my mouth..." But, of course, his words had fallen on ears now deaf forever, and Helma-Rar only wept and wept.

He'd found her that night, only hours following his treason and subsequent departure from the lines. His mother's gigantic form toppled over among her newest diorama, a piece cobbled together from the thin, tough branches of talji saplings and totra roots. Their sinuous fingers coiled about one another tightly, expertly combining to create the semblance of her very own humble little home, her place of haven and sanctuary from the insanities living outside its walls, complete with tiny replicas of both her and her son, sculpted expertly and with her patient hand from the difficult material of bosool weed, twisty and unreliable. Her life-colour faded, her skin pale and pink and her body motionless. A pool of her bright blood surrounding her, from the place in her skull where she'd shot herself with the speargun. The long spear incongruous in her serene home, spiking her clean through, grey and ugly and savage where it entered her head on one side and stabbed through terribly on the other, red and sticky with brain- and bone-gore.

A peaceful woman, unable to bear the scene playing in her head, over and over like a nightmare snippet of film. Her son the executioner. Her son the soulless. Her boy like a human being, *raiding and raping and reaving and eating the young as if they were morsels in the changing galaxy's new food chain hierarchy.*

Helma-Rar, writer of murderous letters, who killed his own mother with the evil deeds he'd committed and foolishly documented as if in some weak hope of forgiveness.

Helma-Rar plucked the noisy human fruit from the branches over his head, easily, holding it aloft for the others to see.

The lanky man with weeks-stubbled cheeks and wild eyes, futilely brandished the small Old World pistol in his fist, the weapon's barrel twisted upward grotesquely where the Varkoom's fingers had wrenched and pinched the steel like paper. He squirmed in silence a moment, until Helma-Rar deposited him roughly on the grass and held him beneath his volcanic gaze. Firelight played over the man's frantic features, sent shimmers along his strange, scaled hands. Peering closer, the group saw that these were gloves of a sort, and when the man snarled at them it was Big Darla who tried to calm him before violence erupted.

"We won't hurt you," she said, pudgy hands raised high in the air. "We just met each other today, too. Maybe you're here for the same reason we're here, stranger."

The man's eyes grew less livid at this last, his demeanour more relaxed as he allowed himself to settle in his place before the fire. He breathed heavily and shook dirt and grass bits from his filthy clothes. He was nodding his head, and when he found his voice, it was low, husky. "I crashed my ship a few miles back, in the desert. I been wandering all day and night. I—I heard you a while back, and snuck up, in case you was... dangerous." He offered the group a wan attempt at a smile, looking eerie and gruesome in the fire glow. "But maybe... maybe this place isn't so dangerous, huh? At least not the... the place I'm looking for."

He saw the solemn look in the strangers's faces, only now allowing himself to ponder the bizarre, rag-tag look of the group. Something in their silence, in their sad yet hard eyes and slumped shoulders, told him that he'd met up with fellow searchers. He muttered, "I'm Harry Dalmar. And I'm so damn tired. Maybe can I grab a couple of those fruits you got there, to quiet my belly?"

●　　●　　●

Harry Dalmar settled himself near to the man, maybe because he was the most silent of the group, much like himself, or perhaps because he looked to be the loneliest of them all. Harry Dalmar was just laying down on the grass and getting set to close his weary eyes on the moonlight when the man's voice chilled him from the darkness.

"You got the skin of the snake around your fists, brother. I don't know if I can trust the look of you." The old man's gun hung motionless in his hands on the silvery-blue air. Moonlight glinted from its long barrel. His eyes watched Harry Dalmar's eyes, though, and not his hands sheathed in snakeskin. Something burned there that he recognized. Some awful thing. Some lost, burning thing that kept his own eyes trained there and nowhere else. He murmured, "What'd you do, Snake Man? What happened to you? Why are you here? You're among fellow lookers now. You can tell. Why are you here?"

Harry Dalmar, very close to the flickering fire, felt winter in his bones, in his heart.

Harry Dalmar saw sweet Jane Smithsa the way he used to look at her for hours every night back in the old world: rope loops wound tight around her wrists and ankles where she lay naked and beautiful and terrified in the attic room of his little shack hidden away in the gulley, spread-eagled across the bed like some kind of present for him and no other man in the universe, eyes only for the silver gun always itching Harry's finger while he circled her slowly, naked and sweaty and frightened, too, at the awful things the universe allowed him to do if he wanted. His only garment the long, severed tail of the Dalbidian female he kept strapped to his bed, the member hanging like an exotic shawl across his shoulders as he paced the small room, admiring the perfection of her, one-tailed though she now was.

Her lips blood red, her skin like virgin-white lilies.

●   ●   ●

"I done bad things."

And it was all that Harry Dalmar said, and the tears that beaded from his eyes gave him away for certain, he thought. And with suns of shame burning in his cheeks, he turned his face toward the rustling green roof overhead and tried to breathe, and tried to sleep, and tried fruitlessly to shut out the old pictures playing behind his eyes, relentlessly, relentlessly.

Harry Dalmar's silence chilled the old man deeply. Something inside of it spoke to him. He curled into himself before the wheeling embers of the fire, numbed with cold, and barely stirred when the heat touched the bare skin of his old, scarred hands. His eyes clouded over, and in the flames he saw things as they were, as they could never be undone.

His fist crashing against her chin, sending her tumbling into the stall with the baby honji. Descending on her and letting loose with words and his fists, too, always his patented dual attack on the only woman he'd ever loved. A booted foot found her side, and another her belly, bowling her over while he pummelled her head and neck relentlessly. His words grunted, curses in the cramped wooden arms of the stall while the frightened honji kicked anxiously at the hay, unable to break away from the commotion because of the tether holding it helplessly in its place.

"My woman won't make me small in front of my son, not ever again. That won't happen again, will it? This land is ours, just like the government companies say it is. I won't go on defending myself from you like I got to from those goddamned Varkoom raiders every day."

Delivering punches until his arms had grown numb. Lashing a discarded loop of rope around her wrists and securing it alongside the honji's tether where it was fastened to the bracket in the wall. Leaving her bleeding and weeping in the straw with the flustered animal still pawing at the earth.

The last time the man had touched his wife before the dawn attack. And then he was blinking sleep from his eyes, staggering

410

outdoors with his old rifle in his hands to the song of alarm sirens wailing. Watching the sickening sight with a hollow, sinking feeling filling him up everywhere. The flailing arms of his wife as she was carried away by the wing-borne Varkoom horde, through the rend in the overhead roof of mesh cage fence. The doors of the barn across the yard thrown wide where the raiders had pilfered the building of its supplies of animals and feed and imprisoned woman.

His own knee bleeding and spiking suddenly with pain as the shells exploded in the dirt about him, shrapnel finding his flesh and crippling him into immobility. His right hand mangled, fingers lost in the dust and chaos. He dragged himself futilely in the dirt, spreading blood and bone bits into the earth where the spikes had severed his limb clean through. Screaming, his voice hoarse as his woman disappeared into the rising sun in the hands of the savages that men feared more than any other demon in the universe.

"There she goes. Oh, sweet Lord, there goes my sunlight..."

And weeping into the dust, and cowering into the small embrace of his trembling son, the loneliest creatures in the universe at that awful morning moment.

Into the nocturnal silence, broken only by the crackling of fire and the electric whirring of crepuscular insects, Big Darla whispered to Harry Dalmar, or to the man and his boy, or to the Varkoom. "I killed someone, too. A long time ago, it seems. The... It's a tough place, this crud universe. Any world, any place. They're tough places. Right? And you got to be tough to live in tough places. Right?"

Harry Dalmar nodded and wiped surreptitiously at his closed eyes with a dirty finger.

"Tough," Big Darla muttered. "Tough. Tough." And she muttered it again and again and again, as though she was trying very hard to convince herself of something.

She'd only ever felt pity for the young Varkoom, slaves in chains dredging in the fields in the name of the Colonialists. Working to further man's goal of stealing from them all of their worlds, with all of their lands, these outer rim backyard worlds that should only have been left alone, in peace.

She'd only started to spill the beans about her father's plantation to the town boy because he'd been so pretty. His blonde hair with its curls. His green eyes like summer grass. How could she have known that her big blabbermouthing would get him and all his cronies up in arms? How could she have foreseen that his rescue operation would turn out so altogether different from its original plan?

She shouldn't have told about the mistreatment of the little red ones, poked and prodded with electric lances in the fields if they slacked off in their work. She never should have said that those young kiddie Varkoom got their wings clipped nice and early, while only in their thirtieth or fortieth year, so her father wouldn't have to worry about fly-aways every long work day, a lot harder to handle than grounded children, even with the security cage surrounding the property. She shouldn't have leaked about how when they got to be too old, and the muscles started bulging in their backs and along their arms and legs, that this was when the farmers and plantation hands would take the pretty, blood-red children to the furnaces and throw them in like wood into a fireplace.

Big Darla shouldn't have, but she did. Because of a boy's lovely eyes and hair, and because he talked to her for a long time, and he didn't seem to mind her tree trunk arms and legs, and the hills of her many bellies and the fat cheeks squashing her features so ugly. She'd do anything in the universe to turn back time and undo her bad deed of shutting off the electricity and snipping the security cage wires with the pair of big shears the way her pretty-eyed boy had instructed her, just to help out his group's small rescue mission. Get those poor kids and get out, and good riddance to slavery on the New Worlds. One two three, mission complete—easy as making pie, or even eating it.

But Big Darla never even guessed that what happened could have happened. That the rescue would turn into a slaughter of her whole family, and all the hired hands, and her fathers' house and property all burned down around her ears, while her sisters and momma got touched by all the bad men disguised as pretty and nice boys with good reasons for sneaking onto Colonial farms in the deep, dark night.

If only she'd been smarter. If only she'd been less ugly and weak, then she never would have thrown her darling sisters into such an easy and evil trap.

If only God hadn't left her, when she'd needed His guidance most.

The group lay about the fire, tired from their long journeys, and drifted. And they each of them wondered what meaning they might find in this place like a dream or myth from their youths, among the grass and mountains and strange and beautiful flowers and fauna. And the thought chanced to flit through each of their minds, too, that perhaps they'd already discovered something very important and vital by finding each other and the distant, forlorn looks in their eyes that they all recognized.

The old man dreamed, and in his dream he saw certain of the same pictures as his son saw in his own dreams, only neither would tell the other and so they would never learn how similar their deepest wishes really were.

A green valley.

Lush and verdant.

Birdsong in the trees instead of bullet symphonies.

Life everywhere instead of death gathering clouds of flies on the corpse-littered ground.

His wife held his crab-hand and she smiled, and she wore no bruises to blemish her sweet, rugged features.

Flowers and trees and all their guns discarded on the grass, useless and unneeded in this new place of wonders where violence was a fable of some dark and far-away past.

Harry Dalmar dreamed...

The girl in his arms held him back.

She wore a smile, red-lipped.

She forgave him and squeezed his hand in hers.

Her tails coiled around his legs, kept him close to her.

Together, they strolled among flowers, beneath a canopy of trees.

Together, they sang along with the birds.

Together, with the girl on his arm, Harry Dalmar felt un-alone and loved...

The boy dreamed, too, and he watched them from above, from his sky-vantage because in this dream he owned wings which sailed him high and far, amid clouds and birds.

Below, far, far below, his mother and father waved upwards at him. They were smiling and beckoning him to join them. He declined with a playful laugh and urged them to join him with his cloud friends.

He watched them sprout their own wings and lift from the lush grass and come to him through the still, bright air...

Big Darla dreamed of Little Maria.

In her dream she cradled the child to her immense bosom, cooing like a pigeon into her ear. Soothing, comforting, her words and non-word gibberish alike, reassuring the child that they were headed through the forest of flowers and fruits and secret magic, and toward the rest of their family waiting safe and happy at the end of the path.

In the dream, Big Darla could sense her sister's ease, her tiny gurgling noises of comfort as her older sister held her closely, tightly, protectively, just in case, just in case...

Helma-Rar dreamed...

His wings took him into the emerald reaches.

The air tasted delicious, moist and cool.

Below, sun-speckled lakes and rivers nestled among the green landscape of trees and rolling hills like sparkling flashes of light.

Beside him sailed a ship. Her wings gigantic, elegant, his mother was wrinkled and beautiful and vividly crimson, the most gargantuan ship owning the sky.

He stretched his long wings and revelled in the sensation. No Colonial sniper threatened him in his high flying. He slipped his spear-gun from its holster and let it fall earthward. He watched its slow descent as it turned over and over, headed for the sparkling blue of a sun-blazing lake. He unveiled the pink baby inside of his belly-pouch and transferred it, mid-air, into the waiting embrace of his mother.

Together, he and his mother watched the weapon fall, and when it was lost in the shimmering distance, they turned to examine the tiny baby with her soft eyes. And Helma-Rar felt something in his chest lighten, tear away from him and drift off into greenness like an old thought or memory...

When they awoke, a path had appeared.

A narrow, balding trail leading off through the overhanging trees to the east. Beyond them, the morning light shone brilliantly, enticingly. They exchanged sleep-blurred glances, struck anew with the awe of this place. They scrambled to their feet, wiping the sleep from their eyes, and looked, incredulous.

A wooden sign that hadn't been there in the night stood amid the tall grass and colourful nodding flowers, its message carved deeply into its face in a patient, looping scrawl.

They stared at the sign together, the young boy helping them all with the longer words, because the boy had his first few years of schooling done, unlike most people he ran into, and, strangely, despite this being an alien world, they were in the only language he understood.

"We, the sufferers, have gathered here. We, the once broken, convened in this valley haven long ago, and here we shall remain until the end of times arrives and sets us free of our bad memories. Welcome, or, perhaps, be gone..."

They stood in awe awhile. The world about them was still, only the distant whirring of insects in the trees, the grass. A wind gusted, stirring their clothes and the branches surrounding them.

They looked down the sun-stippled forest path and saw their ghosts, waiting.

"My God," murmured the father. "It's true. It's all true."

They saw them through the trees, down in the valley beyond, hanging like peculiar, hazy cumulus low over the sloping plain: thousands of spectral lights, ephemeral and shimmering among the tall-grass and sparse trees and tumbleweeds drifting like

415

gigantic spiders over the valley floor; intangible orbs and eddies and halos of light whose languid movements floating over the grass and among the flowers carried a melancholic deliberation, an indisputable sentience.

The path upon which they stood was verdant on either side, and canopied overhead with entwined tree branches. They felt safe beneath this shelter, where no eye might find them, judge them.

"We got to think," said the man, shielding his far-roving eyes with his crab-hand. "About exactly what we're going to do now. We got a lot of thinking ahead of us."

"You know what the stories say," murmured Harry Dalmar quietly. "This road isn't for everyone. Not many make the walk. Just look at the place. A dead sea over there."

They followed his squinting eyes and saw the graveyard plain to the west: bones burning in the shimmering heat, the calcified remains of countless wanderers making a rolling landscape upon the earth, baking in the early morning sunlight. The unworthy or the unprepared. The weak or the too-strong. Among the bonescape, riddling its white-grey surface, sunlight glinted dully from countless implements of violence: rifles new and old, pistols and daggers and sabres and spearguns, like an exhibit chronicling a history of inter-species relations in the Rim.

Harry Dalmar laid a tentative step forward along the path but Big Darla stopped him with a hand on his elbow. He recoiled at her touch, the unfamiliar warm feel of it on his skin, so foreign, this kind of intimacy. His eyes found hers and he noticed suddenly how pretty she was, beneath her fleshy cheeks and many hills of chins. Maybe he could love her, too.

Her whisper was emphatic, frightened. "Let's not make a mistake now. Let's not become skeletons today, okay?" And she unslung her rifle and tossed it from her into the fringe of the skeleton-field, adding to its collection of silenced weaponry.

Harry Dalmar eyed her nervously, shaking his head a little. "I don't know, lady. I don't think so," taking another step in the direction of the valley, and then another and another. "I don't know if I feel right about going down there without no..."

Something roared.

They became still in their places, frozen bodies and numbed minds. Nothing stirred in the forest, only the deep roar that they

416

felt seeping upward from the earth itself, and from the air and trees, too, it seemed. And a moment later, the sound had ceased.

Eventually, they all breathed again, casting shivering glances to the skeleton-field on one side, and then longer looks along the canopied path before them and the openness of the valley shimmering beyond.

Harry Dalmar had stumbled back several steps, throwing his weapon away from him like an accursed thing when the deep roar had begun. Now that it had ceased, its absence left the forest around them in a huge and deep silence. He stammered apologetically, "I don't want no trouble from this place. I don't want to bring anything at all like that here. You were right, Darla. That was a warning... like we got to watch what we do here in this place. It's not... This isn't the Colonies. Or the spaceports and slum towns and Extermination Worlds. This... This place isn't those places."

They nodded silently at Harry Dalmar's wise words.

Helma-Rar slipped his gun from its sheath. The group watched in awe the strength in the Varkoom's arm as he hurled it skyward, to join the ancient graveyard of weapons and bones, far, far out on the plain. The boy's eyes twinkled in admiration. He liked how this Varkoom was different from the ones he'd always heard people tell about. This one carried human babies in his belly and threw his weapon away because peace was better than shooting up the quiet morning forest. He liked this Varkoom alright.

They felt it beneath their feet.

They felt it course through their bodies, rattling them deeply. A distant tremor, rising quickly and quickly in volume. The roar returned, only so much louder. Filled with fury, indignation. A bellow from within the earth beneath their feet, a warning or reprimand. The voice of the world on which they stood making itself known, explaining some little part of itself to these new searchers.

They turned and saw the man with his Old World shotgun, sunlight glinting from its long stalk where he levelled it at Helma-Rar's bright red chest. The man's eyes sighting unwaveringly along the sleek barrel. Hatred burning there. His lips a tightly drawn line stabbing across his unshaven face, grimacing with his disdain.

"I got you, Varkoom," his words whispered, low and heatedly. "I got you dead on, cocksucker." His finger tightened on the trigger, and he whispered, "You took the sun, demon. You took the sun from me, and now...." He trailed off, his eyes burning.

Helma-Rar stood rigidly in place, stooping to lay the baby he'd been cradling onto the grass beside him, out of harm's way. Then he stood once more to his full height, chest thrust forward, head grazing the tree branches, eyes watching the man's, grimly, proudly.

The grass beneath them shook. Fruits dropped from the trees over their heads, pelting them like a heavy rain. Birds scattered frantically, their anxious cries adding to the chaos. The warning in the planet was a cacophony. The new searchers toppled like pins in its throes, but for the man with the gun and the Varkoom, who managed to stand their ground. It deafened them all, put tears in their eyes as they awaited their unfathomable end.

And the man lowered the shotgun and hurled it up and away from himself and into the graveyard field.

The earth trembled a while longer, an uneasy grumbling, a fading thunder, and then was no more. Birds sang again, nervously. Insects buzzed like electricity. The searchers looked about themselves in awe. Big Darla's Lucky Lecki lizard poked his tiny bullet-head from the pocket of her dusty coat and blinked his revolving eyes in the sunlight.

"We got a long way to walk still," said the father to his son, and to the Varkoom, and to the others, his ruined hand gesturing down the balding trail and the valley beyond. "We got time to get to know each other ahead of us, I'm guessing. We got time to get to know each other real well. The good stuff and the bad, and how come each of us is here today." He looked to the Varkoom, noting how it once again cradled the human child so gently to its massive breast, so lovingly. He laid a hand, his good hand, with all of its fingers, on his son's shoulder, and squeezed, clumsily yet warmly, winning him a confused smile from the boy.

They stood in stunned silence, puzzle pieces baking in the air, confused as to how to arrange themselves for answers, perhaps only dimly aware that their tenuous union may have been clue enough. A fat girl, a rapist, a winged demon or angel, and a father and son, all with aching thoughts and breaking hearts, stepping into the path together. Stirring dust and ghosts. Bathed in the bloodlight of the dawn sun. Steeling themselves to

418

drift among spirits, the mysterious valley's and their own, toward their dreams of peace while around their ears sang the songs of their pasts. Making their way, slowly, surely, toward truth and revelation, toward peace or a place like Paradise where nothing would ever hurt them again, or maybe these things were one and the same.

AFTERWORD

Twenty years of published fiction, gone by in a flash. Putting together this compendium has been a good reminder to savour the next twenty and to write the hell out of them.

Beyond my brief introductory notes throughout this book, I hope that these stories speak for themselves. And hopefully, some day when I'm gone, they'll live on and speak to someone, somewhere.

Thank you for reading. I'm truly honoured.

It's been a good run so far. Here's to all the stories tomorrow. *Onwards!*

—AZ
Windsor, Ontario, Canada, 2019

The following stories were originally published in a variety of publications:

"Maria, Here Come the Death Angels!" *Songs for the Lost* (Eibonvale Press, 2014; Independent Legions, 2016); reprinted under the title "Maria" in *Hellfire Crossroads*, Volume 5 (Midnight Street Press, 2015).

"The Potato Thief Beneath Indifferent Stars." *Unparalleled Journeys II* (Journey Books, 2007); *Experiments at 3 Billion A.M.* (Eibonvale Press, 2009).

"The Priests." *Blacker Against the Deep Dark* (Eibonvale Press, 2018).

"A Roman Plague." *Songs for the Lost* (Eibonvale Press, 2014; Independent Legions, 2016).

"Blacker Against the Deep Dark." *The Beauty of Death* (Independent Legions Publishing, 2016); *Blacker Against the Deep Dark* (Eibonvale Press, 2018).

"Highway of Lost Women." *Ghost Highways* (Midnight Street Press, 2016); *Blacker Against the Deep Dark* (Eibonvale Press, 2018).

"On Tour with the Deathray Bradburys." *Songs for the Lost* (Eibonvale Press, 2014; Independent Legions, 2016); portions of this story published in *Ballads to the Burning Twins: The Complete Song Lyrics of the Deathray Bradburys* (Eibonvale Press, 2014).

"Journey to the End of a Burning Girl." *Blacker Against the Deep Dark* (Eibonvale Press, 2018).

"Your Bone Spider Will Find You." *Rotten Leaves* (2011); *Songs for the Lost* (Eibonvale Press, 2014; Independent Legions, 2016).

"The Prison Hulk." *Revelation 3:4* (Fourth Horseman Press, 2006); *Revelation: Volume III* (Fourth Horseman Press, 2006); *Experiments at 3 Billion A.M.* (Eibonvale Press, 2009).

"Gladiators in the Sepulchre of Abominations." *Experiments at 3 Billion A.M.* (Eibonvale Press, 2009).

"Dying Days of Treasure Spiders Everywhere." *Structo*, Issue 6 (2011); *Songs for the Lost* (Eibonvale Press, 2014; Independent Legions, 2016).

"Elopers to Sirius." *Songs for the Lost* (Eibonvale Press, 2014; Independent Legions, 2016).

"We Are All Lightless Inside." *Midnight Street Magazine*, Season 2, Issue 1 (Midnight Street Press, 2017); *Blacker Against the Deep Dark* (Eibonvale Press, 2018).

"Love in Uncertain Times." *Blacker Against the Deep Dark* (Eibonvale Press, 2018).

"An Angela Named Vengeance." *Sex and Murder*, Issue 17 (2011); *Songs for the Lost* (Eibonvale Press, 2014; Independent Legions, 2016).

"Through Fogs Deep and Fires Long." *Sex and Murder*, Issue 20 (2011); *Songs for the Lost* (Eibonvale Press, 2014; Independent Legions, 2016).

"A Valley for Dorothy." *Songs for the Lost* (Eibonvale Press, 2014; Independent Legions, 2016).

"Another Light Called 1-47." *Experiments at 3 Billion A.M.* (Eibonvale Press, 2009).

"In the City Where Dreams Wander the Sidewalks." *Experiments at 3 Billion A.M.* (Eibonvale Press, 2009).

"The Homes We Deserve." *A Test Tube Family* (Eibonvale Press, 2018).

"The Bloodmilk People." *Blacker Against the Deep Dark* (Eibonvale Press, 2018); Scum Magazine, Issue #1 (Scum Publishing, 2019).

"Let the Firefly Men Remind You." *Experiments at 3 Billion A.M.* (Eibonvale Press, 2009).

"This Lustful Earth." *Blacker Against the Deep Dark* (Eibonvale Press, 2018).

"The Demon Takeover of Windsor, Ontario." *Revelation 2:1* (Fourth Horseman Press, 2004); *Revelation: Volume II* (Fourth Horseman Press, 2005).

"Poppy, the Girl of My Dreams, and the Alien Invasion I Can Detect Like Radar Through My Braces." *Front & Centre Magazine* (Black Bile Press, 1999); *Experiments at 3 Billion A.M.* (Eibonvale Press, 2009).

"Songs for the Lost." *Way Out West* (Fourth Horseman Press, 2009); *Songs for the Lost* (Eibonvale Press, 2014; Independent Legions, 2016).

ABOUT THE AUTHOR

Alexander Zelenyj is the author of the books *Blacker Against the Deep Dark, Songs for the Lost, Experiments at 3 Billion A.M., Black Sunshine*, and others. He lives in Windsor, Ontario, Canada, with his wife Elizabeth and their cats and dog.

The author's fourth-grade book, *G.I. Joe: The Sea of Lost Souls*, was the recipient of a Young Authors Award, and he hasn't looked back since.

www.ingramcontent.com/pod-product-compliance
Lightning Source LLC
Chambersburg PA
CBHW051057030726
47504CB00006B/1670